SONG THAT MOVES THE SUN

ANNA BRIGHT

HARPER TEEN
An Imprint of HarperCollins Publishers

ALSO BY ANNA BRIGHT

The Beholder

The Boundless

HarperTeen is an imprint of HarperCollins Publishers.

The Song That Moves the Sun
Copyright © 2022 by Anna Shafer
Map art © 2022 by Cocorrina & Co LTD

Library of Congress Cataloging-in-Publication Data

Names: Bright, Anna, author.
Title: The song that moves the sun / Anna Bright.
Description: First edition. | New York : HarperTeen, [2022] | Audience: Ages 14 up. | Audience: Grades 10-12. | Summary: After seventeen-year-old best friends Rora and Claudia discover there are secret cities, ruled by astrology-based magic, on other planets in our solar system, they travel into the spheres to solve a mysterious disharmony threatening the balance of the outer worlds and their own.
Identifiers: LCCN 2021048399 | ISBN 9780063083523 (hardcover)
Subjects: CYAC: Fantasy. | Best friends--Fiction. | Friendship--Fiction. | Love--Fiction. | LCGFT: Fantasy fiction. | Romance fiction.
Classification: LCC PZ7.1.B754725 So 2022 | DDC [Fic]--dc23
LC record available at https://lccn.loc.gov/2021048399

Typography by Michelle Taormina
22 23 24 25 26 PC/LSCH 10 9 8 7 6 5 4 3 2 1

First Edition

for my brother, zack,
whose heart is shaped just like mine

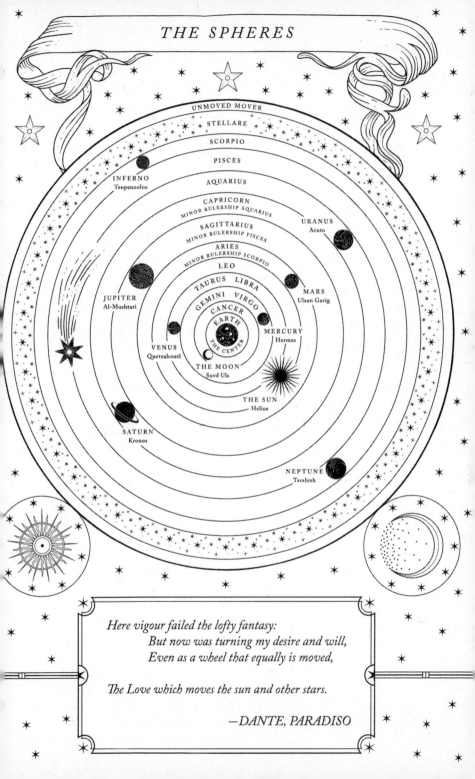

THE SPHERES

UNMOVED MOVER

STELLARE

SCORPIO

PISCES

INFERNO
Teopanzolco

AQUARIUS

CAPRICORN
MINOR RULERSHIP AQUARIUS

URANUS
Acuto

SAGITTARIUS
MINOR RULERSHIP PISCES

ARIES
MINOR RULERSHIP SCORPIO

LEO

TAURUS LIBRA

JUPITER
Al-Mushtari

GEMINI VIRGO

CANCER

EARTH
THE CENTER

MARS
Ulaan Garig

MERCURY
Hermes

VENUS
Quetzalcoatl

THE MOON
Suvd Uls

THE SUN
Helios

SATURN
Kronos

NEPTUNE
Tarshish

Here vigour failed the lofty fantasy:
But now was turning my desire and will,
Even as a wheel that equally is moved,

The Love which moves the sun and other stars.

—DANTE, PARADISO

1287

WE BEGIN AT the center.

In June of 1287, Dante Alighieri would have sworn the Republic of Florence was the center of the universe. It was the crown jewel of Toscana, a bright carnelian bead threaded on the River Arno, the city that would one day be the beating heart of the rebirth that would change all of Europe. It had raised him on gossip, nurtured him from a tender age on rivalry and intrigue.

But Dante saw clearly that night the fate that awaited him amid Florence's high stone towers and warring families, and his heart quailed.

He was nothing special among the family of Gemma, his affianced bride. Her cousins and brothers and uncles—the Donati men—were brawlers, fighting men who earned their coin as mercenaries.

In their household, he would be nobody.

Gemma Donati had been his father's choice following a shrewd evaluation of potential brides from the city's great houses. Dante had circled Florence alongside the elder Alighieri, feeling as though he were winding through the circles of hell.

And here was its lowest point: just outside Arezzo, some two days' journey from Florence. The city was in flames.

The warring factions that dominated Toscana and its neighboring states professed devotion to one mother Church. But theirs was a bloody, vicious sibling rivalry, with each insisting it was her favorite child and adherents switching sides over the years. Such a change in loyalties was the source of the coup in Arezzo, where the Donati men had been summoned to aid the besieged members of their faction. And they had brought Dante with them.

Great crowds of soldiers jostled and shoved in the dark as they made ready outside Arezzo's walls. Torchlight gleamed on steel plating and leather armor, on the chestnut flanks of their mounts. The air was full of the singing of swords and the stamping and snorting of horses, of the shouts of the fighters. Of the stink of flame and spilled blood.

Dante's head swam with it all: with the noise and the light and the salt-smell of bodily humors.

He had trudged here with Gemma's male relatives to battle alongside them. To prove himself one of them, however reluctantly.

But Dante was not a fighting man. He would never be one of them. He would only humiliate himself if he tried.

Heart full of fear and resentment, he turned his eyes away from the besieged city to a dark forest at its edge. It was dark as a dream, dark enough to hide him.

It called to him. Dante ran.

I AM AFRAID of thirty-one things.

I counted once, after that night a few weeks ago. The list runs through my mind as I wash my hands again and again in the Millers' bathroom.

Steam rises up from the basin of the sink. My hands are bright red. I snap off the faucet and reach for the towel to dry them off, then stop, arrested by nerves.

I wash my hands a fourth time.

Mr. Miller's been upstairs since he got home at half past three, looking glassy-eyed and feverish. I spent the next few hours spraying and wiping down doorknobs and light switches while Luke and Mia finished their homework and ate the pasta I'd fixed.

"Rora?" Mrs. Miller's voice follows me as I slip down the front hall toward the door. "I'm sorry again about canceling the trip. I can still pay you for the days you were going to be with us." She grimaces, her round, rosy face sympathetic. Mrs. Miller is an overworked HR rep at the hospital where my dad works as a custodian; she really needed this vacation. Luke and Mia had been excited, too.

I feel bad they're missing their trip. I feel worse to lose the pay for going with them. But pride won't let me take the money for nothing.

"Thanks, but it's okay." I slide my arms into my jacket. "Text me when you want to get back on our regular schedule after the holidays? I'll come pick up my stuff soon," I add, eyeing the suitcase I brought over after school. It was supposed to be waiting for me here after the show, all packed and ready for us to leave in the morning; I can't take it with me now.

"Sure, hon," she reassures me, glancing out the front window and grimacing. "Are you sure you don't want me to call you a—"

"No, thanks," I cut her off. I'm being rude; I can't help it. "Good night."

I dart outside and lock the front door behind me, fighting the urge to go wash my hands again. Pushing the thought aside, I hurry up the sidewalk toward Union Station.

The stars overhead are bright in the cold sky despite the light pollution. I can see my breath. It's December, two weeks till Christmas.

On my way, I text Claudia.

Be safe <3, she replies immediately.

I catch the Red Line below Union Station, pick a seat by the train window, draw my knees up to my chest around my backpack. I let my eyes sink closed to the sound of Jude London singing through my earbuds.

I was surprised at how prominently cleaning products featured in my litany of fears. I'm afraid of accidentally spraying them near people's food in the kitchen. Of cleaning the bathroom and still having them on my hands if I touch my eyes later. It's why I was still washing my hands long after I'd stashed the bleach bottle.

The Metro is always crowded during rush hour, people crammed into seats with laptop bags and purses, lining the aisles with suitcases and briefcases. I always wonder if everyone else is counting as they inhale and exhale, forcing their focus on their books or the music in their ears. If they're trying as hard as I am not to feel the crush of bodies behind and beside and in front of them, trying not to smell the perfume and body odor and weed and nicotine and coffee whose scents press against their noses from clothes and mouths all around, pervasive as the list of fears that runs in circles through my mind like the trains winding in endless loops through the city.

Of missing my Metro stop.

Of losing my phone. My wallet. My keys, especially when I have Luke and Mia.

Of leaving the Millers' house unlocked and getting fired. Of driving, even in their beat-up nanny van.

The anxiety has always been with me—a too-tight scarf around my neck, a too-warm sweater clinging to my skin.

But since that night—the one I try not to think about—the fear feels close and tight and thick enough to choke me.

The ancient train rattles my teeth in my jaw, but the window is cool against my cheek. In the quiet—but not empty, never empty— car, my neck and shoulders start to unknot.

It's the holidays; we ought to be full of comfort and joy. But mostly, we're all on edge.

The news is strange these days. For the last several weeks, sea levels have been falling. Mountains have shrunk by full inches. Week before last, a sinkhole ate half a small town in the Pacific Northwest. And if the weather is weird, people's behavior is even weirder. It's like Earth's somehow tilted on its axis, and we're all clinging to its surface by our fingernails.

I pull out my phone to text my dad that the trip is off. There's already a message from him on my screen. *All set to head out of town?*

Have fun tonight, sweetheart.

Quickly, I tap out the start of a reply. *Thanks, Dad.*

My parents never stop working. But if my anxiety's always in endless supply, it feels like there's never enough of anything else. Money. Energy. Time.

Mom and Dad are always exhausted. And worrying about me just makes everything harder.

Laughter bursts out across the car and I nearly drop my phone. The group of boys must be headed out for the night, maybe to 14th Street or Georgetown. It's below thirty out, but one of them wears a pair of Nantucket red shorts and loafers with no socks. I wonder if his feet are cold.

Claudia loathes preppy style. But they seem loose and comfortable, with their shaggy hair and shirts embroidered with whales or pigs.

I wear my leather jacket—hunted down over months at thrift stores—like armor. But they don't seem to need any.

The five of them look like an indestructible circle beneath the fluorescent train lights. Or like they think they're indestructible. I wonder if it's the same thing. Either way, I envy them. Hands shaking, I stick my phone back in my pocket.

Other fears that live beneath my skin, beneath the beds of my nails, that wake me up at night in a sweat, that strike my heart like a bolt of lightning:

Of being watched through my laptop camera.

Of getting germs in people's food when I cook. Of getting acne medication in my eyes.

Of being mugged, or raped, or murdered.

Of leaving the oven on, or my flat iron.

Of cheating on a boyfriend someday. Of being cheated on.

Of finding my drink spiked with alcohol, or something worse.

Of being called on at school when I don't know an answer. Of being called on, period.

Of something happening to Claudia. Or to my parents, or the Miller kids.

Of cancer, of heart attacks.

Of roaches. Of bedbugs. Of lice. Of rats. Of mold.

Of someone breaking into my parents' apartment. Of someone seeing the place where we live and judging us for how it looks.

Thirty-one things. One for every day of the month.

Some of my fears are colossal. Some are small, burrowing anxieties. But I feel them all. They get heavier every day.

Summer is coming! my horoscope promised this morning. Claudia always goes on about *confirmation bias* and how vague the predictions are, but I say vague guidance is better than none at all. Today, though, I wanted to agree with her.

Maybe summer's coming. But it's been gray here for months.

I push it all aside as I change trains in Chinatown, turning the volume up when the track changes—"An Early Cold," my favorite Ad Astra song. I let Jude London's voice and the impatient snare drum hurry me downstairs to catch the Green Line, the song leaping and diving as my train races through the tunnel. They're my favorite band for exactly this reason.

I try to imagine what it will feel like to finally see them at the 9:30 Club tonight.

But it's hard. It's hard to sit on the Metro and calculate, minute by minute, the risk I take just by being female and alone after dark.

Because one of my fears has already come true. And everything— the night around me, my very breath in my own ears—sounds different now.

CLAUDIA

2

I CROSS THE hall to Jack's door without even thinking about it. But it's closed. And then my brain remembers what habit still forgets sometimes: he's not there.

"Claudia!" my mom calls, clattering around her bathroom. The house is so quiet, I can practically hear every step of her nighttime skincare routine. "Your car's here."

I slide my coat off its hanger and move through the dark house, following the sound of her humming and the sink turning on and off. When I enter her marble bathroom, she's rubbing a jade roller over her neck, a towel wrapped around her hair, though it's only quarter to nine.

"Making a late night of it, I see?" I'm trying for humor, but my voice comes out tight.

"Your dad's at dinner with a client. I should be in bed already," she sighs. "I was at the embassy at seven this morning." My mother is the cultural manager at the Italian embassy here in DC. That Rome is six hours ahead of us means she's perpetually behind.

"Well, I'll be home before midnight," I say, checking my phone. Rora texted me a minute ago; I'll be just in time to meet her.

Her black brows arch sharply. "You're not going anywhere after the show?"

"Maybe to get coffee or something," I say, shrugging.

"I want to know where you are at all times."

I frown. "Aren't you going to sleep?"

"Claudia." Mom sets down the jade roller, one moisturized hand rubbing her temples. "Please, just do what I ask. Is that so hard?"

I'm honestly surprised she has any energy left for this kind of thing. I thought she'd spent it all on Jack.

I wave my phone at her. "I'll text you."

"Use your head," she cautions as I make for the door.

Always, I don't say. Because the water's already running again, and there's no one else in the house to hear me.

The black car is waiting out in the driveway, next to the uneven redbrick sidewalk that lines so much of Georgetown. I climb in, cashmere coat gliding over the leather seat. "Says here we're—" The driver pauses, frowning at his phone. "I'm taking you to the U Street Metro exit?"

It would really make more sense to just have him take me straight to the 9:30 Club, where Rora and I are headed. But Rora was mugged six weeks ago, and she's spent the time in between jumping at every sound. I'm not letting her walk alone in the dark.

"That's right." The driver just nods and pulls away from the curb, streetlamps and yellow-lit windows blurring past in the dark street.

I've lived so many places—my nonna's villa in Siena, New York City, Georgetown. Nonna's house was our home until I was eight. My old bedroom looked out over a terraced city of terra-cotta roofs sheltering homes and churches and the pigeons who lived in their eaves; my twin brother Jack's looked out on Nonna's garden, where she'd spend her early mornings fussing over her tomatoes and radishes before she went into the lab for work.

Jack's there now. I wonder if he's sleeping in his old bedroom, or if he's outgrown that like he outgrew me.

We moved to the States for my father's hedge fund job when I was nine. The change of pace—the shift between Siena and Manhattan—should have been jarring, but it suited me.

When I think of New York, I think of speed, of connectedness. Of never being alone. I think of five boroughs held together by subway lines, of the height of skyscrapers and the regal facade of the New York Public Library, where my mother organized *the* exhibit—the one whose success landed her the job she loves so much at the embassy. I think, too, of the series of underground EDM venues that Jack dragged me to on weekends, and the series of Jesuit schools that kicked him out.

I can't help analyzing our timeline, like I always do. I can't help wondering if even as he was pushing me to come out with him on Friday and Saturday nights, some part of him was pulling away from me.

Outside the Metro, I thank the driver, climb out of the car, and wait, shifting inside my coat as a snowflake hits my cheek. Delicate bits of white swirl in the light of the lamppost above me. It's December, too early for snow in DC, but unseasonable weather is par for the course lately. It's certainly no odder than sinkholes all over the globe or sea levels *falling*, when scientists have worried for years about climate change raising them.

"Claudia!" Rora calls, grinning as she races up the escalator. Happiness to match hers rushes up through me.

I tend to wear loose shapes and neutral colors—gray, olive, café au lait—but Rora is all black and white and as tightly fitted as she is tightly wound. Black moto jacket over a black hoodie. White skin pale beneath black eyeliner and dark bangs. White knuckles around her backpack straps.

We must look mismatched, standing side by side. And we're not much alike on the inside, either. But with Jack gone, I'd be lost without her.

Jack makes me look uptight by comparison. But maybe if Jack were a little less relaxed—a little more like Rora—he'd still be here.

"Did you have to wait?" she asks, catching her breath.

I shake my head. "Just got here."

"Mobile ticket? Or—"

"Nope. At will call."

Rora nods, approving. "Real tickets are better."

I grin despite myself. "I'll have to start a ticket wall like yours."

It took months for Rora to invite me to her house. But once she finally did, I was impossible to get rid of.

When I look back on DC someday, from wherever I land next, I know I'll remember cobblestoned Georgetown streets, Union Station standing like a soldier in the snow, l'ambasciata where my mom worked in a line with all the other embassies up Mass Ave.

But more than any city landmark, I'll remember Rora and me doing homework surrounded by Georgetown students at Compass Coffee, Rora and me eating pupusas at her favorite Salvadorian restaurant in Mount Pleasant. I'll remember Rora picking through thrift store stock as carefully as any buyer at Bloomingdale's or Barneys. And more than my own room in our town house here, I'll remember hers—the song lyrics scrawled around her mirror, the scrounged concert posters taped above her bed, the concert tickets that cover her wall like modern art.

DC isn't Manhattan. It lacks its height, its speed, its light. But until six weeks ago, it's been unimaginably easy to be happy here.

"Your mom would never let you tack a bunch of crap all over your room." Rora laughs.

I make a face, agreeing. "She was all over me tonight. *Use your head. Come straight home.*"

She sighs. "Your mom's such an Aquarius."

"I have literally no idea what that means."

"It means when she's at her worst, she's stubborn, detached, and unempathetic," Rora says, looping her arm through mine as we hurry past Lincoln Theatre, past Ben's Chili Bowl and U Street Music Hall. "Go easy on her. Her horoscope has been a nightmare lately."

"Really?"

Ro nods. "Aquarius, Pisces, Capricorn, and Sagittarius have been doom and gloom for weeks. It's been depressing," she admits.

I squeeze her arm. I think she's conflating fantasy with reality—I don't think there's any help to be found reading some vague, contrived fortune on the internet. But there's no denying Rora's anxiety has been worse since she was attacked six weeks ago. There's no denying it's been a bizarre six weeks.

My nonna tried to talk about it with me last week. She's a physicist at the University of Siena, and more curious than anyone I know, except Jack and me. While we were on the phone—neither of us mentioning my brother—she went on and on about how even though the sea levels on both the east and west coast of Italy are falling, strangely, the depth of the water above the coral reef off the coast of Monopoli hasn't changed at all. She said some of the researchers in the geology department are wondering if, somehow, the seabed is sinking.

The idea ought to have chilled me. But I couldn't muster the energy to chase the question. Somehow, the spark that always flares in me when Nonna strikes out on one of her intellectual investigations just wouldn't light.

"Yep. Bad omens all around. Except—" Rora pauses, steps slowing.

I gesture for her to continue. "Except what?"

"Except today," she says, brows drawing together. "Do you really want to know?"

I roll my eyes and hold up my watch. "Did your horoscope warn you that we're going to be late if we don't hurry?"

Rora laughs, long and loud, and we race down the sidewalk. And whatever the stars promise or threaten, her smile gets broader with every step. Because, for her, the warehouse-looking building across the street is home.

The only safe place in the world, she told me a few weeks ago when we bought our tickets. Back when Jack was supposed to come with us, too.

Concerts aren't therapy, Rora, I'd insisted. Her eyes had gone flat when she'd replied.

They're as close as I'm going to get.

I knew what she wasn't saying. Ro's mental health resources include music and her horoscope and not much else. If her parents have insurance, it's not the kind that'll cover therapy.

Money's never been a problem for my family. My dad constantly reminds me if I ever need to talk to someone, they'll set it up right away.

I suggested once that I could give Rora the money, or lend it to her. She didn't speak to me for the rest of the day.

Rora's my best friend, but we've only known each other for two years. We've never even been to a concert together until tonight. My misgivings always tell me I'm doing too much, that Rora suspects I latched onto her because Jack got his own life sometime when I wasn't looking. That I didn't know what to do about her anxiety *before* her assault, so how should I know what will help her now that things are worse than ever?

I think I'm right. But Rora's proud. So I let her keep her music, and I keep my worrying to myself.

"Aurora Sonder," she says to the guy at the will-call window.

"And Claudia Portinari," I add over her shoulder, flashing my ID.

The venue employee pushes the tickets at us through the little window. "I have one for a Giacomo Portinari, too?" she asks, pronouncing Jack's full name with difficulty.

I swallow hard. "Not us," I say, shaking my head. I try to ignore the ache in my chest like I ignore Rora's sidelong glance as we step aside.

She turns to me, seizing my hands, face going solemn. "Are you ready to enter, for the first time, the sacred temple that is the 9:30 Club?"

For her sake, I put on a smile, then squeeze her arm and push her toward the tail of the line. "Let's go."

1287

DANTE STARED UP at unfamiliar city walls, tantalized by the sounds of life singing from inside. An orange sunset sky blazed above the sepia-colored ramparts lined with roosting pigeons, and people of all kinds—soldiers and beggars and housewives and merchants, old and young and busy and loitering—crowded the great gate before him.

Dante had shot out of the siege at Arezzo like a comet, slipping over ground damp from blood or dew. He had not paused to assess what lay beneath his feet or what lay ahead; he had merely dropped his borrowed Donati sword and disappeared into the woods.

After passing through the forest, he came to a caravan, where he'd leaped into the back of a wagon and hidden under a blanket. The wagon had carried him west until the driver's wife tried to lie down in back, discovered him, and, shrieking, threw him out into an olive grove.

Shoes full of sandy soil, philosophically nursing his bruises, he'd thought the squawking wife not unlike his own fiancée. Gemma was forever asking questions. Even as he'd staggered from the poor shade of the olive trees into a tavern near the castle in Gargonza, he could picture his bride-to-be, her sallow face serious, eternally wishing to know his thoughts and demanding answers of him. *And what will you do, Dante? What do you desire, Dante?*

Thoughts of Gemma only soured his mood further. And when the barkeep had questioned how Dante would pay for the tumbler of *vino rosso* he'd ordered, Dante mouthed off to him before considering the wisdom of such a choice.

Patrons had trailed after them to jeer as the big man had belted Dante on the head and driven him out the iron-studded tavern door, then wiped his hands on his apron. *La forza* had captured Dante then, bound him and tossed him into a prison cart that had carried him to Monteaperti before—as he'd escaped the Donati men and their siege—he'd slipped through its wobbly bars.

Dante found himself now before the gates of the city of Siena. Motionless, exhausted, he watched them, watched people pass in and out of the city. But as he stood shivering in the sinking sun, cypress groves and rolling green hills at his back, his shirt bloodied and shoes broken, the gates began to grind closed.

He had sleepwalked and staggered through his journey. But suddenly, Dante awoke.

Again, he ran. *Aspettate!* he cried, afraid no one would hear him.

Dante scrambled through the gates, into the town, past crowded taverns and hay-scented stables and the city's fledgling university, the Studium Senese. Since he had left Arezzo, he had run *from*, not *toward*; he had been alone, an aimless object in space. Dante did not know that he was standing on the precipice of another world.

There at the Studium, high in a tower of honey-tinted stone, a woman stared out the window and watched the gates close beneath the setting sun.

She was running out of time. Mere weeks were left to her.

Dante did not yet know what would come. He did not yet know that this woman was the door to another world, and that she was another world herself.

He did not know yet. But he would soon.

RORA

3

YOU'D NEVER GUESS what this place is from the outside, if you didn't already know. It doesn't have a brightly lit marquee, like the Fillmore in Silver Spring or the Black Cat a few blocks away. It sure doesn't have color-saturated video screens outside like the big concert arena in Chinatown. 9:30 and its neighbors just look like warehouses, the venue a gold-brick building with an unexpected blue face beneath its low awning. I watch Claudia study the club's windowless exterior as I shiver in the cold, dancing against the air that bites my knees through my ripped jeans.

Claudia came to our school spring before last, after a second DC prep school had kicked Jack out and she hadn't wanted to stay without him. The twins are more or less attached at the hip. Or they were when I first met them. Back before Jack started acting out more and more and finally earned himself a one-way flight back to their grandmother's.

Claudia's family is fancy. They're the kind who go to fundraisers and gallery openings, who rent houses in other countries for whole seasons.

My parents may be perpetually broke. But I've never seen them

18

look as crushed as Claudia's did the last time Jack disappointed them.

Maybe that just means my mom and dad don't know anything about my life anymore. But apparently, being rich doesn't mean your family can't break your heart.

The day I met Jack in geometry is clear as a bell in my memory. He's the kind of guy you notice immediately, who prefers the center of the room to a spot on the wall, who pronounces Ibiza like *Ee-bee-tha* because he went once when he was eleven. But he's also the kind of guy who'll go up to someone looking awkward and lonely and poke an AirPod in their ear and tell them all about the horrible DJ he discovered last night. It wasn't long before we were swapping playlists and Jack was telling me all about his sister, who was already taking calculus and could totally help us get ready for our next quiz.

A pang chimes through me at the memory. Jack may have been Claudia's brother, but he was my friend, too. I think of his ticket, abandoned at the box office, and wish he were here.

Again, I check the time on my phone. We've missed the opening acts, but with my schedule, there was no avoiding that. The line inches forward, bringing us to the mouth of the alley beside the venue.

I don't see where the noise comes from. It's like a window shattering. No one else seems to notice.

But I feel the shock of it in my whole body, rushing from my teeth to my fingers and into my gut. I jump, twisting around, tripping over my feet.

"What was that?" My voice is knife-sharp, tight as my chest and my clenched fingers.

"Rora," Claudia cautions, voice soft. "Rora, it's nothing, it's fine."

I ignore her reassurance, straining my eyes to peer into the shadows. Deep in the alley, something silver glows against the bricks, cold and strange, like light off water or a mirror.

Claudia's wrong. It's *not* nothing. That lesson burned itself into me six weeks ago—that sometimes, it's not nothing.

I've always been anxious. A *what-iffer*, my dad gently calls me. But this last month and a half—this is worse. This is jumping every time I meet a stranger around a corner. This is riding a constant tension that keeps me sweating, jaw clenched, shoulders tight. This is a specific, drowning fear for every day of the month.

"Honestly, it's probably just people drinking or something," Claudia says soothingly. But I know the shape and sound of my best friend's voice. There's uncertainty there, and it only rattles me harder.

"But the light—"

"It's just a phone," Claudia insists.

No sooner has she spoken than the glow disappears and two boys cross out of the dark. The first lopes casually out of the alley, a tall white guy with long limbs and a tangle of blond hair. Another follows him, bronze-skinned and dark-haired, slighter and more cautious than his friend.

My conscious mind tells me what Claudia already has. That whatever they were doing in that alley, it had nothing to do with me. And still, my instincts hiss their warning. *Male, bigger than me, not safe.*

This is my life. The alarm never stops shrieking.

But beneath the apprehension coiling in my gut, tight and ready to run, something else tugs at my senses. A sound, like a high, sharp ringing in my ears. The silver light has disappeared, but a vague gleam still shimmers on the air, fading when I wipe my eyes.

It's a long moment before I realize I'm staring. The blond boy pauses—is he picking *glass* out of his knuckles? Either way, they're bleeding—to give me a curious, crooked smile. I jerk my gaze away and face the front of the line, ignoring them both as they come to stand behind us. Claudia squeezes my hand, her sidelong look significant. She doesn't let go until we're inside.

And somehow, my racing heart slowly calms.

Somehow, the alarm falls asleep.

CLAUDIA

4

WE DROP RORA'S backpack and our layers at coat check. I reach for my wallet. "Let me get it—" I start. But Rora just scowls at me, paying her fee and sliding two precious nannying dollars into the tip jar.

Her hands have stopped shaking, but she's still quiet, and her cheeks are still pale. Frustration burns through me.

Rora's been waiting for this show. I refuse to let her night be ruined.

So I pretend nothing's wrong—that the little interruption from the alley never happened. Since I'm taller, I slip through the crowd ahead of Rora and get us a spot near the stage, amused by how easy boys are to shift with just a hand laid on their shoulders. It's the same reaction, over and over: the turn, the surprised smile, and then I glide past, Rora in tow.

But apparently, tonight, it's my turn to be surprised. Because no sooner have we picked a spot to stand than the boys from the alley stop right beside us.

You've got to be kidding me.

Abruptly, I feel my jaw set, my tolerance and good humor starting to evaporate. Tonight is about cheering Rora up. These guys need to take a hint.

"Are you following us?" Rora bites out over the Green Day song tearing through the speakers.

"Why would we be following you?" one of them demands, pushing black hair off his forehead. He looks like a *Vogue* model, with guarded brown eyes beneath long lashes, bronze skin, and veins running like seams over his crossed arms.

The blond one raises a hand, like we're in class. "Uh, I'd gladly follow you around, if that's something you'd be interested in." *Blech.* "What were you doing out there in the alley?" Rora demands.

"Nothing," he says, too easily.

She hisses a breath. "Then what was with the weird light? With the—the music?"

I frown at her, confused. I didn't hear any music.

A pause. "You're imagining things," the dark-haired boy says stiffly.

"I am not imagining—" Rora begins, incensed. "I'm not crazy!"

"No one said you were crazy," the blond guy soothes her, glancing around nervously. A few people around us are starting to stare.

The dark-haired boy's voice drops. "If you make a scene—"

"She wouldn't have to make a scene if you guys could read the room and back off," I interrupt, glaring.

"Look, please just leave us alone," Rora bursts out. "Do you want us all to get kicked out?"

"No one's getting kicked out," the tall blond boy insists. But the security guard standing on the wall is looking our way, and I'm not so sure.

"I don't care if you were getting lit in the alley. You don't have to explain. Just please don't screw this up for me." Rora's voice catches. I put a hand on her arm as she grits her teeth and looks down, seeming smaller than usual inside her worn black hoodie. "It's all I've got," she finally says. "The music fixes me."

It's Rora's byword. The hope that carries her forward. It's all I want for her tonight.

But at her last words, the boys go still. They stare at Rora, and then at me, like we're the answer to a question they asked with no hope of response. The slighter dark-haired one tugs at his shirt collar, something sparking in his eyes.

And that spark—for no discernible reason, I want to keep it there.

My own interest annoys me. And then that glimmer, whatever it was—it's gone.

"Well, now I'm really excited to hear the band," the blond boy finally says, gaze flitting toward the stage. He clears his throat, glancing back to Rora. "I'm Major," he blurts out, then jerks his head at his friend. "This is Amir."

Amir clears his throat, posture stiff and uncertain once again. "Hello."

"I'm Claudia." I brush my hair back and smile, determined not to be affected by him, not to be curious. I haven't been interested in anything in six weeks; why start now? "This is my friend Rora."

"It's really great to meet you," Major says, nudging Amir. He's overeager, almost puppyish.

"Would either of you like something to drink?" Amir asks stiltedly.

Rora turns to face the stage again, huddling uncomfortably inside her hoodie, flashing the massive black X on the back of one hand. "We're seventeen."

"Water is a drink," Amir deadpans.

"We're fine," Rora says.

Amir shrugs, shouldering off toward the bar. "Fine."

"Fine!" Rora snaps back.

I stifle a groan and then—I can't help it. I follow Amir toward the bar.

"What's 'getting lit'?" I hear Major ask as I walk away.

1287

DANTE FELL EFFORTLESSLY into rhythm with the new city. It was so easy—so familiar feeling—that he did not sense, at first, that a new world was close at hand.

For Siena was not so unlike Florence. The same ragamuffin children scampered over its cobblestones, answering their mothers' calls to come in for supper as the evening gathered; the same pigeons cooed from the eaves of its red-tiled roofs. Laughter and lamplight and music spilled out of taverns; cats and vagrants picked over piles of rubbish in the streets. As in Florence, the smiths and coopers and carters who hawked their wares by day lit their lamps and stoked their fires to carry on working into the night, and messengers rode on horseback between the city's grand houses.

The difference, of course, was that here, none of those houses bore the name *Donati*.

Here, Dante was free of them. It was the only difference that mattered.

Or so he thought.

Dante was not accustomed to sleeping rough, but the summer night was warm. He hunkered down in an alley near a tavern, drew his ripped coat close about him, and slept soundly. In his narrow, shadowed little street, he did not awake again until the sun was directly overhead, blistering the earth and drawing the scents of dust and refuse into the air. He arose and stretched, his buoyant mood not diminished by the dingy laundry strung between windows above or the woman loudly berating her husband somewhere up the lane.

He felt like a new man. His own man.

Within a day, Dante had circled Siena's sepia-colored city walls, had stared in awe at its Studium Senese and its cathedral, il Duomo, with its grand rose window and its frescoes. Within two days, he'd felt the heat of its smithies, recoiled from its foul-smelling leather tanneries, allowed himself to lift, light-fingered, what he required from its covered markets. Within three, the drunks in the tavern near the alley where he slept greeted him like an old friend.

That was where Dante met him, holding court before intoxicated men and disreputable women like a prince, like a favorite son.

He was in his early thirties, olive-skinned and weather-beaten, with curly brown hair and a voice that projected to the very back of the tavern and eyes that looked like they'd seen long and far. Indeed, they said he'd made a fortune and a name for himself in the Far East, at the court of Kublai Khaan.

His name was Marco Polo.

Dante—he of the academic features and pale cheeks he thought too smooth for a man of twenty-two—was in awe of Polo's stories of adventure from the first. He felt as insufficient before him as he had among the Donati men. And again, he felt the desire to distinguish himself in distinguished company. He wanted to impress Polo in return.

He could never have made a name for himself in a family of fighters. But Dante had always had a way with words. This, he could do.

He was careful. He listened to Polo for almost a whole night before he ever opened his mouth. Then Dante began to do what he did best—better, even, than running away. He talked.

Dante, who had hardly ventured more than a day's journey beyond his home city of Florence, fabricated a few travel stories of his own. To his surprise, Polo listened.

When Dante was done, Marco tossed a coin to the barkeep, grinning with pleasure. "A drink, for my new friend Dante."

When the tavern finally closed, its owner began to shoo the drunks and the dancers and the tipsy singers from their benches. Marco and Dante staggered into the night together.

"Where do you travel next, my friend?" Dante asked. He tried to sound grand and unconcerned, but his tongue felt heavy and inept from the wine.

Polo shrugged, reticent. "Why?"

"I want to go with you," Dante said, plaintive as a child. "I want to see the world."

Polo seemed to tense, grimacing, and Dante flushed; his words must have sounded too pleading. Quiet fell between them.

When they found themselves outside the Studium Senese, the great university, Marco rolled one broad shoulder and pitched his empty wine bottle at an obliging window. The sound of glass smashing against the bricks—he had missed—shattered the quiet night; a cat yowled somewhere in a nearby alley.

"Ehi!" came a woman's cry from inside. "Smettetela! O chiamo le guardie!"

Polo laughed grimly and began to back away. Having no wish to meet the guard again, Dante did the same, throwing a final dizzy glance backward.

But when he saw the face leaning out the open window, he stilled, wiping his wine-bleary eyes.

"Beatrice?" He spoke her name philosophically, as if contemplating an ideal.

She blinked. "Dante Alighieri?"

Dante said nothing. He was too drunk to take her in properly, so he stared at her in pieces: auburn hair that swung over her shoulder, broad cheeks and full brows, red gown.

She'd always worn red.

Beatrice glanced up and down the street, then bit her lip. "Come up," she ordered softly. At once, Dante obeyed.

RORA

5

OF COURSE CLAUDIA would be into Amir. Of course.

They wait together at the bar. His whole person screams *I will require extensive emotional labor!* and Claudia never could resist pitching time and energy after a lost cause (exhibit A: Jack; exhibit B: me), so she's going for it. I watch the empty stage in silence, feeling myself climb down, step by step, from my earlier panic. Major glances idly between me and the crowd, me and the stage, seeming completely unbothered by my crossed arms and half-scowl.

His easy bearing reminds me of that group of guys from the Metro, and I'm abruptly grumpy that he can be so relaxed while I stand here, raw and worn out, like a troll in smeary eyeliner.

He's too tall. It honestly shouldn't be allowed. It's inefficient for people to be taller than five foot eight and he's easily clearing six feet.

When he stretches, I definitely do not watch his chest and shoulders lift beneath his shirt.

"You said before that the music fixes you," Major begins abruptly. The dull roar of the waiting audience is so loud he has to bend toward my ear to speak. Blond hair flops into his eyes when he leans over and he pushes it back again with limber tanned fingers. "What did you mean?"

I cross my arms tighter, hunching. "I don't know. It just does," I hedge, then attempt to change the subject. "Is Major your real name?" *Major what?*

His grin shifts into a wince. "No," he says, "it's a nickname." A guy shoves past, arms full of beers, too busy chewing the drawstring of his hoodie to watch where he's going; Major steps in front of him just in time to keep him from plowing right into me.

"I'm guessing you're the fan," Major begins again, jerking his chin at the stage. "More than Claudia."

I nod briefly, fidgeting and avoiding his eyes. "What about you? Are you coming to the Solstice Show?" Ad Astra's actual tour ends in Atlanta in four or five days, but they'll be back at the 9:30 Club the night of the twenty-first for a charity concert with a few other bands. I wasn't supposed to be in town that night, and neither was Claudia, whose family typically escapes somewhere warm for the holidays. But now that my work trip's off, I'm wishing I could afford a ticket.

Major shakes his head amiably and grins. His right incisor is a little crooked. "I've never heard them before. Amir found this concert."

"Ah." I clack my teeth together. A roadie onstage is securing a bunch of cords and I watch the duct tape roll like it's the most interesting thing I've ever seen.

Am I the most boring person in history, or just in this room? Only time will tell.

I push the feeling aside, letting anticipation shiver through my bones as I face the stage again and check my phone out of idle habit and nerves. Ad Astra's set should be starting in just a few minutes.

But Major keeps talking. Somehow, he keeps talking to me. "How do you hear their music?" I glance over, and my cheeks heat as

I find him scrutinizing my bangs, my face, my tight jeans, my chippy nail polish.

"How do I—?" I break off. It's a weird question, but he seems genuinely curious about my relationship with this band. And I don't know what to do with that.

How do I even explain what I feel about Ad Astra? And why do I feel like, if I do, I might as well start pulling my clothes off right here in the middle of the venue?

The magazine with the big piece on Ad Astra's new album had been so expensive I almost hadn't bought it. Then I'd pitched it across my room when I read the review, full of words like *tired* and *pretentious*.

You know who's tired? I'd asked the glossy pages. *I'm tired.* I have risk assessments running endlessly through my brain. On the hard days, Ad Astra's songs are all that pin my muscles to my bones and keep me moving forward. On the worst days, they're about the only thing that keeps me from lying down in the street.

The reviewer didn't get it at all. And if he didn't—maybe no one will. Maybe it's not even worth it to try and explain what this band means to me.

When Major arches his brows, I realize I've just been staring at him without replying. I hesitate. "I hear—"

But a roar from the crowd cuts me off. I whirl toward the stage, a grin splitting my face.

The lights go down. Ad Astra's on.

Claudia and Amir reappear beside us. She hands me a bottle of water, and I grip her shoulder. "It's starting!" I shout in her ear.

"I know!" Her hazel eyes are inches away, as bright as mine. "It's starting!"

"I know!" I yell again, shaking her a little, giddy. On her left, Amir's fighting a smile like he's afraid it's going to break his face. Not that I'm surprised he's warmed up a bit. Claudia's hard to put off when she wants something.

"Can you see?" Major bellows to me over the crowd, bending down. At my shrug, he maneuvers himself behind me so I've got a clear view of the stage. How did we get this far forward? We're practically in the second row.

But I forget my questions when the music begins.

"Ave Imperator" is brash from the get-go, a snare drum that chases my breath faster and faster, a guitar riff that has the entire hall jumping and clapping in seconds.

The lights go up. Jude steps up to the mic.

I sing with him. Every last word.

CLAUDIA

6

RORA IS EUPHORIC. And, as always with Ro, I'm having a better time than I expected.

That's who Rora is. She makes things louder. Brighter. Better.

I really like Ad Astra. Ordinarily my tastes run a bit more experimental, a bit less earnest. But this band is Rora's favorite. Experiencing this with her is what makes it worth it.

"Ave Imperator" ends, and the next song begins, and the cheer is deafening. Even I can hardly resist the spirit rising in the room, victorious and skyscraper high. I'm surprised at how many of these songs I know.

But the show feels almost like a distraction in light of our new friends' presence.

Major isn't watching Ad Astra so much as watching Rora watch them, and I can hardly blame him. In under four minutes, she's gone from sentry on defense to actual girl. Major's blocked at least one guy she didn't notice trying to invade her space, not to mention a crowd of spontaneous moshers—come on, guys, this is Ad Astra, not a Slipknot concert—and watching him, the knot of my worry loosens just a little.

Before Jack got shipped back to my nonna's, *Where's Jack? What's*

Jack doing? was my default setting. But the night Rora got held at gunpoint on the way to a Georgetown party—a party *I* invited her to—and had a panic attack in someone's English basement, my concern mutated into constant apprehension. It was the same night my parents decided they'd had it with Jack.

Jack and Rora. My twin and my not-twin.

Rora is still my best friend. But somewhere along the way, sometime when I wasn't looking, Jack and I stopped matching.

No one knew when Jack was swaggering around school or talking about learning Portuguese because "Brazilian girls are hot" (he's never met one) that the reason he never has cash is because he's always giving it away to people asking for help. Or that when we were fourteen, he smacked my mom's *Vogue Italia* out of my hands because he'd caught me obsessing over editorially thin models. There's more to him than most people know, and beneath all his attention-craving antics, there was always genuine joy. But that didn't make the acting out any less frustrating for the rest of us. And Jack never stopped pushing.

In ninth grade, he filled the staff lounge with lacrosse equipment; in tenth, he made some "educational additions" to our American history teacher's Columbus Day bulletin board. But that wasn't enough for him. Saint Teresa's finally took issue with the *entire wall of mural* he added about Columbus's crimes against humanity.

"I paid to have it painted over," Jack protested to my parents over dinner that night. "I left the cash right on the headmaster's desk. I don't know why he was so mad." Then he'd winked at me.

"Giacomo," my mom had sighed, rubbing her forehead, "you won't always be able to charm or buy your way out of tight corners." Jack had ignored the massive warning sign that was our mother using his proper first name and took this as his cue to embark on a long rant about art as protest and everything we weren't learning in school.

That's the thing about Jack. He's charming because he's sincere. He believes every word he says, whether it's the truth or he's stretching facts like a canvas to fit a frame he's already bought and paid for.

But Mom was right: Jack's luck eventually ran out, right around the time his behavior dove off a cliff. And I feel like I've been chopped in half with him gone. He's still posting online every day, but he hasn't returned any of my messages or calls.

I don't feel anything like myself anymore. Only being with Rora helps.

Until tonight. For a full hour, I haven't worried about Ro, or checked my phone to see if Jack's caved and texted me back.

Part of me is annoyed that it was Amir—not bizarre weather or scary news, but a boy—who finally managed to distract me. The other part is just glad to be distracted at all.

He doesn't seem to know any of the songs, but he's focused on the show, palm pressed to his sternum, thumb tapping the space between his collarbones in time with the beat. A metal cuff curves over the boy-veins in his wrist and forearm.

Amir catches me studying him and bites back a smile, then sobers, glancing at Rora. "She was really frightened by us earlier."

I feel my own smile falter. But Amir's only taking his cue to focus on Rora from me.

Jack may be gone. But Rora's still here, and it's my job to take care of her. That's what friends do.

"You didn't mean any harm," I say, raising my voice over the cheering from Rora and Major and the rest of the venue.

"But the music." Amir shakes his head. "She's right. There's something special about it."

I lean closer. "These all feel like questions, but you haven't asked me anything yet."

He glances restlessly from the stage to Major to Rora and back to me, gaze never quite settling anywhere.

"When the music stops," he finally says. "Then we'll talk."

1287

DANTE HAD BEEN nine when he had first seen Beatrice Portinari. It had been at a May Day party at her house, and she had worn red that day, too. Her hair had been lighter then, closer to ginger than auburn, and her cheeks had been pink and full like a cherub's in a fresco. He'd tried to ask his father who she was, but Signore Alighieri hadn't noticed.

People had often failed to hear Dante when he spoke. He was determined to change that.

He and Marco swayed now as they entered the library—for that was the building they'd laid siege to, the library of the Studium Senese—and climbed the polished wooden stairs. Beatrice did not speak when they reached the room where she sat alone, glancing between the skies and the documents before her.

He had seen her scant few times through the years—once or twice at grand affairs, a few more times on the streets of Florence. Once, he had passed her out walking with her mother and sisters and maid and she had greeted him, right there in the piazza. Dante's heart had soared. He hadn't even been certain she knew his name before then.

Though he was long engaged to Gemma Donati, he had mourned

when Beatrice had become betrothed to Simone dei Bardi, a grand banker from a grand Florentine family.

The choice of bride had never been his. But still, he had grieved.

Gemma was too thin, too loud, too opinionated. Too used to managing and shouting down her male relatives. Her strident voice cut through his dreams.

And Beatrice was here, away from all of them.

He had taken flight, had—however gracelessly—taken destiny into his own hands. And it had led him to her, to his purest childhood dream, like a damsel in a tale at the top of a tower, waiting to be rescued.

Dante watched her dazedly, unable to look away from the net of pearls pinned around her hair, from her gown red as a cardinal's robes against her pale skin. She looked a little weary in the candlelight, her deep green eyes shadowed from the late hour—perhaps many late hours.

Finally, Beatrice put down her pen. "Why did you throw things at my window?" she asked, voice dry, expression arch.

"The building," Marco pronounced, somewhat exaggeratedly, "offended me."

But Dante hardly heard Marco at all. "Bice," he said, "what are you doing here?"

Bice. Two little syllables, the childish nickname given by her sisters. It was the name of a girl who would rather stare out the window than at her embroidery, who crept in to listen when the learned old tutors came to visit her cousins just because they were boys.

"Studying." Beatrice's voice was steady, but she was clinging to her calm by a thread.

Beatrice and Dante had been raised mere houses apart. She'd

watched him grow tall and handsome. She'd watched him become engaged to Gemma.

She could hardly stand to look at him, here, where he should not be, where she had come to lick her wounds and enjoy one last twelve-month of liberty.

"Weren't you to be married?" Dante ventured.

Bice stiffened. "I will be. Just before the Feast of the Assumption of Mary in August." The feast day was not two months thence. She hesitated. "My parents gave me a year's reprieve to come to Siena, to the convent at Santa Petronilla."

Marco's gaze slid unevenly across the library, across the two rows of books in their honored place at its center. "I see no nuns."

"No," Beatrice said slowly, as if speaking to a child. "This is not the convent. This is the university."

"Then why are you here?" Dante asked again. She was not sure when he'd stepped nearer to her, but he stood barely a foot away.

Had he always been so tall? His features had been softer in childhood, the bridge of his nose less distinguished, the cut of his cheekbones less blade-sharp. They cast shadows across his face now; they made him look like a man.

"There is a professor of medicine here at the university," Beatrice finally answered. "He was aiding the sisters in their care of the sick at the convent one day, and when he finished, I assisted him in carrying his things back here."

"And you . . . never left?" Marco asked. "How simple it must have been. Would that we could all stumble into our vocations." He laughed, his mouth wine-stained and surly.

Beatrice felt herself flush. "My path has not been *simple*," she bit out.

They did not understand how little time she had left. How skillfully and persuasively she had had to plead to leave Florence at all.

They could not fathom how little power she had. How could they—two young men, with all the world and the heavens before them, and only a lack of will or wit to impede their ascent?

"I sleep at the convent," Beatrice said, her eyes aching at the very thought. "I pray Lauds with the sisters of Santa Petronilla at dawn, attend to the sick until midmorning, and then I come here to work until midnight or so."

"For this—professor?" Dante frowned.

Beatrice glanced away. "So he has informed the university."

"So much study," Marco mused, and Dante *hmm*ed in agreement. Beatrice felt her flush deepen.

"Do you fear I will lose my bloom?" she demanded. "That my eyesight will fade, that I will develop a squint?"

"No—no, of course not," Dante replied, stammering apologies and compliments. Staring at the unfinished pile of work before her, Beatrice hardly heard him.

"The sisters are aware that my opportunities for study may be somewhat . . . limited in the future," she said when she thought Dante had finished. "They have been very lenient with me. As has the professor. He has allowed me to embark on an independent course of study."

"How unusual." Marco reached with one handsome, blunt-fingered hand toward a small metallic model beside her on the table. It was circles within circles, a blue sphere at its center.

"Please don't touch that," Beatrice said, almost breathless with frustration. Cheeks coloring, Marco snatched his hand away and turned toward the bookshelf, putting his back to her and to Dante.

Dante cleared his throat. "What are you studying?"

"Ptolemy's model of the heavens, Pythagoras's theories. Among other things," Beatrice said vaguely. Then she paused. "And you, Dante Alighieri? What are you doing in Siena, so far from the fair Gemma Donati?"

At the mention of Florence—of everything he had fled—Dante was suddenly stymied. He had been a new man for three days so magnificent that he had nearly forgotten the Dante he had left behind.

That old Dante had run from the siege at Arezzo. From the family where he would never fit.

But nobody in this room had to know that.

Dante shook himself, remembering his new friend. "Polo?" he prompted. Marco straightened and turned from the books he had not been studying, facing the young pair.

"We," Marco said resolutely, "are explorers. I have come of late from the court of the Great Khaan, and Signore Alighieri is to join me on my next adventure."

"Indeed?" was all Beatrice said. But something lit behind her eyes.

Dante and Polo were to have an adventure together—and Beatrice as well, one that would far outstrip any of the tales told in the tavern that night, whether true or false.

Each of them would tell of it in tales both true and false for years to come.

RORA

7

TOO SOON, THE band leaves the stage, but we summon them back for their encore. I've been tracking their setlist, so I know what's coming.

I don't expect Major's touch. I glance up, startled at the brush of his knuckles against the back of my hand. It has to have been an accident; the room is packed. Still, I grit my teeth and wrap my arms around myself, because I can't handle the way my insides thaw when he looks at me. I can't afford that slushy softening feeling in my chest.

And beneath it all, though the room is still bursting with the noise of the crowd clapping and cheering for their encore, I hear that sound again. The same high, sharp sound I heard in the alley—music. It's elliptic, surging and fading in my ears. And like heat radiating off sand, it's coming from Major.

I don't know why I remember it now, but as Ad Astra begins their final number, I think of my horoscope.

Summer is coming!

The song starts with a synthesizer, with a circular two-note back-and-forth that kicks at my pulse and raises goose bumps on my skin. Then the drum, unassuming but steady. The beat resonates in my chest, rounding, rising.

Someone starts clapping. Then someone else. A chill runs up my spine. They're closing with "An Early Cold." Some part of me has been waiting all night for this song.

My pulse feels like a plane about to take off.

The cold came early, came early this year
It burned my fingers, bit my ears
We laced our boots, we ran outside
The snow found us undignified

The guitar comes in, a little distorted but promising, its double-time strum the burning fuse on a firework. Notes from the synth arc high and clear like crystal through the drumbeat, the pace of the song rising infectious and thrilling as its rhythm multiplies and divides itself.

Winter comes, it will not fail
But do you fear the early cold?
Run, run, make your blood flow
Build your bones up sevenfold

My heart feels like it's been shot from a cannon. I look away from the stage, pressing a hand to my chest because I think I might burst.

Major glances over at me and smiles, and it's like the sun coming out.

And then the chorus comes, and the song shatters into a thousand glittering shards of light. As the crowd roars, Claudia laughs wildly and I grab her hand. We sing, breathless because we're all jumping, even Claudia, even Major and Amir.

> *We the smashed up, we the bold*
> *We will brave the early cold*
> *We chase the highs, we chance the lows*
> *We will brave the early cold*

The room is a launchpad, and we are all bright, high, fighters, fearless, magic and happy and brave and alive, alive, alive. Our feet pound the club floor, the sound like a twenty-one-gun salute, like Roman candles taking off.

Major is shout-singing over all the noise by the second chorus and he won't stop smiling at me and I know if I looked down, I'd find my chest cracked open. This night has restarted my heart, shot it into orbit, set it beating hard and thankful between my lungs. The music halos me, protects me inside its relentless light.

This is why I come here. This is why I came here. Because there is no fear on the air in this room. Because my heart isn't my responsibility to beat tonight. For now, my blood will flow at someone else's bidding.

This is the safest place in the entire world.

The song soars toward its final notes and I wipe my eyes with the hand Claudia's not holding. We're shouting and cheering long after the band leaves the stage.

I glance up at Major again, his chest heaving from dancing, his fair hair and gold lashes caught in the stage lights. When he glances down at me again, his grin is a mile wide.

It shouldn't matter. I shouldn't care, because I barely know him. But I'm suddenly glad Major could see me here, like this. Happy and unafraid.

He's still watching me when the lights come up.

"I told you," I say to him and Amir and Claudia, who already knows all too well. "The music fixes me."

CLAUDIA

8

"WE NEED TO talk," Major blurts at Rora, eyes darting back to Amir.

"About what?" Rora asks.

Amir frowns at his friend. "We do?"

"You did say you wanted to tell us something after the show," I say, nodding to Amir, trying to catch my breath. I don't usually dance; I'm not sure what made me do it tonight.

"Come with us. To the—" Major glances around. "Bathroom?"

Rora scowls, drawing into herself. "Why can't you just tell us out here?"

Where there are people, she doesn't say. *Where it's safe.* My heart sinks a little to see the joy of the show already fading from her face.

"We want to show you something," Major says.

"Major . . . ," Amir begins, slow and cautious. He scrapes a hand through his damp hair, and the iron-colored band around his left wrist flashes in the overhead light. Its engraving says *hic manebimus optime.*

But Major doesn't reply. All around, people are crowding the merch table, finishing up their drinks, paying their tabs. Roadies call to each other as they clear the stage. For a long moment, none of us speaks.

"Look," Major finally says, leaning close to Rora. "You're in pain. You've *been* in pain."

"Yeah, well. I'm not the only one. The world's basically tilted sideways." She glances significantly at me, and my chest is suddenly tight, my phone too silent in my pocket.

"The thing is—" Major hesitates, but only for a second. "The thing is, we might know why you feel this way."

"Major." Amir shakes his head. "What are you doing?"

"But I think you can help us," Major pushes on. "And I think we can help you. Just let me explain."

Rora and I exchange a glance. I will my face not to reveal my rising doubt, but unease takes root inside me. What does Major think he knows?

I think then of the strange light and the sound of breaking glass in the alley, of Rora's earlier worries. I wonder if I brushed them aside too quickly.

Rora relents but doesn't relax. "Fine," she says. "Five minutes."

There's a line for the bathroom, so we kill a few minutes by retrieving our things from coat check. When it's finally emptied out, we slip inside the women's room, its entrance inexplicably marked by an Ariel Barbie doll in a shadow box.

Major pushes a heavy black garbage can against the inside of the door, and my hackles go all the way up. I step shoulder to shoulder with Rora. "What are you doing?" I demand.

"Same question," Amir says, misgiving in his voice. "I'm not sure about this."

"I am." Major holds up his hands, all assurance. "Just trust me."

"I do trust you," Amir counters. "I just don't understand what you're doing. We came here for the song, and we've got it." In the mirror, a confused frown creases my reflection's face.

"No. We've got something better," Major says, glancing at Rora, voice urgent. "Just help me show them? Please?"

Something about that *please* does to Amir what worry for Rora always does to me. Amir relents with a sigh. "Okay."

He leans over the counter toward the mirror, breathing on it and tracing figures in the fog. Beside him, Major closes his eyes like he's making a wish and begins to hum, the sound rising and falling in his chest.

For one moment—two moments—nothing happens.

When Amir lifts his palms from the mirror and turns his unreadable gaze back to me, my heart jumps. And it seems to stop fully when slow circles begin to trace *themselves* across the glass.

Rora draws closer to the boys. To the mirror, and the impossible thing there. I have no choice but to follow her.

Concentric circles, spheres inside spheres. Shining words that cover the mirror from its scratched-up center to its graffiti-scrawled edges.

Luna. Mercurii. Veneris. Solis. Martis. Iovis. Saturni. Ouranous. Neptunus. Inferno. Stellare. Primum Movens.

The moon and Mercury. Venus, the sun, Mars. Jupiter, Saturn, Uranus, Neptune. And there at the edge—Inferno, the stars, the Prime Mover. I've never heard of a planet called Inferno.

"This is the Ptolemaic model of the universe." My voice is unrecognizable in my own ears; I feel like I'm choking. "Pre-Copernican. Geocentric," I add to Rora, my words tripping unfamiliarly.

Rora stares blankly at the map, the rings each set with colorful objects representing heavenly bodies, a blue and green orb to indicate Earth at its center. "As in—when we thought Earth was the middle of the universe?"

"Yeah," I say, airless. "Doesn't explain how it drew itself on the 9:30 Club bathroom mirror, but." I wipe my eyes, but the image of the spheres doesn't fade. The rings cut again and again through Rora's pale, spooked reflection.

Abruptly, she pulls away. In one move, she swings her backpack up off the floor and onto her shoulder and starts around Major. "Okay, five minutes are up. I think we're done here."

"Wait!" he blurts, dismayed. "We didn't even get to explain why we're here!"

"For a concert? To harass some girls you don't know?" Rora asks helplessly. But she doesn't leave; her eyes are fixed on Major.

"If you're going to tell us what this means, then tell us now," I interject. My voice comes out exactly as sharp as I intend it to.

Amir answers first. "Major came here from Mercury and I came from Mars," he says rapidly, the words breaking into my thoughts. "There are cities. Cities on the planets in these spheres. And—something is wrong there."

"What?" The word clatters in the silent bathroom, like a dropped fork at a too-quiet dinner table. I stare between the boys, waiting for one of them to crack a smile and admit they're just fooling around. But they don't.

"What—" Rora clears her throat. "What kind of something?"

"You said the world has tilted sideways." Major looks down at Rora, expectant and hopeful and worried. "Amir and I are roommates at school on Mercury. It's the same there. Has been for about six months."

"Really?" Rora's word is a breath. Her eagerness fills me with apprehension.

He nods. "Six weeks ago, the tides on Venus went out and never came back in, because the sea levels fell."

"That's happening here, too," I blurt. I can't stop myself. "And mountains have been shrinking—literally, their peaks are documented as being lower by full inches over the last six weeks."

Major nods vigorously. "And it's affecting the signs and the songs. No one trusts anyone right now, theft is up—all of Mercury's worst traits in action. Amir's been trapped with his squad on Mars—"

"I belong to Mars, but I'm only supposed to be there weekends, for training," Amir adds, scratching the back of his neck. "But now all of us who belong there are piled up there together, and the squads are constantly fighting."

"What do you mean, *the signs and the songs*? What does *belonging to Mars* mean? And how did you get here if you've been stuck somewhere else?" Rora asks. But all the talk is flying past me now; I'm only half listening.

"Six weeks," I whisper to no one in particular.

It's been six weeks since Jack's behavior took a surprise turn for the worse and he got kicked out of our school. It's been six weeks since the night Rora was attacked. But I can't even countenance the things they're claiming.

The problems out in the world are huge. They are the size of oceans and mountains. And we are just us—just people, even our biggest hurts small enough to fall through the cracks in the universe.

Whatever's affecting the world at large, it can't possibly care for our little aches and pains.

I tilt my head back. "Why are you telling us this?" I ask the ceiling.

"I'm wondering the same thing," Amir says to Major. He addresses me when he speaks again. "The natural disasters and the strange behavior—it's all owing to disharmony in the spheres. They produce music, and it's off. It's gone wrong. So we came here, searching for powerful music—a song to fix things."

I grasp for a reply, watching Amir's handsome, set-in-stone face, but I can't find one. Not a single response presents itself. Because what is there to say to an assertion like that?

Six weeks, six weeks, six weeks.

I'm a skeptic. My physicist nonna's granddaughter and a devout believer in objective inquiry. But a tiny, niggling, frustrating crack starts at the base of my doubt and disbelief.

I patch it up immediately.

"A song to fix things?" I ask. My voice rings through the bathroom. "What does that even mean?"

But Major shakes his head. "No. The song isn't what we need. It's not the music." He pauses, voice full of wonder, eyes full of light as his gaze swings from Amir to my best friend. "It's *you*, Rora."

1287

MARCO AND DANTE visited Bice night after night in the library. Sometimes, other students joined them—one or two women who had made their way into the university under the pretense of keeping house for a professor or visiting a brother, and a few proper students too poor or too passionate to spend their evenings in more idle or fashionable fashions.

They were secretive about the nature of their work around the two interlopers. But one thing was clear: all wanted, desperately, to be there. In this, Dante was no different from them.

Dante could not stay away from Beatrice. He could not stop studying her hands as she worked, could not stop watching her face as she laughed aloud at a joke from a fellow scholar. Though her eyes were ringed with weariness from her long hours, they were bright when fixed on the model at her side, as she made her calculations and contemplated the books around her.

She loved her studies. And Dante loved to be near her.

Little more than a month after he'd left, Dante's life in Florence already felt far behind him. He had heard rumors the Donati men were looking for him, ready to drag him back to his betrothed and to his old life; but Siena sang to him.

To be near Bice, after all these years, sang to him.

Late at night, when the scholars set aside their parchments and models, their strange assortment of musical instruments, Marco regaled them with wild stories of his travels, arms outstretched, broad mouth full of laughter. And as he narrated his rambles from Venice to Jerusalem, across the Steppe to the court of the Khaan, the students listened in awe, glasses of cheap Chianti held in suspension, knees drawn up under chins. When it was Dante's turn, he mimicked Polo, slipping on his friend's confidence like a robe as he blended lesser-known stories from Horace, Ovid, and Virgil with gossip from the highest circles of Florentine society.

As Marco and Dante spoke, the scholars looked again and again to Beatrice, as if gauging her approval. So transfixed was she by the stories, she hardly noticed their glances.

One night, though, she seemed distracted. Dante rose and walked to where she sat at her table by the window. "Bice?"

Beatrice stared out into the night, not looking up at him. "Do you know what day it is, my dear Dante?"

Dante shook his head. Time meant nothing to him anymore, here with her.

"The sun has entered the sign of the Lion, and it is twenty days until the Feast of the Assumption," said Beatrice. When she finally looked back at him, her eyes were red.

Dante swallowed, and thought of Florence, some forty miles and a world away.

Beatrice had only ever had a year, and it was nearly over.

"Do you wish to go home?" he asked.

The pearls in her hair caught the moonlight as Beatrice shook her head. With her free hand she traced the silvery model at her side, Earth at its center.

Finally, she spoke. "Your presence has enlightened me, dear Dante. With you here, my calculations seem to have completed themselves." Bice's eyes rose like stars to meet his own. "You and Marco have traveled so widely, so far. I want to do the same. I want to see marvels."

Dante could not breathe, could not speak.

"You," Beatrice continued determinedly, "will come with us."

They made ready in a mere revolution of the sun. Foodstuffs were assembled; clothes were folded into packs; magicians of various stripes slipped inside Siena's walls to join Beatrice's cadre, bearing well-worn spell books and hard-won arcane knowledge. Dante and even Marco watched, astonished, as the conjurers—some they had thought mere university students—demonstrated their abilities. *Only cantrips*, one of the practitioners replied with a smile.

As they prepared, Beatrice explained to Marco and Dante in fits and starts what she had done: she had calculated the shapes of the heavenly spheres, had studied the texts of the scholars who laid out their order from Luna to Saturni. Most important, she had studied what she called the music of the spheres.

"The celestial bodies produce a harmony we cannot, here on Earth, detect," she explained, effusive. Her red sleeves and skirts billowed behind her as she strode through the library, returning supplies and textbooks to their shelves, determined to leave all in its proper place when she departed. "The planets' sizes, their move-ments, their godly properties, their physical compositions—their summation is a music, a song, conducted by forces that dwell among the stars and beyond. And their harmony or dissonance is reflected in the world around us." Bice whirled on them, smiling, triumphant.

"Does Earth produce music?" Marco asked, frowning, rubbing a hand through his curls.

"It must." Beatrice brandished a page at him, recited the Latin without looking at it. "'. . . Et quod est superius, est sicut quod est inferius, ad perpetranda miracula rei unius.' In short, as above, so below," she said. "And we, my dear Dante and Marco—as Hermes Trismegistus says—shall perpetrate miracles." Beatrice looked up, smiling. It was bright as gold, and all for Dante.

It was impossible to doubt her when she looked at him that way.

"It has all been much clearer with you here," she said to him. "The music I sought, and my calculations. With you here, I have rendered sheet music."

It would be blasphemy to worship her as Dante wished he could. With her arms full of books and her auburn hair falling around her face, she looked passionate, beatific. She glowed like a star herself. He struggled not to fall to his knees.

Dante the blasphemer. Dante the fraud, with unconfessed false-hoods piling up around him. He was grateful that Marco, at least, was a true adventurer—not a runner, not a mere spinner of tales.

When the time came to depart, they numbered twelve in the library of the Studium Senese—four magicians, five astronomers, Marco, Dante, and Beatrice herself. Twelve for the passing hours of the day, for the twelve astrological signs.

Beatrice produced a small set of pipes from her pocket. She,

Dante, and Marco stood close together, the magicians and the scholars assembled behind them.

Dante felt bloodless, faint, fragile as the parchment in Beatrice's pale fingers. Her brow knitted in concern at his sudden pallor, her gaze flashing from Marco to Dante in confusion.

Would she learn that he was a fraud? Would the Church burn them all for witchcraft? Would the Donatis hunt him down and drag him back to the life he'd left behind?

Not if he could run far enough. Not if he could run fast enough.

"Take my hand," Beatrice said to Dante, and he did.

"WHAT DO YOU mean?" Claudia asks again. She's close to my side; I breathe in comfort with the familiar smell of her cashmere coat and Marc Jacobs perfume.

Major reaches for me with his gaze, and this close, in the light, I can finally see his eyes are some color between light blue and gray. "Rora, you said that the music fixes you. I saw right away what you meant."

I might not have blurted out that confession if I'd known Major would still be chewing on it hours later. Again comes that feeling that I've stripped to my underwear in the middle of the venue. "Okay. So the concert was amazing. So what?"

"The concert was great," Major agrees. "But Rora, you made it *powerful*, because you feel the music so fully."

"What?" Claudia's expression narrows.

Major leans his head down, forcing me to meet his gaze. "Rora, you're an amplifier," he says, warm and a little awed.

My cheeks flush at his tone. "I don't know what that means."

"Each of the spheres produces music," Major says, gesturing back at the mirror. "And the music is more than just sound. It's magic, it's atmosphere, it's the properties of a planet."

"But what does that have to do with me?" I ask helplessly.

"Being an amplifier means music resonates in you so intensely you actually strengthen it. It means that you're powerful." Major's voice is earnest. "All the early explorers had an amplifier—it made them able to travel through the aether. Into the spheres."

Powerful. I don't feel it. The word glows on the air between us, as strange and unlikely as the light I saw in the alley.

At my side, Claudia presses her lips together and looks away, her posture all defensiveness and disbelief. Amir looks just as unconvinced. "You have no way of knowing that. Amplifiers show up once a century, if that," he interjects, voice sharp enough to cut glass. "We don't even know that much about them."

"Amir, I'm *sure.*" Major huffs a breath, breaking my gaze just long enough to dart a lopsided grin at his friend. There is light in every line of his face. "Weren't you watching her?"

Amir looks incredulous. I feel myself color from head to toe.

"I want you to meet Dr. Qureshi, an astronomy professor at school," Major says.

"What for?" I ask.

Major takes a step toward me. "We came searching for a song, but we've found something better," he says, effusive. "With your ability, we could solve the disharmony. We could solve what's hurting you."

A flash of that night comes back to me. The old man. The gun.

Everything about the memory is stark-etched in my brain, ugly and real and mundane as a negative bank balance. But their story casts it all in a different light.

Was it just ordinary evil? Or was it magic—magic strong enough to cut down mountains and shrink seas, magic made of music in the heavens—that stopped me in the dark that night?

If it's magic, I should be afraid of magic. But somehow, reality is infinitely bleaker and more frightening.

"And why is this your job?" Claudia asks. The line of her jaw is sharp. "Also, even if we concede that Rora has *powers*, how are you going to fix music by amplifying it? How will making it louder or stronger help? That doesn't make any sense."

Amir studies Claudia before answering. His demeanor is cool, but his eyes rove over the long angles of her face, the swing of her long hair, the drape of her coat over her long frame. "Correcting the music could be a question of restoring balance. An amplifier, if she is one, could do that."

I pay attention just long enough to notice he doesn't answer her first question. After that, I don't hear anything at all. I sit heavily against the counter as they bicker, ignoring the water puddled around the sink and soaking into my jeans, still watching Major.

I don't understand it all. This conversation has gotten away from me entirely. But I want suddenly, more than anything, to believe that the things these boys are saying could be true.

Hope swells like a bubble, rainbow-bright in my lungs, and I'm afraid if I breathe it'll burst. It's too dangerous to let myself believe things can really get better.

All of it's impossible.

But until six weeks ago, a gun pointed at my chest was impossible.

And the map still hovers over the grimy bathroom mirror, shining like light on water. It doesn't care that logic dictates it should not be there.

It's not a phone projection; the mirror isn't some kind of screen. This bathroom doesn't even have soap or paper towels or working stall locks half the time.

I know this place. I know which stalls have stickers on their doors, which have my favorite graffiti. And I know that besides the pure alchemy that happens on the stage four to six nights a week, if there's anything magical at the 9:30 Club, then Major and Amir brought it with them.

I believe—or, at least, I *want* to believe. That what they insist is wrong on Mercury, on Mars, can explain what's undeniably wrong *here* on Earth, with us.

With me.

"You're a Capricorn, aren't you?" Major asks me suddenly. "You belong to Saturn."

I fix him with a look. "What is this, an exhibition of weird pickup lines?"

"I'm *telling* you," Major says, intent. "I see you. I think we can help."

Claudia suddenly straightens. "No. This is all—it's ridiculous. Why should we even believe you? Why do you think you know who Rora is? You just met her."

"I agree," Amir says, turning to Major. "We came here for a song. We can't go back with a *person*. Not with—" He breaks off, brows arched, looking significantly at his friend.

"But an amplifier is *better*," Major says, baffled. "An amplifier is—it's *fate*, Amir. Don't you want to fix this?"

"You know better than anyone that I do," Amir says, voice and eyes tight. Silence hangs between them, full of old worries and rehashed conversations—things they could never explain to us here and now.

"Rora, this isn't the answer." Claudia's voice is even, rational. "You need therapy. Maybe medication. You need to *talk* to someone. You don't need weird space magic."

"Except you know none of those are options for me," I say,

frustrated. I hesitate, watching her.

Claudia cares. But sometimes, I'm afraid she doesn't understand.

"We'll be right back," I say to Major and Amir, pointing between them. "You two, figure yourselves out." Then I drag Claudia three paces into a bathroom stall and squeeze in after her.

"You can't seriously be thinking of going with them." Claudia's words are quiet, but her eyes and her gestures are huge.

My whisper back is taut, sharp enough to guard against treacherous hope. "Do you think they're lying?"

"Do you believe them?" she demands.

I take Claudia's fingers in mine, force her gaze to mine. "Claudia. Tell me. Do you think they're lying? About where they come from? About—what I am?"

We both know Jack has a creative relationship with the truth. It's made Claudia an expert interpreter.

Claudia sighs, tugging on her necklace. "I don't understand how what happened to you and Ja—how *that* could have anything to do with all the natural disasters. And I don't know if I believe you have magical abilities, even though you know I think you're amazing," she adds, squeezing my hands, her brow creased with love and concern. She hesitates.

"But?" I prompt.

"They could be delusional. But"—she finishes with a grimace—"they don't seem to be lying."

"Okay," I say slowly. "Okay."

Major thinks they can help me. Major thinks I have the ability to help everyone. My heart begins to race.

Claudia sighs, dropping my hand to pick at an All Things Go

festival sticker on the wall. "What about real life? You're supposed to be leaving with the Millers tomorrow. You're due back there in, like, two hours."

"About that." I peek through the gap in the stall. Amir and Major speak in agitated whispers, gesturing at our door. "They canceled the cabin trip. Mr. Miller has the flu. They don't need me to watch the kids."

Claudia twists her fingers together. "Have you told your parents yet that you aren't going?"

I shake my head, silent. "Started to. Forgot."

"So they're not expecting you home until Christmas Eve."

I shake my head again. "And you guys haven't resurrected your travel plans." It's not a question; she would've told me.

Claudia laughs dryly. "My mom 'couldn't handle' Saint Lucia after everything happened. Like it takes so much effort to overnight gifts and sit in an infinity pool."

I hesitate then, all my misgivings flooding back in. "But what do they *mean*, Claudia?" I ask. "'A song to fix things'? And what does it mean that all the stuff that's happening there—the sea levels falling—that it's happening here, too?"

"I don't know." Claudia shrugs, her expression careful, her voice solemn. "Look. We can bail. We can be at Ted's Bulletin in twenty minutes and take homemade Pop-Tarts back to my house and forget this ever happened." She pauses, her jaw working, then glances out the gap between the stall doors. Her eyes linger first on the mirror, then on where the boys stand, still whispering.

"Or?" I prompt.

"Or, I can tell my parents I'm going with you and the Millers

63

to the Shenandoah cabin and we can find out what they mean. Go meet this professor. See if the chaos out there matches what's happening here on Earth." Claudia's expression shifts, analytic. "See if this . . . disharmony is responsible for what happened to you."

"But you aren't buying any of this." My voice is barely a breath.

"Doesn't matter," Claudia says. Her voice is hard and her thin shoulders are stiff. "Where you go, I go. Period."

I shake my head. "But you don't even think it'll work."

"I think you need medical help, not magic. But . . ." She pauses, dipping her head.

"But what?" I press.

Claudia glances up, uncertain. "But I'm not in the habit of disbelieving my own senses. And that model on the mirror—I can't explain that away." She hesitates. "And it does make me wonder."

I'm wondering, too. Wondering if my problem isn't *just* my problem but a piece of something larger. If I am part of something larger.

If my newest cause for pain isn't just some crime statistic, the kind of thing that happens every day and means nothing. If it's something cosmic and magical. If it means everything.

"Your parents are gonna be so pissed," I say, suddenly fighting a laugh.

Claudia smiles grimly. "They used all that up on Jack."

"Fair." I swallow, nod. "Then let's go."

I push through our stall door, backpack clenched in my fist, glancing first at Amir, lingering on Major.

Hope is dangerous. But for the first time in a long time, it's a risk I'm willing to take.

Claudia fires off a text to her parents and then, decisively, puts her phone on airplane mode.

"So?" I ask Major and Amir.

"So," Amir agrees. His expression is tense. "I have to be the one to fix this. I just do. So you should come with us."

I don't know where the weight in his gaze comes from, but I recognize it all the same. Is it guilt? How could he be responsible for cosmic disharmony—for something larger than any of us?

Amir turns determinedly back to the mirror, glancing down at ink scrawls on his palm as he traces numbers in the fog.

"How?" Claudia's voice catches.

"C-sharp," Major says, speaking to Claudia though his eyes are on me, full of expectation. When he digs into his pocket and produces a silver pitch pipe, I take it, and the fingers of his injured hand brush mine. I realize I never asked how he hurt himself—why he was picking glass out of his knuckles when he walked out of that alley.

"The planets produce music in a specific tone, based on their speed, their size, their nature," Amir says, glancing over his shoulder as he writes. "We can travel with the tone that belongs to a particular sphere, and coordinates to guide us to a particular point on the planet, because all things seek their place."

"I still don't understand," I falter, turning the pitch pipe over in my hands. Major stretches out his palm, and I pass it back.

"Watch," he says with a lopsided smile.

He plays himself a tone, and once he's got it, he begins to hum. Major's eyes fall shut, C-sharp swelling on his voice, his tanned forehead wrinkling over fair brows.

And then: magic.

Magic like the glow of light where there was none before. Like stars against blackness. Like the smile on Major's face at the amazement I feel taking over mine.

A portal takes shape on the air in the middle of the bathroom. Circular, glassine, not much taller than us, quivering but substantial. I'm completely alive with wonder, my nerves tingling from my head to my toes, struck that it's not only the impossible horrors that come true.

Sometimes, the impossible beautiful things become real, too.

Holding my breath, I step closer to look through the portal and find it's the entrance to a tunnel. Somewhere down its curving length, a gray planet hovers in the distance. Its stone surface is pitted, scarred and scored with lines like connected highways, but it shines quicksilver-bright.

We're looking at Mercury. And emerging from the planet, soft and elliptic but unmistakable, I hear music, a richer and wider echo of the note Major sang.

Amir pushes against the wavering portal before us, then presses harder when nothing happens. It shivers like a soap bubble.

Major makes a frustrated sound, leaning around Amir to put his good hand to the surface. Still, nothing.

The boys exchange a glance.

Amir sighs, wraps his hand in his T-shirt, and punches the quivering portal.

I can't even hear my gasp above the sound of its shattering. Light pours onto the grimy bathroom floor through the cracks that spiderweb across the crystal, then through the larger gap Amir clears with his elbow like he's knocking shards out of a window frame. Shirt torn here and there, he steps halfway through and offers Claudia his hand. "Let's go."

My breaths come heavy and fast. A lump grows in my throat as I stare around the dingy bathroom. Stall doors sag on their supports; paper towels straggle from dispensers.

Suddenly, someone tries the main door—but it's blocked by the massive trash can Major shoved against it. They knock loudly, their annoyed shouts floating in from the hall, and my heart begins to race as I wonder if a club employee is about to burst in and throw us all out. "Let's go," Amir says more urgently, glancing at the door.

Am I really doing this?

My whole life, I've managed my fears on my own. Even these past six weeks, I've soldiered on, pushed the thing that happened out of my mind, pushed forward, tried not to burden anyone else.

But you can't go on like this, whispers a small, tired voice in my head.

I've been scavenging bits of strength and stability from Claudia and the music I love, trying to cobble together a full life out of them. But it's not enough. It's not enough to feel like an alien everywhere but here, drowning my anxiety in music one show at a time.

And if the entire universe is swinging off its hinges, what are the odds that I alone can find a way to be safe?

This magic is too big—too strange—to face on my own. Much as I'm afraid to admit it, I need help. I need help finding out if the change I've felt these past six weeks isn't just something that's happening to me.

More than that, if somewhere in this vast, unknown circle of worlds, someone understands the problem and what we have to do to solve it, then I have to try to help them.

Claudia steps through after Amir, avoiding the shattered edges of the crystal, and I watch her feet leave the bathroom tile for the portal's gleaming floor. She stares around, hazel eyes wide as she takes in things I can't see from where I stand.

I look up at Major, the gold of his skin and hair, the grin hovering at the corners of his mouth as he tips his head toward the portal in a silent question.

"Let's go," I say.

"Let's go," he agrees.

I step after him into the sphere.

1287

SHE WAS BEATRICE Portinari, the maker of doors between worlds. It was his fate to follow her.

Dante had already seen his future. One of Beatrice's magicians had taught him the art of bibliomancy, and he had consulted Virgil's *Aeneid*, choosing at random the page and line that would illuminate the path ahead.

Go happy hence, and seek your new abodes.

Beatrice lifted the pipe to her lips.

A fraud, Dante might have been. But if Beatrice wished him to accompany her, he would do it. He would stand before her, adoring her; he would observe, and remember what he saw. With Marco broad and unshakable at his side, he followed Beatrice with all the devotion of an acolyte behind a priest.

And when her calculations and the musical note she played on the pipe conjured a portal on the air, he passed through it, into the aether.

Suddenly, they stood in an infinite, curving tunnel, a ring set within rings. All around them was darkness and distant stars.

With no warning, Dante's lungs seized.

He had not known such fear even at the siege of Arezzo. Though his mouth pulled at the air, emptiness filled his chest. Pale, cold light illuminated the panicked gasps and silent cries of the scholars and magicians around him.

Bice drew herself up, muttering as she pressed a palm over her own breastbone. As color returned to her face, the other magicians did the same, filling their lungs.

But Dante had not studied magic.

He hit his knees, and his knees hit something solid and cold. His eyes met Polo's.

Marco whirled, clutching his own chest, searching the faces of the magicians. "Do something!" he mouthed. Even soundless, he commanded attention; a magician was at his side at once.

Dante gasped like a beached fish, alone on the tunnel floor.

Perhaps suffocation was his punishment for venturing, like the builders at Babel, to touch what lay beyond. Perhaps he was merely reaping the lies he had sown.

His vision began to blacken at the edges. Dante gasped again, pain knifing through him.

But then Bice was there. She pressed her warm hand to his chest and whispered words of magic in his ear, the movement of her lips stirring his hair.

At once, Dante's lungs swelled with breath. Life rushed through his body again, and the blackness receded from the edges of his sight. "Thank you," he gasped.

For the briefest of moments, Dante did not feel like an imposter. With Beatrice's fingers curled in his shirt and her pale brow resting against his, her hair falling around him, he felt he was precisely where he belonged.

When he finally tore his gaze away, it was to stare in wonder through the tunnel into the endless expanse of spheres and to the stars beyond, a cathedral of night. Bice watched with him the marvel they had found. The miracle they had perpetrated.

CLAUDIA

10

HERMES, MERCURY

WE'VE LEFT THE 9:30 Club bathroom behind. We've left everything—*everything*—behind.

The size of the sphere threatens to bend my brain; shaped like a tunnel, it stretches forward as far as I can see, curving slightly to the left ahead. Fog shifts like clouds on its translucent aether walls, with patches of blackness emerging where the crystal seems to grow thin, revealing the cold dark of space above and the neighboring spheres to our right and left.

Standing here, I remember every story my nonna ever read me. Epic tales of science, of discovery, of the circles of heaven and hell.

Circles. Spheres—but not precisely shaped like spheres, not globes inside globes. All around us are rings within rings, tunnels glorious and grand enough for the planets to move in their orbits.

I am openmouthed, wide-eyed with wonder—and with fear.

Because the tunnel has begun to creak, ringing with a skewed reprise of the note Major played to conjure the portal. A chill runs down my spine and I step closer to Rora. The whites of her eyes are stark against her smudged eyeliner; she's still white-knuckling her backpack straps.

"We have to move." Amir tugs at my coat sleeve, his voice all urgency in my ear.

I push back my nausea, let him hurry me forward. I try not to work out the physics of our combined weight crossing what feels like thin ice over a pond.

The sphere engulfs the entire planet while somehow still guiding us to a spot on Mercury's surface—but no. We don't stop at the surface; we pass through its scarred gray stone like a train through a tunnel.

All at once, the sphere disappears, and we find ourselves in an alley of silver-gray brick and cobblestone. Rora turns in a circle before flopping onto the ground beside an abandoned bicycle, her fingertips with their chipped black nail polish pressed to her forehead.

For a long moment, all I can do is stare at that bike. Its wheels, its handlebars, its smooth metal frame. Not exactly like the Huffys and Schwinns chained up outside our school, but close enough to temper the shock of our arrival.

I lift the bike off the wall, throw one leg over its chassis, sit on its seat. The frame doesn't feel any lighter than a normal adult bike; more to the point, I don't feel any lighter, though Mercury's gravity is about 60 percent weaker than ours. Though I can feel myself trembling from our trip, I don't feel faint, so oxygen levels here must be about the same as on Earth.

Amir is staring at me, clearly wondering why I'm sitting on some stranger's bicycle, but the momentary pause clears my head.

And yet—it isn't just the moment. Something more than that is at work.

Before we left Earth, I couldn't understand what the boys meant about music produced by the planets. I didn't believe them. But I hear it now.

It's the pulse of the city, a silent song on the air. It feels like espresso and fast conversation, like done-up buttons on a coat and sprinting in heels to catch a train.

Though I've never been here, it feels like home.

Even so, I can hear the faintest false note. Some disproportion, some skipped beat in the music. Is this the disharmony Amir and Major were talking about? Would I hear it if they'd said nothing?

"All right," Amir says, eyeing Rora and me seriously. "Two rules: stay close, and don't tell anyone you're from Earth."

Rora nods, throat bobbing nervously, but I hold up a hand. "Wait. Why not?"

"So you don't get lost," Amir answers smoothly. I cross my arms and cock an eyebrow at him, waiting. Finally, he heaves a sigh. "Because we need to keep it a secret for now. Can you accept that?"

I grimace. "For now," I finally say, repeating Amir's words back to him.

Major slips to the alley's end, popping his blond head around the corner, palms pressed to bricks the silvery shade of mercury. "Come on."

We follow him out of the shadowed alley and into the street. Into a galaxy of light and sound.

The city is a mass of spires stretching toward a high stone ceiling, cobblestones and ancient buildings in the same cool mercury-colored brick as the alley wall. Lights fill every window and burn from the pinnacle of every tower, illuminating the faces of the crowd hurrying around us. High overhead, a silver train sings across an elevated track.

Something knocks against my shoulder. I glance up and find

Amir's brows arched as if in question. The city lights glow against his cheeks, reflect in his eyes and in the sheen of his hair.

I can't remember the last time anyone observed me this carefully. Anxiety races across my skin.

He nods at the streets branching out before us without looking away from me. "Welcome to Hermes," he says.

In seventeen years, I've seen dozens of cities, from Rome to Rabat and beyond. What never fails to amaze me is how specific each of them feels—old or new, bustling or serene. Cities tell you what their inhabitants care about. How they want to be remembered.

This city is ancient, a bit like Oxford or my grandmother's beloved Siena, but there are no honey-colored stones here, and no red tiles on the roofs; everything is rendered in the same dove-gray, silver-limned rock of the planet's surface. High above, the stone cavern's ceiling is covered with magnificent frescoes, faded with age. But despite its antiquity and its dreaming spires, there is a swiftness to this place—an almost liquid brightness in its shadows, something sharp and clever and tricky.

What did the builders of this place want us to know about them? What did they want us to remember?

"I thought it would feel more . . . modern," Rora confesses as we make our way up the cobblestoned street. She laughs, the sound a little faint. "I guess I was expecting a space station."

"Some of the other planets' cities do feel more experimental," Major answers her. "But Hermes was built in 1287. It was modeled after a medieval Italian city."

My breath catches in my chest; I knew it felt familiar.

But how? Who built this place?

I turn my eyes from the skyline to the streets. A busy crowd flows around us, seeming entirely comprised of teenagers and younger kids. Their clothes are mostly like ours, if a bit more bespoke-looking, in a variety of colors, reflecting a variety of traditions—here and there I see girls in headscarves, boys in kippahs. It takes me a minute to figure out why the ones our age are wearing robes over their outfits, but then I realize they're in academic regalia.

"Why are we underground?" Rora asks.

I'm glad Rora's asking questions, because I have so many I'm not sure where to start. About the city around us, about the inexplicable magic of the music I can feel working on me even now. About how my parents will react when they realize I'm gone and whether they've texted me back yet.

One issue at a time, I tell myself—except for that one about my parents replying, because I doubt I've got cell coverage here. I smooth over my thoughts, compose myself, like running a lint brush over my clothes. "Well, Mercury has a really thin atmosphere," I venture. "I assume we're below ground for protection."

Amir nods. "Magic is a finite resource. The city's founders could have used magic to construct a strong barrier, but it was simpler to build Hermes belowground." He tips his chin at a park in front of a parade of shops. "Plant life helps keep the air breathable."

A cluster of kids about twelve or so surges around us, then dives like a school of fish into a candy store. "Why is everyone here so young?" I ask.

"Hermes is where we go to school," Amir says. "We live here from age seven until we're eighteen—longer if we're planning university studies, though I'm not. Then we move on to the planet we're born to."

"You're not going to college?" I'm not sure what being *born to* a

76

planet means, but I'm stuck on his earlier comment—oddly scandalized, though it's kind of judgy. My nonna is a physicist; my dad's an MBA; my mom has an art history PhD. I've never *not* considered college and grad school.

Amir shakes his head. "I think I mentioned before that I belong to Mars—we call it Ulaan Garig. At weekends, I go there for training, but we're eighteen and nearly finished with school now. So I'll live there until—" But he breaks off, a muscle feathering in his jaw. It's hard to tell beneath his light brown skin, but he almost looks like he could be blushing.

I frown. "Until . . . ?"

He clears his throat, exchanging a furtive glance with Major. "Until my unit is sent elsewhere." The answer hangs strangely in the air, feeling unfinished.

There are many ways to dodge a question. I'm familiar with them all, in all their variety. Silence is simple, elegant. Redirection—skirting a question altogether—is noninflammatory. Jack's signature method of avoidance is humor. Amir, it seems, favors the half-truth.

He told Rora and me not to let anyone know that we're from Earth. It's clearly not the only secret our little group is keeping.

I glance over at Rora, suddenly realizing she's been quiet for a couple of minutes. Major follows my gaze, and his face falls. "What's wrong?" he asks her.

"Nothing." Clearly false. Ro's scowling, her body curled inward against the buffeting crowd. She waves one hand, the other gripping her backpack strap. "How does this place even exist? How does NASA not know it's here?" Amir and Major exchange a confused glance, and I understand why.

Rora reads as irritable. But I know her; I know what her moods mean and what they hide. And right now, my best friend isn't annoyed; she's freaking out.

Confusion flashes through me. I feel *alive* right now—like I've caught every train on a subway trip, like my luggage is rolling feather-light behind me, like my Americano is just right and searing hot. But Rora looks like a cardboard box ready to fold in on itself.

Whatever Major and Amir's plan is, we need to get to it.

I hold up a finger to Ro. "No. For now, we need to focus. History lesson later—and we *will* get one," I say firmly to the guys, then switch to my best alien voice. "Take us to your teacher."

Rora laughs weakly at my horrible pun, like I hoped she would. I squeeze her shoulder, reminding her I'm still here and she's not alone.

This is my dream. My kind of place. It hadn't occurred to me it wouldn't be hers, too.

My whole life, I've had my eyes on the road, my eyes on the horizon. It was inevitable I'd eventually look skyward and beyond.

I've watched video of the moon landing, tracked the Mars rovers and the Juno mission to Jupiter. And my nonna always shepherded my enthusiasm. She told me every door was open to me, that our family history was full of brave, brilliant, remarkable women— impossible, apocryphal stories I never dared to believe.

But here in the unknown, they feel less impossible.

Here, with my not-twin beside me, I am beginning to dare.

RORA

11

I *WANT TO* let the wonder consume me.

We've passed into space, into a world of magic. We've left our home city behind for one we never knew existed. The cavern is dark and the city is bright and I want to let it fill me up and sweep me away.

But I can't get my feet under me long enough to breathe it all in. My body feels sluggish compared to the city's jarring, jittery pace, like I'm trying to dance to music with a rhythm I can barely pick out.

Shoving through the crowd, even with Claudia and Major beside me, panic and dread seem to surround me on all sides. They cut me off from the wonder I want to feel.

I am eyes and legs and a swirl of nerves as we ping-pong through the streets. A gleaming staircase stretches up-up-up to a massive metallic platform; as we climb, trains shriek quicksilver fast into and out of the station, ferrying people back and forth beneath Mercury's painted sky.

Claudia's whole being is straining upward, toward the top of the stairs. She glances back over her shoulder now and again to check on me, and just as always, I'm in awe of her confidence.

This place hasn't rattled her at all. Though the crowd and the music winging on the air grate against my skull, I can almost see her blue blood racing with excitement.

Breathe, Rora. Breathe. I take long breaths in through my nose, push them out through my mouth till my diaphragm feels hollowed out, just like I do on the Metro at home. I try not to clench my fists so tight, try not to look down from the sleek metal stairs at the street a hundred feet below.

I'd shut my eyes, but we're still climbing. If only I could shut my ears to the song skittering around me.

I try to focus on Claudia, her eyes glittering as she watches it all. Despite everything, affection for her surges through me. She's just as sophisticated and powerful and sharp now as ever, and it's nice that some things don't change, even in secret magical cities, even lifetimes away from home.

Amir drops coins in a slot and passes through something like a turnstile. Claudia follows him, never breaking her stride.

I slide my backpack off and plop it between my feet when we reach the platform. "You're doing great," Major says confidentially at my side, inclining his tousled head. He smells like the beach somehow, like sweat and *boy*; and there again is that music, glowing and reverberating off him when I get close enough to hear.

We aren't even touching. But it's hard to decide if his proximity feels more like I've just pulled on a sweatshirt warm from the dryer or like a thousand burning sparks.

"Would we call this 'great'?" My voice is breathless, dubious. "There are so many languages. So many *people*."

"Oh—well, here. This might help with that." Glancing around to be sure no one's paying attention, Major slides his fingers just behind my ears and whispers a few more words I don't understand.

His touch makes me tremble. Then suddenly, magically, the tumult around me clears.

Even as I still hear the words in their own languages, I can understand everything being said. Major quickly does the same for Claudia before turning back to me.

"Look," he says, leveling me with his steady gaze and a grin. "You've made it. You're with us. And it's impossible to get lost here. See?" He shifts behind me and points along the train tracks that streak into the distance. "It's laid out like a wheel. We're headed toward the Centrum."

"What's at the Centrum?"

"The college," Major says. "That's where we'll find Dr. Qureshi."

Dr. Qureshi. And the answers I've begun to hope for.

Major doesn't speak when I don't reply. But he doesn't step away, either.

For a half a second, I shut my eyes and let myself imagine I can feel the unhurried rise and fall of his chest between my shoulder blades. He is so absurdly tall and so preposterously warm and for a split second, the scattershot music on the air drowns in the song that clings to him, the one like lazy guitar music after a long day.

I'm startled by how comfortable Major and his music make me feel. The way my senses grasp after that other melody. I'm startled again by how quickly Mercury's song closes in when the train pulls in and I pull away.

"The train track mirrors the crater and channels on the surface," Amir adds quietly as we board. "'As above, so below.'"

"I thought it was 'on earth as it is heaven,'" I mumble.

"That's Jesus," Major says patiently as we weave up the aisle past occupied seats. "This is Hermes Trismegistus."

"*Who?*" But Amir glances significantly at the other passengers, and I fall silent.

We find empty seats, Claudia and Amir across the aisle, me beside Major. When our elbows brush, I hear a snatch of that music again, and just the sound of it settles my nerves.

"So. This big secret we're keeping." I raise my eyebrows, and he grins. "Do people from—you know, from our place—ever come here?"

Major shakes his head. "There hasn't been a major expedition since the 1700s." He frowns. "I think that's right. Maybe the 1800s."

I nod slowly. "Can you guys . . . see us? Like, can you watch us?"

"No. Well, not most of us," he amends. "I'm sure some people do. The palace must—"

"The *palace?*" I blurt. Amir glances at me sharply across the aisle, and I wince; I'm being too loud. "Sorry. So how did you figure out how to get to us?" I ask more softly.

Major winks, leaning closer. "We know a guy," he says, and I can't help laughing. When he laughs, too, it feels like someone's injected glitter directly into my bloodstream.

Then I sober. "So—does everyone up here just think we're oblivious?" I ask. "Their less-intelligent cousins who have no idea what's happening right above their eyeline?"

He shakes his head again, more vigorously. "Not at all. Earth would know we were here if we didn't hide ourselves with magic." Major hesitates, glancing out the window behind me for a moment, sun-kissed brow furrowing. "We all know a little about life there. Some of the cities even mimic things about your world. There are research labs in Acuto, on Uranus, that follow Earth's scientific progress. Hermes reveres your speed, and built its infrastructure to keep pace," he adds, gesturing at the train around us. Then he pauses, searching my face. "I just don't understand how you live. Cut off from the music. Most of you not believing in magic."

I think more people on Earth would believe in magic if they could see this place. But I'm sure some of them would feel how I feel: too afraid for wonder.

Major looks nervous, like he wants to say something else, and my shoulders tighten. Finally, he nods shyly at my phone in the mesh pocket of my backpack. "Can I look at that?"

Relief zips through my muscles, and I can't hold back my laugh. "Here," I say, and hand it over.

1287

THE SKY ABOVE him was black, the color of eternal night, the ground pale as crushed pearls.

Dante had been preparing himself for this moment since he had agreed to follow Beatrice into the heavens. And yet he was unprepared.

The moon. Dante's two feet stood on the moon.

Far from Siena. Far from Florence. Far, far from the Donatis and all his failures.

"Conjure a barrier," Beatrice called out to one of the magicians. "Something self-sustaining, so that we may breathe without the charm on our lungs." She had told Dante, as they had passed through Luna's sphere, that she had learned three incantations before they ever left Siena—one for light, one for breath, one to stanch bleeding. But Bice was an astronomer, not truly a student of magic; she could not maintain indefinitely the spell over both her lungs and his. Now she turned to Dante and Marco, eyes alight. "What, my explorers, ought we do first?"

Dante's stomach filled with cold water.

The Donatis had called Dante soft; he was a pupil of poets and philosophers, a keeper of grudges and gossip. He hadn't the faintest idea what they should do next. He turned to Marco.

But one of the magicians spoke before Polo could. "Signorina Portinari—I cannot create a barrier here."

Beatrice paled. "What do you mean?"

The magician shook his head. "One has already been cast."

They all looked upward. There against the deep night sky, there was indeed already a shimmer of magic on the air.

Dante turned to Marco, who had not yet spoken, and found his face rigid with horror. Confused, Dante followed his gaze, and likewise fell silent.

None of the party from Siena moved or spoke as they watched the three figures riding across the plain toward them.

CLAUDIA

12

WE SKATE HIGH above the city, passing stone houses, quaint shops, and tree-lined parks, the horizon unnaturally close where the city's edge meets the frescoed ceiling that arcs above and around us. Beneath the paintings of kings and miracles and prophets, our train is a bright silver bullet, wings illuminating its nickel surface like the margins of a medieval manuscript.

Wings of angels. Wings of butterflies. Wings of birds. The jewel-toned illuminations cover every inch of the train walls, a nod to the Greek god of messengers and tricksters and speech and travel—to Hermes, the city's namesake.

For the first time all day, I find myself unsettled. Not because any of this feels foreign, but because it's familiar.

Back in the station, just like in New York, just like in DC, the crowds streamed through barricades, dropping coins into slots and carrying on. The guys paid for our trip with silver coins about the size of a thumbprint, circular and stamped with a face. And as we passed onto the platform, I looked around for the other thing you can always count on in a busy train station.

"What's wrong?" Amir asks beside me. Across the aisle, Ro's

discreetly pulled her phone out, and she's explaining how it works as Major runs his fingers over its cracked screen.

Here, where the folds of my coat cover us, Amir's knee rests against mine.

We both know it—he *has* to know it—and neither of us is moving. I steady myself, determined to follow my thoughts and not the rush of my blood.

Earlier, in the train station, I glanced around for anyone consulting a map or fumbling with money, for anyone standing in the wrong place, oblivious to the flow of traffic. As on the street below, half a dozen languages surged around us—Arabic, German, Spanish, something I thought might be Mandarin and something else that sounded a bit like Welsh (but was definitely not Welsh). Without Major's language charm on me yet, I didn't understand any of it. But I didn't see a single obvious marker of unfamiliarity. Everyone seemed comfortable, purposeful, at home.

But where there are cities—where there are sights to see, trains to take—there are always strangers. Visitors. Tourists. *Always.*

And if there aren't, should we be here at all?

"I want to hear why we have to keep mum about being from— you know," I say to Amir, pitching my voice as low as I can.

Amir's throat bobs. "It's complicated."

"I'm pretty smart," I say flatly. "Explain it to me."

He sighs, shifting infinitesimally nearer, and my heart gives a disastrous little *thump.*

"Setting aside that people from Earth don't really visit the spheres," Amir says, "there's been a ban on travel since about a month after everything began."

I pause. His warm brown eyes are so calm I want to shake him. "A travel ban that I assume we've broken?"

"Yes," he admits. "We adhere strictly to the exclusion of the spheres during emergencies."

I shake my head. "You know I don't know what that means."

"As adults, we all live on the planets we were born to. We call that the exclusion of the spheres. But everyone travels—though there are quotas to keep and permissions to be obtained and things," Amir says. "During crises, though, everyone is supposed to stay on the planet where they and their music belong, to protect the spheres from further damage."

His explanation only confuses me more. I huff a breath. "What does that mean—'born to'? 'Belong to'?"

Amir's eyes widen a little, and I cross my arms, irritable. I'm used to being the tutor, not the student needing help. "Astrologically," he clarifies. "Every person is born to a given sign, which is governed by a particular planet. As adults, we belong to that planet, that sphere, so during crises we repair to our own places and wait for things to pass." He pauses. "The school on Mercury is the exception, the theory being that since we're all children, our songs aren't developed enough to do much harm. For now, anyway." He pauses, watching me.

"For now?" I prompt.

"Yes. If things get worse, they'll send everyone—even the children—to the planet where they belong. For who knows how long."

"And this is a point of conflict? The—exclusion?" I stumble over the word. My thoughts are swimming.

"For some people." Amir may think his glance across the aisle at Major is subtle. But I don't miss it.

I don't know what Major might find so terrible about going somewhere else for a little while. But I can't worry about that right now. "Does it happen often?"

"No, it doesn't." Amir's thick lashes flicker uncertainly. "So, yes. We're breaking the rules bringing you here. Is that an issue for you?"

I study him for a long moment.

One time, about a year ago, Rora tried to explain the difference between herself and Jack and me by pulling out that Dungeons & Dragons personality chart people love to talk about in internet memes. (I refuse to play D&D. Ro plays with a group at her library once a month. We do not speak of it.)

Jack, she explained instantly, was a chaotic neutral—a person with a strong-enough moral compass, but zero regard for the rules. Rora herself was a lawful good—both a rule-follower and possessing an almost crushing internal sense of right and wrong.

And what am I? I'd asked her, rolling my eyes and laughing.

You're true neutral, she'd explained seriously. *You respect right and wrong, and you respect rules, but only to a point. Because you're also very . . . practical.*

I would have been offended, except it was entirely true.

Travel has been paused for a reason. But we're breaking it for a reason, too. And even if the universe weren't at stake, protecting Rora would be motivation enough for me.

"Sometimes, breaking the rules is the only wise choice," I say quietly.

I have been smiled at by enough boys to recognize the admiration in Amir's grin, but evidently not by enough to inoculate me against the flutter that begins in the pit of my stomach.

Wings, wings everywhere.

"Don't tell Rora," I whisper softly. "She'll just get upset, and I want to help you solve this."

It feels like treason. But she'd only torture herself if she knew.

"Our secret," Amir agrees.

He is close. Close like the woodsy cologne I can only just catch when I'm near enough, like the unexpected little patch of silver in his black hair at the crown of his head, like his knee still pressed against mine.

Across from me, Rora laughs, off-kilter and silly, at something Major's said. It does nothing but egg him on; he keeps telling his story, even more exaggerated than before.

I don't look away from Amir as I smile.

This is my place. I can feel it. With every step—every click of my stacked boots on the platform as we step off the train—I feel it.

And then the music slides farther out of key. The tempo changes, skipping beats.

Something is wrong.

Instantly, I whip around. "Rora?"

She meets my eyes, and immediately I know. She hears it, too.

When I hear the rumble somewhere far below, I'm moving before I can think. I get out of the way, get behind a pillar so no one can accidentally shove us toward the train tracks, dragging Ro with me. And there, my back to the pillar, I watch it happen.

A sinkhole opens in the ground a few hundred yards from the platform, on the far side of the Centrum. Blackness opens like a mouth and swallows two houses and half a street. Wood and cobblestones shatter. Screams rise all around us.

The platform lists, sliding a cluster of four teenagers onto the train tracks as easily as you'd drop loose change into a tip jar.

I can hear my mother's voice in my memory—*stay away from the tracks, stay behind something solid*—and with Rora safe beside me, I reach for Amir and Major. But I'm not quick enough.

Amir's face is slack, horrified. He rushes toward the tracks, stretches toward a boy trapped there. "Come on!" he shouts. "I'll pull you up! You have to—"

But Major has to drag him out of the way. He's too close.

The next train is careening into the station, too close.

"No, no, no." Ro's voice is keening as Major hauls Amir back toward us.

A quicksilver line of cars squeals into the station on bent tracks. The sound is horrible.

And then four people are gone.

A ragged cry drags itself from somewhere deep in my stomach and I press my palm over my mouth to keep from being sick. Mercury's song is shrieking so loudly that my brain throbs in my skull. I stare wildly around, wondering if anyone else hears what I do, but it's impossible to tell in the chaos on the platform.

People crowd the edge of the track. Passengers are staggering off the train and the onlookers who'd been waiting to board are talking over one another and Rora is utterly bloodless at my side, her eyes wide and streaming with tears.

Major looks like he's going to be sick, too. Amir says nothing, just drags his hands down his face, looking drained.

I wanted to see him rattled. But not like this.

"Four kids," Rora says quietly. "*Four kids.*"

We watch each other, none of us speaking. This is the worst thing I've ever seen.

Suddenly, a tall man with deep brown skin wearing a red uniform races across the platform toward the crowd. "Everyone, please, remain calm!"

I'm not sure if he's fire or security or emergency medical, but he's clearly here in an official capacity. More people in red arrive and start questioning onlookers and clearing the platform. At my side, Ro relaxes ever so slightly, soothed by the presence of an authority figure.

"We should talk to him," she says, voice trembling. "Tell him what we saw. They'll have to find their families—"

"No," Amir says quietly, eyes avoiding the officials. "No, we have to go."

But at that moment, the first man turns, spotting us across the platform. Though Amir's been looking anywhere but at him, Rora has been staring holes through his deep red uniform. "Amir?" the man mouths, confused.

The boy in question is suddenly rigid beside me.

"Go," Amir says quietly, turning away, pulling me with him into the crush. "Go, go, go."

"Don't run," I say in a low voice to Rora and Major as we walk. "Just follow the crowd and look like you have someplace to be." Amir hustles us toward the station exit and, once out of sight, the four of us race down the crowded steps. We are a jumble of feet and elbows as we knock into one another, looking over our shoulders, grateful just to still be here, to still be alive and whole.

"Did they follow us?" Major croaks.

"Tried to," Amir said. "But they got stalled."

Rora grips the straps of her backpack, cheeks pale. "Why did we have to run, Amir?"

Amir glances at me guiltily, his throat tensing. This must be to do with the travel ban, and I don't want Rora thinking about it right now. "Let's focus on getting out of trouble before we analyze it," I interject.

Rora searches my face for a beat. "Fine," she agrees. There's no reluctance in her voice, because she trusts me.

Will she still trust me when she finds out I've hidden the truth from her, even a truth this small?

No. I set the thought aside. We are here with an idea, here to see someone who may have answers. With this person's expertise, we may be able to fix what's happening. We'll probably have official permission to be here in the next half hour, and she'll never know the difference.

This is for her own good.

But I think about my family, pulled apart, and all that Rora's gone through and, dear God, the people who just fell onto the tracks, and fear settles into my chest.

Part of me is afraid it doesn't matter if we can solve the problem in front of us.

Part of me is afraid too much has already been lost that can't be gotten back.

CROWDS OF TEENAGERS and children push and press through the cobbled streets of the Centrum, exclaiming to one another over the quake we all felt.

When I glance at Major beside me, he doesn't speak. His expression is stricken, taut with grief.

None of these people around us have any idea what just happened on the platform. None of them know that four kids—three boys and a girl who looked a little younger than me—just died on the train tracks, even though I'll see it every day for the rest of my life.

But as we push through the packed streets, Major and Amir constantly glancing back for red uniforms in the crowd, I see people are on edge. They may not have seen what happened, but they felt it. Most are just nervous, but here and there I spot shifty expressions, hands reaching for pockets that aren't theirs. When something brushes against my fingers, I jump, clutching the backpack I've moved to my front.

"Sorry." Major's face goes red. "I just didn't want you to get separated. Or spotted." Mouth dry, I search the street; there's no sign of the red-coated guards, but I've fallen behind the others. Amir and Claudia are half a block ahead.

The crowd pushes and swells around us, and a group of boys who look about eight or nine dart past and nearly knock me over. But then Major's hand is in mine, bracing me.

I don't quite dare meet his eyes. But I cling to his fingers as they lace with mine, warm to the touch, like stepping into a patch of sunlight.

With Major's palm pressed to my own, I can hardly hear Mercury's discord anymore. So I let him tow me through the crowd, and tell myself it's the only reason I like his hand in mine.

Around a corner, we find ourselves in a cobblestoned courtyard dotted with vendors' stands and filled with students. Seven ancient stone buildings surround the plaza, different words carved over the main door of each. *Gram.: loquitur, Dia.: vera docet, Rhet.: verba colorat, Mus.: canit, Ar.: numerat, Geo.: ponderat, Ast.: colit astra.* The words bounce off my brain as the smells of coffee and tea and hot food flood my nose and remind me I haven't eaten in hours. But I start at the last word emblazoned over the building immediately before us.

Ad Astra's band name comes from a Latin phrase—"ad astra per aspera." *Through hardship, to the stars.* I say it to myself all the time, when I'm sad or tired. I say it to myself now, as I try to set aside the grief that could immobilize me for hours or days or longer if I let it.

"What does it all mean?" I ask, nodding at the words as we join Claudia and Amir. Abruptly, Major drops my hand, and I wince as Mercury's music closes in again.

"They're the seven liberal arts," Claudia says. "I'm blanking on some of it, though. Getting rusty."

Amir nods, leading us toward the nearest building. "This is the Astronomy College."

"Don't relax yet," Major adds quietly as we slip inside. "That guard will have texted the others, maybe even the professors."

I want to ask what he means by *texted*, since Major had clearly never seen a phone before twenty minutes ago, but there's no time. More students in robes rush around us to class through the corridors, their voices echoing off the silvery stone walls and vaulted ceilings. Amir keeps his head down as we push past them.

Finally, we reach the end of the corridor, stopping in front of a closed door. Words in different alphabets mark its placard. Three of them say *Prof. Nadeema Qureshi*.

I exchange a glance with Claudia. This is it.

I'm going to meet someone who—maybe, maybe, maybe—can help us. Someone who could figure out what's wrong with me. Someone who might know what's wrong with everything.

Someone we've crossed worlds for.

"Remember," Major says. "Don't tell her who you really are."

Amir shakes out his hands, takes a long breath, and knocks.

Mercury's song is relentless in my ears. Without thinking, I step closer to Major. He presses one hand to my shoulder.

But the door stays closed.

Amir knocks again, hesitant. There's no sound from inside. No one comes to the door or calls for us to enter.

With a grunt of frustration, Major reaches around us both to open it. "What are you doing? You can't just—" Amir protests.

But it doesn't matter. The office is dark.

"Hey, what's this?" Claudia asks, pointing to a note just to the right of the doorframe. It looks like Arabic.

"'Leave of absence until further notice,'" Amir narrates. "'Students should attend Dr. Lewis's sections. Refer questions to Dr. L., Dr. Barfield, Dr. Tollers, or Dr. Williams. Best, Dr. Qureshi.'"

Disappointment feels like an overturned glass inside me. It spills everywhere, cold and ruinous, soaking everything.

It's a complete anticlimax, a song cut off just before it's finished building. A great adventure that leads to a treasure already unearthed.

Claudia and I crossed through *space* to talk to this person. We braved disaster to come. And the professor's not here, and she's not coming back anytime soon.

My throat goes tight. I zip up my jacket and catch up my backpack. "Well," I say shortly, "this has been fun."

"What—but you just got here!" Major drags a hand through his hair, expression raw with dismay.

Amir shakes his head, confused. "Why do you keep trying to run away?"

"I'm not running anywhere," I retort bitterly. "We came here for answers, and the person who has them is gone."

I let myself hope this could work. But all of it has been for nothing. Defeat yawns so hollow in my chest I want to cry.

"Do we need to take the train back to where we started to—you know, teleport home?" I grip my backpack straps, trying not to look at Major. Then I remember. "Wait. Is it okay for us to go back out there? Why did we have to get away from that guy in the red coat to begin with?"

I'm looking to the boys for answers. But then I catch sight of Claudia, avoiding my eyes with her lips pressed together, and a funny, sick feeling begins to spread through my insides.

Amir swallows hard, glancing at Major. "Do you remember how we had to smash into the spheres to travel through them?"

I squint, rubbing my eyes. "No. Yeah. I guess so."

Amir nods, uncertain. "Right. Well, the spheres are brittle and fragile at the moment. That makes travel risky." He hesitates. "So, technically, there's a travel ban on right now."

Their expressions are as careful as their words. But Amir's admission pokes a hole in my composure; anxiety seeps into my voice and it slants upward, panicky and sharp and too loud in the stone hallway. "What do you mean, it's not safe to travel?" I demand. "What if something terrible had happened?"

Happened *to us*, I ought to have said. Because something terrible did happen to those four on the platform.

Not safe.

I should have known.

"Did you feel safe before, Rora? Were you comfortable with the way things stood?" Amir's expression isn't unkind, but it's not apologetic, either.

"We need to take this somewhere else," Claudia says. I'm so angry and Mercury is grating so loudly in my ears that I don't argue as she shepherds us into Dr. Qureshi's office and shuts the door. Lamps flare to life on the wall inside.

I haven't felt *comfortable* in weeks, and that's an understatement. I've been tense, more anxious than I've ever been. Jumping at innocent sounds, crawling out of my skin when I have to walk alone at night.

No. I didn't feel safe. But the decision to chance danger or not should have been mine.

Finally, Claudia speaks again. "Rora, we took a calculated risk," she begins, voice calm. It pisses me off.

If her expression before hadn't tipped me off, her tone now would. She totally already knew about this. "Oh, I'll deal with you in a second," I snap at her. Claudia shrinks away, hurt and startled, but I'm too upset to take it back.

"Rora, we wouldn't put you at risk," Major says, blue eyes calm. "We were paying attention. We were careful." He steps a little closer to me and the very sense of him makes me feel better, and it *infuriates* me.

"That's not how rules work!" I explode. None of them says anything.

I glance over at Claudia. Her expression is still stung, eyes cast down, hands in her pockets. I hate that I put that look on her face. I feel like an absolute piece of garbage.

But looking at her, I remember something.

I think of Jack—kicked out, yes, in the end—but accepted so many places, offered a thousand do-overs. I think of the way rules work in Claudia's world.

"That's not how rules work," I say slowly, "unless they don't really apply to you."

Neither of the boys speaks for a long moment. But I wait.

Finally, Amir meets my eyes. When he speaks, his voice is small and unhappy.

"My parents are the king and queen of the spheres," he says.

I scoff. I can't help it. "Of course. Of *course* they are." I glance at Claudia. "And you knew all of this, and just . . . what? Didn't tell me?"

"I didn't know that last bit," she says, and I know Claudia's face like I know the way around my own house; she's not lying.

"But you knew the rest of it," I say softly.

That we were breaking rules. Crossing lines. Doing things I never do, because I can't handle any more risk, any more consequences.

It's by unspoken agreement that we step into a corner of the office, beneath a miniature model of the spheres, and the boys pretend not to listen. "How could you keep this from me?" I ask her under my breath. In the opposite corner, Major shifts irresolutely back and forth, while Amir stands before Dr. Qureshi's bookshelves, arms stiff at his sides, face full of frustration.

I couldn't care less if he's frustrated. Even if we weren't actually in danger, he kept this back—that we were breaking the law by setting out on his little quest—and he kept his ace in the hole a secret.

He wants to solve the problems of the universe: cool. But there's a difference between bravery and knowing you'll never have to pay for your choices. And friends don't lie to their friends.

Maybe I was naive to think that was what was happening here. That we could be friends.

"I kept this from you," Claudia says levelly, "because I knew you'd react precisely like this."

"Because I'm the crazy one?" I scoff again and swallow, hard. I can't cry right now.

"No." Claudia's voice is forceful. "Because once I found out, it was already too late to go back, and because you're more important than rules. Because you would sacrifice *everything*, including a chance at getting help, for the sake of not crossing some arbitrary line, and I wasn't going to let that happen. The—" She falters. "The Amir-being-a-prince thing? I guess he's a prince? That's a bonus."

"Right, because rules are only for normal people. So now everything is okay."

"Why can't you just take a favor?" Claudia bursts out. She looks angry now. "If, for *once*, life deals you a lucky hand, why can't you just say yes and thank you and go with it?"

"What are you saying?" I fire back. "That I'm fortunate I made a friend in high places? That my odds are so bad that I have to cheat when I get the chance? Because I don't need to cheat," I spit. "I can do the right thing and come out okay."

"Do you really think that's what I—me, your very best friend— am saying?" Claudia demands. Her palms are upturned, pleading. "Do you really trust me that little? And honestly, Ro, are a series of choices where you *never* get the help you need really *the right thing?*"

I cross my arms. The sleeves of my leather jacket pinch my skin. My throat feels swollen. Claudia is blinking hard.

"Rora, you are my best friend in the entire world. In *any* world," she finally says, tucking her hair behind her ears. The gesture is vulnerable and it makes her look like the middle school version of her I've only seen in pictures and it makes me feel intensely protective, despite how pissed I am.

"You're my best friend, too," I whisper back brokenly.

"And you are miserable," she says. "I have watched you in so much pain. And I just want—" Claudia pauses, voice catching. "I just want you to be happy. And it just seems like—for you, no obstacle is too small to get in the way of that. No rule is too pointless to follow. And I think you're wrong about that."

Happy.

When was the last time everything felt that easy?

It's been ages. I'm exhausted. Whether the cause is magic or not, I feel like I've lived in this body, carrying all this weight around, for a hundred years.

"Look." Claudia glances around the office. Her voice grows desperate, focused. "Look. The way I see it, there are three doors in front of us: either we go home, we go consult the other professors Dr. Qureshi mentions in her note on the door—Tollers, Lewis, Barfield, whoever—or . . ." She pauses, glances around.

"Or?" Major asks hopefully, completely dropping the pretense that they weren't listening.

"Or, this office is a gold mine, and I'm good at research. Give me thirty minutes in here. Half an hour," Claudia says to me. Her voice says cool resolve, but her expression says *I promise.* "Give me thirty minutes and I will sort out our next step."

"Thirty minutes?" I scrub my hands over my face, my oily bangs; our argument has wrung me out. "That's all you think this'll take?"

"Dr. Tollers walked into the lecture hall talking so hard last week he spat out his dentures," Major offers into the silence. With one hand, he mimes false teeth sailing out of the professor's mouth and onto the floor. "Smart guy, though." Claudia and I stare at him, silent for a beat. Then she turns back to me.

"No, I don't think it's all it'll take," Claudia says quietly. "But maybe if you sit for thirty minutes and catch your breath, you'll see I'd never do anything to hurt you. And I can come up with a plan."

"It's not your job to fix this, Claudia." *To fix me,* I don't say.

She winces. "I know it's not. I don't—just let me try."

I look around the study, from its two walls of books and its celestial model to its desk and its stacks of letters. My head hurts from trying not to cry. "Ransacking a professor's office feels like the wrong way to go when we're already in trouble," I say. "But in for a penny, in for a pound, I guess." I look at Claudia. "Thirty minutes."

1287

THEY WERE NOT the first to breach the spheres. Dante could not believe it. Though his body moved more slowly there on the surface of the moon, his heart raced.

The three strangers rode slowly across the great dusty plateau toward them, expressions cautious, horses restrained.

"Who are they?" Beatrice breathed.

Dante had expected to find resentment painted on her features; after all, she had been beaten. The first glorious steps into uncharted territory were not to be hers. But Beatrice's face only glowed with delight.

The greater surprise, though, was the fear he found upon Marco's face—Marco, the worldly and well-traveled. "What is wrong?" Dante asked him as the strange party drew nearer.

Marco schooled his features with apparent effort. "Nothing."

"But who *are* they?" Beatrice asked again.

They were not the first. Beatrice could not believe their party's good fortune. They had met fellow travelers here—like-minded companions, perhaps—where she had expected only to be alone.

The strangers reached them, and the two parties faced one

another on the great pearl-colored plain. The man who rode at the fore of their trio was broad-cheeked and brown-skinned, with long braided black hair and narrow dark eyes. Like the rest of his party, he was dressed in boots with upturned toes, trousers, and a fur-lined hat; but where the others wore dark clothing, his robe was of silk the color of a blue jewel, embroidered with gold. Beatrice longed for a garment even half so beautiful.

When the man finally spoke, her heart sank a little.

It was not, of course, that Beatrice had expected these strangers would speak the language of Toscana. But she had hoped that, somehow, she would understand. That somehow she might learn their provenance, learn what they knew—befriend them, if they wished it.

She had borne witness to miracles already today; she had hoped for just one more.

Beatrice turned, openmouthed, to face Marco Polo when he issued a painstaking response in the strangers' own tongue.

She would wonder later why she had been surprised. After all, was this not why she had wished for Marco and Dante to captain her journey? Because they had traveled widely and seen much?

And still, Beatrice found herself astonished. "How?" she asked, wide-eyed. "Polo, how?"

His throat bobbed. "They are from the East," he said, tone careful. "They are come from the court of the Khaan."

Dante could not say, of course, but the strangers seemed mildly pleased by their arrival. Polo translated their conversation as their hosts guided them across the sunlit plain and into the caves below.

A great camp rose up from its depths, centered around a massive round tent of white felt. Horses walked and trotted freely amid scores of smaller tents like it, and sheep inside a paddock grazed on prickly-looking dry grass.

He was not sure if it was his own weariness or the too-bustling atmosphere of Luna around him, but Dante felt as though he were caught in a dream. Most of all, he could not help but be reminded of the Donatis among such obviously powerful people.

He controlled his expression, refusing to appear daunted. Not in front of Beatrice.

Still, he jumped when Marco spoke, gesturing to their blue-robed guide. "This is Yelü Xiliang, administrator of the camp's astronomers." Marco paused as Xiliang nodded and spoke again. "The camp is called Suvd Uls," he translated, "or *Pearl Country*." Polo formed the words carefully, the *sohv* slipping out softly before the taut stop of the *d*.

"How fascinating." Beatrice studied the tents, their ornately decorated entrances in a rainbow of shades. "These shelters must be very useful for travel."

"Indeed," Marco said, after translating to Xiliang. "He says that the gers—that is what they are called, gers—are also quite warm inside." Reaching the largest of these at the center of camp, Xiliang pushed open its deep blue tent flap and gestured for them to pass through.

Further introductions were made as the party from Siena—most of whom were shivering with the chill—were offered food and drink, and accepted gratefully. More and more inhabitants of the camp came to greet the strangers, or to join their impromptu meal of noodles with mutton and vegetables, accompanied by mutton dumplings their hosts called buuz.

"Do you know anyone here?" Dante asked Marco as they sat eating. Merely to ask the question felt like a struggle; Dante thought Luna's panpipe-like music, slow and surreal, must indeed be at work on him. Beatrice, who had been staring dreamily at the geometric patterns formed by the tent's frame, came to attention.

Polo frowned. "Know them?"

"From your time at the court of the Khaan," Dante prompted, confused. "Do you see any of the courtiers whose acquaintance you made?"

"No," Marco answered quickly. "Xiliang informed me that his grandfather, Yelü Chucai, organized astronomers for this expedition over three generations ago at the behest of Chinggis Khaan, under a leader called Möngke. A man named Jochi is their leader today," he added.

"They are such a large party," Beatrice marveled; for their new acquaintances numbered at least two or three hundred. At Xiliang's questioning, Polo relayed the comment.

His translation came almost reluctantly. "More of them travel regularly from Kublai Khaan's court at Khanbaliq here to the camp."

"So you might know someone!" Dante's head swiveled back and forth. Marco looked away, seeming not to hear the comment.

Beatrice frowned, speaking for Marco himself, not Xiliang. "Polo, are you well?"

He swallowed. "Yes, of course."

"Good," Beatrice replied at once, relieved. "Because I have so many questions," she said, turning again to Xiliang.

Their guide spoke genially, and Marco translated, looking

hesitant. "He asks what you wish to know."

Beatrice beamed. "*Everything.*"

In the days that followed, Beatrice beleaguered Marco with questions for Xiliang and his astronomers, slowly learning a few words here and there herself in their hosts' various tongues, Kitan and Mongolian and Chinese. As the rest of the small city went about its business, Beatrice inquired of Xiliang about their travels—first from Chinggis Khaan's capital city of Kharkhorin, and presently from Kublai Khaan's city of Khanbaliq. She asked about what they had seen of the spheres that lay beyond, about their calculations for reaching them. Xiliang seemed pleased at her quick mind, and just as pleased to oblige her with answers.

Xiliang informed Beatrice that under their first leader, Möngke, their company had explored as far as Mars in their travels, per the Khaan's orders to conquer what spheres they could. But they had been a lean party at the outset, their numbers too thin to occupy many spheres, so they had decamped in the end to the Uls on Luna. Many years had since passed, however, and some of their city's newer inhabitants had expressed the wish to travel on to the settlement they had abandoned on the red planet. Xiliang also mentioned that explorers from another land had preceded even them, and that the party from Siena might meet them, should they carry on far enough.

The Sienese explorers ranged far and wide over Luna, meanwhile, climbing its peaks, clambering down its valleys, wandering its caves. Dante made notes, voraciously observing it all. But he wondered at Marco's restlessness, at his apparently endless energy to stride up and down the pale, rocky land, never sitting still, inclined to avoid the Uls altogether.

Beatrice divided her hours between wandering the white plains and consulting with Xiliang and the rest of her new friends, learning of lands she had never seen and plotting their course beyond.

Beatrice watched the stars, and Dante watched her. She never ceased to glow.

CLAUDIA

14

I PUT MY back to the door as soon as I shut Rora and Major out in the hall. My heart is in my throat.

I can't deal with Rora this upset.

I'm afraid she's right. That I've gone too far, even if my intentions were good. I'm afraid I'm doing too much, that I'm only clinging to her this hard because Jack's gone.

The thing is, maybe if I'd done a little more while Jack was still around, he'd never have had to leave in the first place.

"So." Leaning against Dr. Qureshi's desk, Amir lifts his chin. "What's your plan?"

"Kind of adorable that you think I have one, *Prince* Amir," I say briskly. I step farther into the room, spin, survey. There are two long rows of bookshelves, a desk littered with papers, walls covered with art and mathematical models. I feel a kinship with Dr. Qureshi already.

He cringes. "Don't call me that."

"Is that what those officers in red would call you?"

"No. They'd probably call me *Squad Leader al-Kindi.*"

"Well, I'm not going to call you that." I tug a book down idly, then slide it back into place.

"Look," Amir says, sounding drained. "Is your family life ever—complicated? Tense?"

The thought of Jack's empty room flits through my mind. I slide out another book but don't even read the title before I replace it. "Obviously."

"Very well. Imagine that, coupled with the pressure of future kingship. With all that's expected of me." Amir doesn't look at me, but I can feel him waiting for my reaction.

I laugh lightly. "Ah. Well, thank you for informing me your problems are so much worse than mine."

He groans. "I didn't mean that—"

"It doesn't matter," I cut him off. Because I can't think about Amir, looking tortured and beautiful six feet away. I need answers for Rora, and I need them quickly. Before my half hour is up. Before those officers in red find us and we lose our chance entirely.

Amir falls silent. Mercury's music still hasn't righted itself entirely, but its jagged edges have smoothed a little. I focus, wrap my skull in the planet's melody, let it clear and speed my thoughts around their professor and what she might tell us if she were here.

If Dr. Qureshi is our likeliest source of knowledge about the wrongness of the music in the spheres, I need to know what's been on her mind lately. Ideally, I'd rummage through her handbag and read her texts and emails. But the office around us is a wealth of information, regardless.

"We start with the desk," I say, trying to sound confident.

"All right," Amir says. "Should I take half and you take half?"

I shake my head. "We need to consider our findings together. I may not recognize that something's significant. You sit."

Amir takes the chair, looking a little startled at being ordered around, and I begin to sift.

Dr. Qureshi's desk in-tray seems mostly full of student assignments. None of them have been graded, and most of them are at least three weeks old. I point this out to Amir. "Dr. Qureshi's been busy with something other than teaching, I'd guess."

"Good point," Amir agrees—though it could simply be that she hasn't had another assignment due in the last couple of weeks, or that she's just procrastinating on student papers.

At the center of the desk is a large calendar, labeled both *December* and *Rabi' al-Thani & Jumada al-Ula*. My eyes widen. "You use Earth calendars here, too?"

Amir laughs. "Yes, the Gregorian calendar, the Islamic calendar, a few others. We aren't aliens, Claudia." He crosses one ankle over the opposite knee and shifts forward in his chair, grinning up at me. "We share a common history, common religions and language—"

"Except you live in secret magical cities across the solar system and you travel between them by music," I fire back, unable to stifle a laugh. "What else did you keep? Earth holidays? The twenty-four-hour Earth *day*?"

Amir lifts a finger to stop me. "Hold on. Just wait." He dives into the rest of the papers littered over the desk, his voice turning formal. "What do we have here? A note from a student explaining her absence from a lecture! She had"—he gives a wry laugh—"she had a cold, *and* a stomachache, *and* a sprained ankle." He sets the note down, and I flush at his smirk. "A medical marvel."

He plucks up another sheet of paper. "We have here . . . a memorandum from the Astronomy College. No, two. One is about an upcoming department meeting. The second is regarding the Astronomy College staff room. Someone's not washing their teacups." Amir pauses. "As to your questions—various religions have kept their holy days, and the spheres have their own holidays. Some planets have kept or slightly adapted the Earth day, and some haven't. In Acuto on Uranus, the researchers are so fixated they've altered their circadian rhythms to fit the planet's sixteen-hour rotation."

I think of Nonna. Her sleep schedule is more regular since she's older now—early to bed, early to rise, just like she taught me—but my dad says when he was young, he used to hear her in her study late at night and find her there in the morning, asleep over her books.

Amir crosses his arms, giving me a knowing smile. "Claudia, we may live in parts unknown, but we're still just human. We're not fundamentally different here to where you're from. Your logic still applied, didn't it?"

I frown. "How did you—"

"I saw you taking the room apart before you set to work. Your brain is a steel trap."

"Takes one to know one," I mutter under my breath as Amir stands and props himself against the desk's edge. "There isn't much else here."

"Look at this note." Amir reaches for a slip of paper, bumping into my shoulder in his hurry. The contact sends goose bumps running down my arm. "It's from the Astronomy College library. Several books Dr. Qureshi requested were delivered just about three weeks ago."

"About the time she stopped paying attention to assignments," I say slowly. "What were the books?"

Amir scans the list. "*Celestial Conjunctions: The Pace of Planets*," he translates awkwardly. "Think it's in German."

"Probably not what we're looking for."

"*Many Moons: The Great Planets and Their Satellites.*"

I shake my head. "Pass."

He shrugs. "*The Settling of the Spheres, Volume III: Beatrice and Her Companions. Beatrice and Dante: Notes and Letters.* Oh, no, wait, that's two different titles. One's in Arabic and the other's in Italian."

I've been sorting through a drawer full of detritus, but I freeze, dropping the pens I'm holding. "Beatrice and Dante?"

Amir nods. "Beatrice Portinari, Dante Alighieri, Marco Polo. They led one of the initial explorations of the spheres."

"Famous on Earth for other reasons," I manage to say. My heart is thudding in my chest for reasons I couldn't begin to explain to him right now.

I don't believe in fate. I don't believe in destiny. That's Ro.

"What's wrong?" Amir asks.

"Nothing."

Nothing, except that my nonna has insisted my whole life that we're related to Beatrice Portinari, Dante's famous love interest. Nothing, except that Nonna always insisted that there was more to Beatrice than anyone else knew, and I barely acknowledged that she was anything more than a character from a poem.

"Um. Two textbooks on the same subject?" My voice is hoarse.

"No, three—no, four," Amir corrects himself. His eyes are bright. "Dr. Qureshi retrieved four books about Beatrice and her expedition just before she left."

"Okay. So where are they?" I whirl, scanning the shelves, and nearly trip over a pile of books at my feet. When I look up at Amir, his slightly dazed expression tells me I've hit him with the full force of my smile.

We commence phase two of our search.

RORA

15

I SLIDE DOWN the corridor wall to the cold flagstone floor, and Major sits beside me, leaving space between us. *Thirty minutes*, I tell myself.

Claudia clearly didn't want me to watch her dig around Dr. Qureshi's office, so we're out here to keep an eye out. But there's no sign of anyone in a red guard's uniform.

"I'm sorry we didn't just tell you what was going on," Major says quietly, eyes trained on the silver-gray stones in the opposite wall. "I'm sorry you're fighting with Claudia."

"Claudia and I don't fight," I say at once.

"Sure," Major agrees readily. He drums on his knees, unconcerned with the contradiction.

Watching him fidget is calming somehow. Major's fingers are long and tanned, the hair on their backs a fine gold, their nails short and clean.

"How did you and Amir talk if you were on separate planets?" I ask, trying to fill the silence. "I mean, how did you come up with your plan?"

"Texting," Major says—and there's that word again. "Mirrored parchments. I'll show you later."

I bite my lip. "Got it."

Quiet hangs between us. I glance up the hall again and again, strain my ears after the sounds echoing off the intricately carved stone ceiling, but we're still alone.

"You're not the problem here," I finally reply. "Claudia, either. The problem is the problem. We're all just doing our best to fix it."

Assuming I even believe that's possible. Assuming that a problem that touches mountains and oceans has anything to do with me, and that my problem isn't rooted somewhere unreachable inside my body or my head.

Major pauses, dropping a knee to face me and shifting a little closer. "I was unhappy when I came here." He cracks his knuckles, shaking his head. "I hated it. I hated all the gray, I hated how dark it always was. I hated taking the train everywhere."

"Really?" I glance up at him, still chewing my lip. "Where'd you live before you came to school?"

"Quetzalcoatl, the city on Venus. Sometimes people call the planet Fortuna Minor. The way it works here is—well." His face twists up a little, like he's preparing a long explanation. "You're born where you're born, you know—"

"Okay," I laugh. "Got that part."

One corner of his mouth curves. "And then you go to school and maybe university on Mercury. But when you're grown up, the zodiac sign you're born under, the song you're born *to*—that dictates where you live."

"What?" I stare at him. "But what if you don't like the—the planet you're assigned?" The sentence feels like gibberish in my mouth; the idea is even more outlandish.

"That's our way," Major says simply. He doesn't meet my eyes as he speaks the words.

I shake my head, staring off. "I think I'd just go to school forever. Put off growing up."

"Good try, but the graduate schools in Acuto are only for those born to Uranus." Major laughs, and it's not quite a happy sound. "I can't decide if it's worse for those who want to go but can't, or those who don't want to go, and have to."

I don't say anything to this. I can't think of anything to say.

He stares at the hem of his pants, a little frayed above the heel. "So I was born on Fortuna Minor, born to Fortuna Major—to al-Mushtari. Jupiter, by its Latin name. The youngest in my family, the only boy. My parents had such high hopes for me."

"Fortuna—Major," I say slowly. "Like your nickname."

Major bobs his head, betraying no enthusiasm. "School friends gave it to me. Anyway"—he blows out a breath that ruffles his hair—"once I got here, all I wanted to do was go home. Back to Quetzalcoatl."

"So what did you do?" I draw up my knees, chin sinking onto my arms. I'm not sure when I turn to face him.

Suddenly, Major looks shy. His mouth curls again. "You're going to make fun of me."

"I promise I'm not," I say solemnly. "Sarcasm is Claudia's department."

He smiles a little more assuredly, picking at that frayed hem. "When I couldn't take it, I would think of three good things."

"Why three?"

Major glances back up to me, testing my reaction, and his voice when he speaks is as soft as his eyes. "One happy memory. One good thing in the present. One thing I was looking forward to in the future."

"Three good things," I say slowly. "What did you think about?"

He smiles. "My family owns an orchard. Have you ever been to one?" I shake my head. "They're green and cool and when the trees start to fruit, they smell like heaven. I love working there. Or . . . not working. Depending on the day." His grin broadens, and my mouth goes dry.

"What else?" I manage.

"So, my father sees to the orchard, but my mother's an artist. She's famous for her mosaics. Our home's full of them." Major pauses and shuts his eyes, like he's back there, lying in the sun. "Did you know the light on Venus doesn't change with the time of day? Long afternoons, sunsets, evenings—they take weeks. Months. And it's always warm, because that's the sphere's character."

"Character?" My voice is almost a whisper.

"The spheres' songs shape us, but they shape our cities, too," Major says, forehead furrowing between his blond brows. "Or maybe the songs make us who we are, and we make our cities to match. But the traits of the signs and their planets appear in the cities. Like Mercury—the pace of life here in Hermes reflects that Gemini and Virgo are quick and clever. Jupiter is the proudest planet, so the king and queen's palace is there. And Uranus governs Aquarius, and the researchers in Acuto are strange but focused. Innovative but weird."

I nudge his shoulder. "And your city?"

"It's full of growing things. Vineyards and fields." Major's eyes are far away. "Growth, warmth, life. Quetzalcoatl is beside a small ocean, and the sand is rose gold, and the houses are painted bright colors. And there are always boats crossing back and forth." He glances at me, expression turning a little sly. "On top of tending to the orchard and being lazy and charming, I'm pretty good at sailing."

I can picture it—Major's long arms stretching into trees, searching for fruit; Major, the muscles in his back working as he adjusts the lines on a sailboat; Major, his face relaxed as he falls asleep in the sun.

I can't help shifting just the slightest bit closer to him.

"But—didn't you say you thought of three good things? Past, present, future?" I ask quietly after a long moment. "Those are so many good things, but they're all memories."

"That's true," he sighs. Major stretches, rolling his neck, then settles again. "Well, things got better. I made friends with Amir. And even though he had to go away to Ulaan Garig—to Mars—on weekends for training, having a friend made life easier."

"How did you meet?"

"Suitemates." He grins. "We fought nonstop for the first three months. I thought he was too serious, he thought I wasn't serious enough. Then one day, we just . . . stopped fighting. Amir had a bad day with a professor—everyone was so hard on him, even when we were young—and I offered to burn the classroom down. He couldn't stop laughing."

"They were hard on him because he's the prince?" I ask, curious.

"All of them. Amir's professors, Amir's parents . . . Amir himself." Major scrapes a hand through his hair. "I think he liked that I didn't treat him differently. And he knew he could trust me." He leans down a little, closer to my ear. "I'm extremely trustworthy. You should tell me everything."

I laugh, startled, and shove him back. But I'm not pushing him away, not really. He catches my fingers in his, and we scuffle and jostle for a moment, and touching him—even just playing around like this—is absolutely electric.

I don't know when I got this relaxed. But this near, Major's eyes are the color of my favorite pair of jeans, washed and rewashed until they're comfortable and soft and fit me perfectly.

When we finally stop goofing around, I'm fighting a grin. "So what's your real name?"

Major stares me down, cocking an eyebrow. "You really want to know?"

He seems nearer than before. I go still. "Yeah."

Major leans toward my ear, close enough that I can feel his breath on my skin. My heart catches. "It's Egbert."

A laugh bursts out of me, and I push away from him. "No, it's not."

He shrugs. "Caught me. It's Humperdinck."

"Come *on*." I make a face.

"Percival. No, Lancelot. No—"

"You're ridiculous." I roll my eyes, then pause, thinking about what he said. That he belongs to Jupiter, but Jupiter is the proudest planet, home to the royal palace. It doesn't make sense—that's not what I hear in the music rolling off him, even now.

Is that mismatch owing to the wrongness in the spheres? Or something else behind it?

But I don't want to voice this kind of question. "So," I begin again brightly. "What's next?"

Major glances at Dr. Qureshi's door. "Well, Claudia and Amir ought to be done soon."

"No, I mean your future." I laugh. "What are you going to do? Amir's going to train on Mars as a guard or whatever, and then someday be king, and you're . . . ?"

But at this, his face falls, and I instantly wish I could take my words back. *Ctrl-Z, ctrl-Z, backspace, delete*, my brain yells fruitlessly. "I don't know," he says, avoiding my eyes. "Amir will be king one day. And since I belong to Jupiter, one day, I'll live there, too."

I grimace. "And you're not happy about that."

"Amir's my best friend. And I'm happy we'll be together. But . . ." Major shrugs. "I don't see a life for myself there."

I understand what he's saying. Having Claudia beside me would brighten up a bleak picture of the future. But it wouldn't be the same as choosing who I wanted to become.

"When I was little," he admits, "I didn't understand. We all travel, as children, to the place we'll live someday—for exposure, to develop our songs. But for the longest time, I didn't get it. Al-Mushtari was just this massive, windy city by the sea, not the place I'd live someday. I thought I'd take over the orchard from my dad when I grew up. Look after my parents as they got older. Our house is huge; there's plenty of room."

My heart aches as I realize how much he's thought about this. He's laid all these plans out, sown himself a field of hopes doomed to be torn up before they can ever see the sun. And for what?

"Why do people have to live in the spheres they 'belong' to?" I ask, quoting with my fingers. "And does that mean your partner has to belong to the same planet? And your children just *leave* you? It . . ." But I trail off at the look on Major's face.

"We take it seriously," he says, staring at the floor. "Some people try and have their children at particular times of the year—either so they'll belong to their home sign and planet, or so they'll belong to some other, particular place. Of course, you can visit family, but you have to live where you belong. And if you marry, you have to marry someone who belongs there, too."

"But it's so arbitrary!" I exclaim.

"We call it the exclusion of the spheres. It's supposed to preserve the characters of the songs and keep the spheres safe," he says to the flagstones. "It's been our rule for over seven hundred years. They say the planets are too different, and *we're* too different, for anyone to just live wherever they want."

And he's nicknamed for Jupiter. Fortuna Major, a place he doesn't want to live, that he isn't happy to belong to. I can't imagine being reminded of that every time someone called my name.

It makes sense, though, whisper my treacherous thoughts. I can feel even now how Major's music seems to counteract the unpredictable Mercurial rhythm all around us. I can't argue with the logic of the rule, even if I can't bear the sight of him so resigned.

"Tell me something good," I say. I turn back to the last subject that made him happy. "Your house. Tell me what it's like."

And he's glad to play along. Major's smile is instant gratification, a shot of sunlight to my veins. "The first floor is mostly an open terrace," he says, gesturing expansively. "Marble pillars, mosaic floors my mother designed. All sorts of colors that you wouldn't think go together—bright green and peach and deep blue and yellow—but they do." He sighs. "There's always a sea breeze, so the terrace smells like either salt or the orchard. Art all over the house. Food whenever you want it."

"Food," I groan. My stomach rumbles; it must be seven or eight hours since I ate pasta at the Millers'. But thoughts of home make me wonder something else. "Does Earth have a song?"

"Of course." Major fidgets again, and his shift puts us knee to knee.

"What does it sound like?" My voice is airless.

He cracks his knuckles, expression growing thoughtful. "Scrappy," he finally says. "And kind."

"Scrappy and kind?" I laugh. "That's how you'd describe us?"

Major laughs, too. "I don't know! I only heard it for the first time last night! How would you describe it?"

I shrug. "I don't know. I don't think I can hear it. Or maybe I've heard it my whole life, so I've just never noticed it."

Major nods. He's so much closer than is friendly and his song suffuses the air around me, clear as day, flushing out Mercury's harsh staccato music.

Why can I hear him? Why not Earth's song—the one I must have heard my whole life? Why not Claudia's music, or my parents', or my other friends'?

My eyes sink shut, exhaustion lapping at my thoughts. This has been the longest night. And even now, I'm supposed to be alert, on the lookout for people coming to find us and drag us off our course.

But I could so easily fall asleep to Major's nearness. To the music hovering around him that feels like the story he just told—like rose-gold sand and orchards and sunshine and boats on the water.

"Rora," Major says softly, and the word stirs my hair and lashes like a sea breeze.

But Claudia pokes her head into the hallway. Flushing, I sit up straight.

"Thirty minutes is up," she says, cheerful and resolute. "Let's talk."

1287

THEY DID NOT remain on Luna. There was more, Marco reminded them constantly, more to see, more to explore.

The day Beatrice was to have returned to Florence to be wed, they left the moon's sphere.

Polo told Dante he was ravenous for new sights. But Dante thought there was an edge to his friend's urgency that spoke less of hunger than of a panic he did not understand.

Marco had expressed reservations, too, about inviting residents of Suvd Uls to travel with them. But Jochi, their leader, granted them permission to go, and Bice's enthusiasm was not to be overruled. So though they had been a party of only twelve when they left Siena, they numbered nearly fifty leaving Luna's sphere, with horses and wagons and gers for the explorers from the Uls besides.

So they traveled on to Mercury, fleetest of the planets, in the sphere just beyond. There, they met no one, and there was no mistaking Polo's relief.

Neither was there any mistaking Beatrice's pleasure at the world that greeted them. She had been delighted at the acquaintances she had made in the Uls, but the air on Mercury was sharper, somehow, and she herself felt keener. Together, they built a city beneath its stone surface, and Beatrice christened it Hermes, for the fleetness that chased her thoughts every waking moment.

Mercury offered none of the gold stone that made up the grand homes and churches in Toscana, and no earth to turn into terra-cotta roofing tiles, but they quarried stones from the cavern walls by magic and built houses and great halls like those in Siena, topping them with magnificent spires. Dante himself supervised the paint-ing of the ceiling to resemble the marvelous frescoes of the Duomo in Siena, of prophets and miracles against a backing of the purest azure.

"I am no astronomer," Dante told Bice one night long after the others had gone to sleep, gesturing to the celestial scene overhead. "But you are. And you must see the heavens whenever you cast your eyes skyward."

Beatrice's mind moved swiftly as she worked with her scholars by day, analyzing what the more seasoned travelers from the Uls had told them of the spheres beyond, calculating their path forward. And her quick mind knew precisely what to say as Dante watched her, waiting.

"Somehow," she said softly, "in your presence, I see heaven every-where I look."

RORA LOOKS DIFFERENT than when I left her.

"What did you find?" she asks, climbing to her feet and following me into the office.

I'd hoped thirty minutes apart would help us both cool off. But she doesn't just look calm; she looks happy. I eye Major critically, wondering how he's cheered her up so thoroughly, and try not to feel stung that hanging out with him did for Rora what I couldn't.

I turn the book I've been studying toward her. "I've been going through Dr. Qureshi's research materials," I say. "She recently checked out a bunch of books on the exploration of the spheres, so I started with this one. It's full of journal entries from one of the early explorers, Beatrice. They're her calculations, her thoughts, notes on the philosophers and mathematicians who guided her." Amir nods at me, encouraging. "She keeps returning to the principle from Hermes Trismegistus that Amir mentioned earlier. 'As above—'"

"'—so below,'" Rora finishes, recognition sparking in her gaze.

"Exactly." I can't stop my smile, can't help the way my hands tremble as I smooth them over Beatrice's writings. Nonna was right. Beatrice was real—not just a character. And she was brilliant, and she was *here*.

I can hardly believe it. I can't even begin to guess what this means.

I refocus, pointing to the images of diary entries, all delicately handwritten equations and musings. "You see here? And here again? *Et quod est superius, est sicut quod est inferius.* It was on her mind constantly." I start to pace, talking with my hands the way Nonna always does when she starts lecturing.

"Amir and I had a conversation about how the rules that apply to humans and human nature on Earth apply to life here, too, and it got me thinking. This phenomenon—this wrongness that we're seeing out in the spheres—it manifests everywhere in parallel." I push my hair behind my ears, trying to explain slowly when my mind and my mouth want to go faster and faster. "All of it made me realize that if we can't examine the universe at large, or talk to Dr. Qureshi about the state of the spheres as a whole, we need to look at the chaos in a microcosm. Because whatever is wrong in the grand scheme of things, we will most likely see it reflected in an affected cross section."

As above, so below. Beatrice's byword.

I imagine her leading Dante and Polo into the spheres, trying to picture her from the diary snippets I devoured in the little time we had. It feels fitting to let her guide me here, now, today.

"What do you mean?" Major leans forward, eyes hopeful.

"I mean what we've known all along," I say. "Ro and I came here to help you resolve the larger problem in the spheres because it might also help correct what's wrong with her. But if they are connected, then the reverse should also work. Examining *Rora* might tell us what's going on out *there*," I finish.

I twist my hands, watching the others consider. Ro's forehead is wrinkled beneath her bangs as if she's thinking hard, treading my spoken thoughts like stepping-stones.

Amir still hasn't said anything—just watches me, arms crossed. But he looks at me like I'm two sides of a chess match and both are winning, and his approval has dopamine and serotonin and every other reward chemical in existence shimmering in my brain.

"Great!" The word bursts out of Major, relieved and cheerful, like we've solved the problem and he's looking for confetti to throw. "That's great. How would we do that?"

Rora's expression lifts. "We could examine my star chart."

"I . . . don't know what that is," I admit. But she just smiles at me, full of steadily rising energy.

"At the moment you're born," Rora explains, "you're the center of the universe. The sun and the moon and the planets and stars are looking down on you. Your star chart shows their position relative to you and one another at that moment. It shows their influence over you. So if a threat or a weakness showed up in my star chart . . ." She gestures, inviting me to complete the thought.

"Then maybe it could tell us something about the larger situation," I finish. But I can't help hesitating. I'm not just out of my depth; I'm taking seriously something I'd have scoffed at mere hours ago.

Except—we're here now. The fact that we're here, by magic, means that I was wrong. That maybe I've held too narrow a view of what's real, what's possible.

"Okay," I finally say. "Let's do it." Major beams.

"There's just one problem," Rora says, grimacing. "I don't know what my star chart looks like."

I deflate. "No?"

"Well, I mean, I've looked it up," she says, shrugging. "I know I'm a Capricorn. I like Capricorn memes on the internet, I read my horoscope. But a star chart is really detailed."

"Our star charts are calculated when we're born," Amir offers, brow wrinkled. "I think mine's in the family vault with my birth certificate."

"Do I know where my birth certificate is?" I mumble.

Rora frowns. "I . . . think my mom has a file?"

"Regardless," Amir cuts in, "they take effort, and time."

"Which we don't have because, quick reminder, guards are looking for us," Rora finishes, slumping.

A pause. "We could conjure it," Major offers.

"Have you done that before?" Amir asks.

"No," Major admits. He faces Rora, undaunted. "But we already know your ruling sign. You're a Capricorn, which is governed by Saturn, so it would answer to Saturn's song."

"How?" I slide my hands into my pockets, pacing again. My mind floods with images from TV and movies, witches tossing obscure ingredients into cauldrons. We don't really have time to run around the Astronomy College on a scavenger hunt for eye of newt or whatever.

"The same way we traveled. I think." Amir's voice is distracted as he scans Dr. Qureshi's shelves. He tugs a book loose and flips through it and I lean over his shoulder, trying to ignore the piney scent of his soap as we study a portion of the Ptolemaic model marked with musical notes and equations and the sign for Saturn.

"Like Major said, Saturn governs your star sign," he says to Rora. "So the song of his sphere, applied to the part of your body that he also governs, should conjure your chart."

"Body part?" I blurt.

Amir grins back at me, fighting a laugh. "Yes. Saturn governs your nails, teeth, and bones." Then he turns to Rora. "So I need you to give me your hands, and show me your teeth."

Rora blinks, surprised. But she flexes her pale, stubby fingers all the same, bares her teeth. Amir takes the tips of her fingers in his, lowers his lashes, bows his head.

"The note is D," he says to Major. "You sure this is a good idea?"

Major shrugs, eyes on Rora. "I don't know what else to do."

He plays a low note on his pitch pipe. Amir picks it up. And suddenly, the air is thick with music.

The melody hangs around us, heavy as fog, so cheerless I want to cover my ears—anything to keep from thinking all the song makes me think, feeling all it makes me feel. If it has words, they slip past me, just as when Major conjured the portal to Mercury.

But nothing appears before us now; nothing happens at all. Rora's only reaction is the flutter of her closed eyelids.

On and on they sing, in low, ponderous bass notes. Amir's natural register accommodates their depth better, but Major's tenor voice strains, his eyes on Rora uncertain. Suddenly, he breaks off.

Amir drops Rora's hands. "What? Why did you stop?"

Major shrugs. "It's not working. It should have happened by now."

Amir turns back to Dr. Qureshi's textbook, grimacing. "Are we doing something wrong?"

"Why would you assume we're doing something wrong?"

"What else could it be?" Amir asks, and I frown. Why is he so quick to assume the fault is his?

Amir sits heavily in Dr. Qureshi's chair, staring up at Rora and me. "I don't know Saturn's song very well," he confesses. "I've only been there once, and neither of us has ever done this before. . . ." But I'm not listening. I'm watching Rora's eyes glaze slightly, a little disappointed, a little confused.

Every time our plans come up short, a little more of her hope fades, and she pulls a little further away.

And with guards potentially scouring the planet for us, we are running out of time.

"Are you sure that's the right song?" I interrupt Amir.

He nods. "Every sign is governed by a particular sphere, and they all have fairly unmistakable traits." He waves a hand. "Cancers are nurturers, Pisces are empaths. Rora's your textbook tough, shrewd Capricorn. Here, let me—" He breaks off, flipping back through the book he's holding. Near the introduction is a chart; Rora and I bend to study it.

The Moon: Cancer
Mercury: Gemini, Virgo
Venus: Taurus, Libra
The Sun: Leo
Mars: Aries (minor rulership Scorpio)
Jupiter: Sagittarius (minor rulership Pisces)
Saturn: Capricorn (minor rulership Aquarius)
Uranus: Aquarius
Neptune: Pisces
Inferno: Scorpio

Rora looks up. "So you're a Sagittarius," she says to Major, who nods soberly. "And you're an Aries?" she asks Amir.

He shakes his head. "Scorpio," he says, a little stiffly. "We can petition to live on a planet we belong to by minor rulership."

"Scorpio?" I frown. "But if you have to live on Jupiter someday—"

"I'm not an ideal fit." Amir looks away, expression hardening, and I immediately regret voicing my half-formed thought.

"Why don't you just listen to someone's song to determine where they belong?" Rora breaks in, to my relief. "It would be so much easier."

Major frowns at this. "Listen to someone's—how?"

But suddenly, Rora's eyes light up. She's already moved on. "Wait," she interrupts, a hand on Major's forearm, not even noticing the breath he sucks in at her touch. "Wait. Try Claudia's chart."

I freeze. "What? Why would you want to look at mine?"

Ro leans forward, speaking quickly. "The thing about astrology is that some planets move so slowly, they hold the same position for *everyone* around the same age," she says. "Uranus, Neptune, and Pluto will fall in about the same place on Claudia's chart and mine. So we should just check hers."

"Because if the problem lives in those spheres, it'll show on Claudia's chart, just like it would on yours," Major finishes, eyes wide.

"Okay, okay, hold on." I put a hand up, shut my eyes. I need to parse this bolt of inspiration.

Rora is our chosen microcosm, but only because I decided we should put her under the microscope. We can examine a proxy for *part* of her chart by looking at one belonging to someone else our age. We could potentially study anyone suffering from the disharmony in the spheres—but no. I don't let my brain consider this; it's irrelevant. No one else in this room has been affected as badly as Rora by what's happening.

When I open my eyes, Amir, Rora, and Major are all watching me, waiting for my take.

Show your work is the mantra of math teachers and physicist grandmothers everywhere. But maybe, just this once, I'll skip the full report.

"I think you're right. That's brilliant, Rora," I say simply, and she grins, straightening.

"When's your birthday, Claudia?" Amir asks. He's propped against Dr. Qureshi's desk again, eyes steady on my face.

This is fine. I'm not particularly moved by the prospect of seeing my own chart, because it's not like there will be anything exciting to see. This is just the next step in our inquiry. This is for Rora.

"June first," I manage. "Gemini."

"A twin," he muses, smiling slightly. His forearms flex as he pushes off the desk. "I see."

I clear my throat, tug my gaze away from him. "Do you know the song?"

"Everyone does," Major says behind me. "We go to school here."

"What do you mean?" Rora frowns.

Major hesitates. "You know how you know your way around a city after you've lived there awhile? You learn it unconsciously. Whether you want to or not," he adds, voice darkening.

"Why wouldn't you want to learn it?" I ask. Ro raises her eyebrows pointedly, watching the ground. "What?" I demand.

"I know you like the music here." Rora sways as she answers, as if she's not sure how much to say. "You've been like a duck in water since we showed up. But . . ." She shakes her head, looking tired. "It's hard to explain. The music's too fast. Off-kilter. It's all over the place and it's so *cerebral*—it hurts my head."

132

"Are you serious? You really don't like it here?" I cross the office toward her, startled. She seemed overwhelmed earlier, but I thought she'd recovered. Rora bites her lip, apologetic, as if she's got anything to apologize for. Wincing, I step back to give her a little breathing room, soften my tone. "You should have said something, Ro."

I should have known, I think. And then, in the same moment: *Jack would have loved it here.*

"It makes sense," Amir says behind me. "I'm not surprised you're at ease here and Rora isn't. Mercury rules you. Saturn rules her. One is wit and movement. The other is contemplation and stillness. The two planets are opposed."

I frown up at him. "Opposed?"

Major makes a noncommittal sound, holding up a hand. "*Technically.* But there are exceptions to every rule." When he thinks I've turned away, he scowls at Amir and mouths something I can't make out.

And when I really have looked away from him, I find Ro staring at me. My best friend, black and white and serious, studying me like we've never seen each other before.

Jack would have loved it here. But she's not him, and she's not me. No matter how hard I cling to her, Rora is only my un-twin.

"Anyway," Amir plows on, and I break from Rora's gaze. "Claudia? If you want . . ."

"Yeah," I cut in, crossing stiffly to Amir. "I'll do it." I don't want to think any more about Rora and me belonging to opposing anything.

I hold out my fingers to him—my manicure is flawless, a taupe-and-silver negative-space design—and curl my lips away from my teeth. But Amir pushes my hands gently back to my sides.

"No." His dark hair falls over his forehead, his deep brown eyes almost liquid as he reaches toward me. "Mercury rules the mind."

Before I know what's happening, he steps so close I have no choice but to sit on Dr. Qureshi's desk, and Amir winds his hands through my hair, fingers threading loosely through the roots and cupping the back of my head.

He is so close his knees knock gently against mine, so close that I can pick out the individual washes of gold and brown in his irises. My heartbeat is an uneven rattle, like a train on old tracks, but his breath never hitches, never changes, like I have no effect on him at all.

Major doesn't produce a pitch pipe before they begin to hum; they don't need it. Mercury's song already lives in their minds, winds around us here and now, rises light and sharp and dynamic on their voices.

I only feel Amir's hands in my hair. And though I expect him to shift his gaze, he looks into my eyes with a steady confidence that makes my stomach clench.

I wonder if I imagine the stroke of his pinkie just behind my ear; but there's no denying the shiver that runs up my back.

Then the room is suddenly awash in silver light, and a halo takes shape over my head. I stare up at it, unable to keep the awe I feel off my face.

But no—not a halo. It's a two-ringed chart, shining like quick-silver, all clear lines and sharp little points of light.

Rora straightens, dumbstruck, dumping her bag on the floor. Silver light bathes her wide eyes and pale face so she looks like an angel. "Is it—?"

"It's her chart." Major grins at her broadly, and she smiles back—a true, infectious, wonder-struck smile. The sight of Rora so happy after so many hard weeks makes me ache.

I turn away, back to Amir. "It's beautiful," I say, then wonder if that's arrogant. But he just nods in agreement. He slides his hands down to my nape before lifting them to prod gently at the chart, and I wish abruptly he'd left them where they were.

"See?" he says, tipping his chin at the icon dominating the center. "Gemini. The twins."

Rora and I exchange a glance. She's still beaming, and I smile despite myself.

After all, I have not one twin, but two.

"Geminis are also travelers, movers," Major says, nudging Rora. "They're tricky. Hard to pin down." He grins at this, but I stiffen. Jack is that, for sure. Maybe I am, too.

I'm suddenly overwhelmed with missing him—missing him the way he was before a switch in him seemed to flip. Before he progressed from pushing the envelope to setting it on fire, stamp, letter, and all. Watching the silver light shift overhead, I find myself wishing I could look at Jack's chart beside mine.

Would they match more closely than we've seemed to match over the last couple of years? Would their differences explain what went so very wrong just six weeks ago?

"Almost all our best professors are Gemini," Amir adds. "They're natural communicators." Though his hands are no longer buried in my hair, he's still standing close. His gaze flicks over my face, my collarbone, the diamond Bulgari necklace that was my fifteenth birthday present.

Everything about his examination sets my nerves on fire.

But Rora is focused on my chart. "Okay," she crows. "Let's analyze Claudia! Gemini sun, um . . . Gemini moon?"

"No, let's not analyze Claudia," I say too quickly; my laugh comes out awkward. I can't seem to shake Amir's attention, but that doesn't mean I have to offer up my entire self to be picked apart. "This is about you, remember? Let's focus on the relevant stuff."

"Fair enough," Rora agrees. "So what do we see?"

In the end, the answer to Rora's question appears to be *not much*.

I don't follow most of what follows, but for an hour, we study signs and angles and houses pertaining to the three slow-moving planets Ro mentioned—Uranus, Neptune, and Pluto, whose presence in my chart should more or less resemble hers—looking back and forth between the glowing chart and a stack of textbooks. But none of what we read or see indicates grave danger or a cosmic problem.

Rora's getting muddled. She keeps rubbing her eyes, smearing liner and mascara so she looks like a sleepy raccoon. She and Major seem disappointed that nothing's turned up.

But though my grasp of the astrology is still tenuous, I'm not feeling put off. This is the nature of inquiry. Form a hypothesis. Test a hypothesis. Hypothesis falls apart upon close consideration. Sweep up hypothesis pieces and set aside for possible later use.

My eyes stray again and again to Dr. Qureshi's library books. To thoughts of Nonna, and Beatrice, and all the stories I've never been able to believe.

But I can't read the books now, in front of the others. For that, I need to be alone, to think in private.

The rings of light still hover above my skull, little replicas of the spheres around us. Their brilliance dazzles my eyes. I'm getting muddled, too. It seems impossible that only a few hours ago we were dancing at the 9:30 Club, trying for a few hours to return Ro to her factory settings. That was the first thing she told the boys: that the music fixed her.

My eyes fly open. "I've got something." The three of them turn to look at me, and I begin to think out loud, afraid to let this thought slip away. "You guys came looking for a song to fix the spheres. Rora's goal, last night, was to let the music fix her for a while." I pause. "Treating Rora as a microcosm: What if she just needs to get in touch with the music she belongs to?"

Ro bites her lip, hunching a little. "We already tried that, though. The guys sang Saturn to conjure my chart, and it didn't do anything."

"Bear in mind that we don't know the song very well," Amir cautions her. He cocks his head, curious. "What do you want to do, Claudia?"

Something about him being here clears my head, helps me think, fills me with ideas.

I shrug, and pitch them Experiment Number Two. "Would Rora be able to connect with Saturn's song better on Saturn?"

Rora's jaw drops and she and Amir begin to talk at the same time, but Major interrupts. "Hey, Dr. Qureshi's getting a text."

And suddenly, words begin to ink themselves across one of the papers on the desk.

Attention, Astronomy College staff: Amir al-Kindi has been seen on Mercury and is believed to be on campus, possibly in company with Major Vieira and two unknown girls. Should you encounter the prince, please text the guard station.

"Well, that settles that." Major's mouth presses into a thin line, and he glances around at the three of us. "We've gotta get out of here."

RINGS OF SILVER still drift over Claudia's head as she scribbles notes from Dr. Qureshi's book about Saturn, its coordinates, the tone we need to travel. Amir puts the office to rights around her, tucking the chair back in, replacing the professor's books.

"Hurry, hurry, hurry, hurry, hurry," Major chants, though this is obviously not helping.

"So, that's not what I thought you meant when you said *texting*," Claudia says, slamming the book shut and shelving it.

Amir's brow creases. "It's text on paper. What else could it mean?"

I'm not moving. Because I can hear it. Claudia's song.

Maybe I've always heard it, but never been listening. Or maybe it's the influence of Mercury around me allowing me to hear her, *really* hear her, for the first time.

Her song isn't a perfect match to Mercury's song around us; there's something a bit softer in its rises and falls, something gentler in its rhythm, a mildly pained minor note somewhere I can't quite track. But it's close.

I understand why she's so at home here.

"Less standing, more moving." She claps at Major and me. I jerk to life, and as my focus pulls from Claudia's music to Mercury's larger melody on the air, I can't decide if the music is threatening to bend the wrong way around us like it did at the train station, or if the dread only lives inside me.

The ground hasn't opened up beneath us. But disaster still feels close enough to touch.

"I can't believe we're going to Saturn," I mumble, zipping up my jacket. "I'm breaking the law on *purpose* now."

"Going to Saturn makes sense." Amir straightens the last papers, his voice low and confident. "His song should correct you. Being around other Capricorns should correct you. The planet will render its own song far better than Major and I can." He hesitates. "After all, this is what the exclusion is for. This is what it's meant to do."

Major puts a hand on my shoulder, and the corner of his mouth curves. "In for a penny, in for a pound, right?"

I try to smile, but just end up baring my teeth. They're trying so hard to help me. They're so certain Saturn's song is the answer.

I can't bring myself to tell them how it made me feel.

We sneak out of Dr. Qureshi's office and through the Astronomy College, careful and quiet as we can be. We check for guards or professors around every corner before we turn, duck into alcoves around diamond-paned windows when we hear voices.

We have to get to the college's heart, its center. That's where Amir says travel is easiest: to and from the points that best represent a sphere's energy.

"And that's why you traveled to the 9:30 Club?" I ask Major as the four of us creep over the silver flagstones. Massive woven tapestries on the walls dampen the sound of our footsteps.

"Yes," Major says. "It's a center of energy and music. It's also why we ended up beneath a train station when we came back here."

"Because travel is another facet of the planet's persona," I finish, glancing up at him. Lamplight from overhead catches in his hair, and when he smiles, pleased that I'm learning, my heart leaps. "Was DC the first place on Earth you traveled?" I ask.

"No. We went to an orchestral concert in Madrid first, and then an underground club in London. But neither of them felt right." Amir throws out a hand and we skid around a corner to hide. Major stands over me, grinning faintly. "Aren't you glad we kept going?"

I bite my lip. It's the wrong time—the worst time—to let myself go loose and warm at his closeness. And though Major may hit on me relentlessly, part of me doubts whether he likes *me* or he likes *flirting*.

But Amir waves us on before I can reply. "All clear," he says. "Let's keep going."

There are three grand lecture halls near the front of the Astronomy College; we're lucky to find one empty. The space is massive, an arena of scratched-up dark wood desks facing a lectern up front. A massive blue stained-glass window glows behind it, and a map of the spheres swathes the ceiling in stars.

"This should do," Amir murmurs to himself, hurrying down the stadium steps. He reaches the blackboard and begins to chalk out the coordinates Claudia wrote down.

"Where will these take us?" she asks.

"Kronos," he says. "That's the name of the village on Saturn."

My stomach twists. Saturn. We're really going.

"Are you ready, Ro?" Claudia asks, startling me; I'd thought she was watching Amir. I catch a flash of misgiving on her face at what I know my expression must be.

I couldn't tell them what Saturn's song made me feel when the boys sang it. But they seem so sure a stronger dose of it is the answer, they must be right.

They have to be.

Suddenly, the lecture hall door opens. We all freeze, heads whipping toward the top of the stairs.

The red-clad guard only glances inside at first. But then he double-takes, narrowing his eyes.

My heart plunges into my stomach. "No, no, no, no."

"I've got them!" shouts the guard. He hovers in the doorway, gaze jerking back and forth between us and the hallway outside.

Major swears a blue streak as Amir finishes scratching out Kronos's coordinates, the chalk scraping and breaking in his trembling hands. Major fumbles the pitch pipe, playing one wrong note and then another before he finds Saturn's tone and echoes it in his own voice.

Running footsteps grow louder. A portal appears, and through it, a planet the color of ash, wrapped in rings.

I'm trembling as I turn to Claudia. "Are you sure about this?"

"Yes. Weighing the relative risks, yes." She takes a short breath, eyes on the gray planet. "This has to be the next step, Rora. This is what makes sense. Correcting you, the microcosm."

It makes sense. She's right. She *has* to be right.

All these weeks, just as right now, I've been frozen in place. And it hasn't served me. Nothing has changed, because I've done nothing different.

I trust Claudia. And she thinks this is the right move, so it must be.

From the lecture hall entrance, the first guard watches us, unmoving, horrified. Then five other guards burst through the door and race down the stairs.

"Ready?" Major steps close to my side, radiating familiar warmth. It's nearly enough to drown out the song I can already hear emanating through the portal.

I can feel the planet calling, in my bones. I try not to let my body's answer show.

Our pursuers are nearly down the stairs when Claudia puts a fist through the portal. "Let's go!" she shouts, jagged crystal scraping at her cashmere coat as she pushes through, beckoning for me to follow.

We have no choice. We have to go.

First Claudia, then Amir, then me, and then Major with a hand on my arm. I feel like a smoker who's slapped on a nicotine patch; his touch is instant relief.

The guards stay back as we pass through. They watch us, eyes wide, a few hands scribbling out texts—but they don't follow.

Mercury's song is quick, jittery, edgy, like an itch in my brain, like a thousand hailstones against my skull. As I leave the quicksilver planet behind, with Major's hand steering me and his warm music sliding over my skin, the itch eases, and I heave a sigh of relief to have left it and the guards behind.

We have another chance. Another shot at answers.

But they're already notifying others that we've gone, and they'll know where to. We don't know what could be waiting for us when we land on Saturn. So we hurry; and yet my blood seems to slow as we move toward the planet in the distance.

A new song moves into my bones, a song like grit, like sand, like spiderwebs; and my body begins to waver like warped old glass.

1287

BEATRICE SPENT HER evenings at Dante's side, drinking wine beneath their city's magical lamps and staring at the heavens he had painted for her on the cavern ceiling. And though she passed her days with her fellow astronomers, eyes on the stars, Dante was never far, his very presence seeming to amplify the music and the magic she heard all around her.

From her vantage point at the mouth of the cavern, with her gaze and her focus sharpened by her telescope and by magic, Beatrice could see one planet beyond sober, ash-gray Saturn. It was a pale, strange blue, and with all her senses attuned to its sphere, she could sense the brilliance and oddity of its disposition.

Everything in Beatrice inclined itself to that unknown planet the color of an aquamarine. It called to her.

So intent was her focus that she startled when a foreign body crossed between her and the pale blue planet.

The substance of the spheres—the aether—Beatrice hardly noticed anymore; it was ubiquitous but insubstantial, and she sensed it only peripherally, as she sensed the songs around her. But when the comet—for that was what Bice thought it might be—crashed into view, careering wildly into the pale blue planet's sphere, the aether grew brittle, glassine, almost as if to close itself off.

The comet merely smashed these defenses, bowling back and forth and seeming to shatter the spheres like crystal before shooting off into the distance and out of view.

Beatrice jerked away from her telescope, heart pounding.

She did not see the comet again, and her fellow astronomers from Suvd Uls knew nothing of it when she described what she had seen. But though she shuddered, she faithfully marked its presence in her charts, identifying it with a key to represent how easily it had moved between the spheres that had attempted to shut it out.

She marked the pale blue planet, as well. She did not name it, not yet—not until she knew if others had already done so. But the comet Beatrice called Chiron, after the centaur of myth.

Centaurs were untamable, not unlike comets themselves; but Chiron had become a healer. Beatrice hoped, with such a name, to manifest a kinder nature for the wild object she had seen.

Its fury—the promise of what might wait farther out in the spheres—frightened her.

But like the comet, Beatrice would press onward, outward. She was undaunted, unstoppable.

Nothing would deter her from her path.

RORA

18

KRONOS, SATURN

I AM DRAWN as if by a magnet into ringed Saturn's orbit as soon as we crash into the sphere. Summoned by its weight, towed by its gravity, something in it calling to something in me.

Yet even as I'm drawn by my very bones, I'm repelled by the tone of its music, mournful and heavy and gray as ashes. My pounding heart resists every step of the way as we walk, repulsed as if by like polarity.

I hate the song that beckons me to the austere planet Dr. Qureshi's textbook called Infortuna Major. But I don't let my face show anything. I turn myself to stone. I press on.

And when we break out of the aether onto Saturn's surface amid flurrying snow, I try not to smell the acrid scent of sulfur and ashes that threatens to smother me.

Claudia searches our surroundings, eyes lit with curiosity. "So there *is* land here," she says. I can hardly hear her over the wind. "But Saturn's a gas giant!"

"Beatrice's expedition conjured this island," Amir answers, scanning the terrain uncertainly. A mountain looms above us; down a hill to our right is a village of a few stone buildings surrounded by little half-timbered homes. Snow is piled on their gabled roofs, on the rock face, around our feet. It can't be more than twenty degrees out, and the boys aren't wearing jackets. "Kepler's people built the monastery and the village."

Major turns in a circle. "No guards coming," he says. Given the texts they sent as we were leaving Mercury, I'd anticipated red uniforms waiting to meet us.

But no sound rises from the town. Not a single window shines with light; no smoke curls up from the chimneys.

Something in me knows—knows for certain, with no room for doubt—that it's not just the cold keeping the people inside.

Claudia tugs her coat more tightly around her, dark hair whipping around her face. "Where is everyone?"

Major just shakes his head. "Do you feel any better, Rora?" He puts his hands on my shoulders, studying me, as though expecting to see some change from this place already written all over me.

It should be a ridiculous idea. And yet, in Hermes, with Claudia—I could. I could see how at home she was almost from the moment we arrived, in the easy straightness of her spine and the clip of her steps as we moved up the street.

Whatever she sensed, I don't. I feel only the fearful creep of anxiety like cold water dripping down my back, only sadness like a weight heavy enough to lay me down in the snow and shut my eyes forever.

Something is wrong here.

Can't the others hear it? Or is Saturn's song already so foreign to them that they can't tell the difference?

Maybe we're all just pretending not to notice. Maybe we're all just hoping against reason that we have any shot at solving the disharmony. At fixing me.

Major is still watching me hopefully, waiting for my answer. I shake my head.

"Is there someone we can ask for help?" My voice comes out raspy, disused.

Claudia grimaces, and I'm afraid I've hurt her feelings. But then her eyes sharpen. "Maybe the problem is that you're drinking from a firehose, Rora." She turns to Amir. "Is there someone here who could help focus the song for her? Channel it?" She glances down toward the dark, silent village, and the three of us follow her gaze. It seems an unlikely source of help.

The problem is that Saturn's song is a ruin. That listening to it is like feeling myself fossilize.

"There's the Abbot," Major suddenly offers. "He's the planet's guardian. He watches over Kronos. Maybe he could help."

"That way?" Claudia nods toward the village.

"No." Amir wraps his arms around himself. "The monastery is up the mountain," he says with a shiver. "Let's start climbing. The Abbot will know what to do."

I don't want to go—to travel into the heart of this place. I clutch at Claudia's sleeve. "Are you sure?" I ask her, as I asked before we left Mercury.

She nods, a little distant, as if she's lost in thought. "It might work," she says. "As long as we're here, it can't hurt."

But I can hear the music all around us. And I'm afraid that whatever we find at the monastery will hurt us—hurt *me*—very much.

The mountains are gray, and the sky is gray, and the music rises like a dirge on the wind as we climb. Twenty feet to our right, the path drops off in a sheer cliff, so we stay close to the rock face on our left.

I can't believe that this song is the answer. The boys called Saturn's music contemplative, but I don't feel any of that as we climb.

Because this is the way the song feels: like a snowstorm, like lead, like a precipice where I could fall and disappear forever. I feel it in my skull, my ribs, my nerve endings.

Saturn's song sounds the way the planet looks. Like danger. Like collapse. It sounds like everything that already waits inside me.

Is this what's supposed to heal my anxiety? Is this song really the fate I was born to?

I can't believe it. I can't fathom subjecting myself to this song forever, as their rules dictate.

We climb higher and higher, Claudia and Amir and Major and me, until the village is a small, breakable thing in the distance, until we can no longer see it through the fog and snow. Layers of icy white suck at our feet, soaking my jeans to mid-calf. I'm shaking from cold and anxiety and the melody that grinds harder at my bones the farther we go.

When I trip in a snowbank, Major's large hand envelops mine, and it is the only warm thing that I feel. He pauses, waiting for me to right myself, staring up the path. "I don't understand. Shouldn't we be able to see the monastery by now?" he asks.

"It's all the snow," Amir calls back. It falls more thickly the higher we climb; his lips are nearly purple with cold.

Major gives a rumble of frustration. "Can't see a thing out here."

Saturn's music is everywhere. It burrows into my bones like termites.

I hang my head, not wanting the others to see the tears pressing into the corners of my eyes. But when Major ducks down to catch my gaze, I can't avoid him. And my relief is stronger than my pride when he makes a small, dismayed sound and tugs me against his chest. "Hey, hey, what's wrong?" he demands.

I don't like my medicine, I want to cry, but I can't. I'm too ashamed to tell any of them how much it hurts.

I lean my forehead against Major's sternum and let his arms wind around me. And there, beneath the keening of the wind—there is the beat of his heart, and his music like the rush of ocean waves, inexorable as the pull of the tide.

I let it pull me under.

"Why are you crying, Rora?" Major presses again.

A tear leaks down my cheek. I give in. "I don't like the song here," I gasp. "I don't like it."

Saturn's music repelled me when he and Amir sang it back on Mercury. But it's worse, here and now. There's an anger and a loneliness to the melody that has nothing to do with quiet or sobriety, nothing to do with who Saturn is supposed to be.

"It's—" Amir clears his throat, glancing away from me wrapped up in his best friend's arms. "I have to admit, Saturn's song is worse than I expected. I've never seen a storm this bad here, and I've never heard its music this . . . vicious." He grimaces, staring up the mountain. "Maybe we should reconsider."

"But we're almost there," Claudia argues, drawing close to lay a hand on my arm, and I drink in the sound of her, too. Mercury's music around her is like a shot of adrenaline to my too-slow heart. "Don't give up, Rora."

Maybe Claudia's right. Maybe the only way out is through.

"We have a plan. We're going to fix you," she vows.

I am made entirely of doubts. But I trust my best friend.

So I nod wordlessly and we carry on, Major's hand tight around one of mine, Claudia holding the other.

But even clinging to one another, even squinting into the snow as hard as we can, the four of us seem to be climbing toward nothing. "Could we be going the wrong way?" Claudia finally asks.

"This is it." Amir's voice is desolate as he stares up the empty path. "There's nothing else on Saturn but the monastery and the village. We've nearly reached the summit. It should *be* here."

"Wait!" Claudia interrupts. "Wait. Is that it?"

The boys shuffle forward, eyes narrowed. "No," Major blurts. "What—what happened?"

Amir plows forward another few feet, then stops dead. When we reach his side, I see why.

CLAUDIA

19

I UNDERSTAND NOW how the boys didn't see it.

The monastery on Kronos is a sober old building—a Gothic thing the color of ancient tombstones, all steep pinnacles and buttresses shuddering in the wind and niches watched by gargoyles. In the snow, beneath a sky streaked the color of ash and bile, it's easy to miss. And where it must once have stood four or five stories high on the mountainside, its three bottom floors have now sunk into a pit in the ground. Slush and frozen mud suck at its walls.

Something has gone horribly wrong. Whatever threatens Mercury and Mars, whatever troubles Earth, it looms larger here.

This was my idea—coming to Saturn, visiting the Abbot. But Rora isn't responding to the planet's music. She isn't being brought into line with herself the way the logic of this place seemed to dictate, the way I expected. *None* of this is going the way I expected.

"Is it supposed to look like that?" Rora asks hoarsely.

"No, it's not." Amir face is unreadable. "Wait here."

"Not a chance," I bite out. "Be right back, okay?" I say, tugging my fingers from Rora's.

"Hurry." Major's teeth chatter as he stands over her, trying to shelter her from the wind.

Her lips are almost blue. And I have to stifle my gasp when I see a light rime of frost on her cheek.

I start to ask if she's all right—but of course she's not all right. None of this is right or normal or *possible*.

Amir darts after me when I take off, skidding down the muddy hill to the monastery entrance, loam smearing my palms and the hem of my coat. A water-stained front door looms over us when we reach the floor of the sinkhole.

He hesitates. I don't.

I hammer on the door as hard as I can. As we wait for the sound of footsteps, I glance back up the sides of the pit and think of Rora's skin, covered in frost.

But just as when we stood outside Dr. Qureshi's office, no one answers.

I stare up the walls of the monastery, wondering what Beatrice made of this place. If she felt fear on Saturn's air as thick as the slush around our legs.

She must have come to this planet—from Jupiter, and then on to Uranus. She—

A weak cry comes from above. Amir and I exchange a terrified glance and bang furiously on the door, calling to whoever's inside.

This time, we're acknowledged.

An old white man with white hair and cataracts in his eyes appears at a crack in the door. "You should not be here," he says in low, harsh-sounding German. There is no welcome on his face.

"Please, Abbot, sir, can you help us?" Amir's words tumble over one another. "I'm Prince Amir. And my friend—she's—please. We need your help."

The monk doesn't speak. But after a pause, he steps back and opens the door wider.

Amir's breath comes out in a rush. He scrabbles back up the hill and retrieves Major and Rora and then we're ushered inside.

It's cold within the monastery's walls. We're sheltered from the wind whistling sharply outside, but the stone foyer and its adjoining corridors are slick with icy damp. The tops of the unlit torches along the wall are burned black, the ghosts of their smoke lingering greasy on the stones behind them.

From where we stand in the entryway, too, I can see a slice of a large dining room. My heart hopes for warmth, food, welcome; but the fireplace is full of ashes, its hearth frosted over, the tables filled with a long-abandoned meal—rotten apple cores and meat spoiled on bones, dirty cups and plates.

Dread slides down my spine. And when I glance back to Rora, I nearly choke. The frost has crept over her cheeks to her neck and throat.

She looks like she wants to bolt out the door, and I don't blame her.

Amir comes close, pressing his shoulder to mine. But more bracing than the contact are the questions I see forming behind his eyes. Because the same ones are troubling me.

"Abbot," he asks for the both of us. "Sir, where is everyone? Why is the monastery so quiet?"

When I was seven, our family took a trip—a pilgrimage, walking the Camino de Santiago de Compostela in northern Spain. Though Jack and I were primarily interested in wreaking havoc and fighting over who got to hold Nonna's hand, I tried to listen, to make her happy as docents led us through a succession of old buildings.

The monastery we visited fascinated me the most. I was bursting with questions for the guide who led us through the sanctuaries and the cells for prayer, the vegetable gardens that fed the monks, the scriptoriums where they'd labored over translations and illuminations. Monasteries were places of contemplation, the docent stressed, but amazing work was done within their walls.

I search for this now, peering around for winter gardens or writing rooms, for sounds of prayer or singing or discussion. But there's nothing.

"They've gone to bed," the Abbot replies to Amir. "They've all gone to bed. Everyone is very tired." His tone is absent and his skin is waxy and pale, blue veins standing out underneath. And though I feel terrible for noticing, he smells awful, like he hasn't bathed in a long time.

"Please—our friend," Major interjects. "Can you help her?"

"We think she needs you to focus Saturn's song for her," I say, trying to sound more confident than I feel. My insides are shaking. "Simply being here doesn't seem to be working quickly enough." Ice crystals have begun to creep up toward Rora's temple, down her neck to her clavicle.

I think again of what Major called Rora: amplifier.

Is this place worse for her because of what she is? Or is something else to blame?

Horrified, I stare between her and the Abbot, waiting for his reaction. But he watches us with flat eyes.

Amir called him Kronos's guardian. He said he could help. And I assumed from his calling—to philosophy, to caring about the human condition, to *whatever*—that he would jump to Rora's rescue. But he barely looks concerned.

"Sir?" Major asks again.

"Yes," the Abbot finally says, almost as if he'd forgotten we were here. "I will attend to her. Come with me."

"Yes," Rora gasps, relief bursting through the single syllable, and follows him down the corridor. "Please."

I stare after the Abbot's back as he walks away, burning up at his apathy. But beggars can't be choosers. And even the fate of the spheres matters infinitely less to me right now than my best friend, who is in pain. So I say nothing.

My eyes scour the monastery as Amir, Major, and I trail behind Rora and the monk. To our right and left, we pass rooms full of abandoned tasks. Candles are burned down in their stands, wax dried around them; papers and writing implements are scattered haphazardly across tables, as if their owners simply walked away from their work and didn't come back. Here, too, the torches are unlit, and black mold limns the seams where the stone walls meet the ceiling.

Not until we come to a residential wing do I see the first signs that anyone lives here but the Abbot. And then I wish that I hadn't.

We pass bedroom after bedroom, their doors ajar, their occupants lying in bed though it's the middle of the day.

Some are asleep, but most are not. They stare at the ceiling, at the walls, *through* us as we walk past.

It chills me to the bone. I'm choking on the smell of unwashed bodies, of other things I'm trying not to think about.

"Is any of this normal?" I ask Amir, pitching my voice beneath the rising wind, trying to keep the fear out of my voice. Because I know it's not.

Amir just shakes his head. He shoves his hands into his pockets, but not before I notice they're trembling.

The Abbot rounds a corner and turns in to a tiny cell. Inside, no personal items decorate the bare walls; an unlit candle sits alone on a hutch. Dirty clothes are piled on the floor next to a bare mattress. He seats Rora on a wooden stool, the rest of us drifting around the room like dead leaves.

Knees drawn up to her chest, Ro looks like a hunted animal. Her eyes scan the floor, slide anxiously along the walls.

Me either, Rora, I want to say. *I don't like this place, either.*

Because I know what she's thinking. Because she's told me a hundred times.

Nowhere is safe.

I try to tamp down the unease climbing my ribs like they're rungs on a ladder.

We're here. We're nearly done with what we came to do. The Abbot will administer Saturn's song to Rora, he will set her right and call up her star chart, and we can examine it to figure out what's hurting her and everyone else.

Rora may only be my un-twin. But I've watched the past six weeks twist and traumatize her. I won't do nothing and watch her freeze over and fall apart when this place has the answers to fix her.

I haven't failed my best friend. We're nearly there.

The Abbot crouches in front of Ro. His voice is heavy and hard as an anvil. "Your nails and your teeth."

Rora grimaces, and holds out trembling fingers.

The monk begins to sing.

His voice is slow and mournful. The song chills me, but Rora must find it soothing, because her eyes sink closed.

Inward, inward, inward, Saturn sings to Ro, to the rest of us. I feel my pulse slacken, the flow of my blood growing languid and my bones growing leaden.

Thoughts press into my hollowed-out mind. Thoughts of Jack's full suitcases and his empty bedroom and the deafening silence of my house after the car doors slammed and my parents drove him away.

I push the painful memories out. *This will work,* I think desperately. It'll make Rora better. She'll—

The frost spreads over Rora's chest, her ears, her lips.

My best friend sinks to her knees, presses her face to the stone floor. She gives one, two, three ragged breaths.

And then she begins to scream.

"STOP!" I SHRIEK. My voice is raw. "Stop, stop, I can't, you have to stop *singing*—"

The song is endless, bottomless, heavy as lead. It wraps around my bones and snaps them one by one, turning them into weapons against my soft, vital parts. My own skeleton is a cage of barbed wire, a crown of thorns.

I curl up, fetal, the stone floor scratching my lips and my cheek. The song leaches all the strength from my heart and pours it out between my ribs like water; it winds my thoughts in a furious tangle, an endless, frenzied, unsolvable knot. Trapped inside my own skull, I have no choice but to chase them.

My vision goes black at the edges. I want to claw the freezing skin off my bones.

All I see, all I hear, all I know is Saturn. He was already inside me, and now he is all around, and there is nothing left but mania and mourning.

I was wrong. Claudia was wrong. This was always my fate—to be shattered against this terrible music. And it was foolish to hope there was any escaping it.

"Shut up!" Claudia bellows. She's at my side, holding my hand.

"What are you doing to her? Stop!" The Abbot goes silent but I am already frozen, already scorched alive. I lie on my side and shake.

At my back, I feel the monk shift away. "Only what you asked. I plied her with Saturn's song. If the music is too weighty or she too frail, it is no fault of mine."

My eyes fall shut. They're too heavy to keep open.

"But—Rora belongs to Saturn. The song was supposed to conjure her star chart and show us what to do." Major's voice seems to come from underwater. My arms are heavy, too, but I reach for him, and there he is. His hands are warm.

In my haze, Amir's answer drifts in and out of focus. "It should have centered her. Harmonized Rora's insides with her outsides. I don't understand why it—"

"No," I beg. Am I speaking out loud? "Not there. Please, please, please."

Claudia brushes my bangs off my forehead. "Not where, sweetie?"

I force my eyes open, feeling tears stream sideways across my nose to the stone floor. My bones ache and I am so cold. "Inside," I whisper. "I don't want to go there anymore."

Claudia and Major and Amir exchange fearful glances. I think my hands have slipped from theirs so I anchor myself in their gazes, in the colors.

If I fill myself with warm brown and hazel and ocean-soft blue, maybe the gray will let me go.

Whatever the answer is, it's not inside me. It's not on Saturn, or in his song. I doubt I'll find it anywhere.

Nowhere is safe.

My nails scrape the stone floor. Cold slime cakes beneath them. I feel bruised to my core. The panic rises again.

Inward, inward, inward.

These cities shouldn't even exist; the monastery is an illusion bound to shatter; and when it does, we'll be lost, drifting a million lifetimes from home, suffocating alone in the cold and the dark, but it doesn't matter, because it's not like there's anywhere safer. Nowhere, nowhere, nowhere is safe.

The horrors press in.

Thirty-one fears. One for every day of the month.

But mostly—that night. The streetlight on the black plastic gun, on the man's scabby white face and gray zip-up sweatshirt.

I try to inhale deeply, but it comes out a sob. My ribs won't give, my belly won't expand far enough; my breaths come short and shallow.

Claudia stands, shaking the Abbot. "Sing something else!"

"I know only Saturn's song."

"Major. Amir," Claudia orders. "Help her. Sing something else."

"What if I get it wrong?" Amir demands. I sense his panic beneath my own and curl up tighter on my side.

If I break every bone in my body, can I make myself small enough to hide from Infortuna Major?

"Pull her out of herself now or it won't matter!" Claudia shouts.

I chase my breath, but it's racing away from me, *in out in out in out in out*—

Major lifts me to the edge of the mattress, aching concern in his eyes. "Am I going to die?" I gasp. My voice is jagged. My chest hurts.

"You're hyperventilating." Major holds my gaze, skims his thumbs across my damp, sticky cheeks. "Can you hold your breath?"

I don't think, or speak. I just bury my face in his neck, try to trap my ragged breathing and the fear with it. Major's arms brace my aching spine and ribs, and I sink against his side. When my head lolls like an infant's, he catches it, cupping my nape.

Everything hurts but him.

Saturn's song still lurks in the corners of the room, beneath the wind wailing outside. But with Major's arms around me, the alto melody that hovers about him is clearer than Saturn's deep, anguished tones. The notes of it don't ring in my head or my bones; they settle warm and forgiving in my blood, in my weakly beating heart, in every curve and soft yielding part of me.

My hands are fisted in his shirt. His slide over my back, not letting go.

When my breath returns, I open my eyes, and there is Major. Tangled hair, tanned skin, soft gold music enveloping me.

The monk seizes his arm. "Not here."

Major starts. "Wh—"

"Not. Here." The Abbot's words are cold. A final answer. "You will not bring your debauched music into this place. You will not sully our song." He points toward the door.

The wind does not hold its breath as it waits for us to make our exit. It howls maliciously as we limp from the monk's cell.

Major bears me down the corridor, boneless and wrung out. I watch as cells drift past, their occupants' eyes empty, their bodies limp and lost as mine, but with no friends to carry them.

"What do we do now?" Claudia whispers raggedly.

Amir shakes his head. "I think we've done all we can do."

Claudia stops. "You're—" she chokes. "You're just gonna leave her like this?"

And then I understand. The Abbot won't help, and the boys are out of ideas. There's nothing anyone can do for me.

But Major interrupts my thoughts, sounding horrified. "Of course not."

"You're going to stay with me?" My voice is hoarse. "I—I don't know if I can help you get answers anymore."

What lesson is there to be learned from me and my scorched-out shell? What use am I to anyone, broken like this?

Major sets me on my feet, looking stunned. "We're not leaving you, Rora."

"But we're in over our heads." Amir looks down the corridor in the direction of the foyer, then seems to think better of it and steps into an empty cell. There is no door to shut against the smells of the hallway—unwashed bodies and untended needs. Exhausted tears drip down my face, and Major doesn't let me go as we follow him inside.

"So we're going to see your parents?" he asks.

Amir nods wearily, tracing numbers into the grime on the floor. "If I can sort out the coordinates we need from here." Claudia crouches beside him, working through figures I can't follow.

Even now, Major doesn't release me. But Saturn's song still circles like a wolf watching prey.

"Tell me three good things," I whisper into his shirt. His skin is golden above its collar.

Major doesn't hesitate. He is summer in winter as he bends down to whisper in my ear. "Once, when I was seven, I fell out of an orange tree," he says. "I'd tried to carry down too much fruit. I fell, and broke my wrist."

"That's not a good memory," I mumble.

"Be patient." He laughs kindly. "The leaves were so green, and the whole orchard smelled like sugar, and I'd decided I would carry

162

home fifteen oranges. Three for each of us, my mother and my dad and my sisters and me."

At this, I can't help giving a damp laugh. "You tried to carry fifteen oranges?"

He nods readily. "My mother coddled me for a week afterward. She propped me up on pillows near the window and moved all my favorite art into my room, and our cook made my favorite foods. I ate nothing but cheese for days."

Another watery laugh. Major squeezes my shoulder. "Better?"

"Give me two more." He's so tall his hip is pressed against my ribs, my chin resting right above his heart. In the icy room, he is impossibly warm.

Amir straightens, clearing his throat. "No time," he says. "We have to go."

I press my nose to Major's sleeve, take in a long breath of warm music, of the ocean, of orange trees. Three good things and more. They steady me enough that I can stand on my own.

We're ready.

Amir knows the note by heart—not the one that hangs in Major's lungs, that clings to his skin and his clothes and his breath, but a new one. It is jubilant and proud, fierce and golden. Despite my weakness, I lunge toward it, desperate to claw out of the cold.

When the portal appears, I'm the one who punches our way out of Saturn's sphere.

1287

THEY DEPARTED HERMES on Polo's birthday, the fifteenth of September. It was a gift, Beatrice joked affectionately, to the most restless member of their party, and one that Polo accepted gratefully.

In Venus's sphere, they found another planet empty—and this one ablaze, like a lake of fire burned dry as a desert. They conjured an island and cast strong barriers around it, and when they filled it with air to breathe, it rose into the sky of its own accord.

They did not build anything of permanence on Venus; even their compatriots from the Uls did not sleep inside their gers when they grew tired. Instead, they covered their floating oasis with earth and pink sand and a salt sea, and soon found that Venus's song rendered it all rich and lush. Moreover, the sky did not change with the hours, as it did on Earth; for the duration of their stay, the heavens were suffused with gold, as if the sun never ceased to rise.

Dante lounged with Beatrice before the sea, suggesting the magicians conjure grapevines out of the soil or magick fish into the water. With the horses splashing in the waves and Beatrice's auburn hair unbound and spilling over his shoulder, he felt like Adam come to his very own Eden. Even Marco seemed more ready to relax here.

For amusement, Beatrice calculated the natal charts of all their company; it was too warm to do much, and one of her astronomers had lent her a volume containing all the signs and meanings of the Greek zodiac. "Marco first!" she had announced, sheet of vellum and pen in hand. "As we have most recently celebrated the most auspicious day of his birth."

Marco laughed. "What must I do, my lady?"

"I need the year of your birth," Beatrice replied promptly. "And the hour, if you know it."

"I do not," Marco admitted. "But I was born on the fifteenth of September, in 1254."

"Thirty-three," Beatrice teased. "Such an old man." But Marco only shook his head, smiling.

It was nearly an hour later when Beatrice produced her work with a flourish. "You, Signore Polo, belong to the sign of the Virgin."

Marco and Dante exploded into laughter. "I assure you," Marco said, red-faced from mirth, "I do not."

"You do!" Beatrice huffed, red herself from blushing. "You were born when the sun was in Virgo and the moon was in Scorpio. Observe, sir." Obediently, Marco took her work and surveyed it with all due care.

"Your sun sign, governed by Mercury, indicates that you are dutiful, industrious, and somewhat of a perfectionist, and your moon sign"—Beatrice grinned playfully—"would seem to mark you quite the man of mystery."

"You"—Marco squinted at her, all friendly affection—"shall never know."

Beatrice produced the rest of their company's charts in turn, completing Dante's and her own after the others had gone to sleep on the beach beneath the ever-rising sun.

"You were born to the Twins," Beatrice said to Dante, frowning down at the pages she referenced, "when both the sun and the moon were in Gemini. You are a communicator, a traveler, and a trickster." She shook her head, bemused. "But that describes you so imperfectly! Your ascending sign, though, is Pisces. That makes a bit more sense."

Dante smiled, smoothing the lines of displeasure between her brows with the tip of one finger. "Lucky for me, my mother delivered me within the sound of Florence's bell tower, and I know the moment of my birth."

Beatrice made a face at him. "And mine was delivered of me mere houses away from yours, but she did not mark the hour, so I do not know my ascending sign."

"Tell me what mine means, then," he said, "since you say it fits so well."

"Dreamy." Beatrice looked up at him through her lashes and smiled. "Sensitive."

"Very well," Dante said. And then he did what he had wanted to do since he had seen her from the alley that night in Siena, since the May Day party at her father's house when they were both just children: he kissed her.

When Beatrice drew back, more flushed than ever, she glanced away shyly, searching for words to fill the moment that hung between them. "Being born to Gemini puts you under Mercury's rulership," she said. "Did you feel at home there?"

Dante looked thoughtful. "I was happy there," he said. "More than that, I cannot tell. Just as I could not say if Marco felt more at home there."

"True," Beatrice agreed. Privately, she was inclined to doubt Dante's assignation to the sign of the Twins. He was no slippery double-talker; his nature was pure, true to his ascending sign.

Beatrice's own chart had placed her in Aquarius, which her astronomers' texts assigned to Saturn's rulership. But Beatrice knew—already, she *knew*—that the pale blue planet she had seen in the distance from Hermes governed her sign. She knew she would feel at home there, just as she knew that when Dante was near, the music was amplified for her, that her calculations came clearer. That everything in her head and heart made more sense.

There, beneath Venus's seemingly eternal sunrise, Beatrice told him so.

There beside the sea, Dante kissed Beatrice once more, and swore himself to her.

She kissed him back, and believed him.

RORA
21

I AM ALWAYS careful.

I think before I speak, before I act. I am wary, controlled.

I've never hit anyone before. I've never broken anything because I was angry. I'm a good girl.

But when my fist meets Saturn's sphere, the aether cracks beneath my fist. Blood wells red against my pale knuckles, where it slices at my skin.

It's satisfying to know that I am not the thing made of glass. I am not what breaks.

I throw my shoulder against the portal. Its shattered crystal edges snatch and grasp at my jacket and my hair and the back of my neck—"Careful, Rora," Claudia gasps—but I shove my way through. She follows me, then Major, then Amir.

Jupiter's song draws me; I chase it. But I should know better than to run.

I should have known Saturn wouldn't release me so easily.

My bag is slapping my back and the others are hurrying after me and then I hear it.

We've stopped running, but the sphere quakes as though we're still moving. And when we look back at Saturn, I see the opening

I smashed into the sphere hasn't closed. It is a jagged wound in the aether, cracks slowly radiating from its edges.

"Go," Amir says to Claudia in a low voice, horror spreading over his face. "You three, go. I have to fix this. I'll meet you in al-Mushtari."

"As if we would leave you," Claudia fires back. "What can we do?"

"Nothing," Amir argues. "It—" But his look at me gives him away.

My voice is grim. I know what's coming. "Say it."

Amir and Major exchange a bleak glance. "Saturn's song should fix the break," Amir finally says. "That's why all of you have to go."

I glance between the three of them, trying to hide my panic.

Saturn's song almost broke me before. I don't know if it has the potential to hurt Amir the same way, or if it's just me.

But we can't split up. I won't abandon him to that music. "We stay together," I say, putting all my resolve into my voice. "We stay here with you until this is done."

Amir gives me a strange look at these words. But I don't give an inch.

"Fine," he agrees. "Major, stay close to her. And all of you, stay back."

CLAUDIA

22

AL-MUSHTARI, JUPITER

RORA STAYS BACK with Major, who holds her tightly. She doesn't watch as Amir retreats toward Saturn.

She's safe with Major. But I feel a low thrum of panic even stepping away from her, trailing ten feet after Amir.

With Rora lost, I feel lost, too. Adrift. A lonely satellite in this sphere echoing with Saturn's ruined music.

Amir stands before the break in the aether, looking into Saturn's sphere beyond, and shakes out his hands. As he spreads his palms over the shattered crystal and sings Saturn's low notes again, I try not to listen. I try just to watch him and make sure he's all right.

But my mind refuses to still.

The nature of scientific inquiry is to formulate, test, and discard hypotheses as you achieve results. It's best not to get attached to specific ideas, and I'm sure another will present itself once I've had time to think.

But I'm unnerved that Saturn's music didn't fix Rora. I don't understand how it only made her worse.

And amid all of this, I'm worried at how attached I've grown—

not to any particular hypothesis, but to the people I've dragged along on my grand experiment.

When Amir returns to me, his eyes are despairing. Under his efforts, the four-foot hole we smashed in the aether has filled, but it's insubstantial, like an early frost, not a solid repair.

None of the spheres have failed to repair themselves behind us before. Is it happening now because things are getting worse? Or—I glance back at Rora, our amplifier. Unusually powerful, unusually connected to the spheres' music.

Are things getting worse? Or is an amplifier—capable of making the spheres' songs louder and stronger—also capable of doing extraordinary damage?

"That's the best I can do," Amir says, voice breaking a little as he glances ahead, past Rora and Major. Far in the distance is a sandy-gold planet, a swirling wine-colored mass of cloud at its heart. "I have to tell my parents I failed. And not only do I not have answers, I've done irreparable damage to Saturn's sphere."

Amir begins to walk. When I stop him with a hand on his arm, he stills.

"You are not going to tell them you failed," I say sharply. "You're going to tell them you *tried*."

His throat bobs. "Thank you, Claudia."

"I'm serious. You've done your best. No one could have done more."

"Someone meant to be king could have done more," Amir says, dark eyes steady. "Someone not born beneath the wrong stars could have."

I'm not an ideal fit, Amir said back on Mercury, in Dr. Qureshi's

171

office. He wasn't speaking in terms of effort or personality; he meant that as a Scorpio, he was the wrong person to be king, to reign from Jupiter. It's so entirely out of his control, and it makes me so unexpectedly angry, and I can't think of a single thing to say.

I press my lips together and press a hand to his elbow, and he gives me a grim ghost of a smile. When he turns again toward Rora and Major—toward his parents and home—I follow him.

We are a bedraggled little parade. We are out of options. So we limp on toward Jupiter.

Beneath the deep red storm blowing high in the atmosphere, the four of us land in damp sand, a few inches of water swirling around our feet. A citadel rises up before us, its twilight torches gleaming against the shallow sea rushing around its gates.

Crimson and purple clouds streak across the darkening sky, and I stare up at the heavens, wind whipping my hair and my muddy coat. "This is your home?" I ask Amir.

"This is al-Mushtari," he says. "This is the seat of my parents' court."

Standing kinglike over the rising tide, the city is a proud mountain of sandstone buildings, crowned with minarets and domes. I remind myself to breathe as we slosh toward the red-clad sentries at its outer wall.

After being chased all over Mercury, I have no idea what kind of welcome we should expect. I'm not sure if the guards are going to jump up and salute Amir, or if they're going to cuff us for breaking the ban on travel.

I don't expect to see fear on their faces. It's nearly as surprising as the apprehensive way Major's hanging back, raising his eyes only to watch Rora and brace her if she looks wobbly. My heart sinks at how sick and pale she still looks, at the frost that still covers one side of her face from temple to jawline.

"Your Highness—" one red-uniformed young man blurts when we get close.

"I can't wait, Marcus," Amir says. His expression is grim, but not rude. He doesn't stop.

The man nods. "Of course." And just like that, the gates swing open, and sand becomes cobblestones, and we're inside the citadel. The wind sweeps through our hair and clothes as we rush through the streets, passing sandstone buildings with grand arched doors and broad walls elaborately carved with geometric shapes and stars and Arabic script. Beneath the dusk, people weaving in and out of homes and shops and markets stare and whisper and move out of Amir's way as he strides on.

It doesn't take long to reach the top of the citadel, where his parents' palace waits, gleaming in torchlight and capped with magnificent domes of red and gold. The massive doors, violet enamel covered with gilt script, open to Amir before he even speaks.

He strides through them, shoulders rounded like he knows what's coming, face set like he knows there's nothing he can do to stop it, and Rora, Major, and I follow.

We trail after him into a foyer where staff take our shoes and replace them with slippers, down high-ceilinged corridors bustling with men and women in black caftans and academic robes. They carry what look like architectural blueprints, hurrying around with purpose. Though I catch glimpses of finery as we walk—intricate crimson-and-gold mosaic floors, sculpted tray ceilings, carved dark wood chairs and spotless white sofas scattered around a salon—it feels less like a palace at the moment than like a hospital emergency room or a trading floor.

One last corner. A large set of double doors. An elegant tableau awaits.

The chamber inside is a work of art, the ceiling overhead all gilt stars against an indigo background, a rug woven with purple and gold geometric designs underfoot. The sea tosses outside a row of large keyhole-arched windows covered in sunburst-patterned screens. But within this room, everyone is very still.

A man and a woman sit at the head of a polished wooden table, he in a robe the color of Jupiter's swirling gold and purple and red sky, she in a hijab and round-necked dress the blue of the sea, heavily embroidered with gold. Both have deep bronze skin and deeply serious expressions.

Their titles are obvious from where they sit, from the way everyone at the table glances to check their reactions, but I could have identified Amir's parents regardless. Amir and the king are clearly carved from the same stuff. He's got the queen's warm brown eyes, but the determined set of his jaw and the curling sweep of his dark hair are all his father.

The table's surface is scattered with blueprints of the spheres, with papers covered in geometric proofs and mathematic equations. At its center is a crystalline model of concentric rings with a blue-green gemstone at its center. The remaining rings hold polished bits of stone or metal to represent planets, asteroid belts, and stars.

"My parents," Amir says to us under his breath. "Queen Inara and King Sameer."

Rora takes it all in beside me; Major watches her, tense and uncomfortable. It's strange to see him so unsure of himself.

Amir can't look away from the table—from his parents, their

advisors. He steps forward, ready to accept responsibility, ready to take the brunt of whatever we're about to face.

I realize abruptly that I'm not ready to hear this.

I'm not ready to watch Amir and Major get shredded. Not after watching it happen to Jack less than two months ago.

The queen is the first to speak. From the horror on her face, I'd expected sharpness in her voice, but it's unexpectedly blunted. "Amir—you're here." She catches sight of Rora's frostbitten cheek. "What happened to her?"

"Saturn's song," Amir says heavily. His gaze is fixed somewhere around the legs of the council table. "We took Rora there because she needed help. Applying Saturn's song on Mercury wasn't working."

They must know all this already. The guards who chased us must have reported everything.

"Where else did you go, Prince Amir?" asks an advisor at the table, a middle-aged white man with blond hair and a German accent, dressed like those around him in a black caftan.

Still hanging back, Major speaks up. "It wasn't his fault. It was my idea."

"Typical Scorpio behavior," mutters one of the councilors, a pale woman with bitter blue eyes. "Can't even lift his head and defend his decision."

Neither monarch acknowledges this, except for a slight stiffening of the queen's shoulders, a new tightness in the king's jaw. But everyone in the room heard it. Even the scholars who haven't spoken yet look uncertain, displeased.

The guys have screwed up. Badly.

I've witnessed the sequence of events that leads to a prince's exile from his kingdom. Since Jack left, I have replayed them again and again in my mind. And I see the opening steps to that horrible gambit in this conversation.

It feels painfully close to the night Jack and Anne-Marie Williams were caught in the principal's office. To the night my family broke.

Jack was hit right away with the difference between public and prep school: Dr. Phillips called the police before he called my parents. He said Jack could have accessed any amount of sensitive information—medical, financial, whatever. My brother insisted that he hadn't gone near the student records, but he didn't deny that he'd stolen the office keys in the first place.

Anne-Marie wasn't arrested, since this was her first strike. But the police cuffed Jack and escorted him to the station.

I was furious.

I didn't even hear about what had happened from him. I heard it from Anne-Marie, who texted me they weren't going to make it to the Georgetown party. That was where I was, trying to figure out by myself how to help Rora while she broke down.

Jack was expelled, obviously. I think his surprise at being kicked out *again* was what made me angriest. As if this was some real shock, instead of the inevitable result of him continuously flipping the bird at authority.

She'd never broken a rule before, Claudia! She'd never had any fun, he'd argued to me later that night, after my parents had picked him up from jail. *I just wanted to show her a little excitement, you know?* he'd sighed, as if he was sure I'd understand.

I didn't.

Not that it mattered. Jack was packing his bags even as we spoke. He'd blown too many second chances.

I didn't go with him to the airport the next day. I didn't return any of his texts or calls. And now that I miss him more than I'm mad at him, he won't answer any of mine.

"Baths and food," the king says suddenly, shaking himself. "Anything else, we can discuss later."

"But my king—they've come here in violation of Your and Her Majesty's edict," exclaims the woman who called Amir a *typical Scorpio* in the same tone you might say *common criminal*. And then another one of the scholars joins her protest.

And as Amir stands silently, not fighting off their criticism, all at once I see the difference between the exile I've already witnessed and the one looming here and now: Amir is not Jack, and this isn't fair.

Jack never stopped bucking authority. But since I met him, Amir hasn't stopped trying to help people—to solve a problem he didn't cause, one that he's willingly taken on his own shoulders.

He's better than Jack. He's better than me. And he doesn't deserve this.

I can't watch another prince banished.

"Enough," Queen Inara interrupts, eyes trained on Rora, and her quiet voice cuts through the scholars' petty scolding. Relief floods my system. "The girl needs a rest and a doctor at once."

As though released by the queen's words, Rora's knees buckle a little. Major catches her before she falls, but the room finally wakes up.

The scholars offer tea and water and damp cloths, scrambling around uselessly. And still, Amir wastes his breath placating them. "We brought her here because she's an am—"

Just as quickly, the relief is replaced by something else, by something burning wrathful and quicksilver-bright in my chest. "No," I say in a low, furious voice. "No. You don't tell them a thing."

It doesn't matter; no one's heard us. They're all watching Rora carried away limp in Major's arms as King Sameer issues orders to attendants.

"Glad everyone's priorities are in order here," I snap, glaring between the scholars. "Would've been a shame if you couldn't tell Amir how disappointed you were before helping someone who needed it." Then I stomp off after Major and Rora, leaving them all with their jaws hanging open, determined not to let my best friend out of my sight.

1287

AND SO, DANTE and Beatrice fell in love.

Venus's song worked on all of them—not with the falseness of a spell, but subtly, drawing out what already lay in their hearts. The friendship of their party grew familial beside the salt sea they'd conjured, talking beneath the eternal dawn and all it seemed to promise.

Dante began to see Polo as the older brother he'd never had. He came to know what Marco would say by the way he spread his hands, or which lines creased in his weather-beaten brow. They were opposites—Dante thin and serious and awkward, Marco broad and physical and restless—but Dante could see Marco bore him the same affection. The two men orbited one another as easily as twin stars.

Dante trusted him and Beatrice alike with everything but the truth.

Guilt pricked him, his lies feeling as heavy as Venus's sultry air. He tried, amid the planet's honey-sweet song, to forget.

But after two weeks—by Dante's reckoning, at least; it was hard to count when the sun never set—they stood on the shores of the sea they had conjured, abandoned fields and vineyards at their back. None would stay behind in the oasis they had created.

Despite the easy warmth of the music on the air, their hearts beat in fear. Dante stood close beside Beatrice, his arm around her waist, her head pressed into the hollow at his neck.

"We will be all right," he whispered to her softly. "I will let no harm befall you."

For the sun moved in the sphere just beyond.

The moon was a pearl, Mercury a drop of quicksilver, Venus a hazy jewel of gold and pink. But what was the sun? Another glittering gem to be plucked up and admired? Or a smith's forge aflame?

Beatrice straightened and nodded, squeezing Dante's hand and giving Marco a bracing nod, though the latter showed no dread.

She traced the coordinates of their path in the sand and played a tone on her pipe, and the note was brilliant and clear in the thick air. A portal appeared over the lapping waves, the light of the sun burning within it.

Steam hissed over the water. Fear sizzled in Beatrice's stomach.

She steeled herself. "Forward."

They marched into the fire.

CLAUDIA

23

WHEN I WAKE in a dim room, I'm disoriented before I remember where I am. I'm dressed in a soft nightgown, and Ro is snoring beside me; she does that when she's got a little bit of a cold, and if she didn't have one before, she does now.

Amir's parents—Queen Inara and King Sameer—offered me my own room. But I wouldn't let them separate us after the doctor had seen to Rora. I knew I'd sleep better close to her, and I knew she'd be less confused when she woke up if I was there.

I rub my eyes and check my phone one last time before switching it off; we've been asleep nine hours. Dusky light streams through the crescent shapes in the carved wooden window screens, washing over our sleigh bed and its heavy duvet, over the matching paneled wardrobe and writing desk. An arched doorway in the crimson-painted wall leads to an intricately tiled bathroom, where I brushed my teeth last night before crashing. And above the wash of the sea beyond the city walls, a man's voice rises, calling its Muslim inhabitants to prayer. This must have been what woke me.

When I roll over and put my elbow in a big wet patch on Rora's pillow, at first, I'm afraid she's been crying in her sleep. But then I see the frost on her temple and cheek is gone, replaced by something that looks strangely like windburn.

I lean closer, trying not to wake her, trying to make sense of it. I can grasp why Saturn—Rora's ruling planet—might affect her. But it's impossible not to connect the wind whooshing over the sea outside our open windows with her red, chapped cheek, and I don't understand it.

That Saturn affected Rora makes sense. But why Jupiter would do so, I can't begin to comprehend.

I try to be relieved. This is good, I guess. I just don't know what it means.

There's a soft knock at the door—soft but insistent. Ro's eyes fly open, and her whole body tenses.

"Hey, relax. It's okay," I say to her softly. "Come in," I call, and the door opens on a pale young woman pushing a cart full of food, followed by one of the scholars we met last night—the blond advisor who questioned Amir. The girl opens the screened windows, places our freshly laundered clothes on the edge of the bed, and sets a small table. Steam rises as she lifts silver lids from the cart, flatware and porcelain clinking.

"Her Majesty thought you'd prefer to dine here," says the scholar. He pauses, hands clasped. "Apologies. My name is Albrecht."

"I'm Claudia. This is Rora," I add, gesturing at Ro, who nods at him between yawns. I hesitate, glancing out the window. "Is it nighttime *still*, or nighttime *again*?"

Albrecht cocks a fair eyebrow, following my gaze. "Night's falling again. The planet turns in a mere ten hours. A day here in al-Mushtari is three rotations—two rotations awake, and the third asleep."

"Thirty hours. Sounds like a long day," Rora rasps.

"And none of us will rest until your presence is resolved," Albrecht says. I exchange a glance with Rora, feeling my hackles rise. "Queen Inara would like you to meet her in the high council room when you've finished eating."

"We'll be there soon," I say stiffly. He nods, the gesture equally wooden, and leaves us. I thank the maid before she follows him out.

Our dinner is a pleasant combination of sick-people food and more filling options—bean soup, soft flatbread, fragrant rice, and roasted lamb. I press a bowl of soup into Ro's hands first.

"Do you think Major and Amir are in trouble?" she asks around a mouthful of broth and beans.

My jaw tightens. "I think Amir's an easy scapegoat for problems that aren't his fault," I say darkly. "Good to know our being here is a thing that needs to be *resolved*."

And it will be, I tell myself. We're safe. We've finally made it.

Now we just have to make them all listen.

Rora's white-knuckling her backpack straps again on our way back to the council room. I can't stop fiddling with my necklace.

She seems to feel better, fed and wearing clean clothes, and I'm relieved every time I look at her face to see the frost gone, replaced with that red windburned patch. But neither of us can be sure what the king and queen will tell us about what's happening out in the spheres, or what it will take to *resolve* our presence.

My nerves twinge as we pass libraries and offices and salons, pausing here and there to ask staff and caftaned advisors for directions. Finally, we round a corner, and there at the end of the hallway are Amir and Major.

"Are you all right?" Major bursts out, breathless. He reaches for

Ro like he wants to run his hands over her and make sure she's okay, but pulls back at the last moment.

"I'm fine," she says. "Food. Sleep."

"They wouldn't let us near your room or we'd have come to see you," Amir says to me in a low voice. Rest has done him good, too, but guilt and worry still hang off him like invisible weights. "We were under orders not to bother you, on pain of—well. Anyway, my mother told us not to bother you."

"Are you sure you're not Italian?" I narrow my eyes. "I couldn't decide if your mom wanted to chase us with a wooden spoon or feed us."

"She wouldn't want to scold me in front of her advisors," Amir says quietly. "They already have their doubts about me. But we got an earful after the two of you went to bed, once my parents got us alone." He pauses. "This is our chance to explain ourselves to everyone."

"Maybe they'll listen." Rora puts a hand on Major's arm, looking hopeful. "Maybe they just want to know what we know."

"Maybe." But Amir's smile is thin. "Or maybe Ingrid will call me a *typical Scorpio* again." He watches my face for a long moment, then tilts his head toward the council room door. "Shall we?" he asks. "No use delaying the inevitable."

We round the corner. The double doors open. And again, the queen and the king and their council are waiting.

They're speaking in Arabic when we enter, and it occurs to me to tell Amir's parents about the language charm Major cast for us, since I forgot earlier. I hadn't noticed in all the uproar that they'd switched to English for our benefit.

"Don't worry about it," Major mumbles before I can. "They all speak about eight languages. English, Nahuatl, Mongolian, German—"

"Are you kidding?" I demand under my breath, amazed. But Queen Inara interrupts.

"Good," she greets us firmly in English, waving us toward empty seats. "You're here."

Albrecht offers us refreshment, pouring us fragrant tea from the top pot of a two-tiered golden tea service and adding water from the lower pot, straining out loose leaves and offering us milk and sugar cubes. I choose distractedly from a selection of dates, melon slices, plums, and little cookies, trying to gauge the king's and queen's expressions and body language, but don't gather much.

Amir frowns at me in concern. *All right?* he seems to ask. I nod, wishing we'd had more than a moment alone to plan.

I like the way he speaks. I like the way I think when we're together.

But Queen Inara interrupts my wishing. "So," she begins, angling toward Amir and Major, the gold embroidery on her dress catching the light. "You've been to Mercury, and Saturn. And judging from your guests and their attire"—she nods at Rora and me—"I would also venture you've been to Earth. Please tell us why."

My fears from last night rise again; I put on my most convincing face. We can't deny the whole truth, but we might be able to hide part of it. "No, we aren't from Earth," I interject. "We're Astronomy College students. We've been working with Amir." The woman beside Queen Inara—mid-forties, olive-skinned, her hair and eyes the same shade of cool, dark brown—arches her eyebrows, and I hurry to add one true detail to my story.

One true detail to make the whole thing taste like truth. To draw out what truth I can from these people. I know a little—but it's so, so little.

"My family lives on Mercury," I say. "The Portinaris?"

But King Sameer only scoffs tiredly, like he's embarrassed on my behalf, like I've made an inappropriate joke. Ingrid, the blue-eyed advisor who called Amir a *typical Scorpio*, sneers and tidies her papers, and Rora stares daggers at me. "What are you doing? You can't come in here and lie to these people," she says, teeth gritted.

"I'm trying to contain this," I hiss back. I'm not above telling a white lie to protect the boys, who've only tried to help us. Honestly, I'm not above telling a white lie for less noble reasons.

Not that it worked. But at least I *tried*.

"It doesn't matter," Amir mumbles. "That's Dr. Qureshi, next to my mother."

"Dr. Qureshi?" Rora says the professor's name like all the air's gone out of her.

"Welcome, new Astronomy College students." She gives a feline smile. "Hello, Amir. Major."

"But why would you put yourselves in such danger, Amir?" King Sameer scrubs a hand across his temple, where the black hair has begun to turn gray. "There's a storm on Kronos!"

"You knew about the storm?" Amir asks.

The queen's brow furrows. "Of course we did."

"Then you know something is *wrong* out in the spheres." Amir's voice takes on a desperate edge. "I wrote to you about it, Baba, but you didn't reply. Nobody would talk to me."

My heart thumps at the desperation in his voice and the softness of the word *baba* and I remember again what Amir said to me when we left Saturn. *I have to tell my parents I failed.*

"The four of us have been trying to sort out what's wrong with the spheres," Rora breaks in. "Because we think it's what's wrong with me, too." Her expression is pugnacious, arms gauntleted in her leather jacket and crossed tightly over her chest.

"*Most* of us," Albrecht says significantly, "hold that the upcoming close encounter of Saturn and Jupiter is the source of the spheres' temporary disharmony. The Great Conjunction often brings some discord to the spheres, as close encounters of multiple songs often do." He casts a cool look at Dr. Qureshi, frowning when she doesn't even look up from her papers.

"Mm. Regardless," she says, still sifting through her notes, "be assured that we're monitoring the situation."

They seem completely confident. They seem to think, in fact, that this puts an end to the conversation. And with none of the facts at my disposal, I have no idea *what* to think, except to wonder how they can just sit here with all the destruction happening outside their walls.

"How long has the disharmony been causing problems?" I ask.

"About six months," Queen Inara says. She doesn't acknowledge Albrecht's point, just gestures at her own cheekbone, where a few hours ago Rora's skin glittered with frost. "Did that happen on Saturn?"

"Yes." Rora hardly opens her mouth to speak.

King Sameer's brows arch. "How?"

So Rora explains. Her voice is small as she details her last six weeks' misery, our failure to conjure her song on Mercury, the disaster on Saturn. Then her tone turns vehement. "There is something *wrong* about that music. There was no way it was going to help me."

I reach for Rora's hand under the table and squeeze it tightly, wondering if Albrecht and the scholars have this right, and we have our answer: that this upcoming Conjunction is to blame, that these problems are part of a cycle that will soon move on. If Ro, and everyone else suffering, has simply to wait for the moment to pass.

It's a theory. But I don't like it.

One, because I'm not big on waiting for what I want. And two, because it's too easy.

Sit tight, children. We know best.

Back on Mercury, right after the sinkhole opened up and those four kids fell in front of the train, I remember thinking that for them, for this life—it was all over. It wouldn't matter if we managed to solve the problem out in the spheres.

Sometimes, lost things are lost, and they don't come back.

What else—*who* else—will disappear for good if we just wait for the storm to settle itself, or for the Conjunction to pass?

"And do you think Saturn's song would have helped you?" Queen Inara asks. "Under ordinary circumstances?"

"It sounds like you already know the answer to that," I say, sharper than I mean to. I don't like teachable moments, and Ro's been through enough. The queen's lips part in something between amusement and surprise; Albrecht nearly drops his glass of tea, scandal written all over his face. But I'm not in the mood to apologize. "Sea levels are falling on Earth, just like they are here. Mountains are shrinking. And you have no *idea* what we saw on Kronos." My voice shakes with anger. "The village looks empty. The monks all act like they're sick. Only the Abbot is awake and moving around."

The king and queen exchange a startled glance. "That is . . . regrettable," says King Sameer, all the dignity of Jupiter's song in his voice. "I'm sorry to hear it. But it will pass, on Saturn and on Earth as well."

"But can you help Rora?" Major's jaw is tight. He looks as tired of groveling as I am.

Maybe we screwed up, but I'm tired of being scolded for doing the best we could. For actually *doing* something, while the people in this room sat and debated.

"I have a hypothesis," I bite out. I still don't know what's going on with the spheres. But another idea's been simmering in my anger since we sat down.

Dr. Qureshi cocks her head, smiling slightly. "And what is that?"

I lift my chin. "I was born under Gemini. Rora was born under Capricorn. And Gemini's song conjured my star chart right away. But Capricorn didn't conjure Rora's." I think of how alive I felt on Mercury, how crushed Rora was by Saturn.

For the first time I hesitate. But Rora can't afford to waste any more time. "I don't think she belongs to Saturn."

Utter silence fills the council room. No one speaks—not Albrecht, not Dr. Qureshi, not even Ingrid, who was so quick to deride Amir. Hardly anyone breathes.

Amir freezes at my side. "Is that possible, Mother?" he asks, sounding winded. "Is it possible to belong somewhere independent of your sign? Can it—is it ever just not that simple?" All the blood has drained from Major's face.

Queen Inara just looks at Rora. "What do you think about all this?"

"Why should I think anything?" Rora grimaces. "I'm too tired to think anymore. I just push forward."

"Interesting." I don't miss the queen's shared glance with Dr. Qureshi.

She rises, moves near Rora, gestures for her to shift her chair. As if anticipating what's coming next—we've danced so many rounds of this dance—Ro holds out her hands and bares her teeth. But the queen hesitates for a moment before returning Rora's hands to her lap.

Instead, she puts a palm on Rora's upper arm and begins, softly, to sing.

I BRACE FOR Saturn's song. But it never comes.

Queen Inara hums a low tune, drumming gently on my arm. Her hand is solid, reassuring. But it's nothing compared to the song.

If I felt Mercury in my brain and Saturn in my bones and Major's song in my fragile, imperfect flesh, this song calls to something in my blood. I feel it in the large muscle groups that make me run and stand and push, in the small muscle groups and joints that shape each little exertion of my will.

Infortuna Major's was anguish. But this song is pure, bracing strength.

My star chart emerges.

Where Claudia's haloed her in silver, this one materializes red and shimmering and knife-sharp over the muscles in my right arm, flashing like a penny in the sun. Low murmurs—some angry, others confused—rise from the scholars around the table.

"Not possible," Major breathes, baffled. He crouches in front of me, blue eyes searching my face, searching my chart like he's trying to memorize it. "We were singing the wrong song. Conjuring from the wrong place. Rora, you belong to Ulaan Garig. To *Mars*."

Surprise punches me in the stomach. I draw back, confused.

"She's Saturnine," Amir says sharply, rising. He pushes up his sleeves, the veins standing out in his arms as he clenches his fists. "She's anxious and moody and shrewd and . . ." He trails off and I can't help scowling at him, like I've just *got* to underline his point.

Queen Inara pauses, tentative, before she speaks. "Perhaps," she says carefully, turning her eyes back to her scholars, "as you suggested, Amir, matters are not always so simple." Mars sings in the chart hovering around my arm, just louder than the whispering that rises from their ranks. King Sameer watches his queen, so admiring I almost feel like I've invaded a private moment.

Shame flushes my cheeks even as misgiving pools in my gut. I slide down in my chair, sinking into my jacket.

Somehow, the queen's gotten me wrong. I know who Mars is, what he means in the heavens.

And he's got nothing to do with me.

The queen stares at my chart, beckoning Dr. Qureshi. "You were right," the professor murmurs excitedly. She's switched to Arabic, but with the language charm, I can still understand.

"Later," the queen says, sotto voce. Then she raises her voice, returning to English. "A strange blend of fire and earth. Such heaviness here, it would appear Saturnine." She glances down at me. "But you're a daughter of Ulaan Garig. A fighter, without question."

My jaw is a steel trap. I stare at my fingers gripping my knees.

I've hoped so hard. I've tried to be patient. But my disappointment is a sharp little object.

It's too much.

"Are you kidding me with all this?" I stand so fast my chair screeches on the floor, kick my backpack aside, peel off my jacket. The scholar opposite me winces. "Look at me—do I look like a *fighter* to you?" My arms are pale and soft beneath my T-shirt; a bruise is beginning around one elbow where I fell back at Kronos, like spoilage on a piece of fruit, and my overtaxed lungs are heaving.

I'm tired. A wreck, the girl who hyperventilates and cries. The cowering prisoner of thirty-one fears.

King Sameer gives an easy shake of his head. "The red planet's strength doesn't reside in your arms, girl. It's in your spine. In your heart."

"And mine keeps giving out on me, so what does that tell you?" I bite out.

Claudia searches my face. "Ro, maybe she's not wrong."

I pause, suddenly embarrassed at my outburst and the staring councilors. "What do you know?" I mumble, flopping back down.

"No," says Queen Inara, adjusting my chart again. "I'm not wrong. Though Mars and Saturn interact so closely here—a conjunction, it's called—I'm not surprised you'd think so. Their blended traits manifest as one influence, one aspect of your nature."

"But if she was born under Capricorn—" Major begins, confused, and a few of the scholars murmur their shared concern.

The queen holds up a hand, all finality, all authority. "I'm working on that." Somehow, I know the sharpness in her tone is for her advisors, not for Major.

"Ad Astra's music sounds a little like Ulaan Garig," Amir says quietly. "Your being drawn to them would make sense."

I scoff. But it sounds more like a whimper.

I've drawn another blank. Dug through my pockets and, again, come up short.

"So what's wrong with me?" I whisper. "I thought—Saturn was off, with the storm and everything, so I was off. But if what's wrong with Saturn isn't what's wrong with me, then—?" I break off, frustrated.

"I have a hypothesis," Queen Inara says, echoing Claudia's words from a moment ago, cracking her knuckles. "I need some of your blood, child."

I hold out my arm. "Take what you need."

An instant of pain. A flicker of red. A touch from the queen, and my forearm seals itself.

Amir's mother spreads my blood across thin air, filmy like a sample on a slide, a twin circle to my star chart.

"We need the room," she says to the scholars without glancing back at them. Albrecht is the first to rise; the rest of them follow his lead and file out. Amir's father gives his wife another warm look, then turns to leave, beckoning Major and Amir.

"Wait," I blurt. Without meaning to, I move toward Major. "Don't—don't go."

Major pauses, brow furrowed. "You want me to stay?"

He always looks so sure, always moves so quickly. But he looks uncertain here in Amir's parents' court. I think of everything he told me about Jupiter and belonging to it.

I wish we could sit out in the hallway and talk like we did on Mercury. I want to know how this place feels to him and tell him how Mars's song felt for me. I need him to help me understand what it means, that the queen's stripped away this piece of my identity like it's nothing.

I wonder how someone I met less than a day ago feels like such a perpetually good idea. Like such a solid, safe place.

I just nod. "Yeah," I say. "I'd feel better if you stayed."

"Okay," Major says. He squeezes my shoulder and I feel the touch all across my skin, like an afternoon in the sun. Then he takes a quiet seat beside me at the table as Amir and King Sameer make for the door.

Well, mostly quiet. "What do you see?" Major asks after a beat. I expect Queen Inara to return to my star chart, as Dr. Qureshi does, but she's studying my blood sample.

Dr. Qureshi's voice is flat. "Patience."

"It's one reading," Major says impatiently. He's leaning forward on his elbows, chewing on a fingernail. On my other side, Claudia is engrossed in watching Dr. Qureshi and the queen. "How hard can it be?"

"Different traditions lend different insights, and we need to think," Queen Inara says pointedly. "Also, hush."

Finally, she turns back to us. "Rora, does your diet include much iron?"

That's a gear shift. I shrug, distracted. "Uh. Maybe?"

The queen nods thoughtfully. "Tell me about your menses."

My entire being tenses in horror. My eyes dart to Major. "What?" he asks worriedly. "What's wrong?"

I feel myself turning red. I've never talked about my period in front of a boy before. "This isn't weird?" I ask. "Or, like . . . disgusting? To you?"

"I'll leave, if you want. But I don't think you're disgusting at all. I just want you to be okay." He tries to push his hair off his forehead but his fingers get caught in the tangles, and his face is so honest and distracted I want to cry.

I turn back to Queen Inara. "They're not great," I mumble. "They come every two and a half weeks. I have bad mood swings." Dr.

Qureshi draws a sympathetic breath through her teeth.

The queen nods again, more decisive. "And when was the last time you saw a doctor?"

"When I got the flu three years ago." I drop my gaze. They won't know what high-deductible insurance is, but figuring out what's wrong with me would mean doctor visits. Bloodwork. Trial and error and *more* visits. And if they figured it out? Medication, therapy—those things cost time and money, and my family has neither.

Queen Inara stands. "Major, will you get—?" She gestures at the doorway.

He's on his feet in a flash, and then Amir and his father return. On his way back to his chair, Major brushes my arm again, like he just wants to remind me I'm not alone.

"So what is it?" Amir is focused, intent. "What did we miss?"

Queen Inara sighs. "Rora, did you know you're badly iron deficient?"

I shrug. "No. So what?"

"Iron deficiency causes fatigue," she says patiently. "Perhaps it's your diet, perhaps it's something else. You're also bleeding too often—you're losing iron there as well."

Amir's eyes go wide. "And if she's iron deficient—"

"Then Mars is blocked," Major finishes. "And that explains why you've been so worn out." Queen Inara nods, and everyone in the room watches me for a long moment, as if that explains everything.

"I don't understand," I say flatly.

Amir holds up his wrist, pointing to his cuff. "Our connection to the red planet is forged in iron. All his sons and daughters wear it, to strengthen our bond to him. And if you're iron deficient, Ulaan

Garig hasn't been able to sing to you. You've been cut off from his influence."

I'm reeling. I don't know what I expected Queen Inara to say, but it wasn't *fix your mineral deficiency*.

Can it really be this simple?

"Wait." Queen Inara's word is an order. Everyone freezes. "Wait."

"What is it?" Major asks. The caution in his voice kills me.

"Did you see this?" the queen asks Dr. Qureshi. "This quincunx. Between Mars and—"

"Chiron," Dr. Qureshi mutters, confused. The two of them approach my chart, murmuring quietly over an icon shaped like a key.

"That word," Claudia says, apprehensive. "*Quincunx*. What is it?"

"Well, a conjunction is merged influences, right?" I venture. Queen Inara nods. "So a quincunx—that's two influences standing opposed. Two aspects of my chart that clash."

"Yes." Dr. Qureshi's tone is careful. "Two points at war. Here, we have Mars in a quincunx with Chiron."

I shake my head. The name means nothing to me.

For the first time since we arrived, Queen Inara seems uncertain. "Rora, Chiron is a harbinger of—of pain," she says softly. "He doesn't appear in every chart. His presence here, in Taurus, suggests an assault on your body or your safety."

I dart a glance at Major, and then at Claudia. I don't speak.

I want suddenly to be far away, with no one to open my wounds and make me bleed, to tell me that my pain was fated and there was never any avoiding it. Because I'm not sure I can live with that idea.

Even if what I need to bleed out is poison, it's going to hurt.

The queen sits down beside me. This close, I can see the fine lines around her eyes and on her brow.

They make her look like a mother as well as a queen. They make me want to trust her.

"What happened to you?" she asks. I stare at my shoes.

I can't offer anything but honesty. I'd better do it fast.

"It was one night after work. On my way to a party, after I was done nannying for the day. Six weeks ago." Claudia winces. My voice cracks a little.

Pale, wrinkled skin. Straggling gray hair. Old gray sweatshirt.

"Not very late. I should've been safe in that neighborhood."

Nowhere is safe.

"He had a gun."

Streetlights on matte black. Six inches from my beating heart.

It had never occurred to me how fragile bodies were.

For the briefest moment, Saturn's song presses against my skull, threatening to drown out Jupiter around me. I cling to the music on the air—all the wind, all the gold, a melody solid enough to live on like food.

But even as I listen to it, I reach back for the iron memory of Mars's song. For the warmth that clings to Major.

"Was the person caught?" Major angles toward me. His eyes are unhappy.

"I never told anyone," I say. "Just Claudia."

He frowns. "Why not?"

I swallow hard, brace myself. "There's enough going on at my house," I explain. My voice is hoarse. "Enough to worry about. Not enough money. I needed to keep working and didn't want a big fuss. Besides," I add, "I didn't have anything worth taking, so the guy let me go. Nothing happened. I made it to the party. Claudia was waiting for me."

Claudia presses her lips together and squeezes my hand.

"Physical fatigue due to iron deficiency. And Chiron's presence suggests what they used to call soldier's heart," Queen Inara says quietly. "They call it post-traumatic stress now."

And just like that, I have my answer.

My problem isn't magical. It's mental, entirely natural.

And I'm right back where I started.

I search the room, feeling myself slump, feeling helpless. "So what do I do?"

Claudia tucks her hair behind one ear, thinking. "Rora, you said you felt Saturn's song in your bones, and Mercury's in your head. But Mars—"

"In my body," I say, knowing where she's going at once. "My muscles. My blood." It was a good feeling—to be in my body for once, and not my head.

I already know what Claudia's going to suggest. But she looks to Queen Inara and Dr. Qureshi first.

"Then you should go to Ulaan Garig," Dr. Qureshi says, nodding at her. "Go, and see if his song can lend the strength you need."

The queen smiles wryly. "And I have another suggestion. Wait here." She leaves the room but returns in a flash, passing me an amber-colored glass bottle, its contents rattling. "Take these. Iron pills," she clarifies. "And you should wear iron as well."

I hesitate. "These are *just* iron pills?"

The queen's face goes serious. "I swear on the life of my son. Let the red planet sing to you, child. Siphon some of his strength." She pauses. "We may have more to say to you in a day or two. But for now, go. Strengthen and exhaust yourself. It may do more for your grief than you suspect."

I glance at my friends. If the queen's right, this could actually fix me, but— "What about the rest of it? The problems on Mercury, on Earth, on Saturn—?"

"We haven't forgotten," King Sameer says, his face grave. "God willing, this will pass. Those on Saturn will heal. But you have to go where you belong, so you can recover as well."

I remember again that we haven't told them what Amir and Major were so startled to find—that I'm an amplifier. That maybe I could help them. But Claudia puts a hand on my arm and shakes her head, as if she knows what I'm thinking.

"And the rest of us?" Amir asks, seeming to force the words out.

Queen Inara's voice turns sharp again. "You will return with Rora to Ulaan Garig, and no more traveling thereafter. God be praised nothing worse happened to you all. And I will be speaking with your commander." Amir winces.

"I need to be on Mars, too," Claudia interjects. "If Rora's there—"

"No. The exclusion of the spheres is essential at this time, to counterbalance any effects from the Conjunction." King Sameer gestures between her and Major. "Major will escort you to Mercury, Claudia, as you clearly belong there, with your charming fibs and fabrications. And you, Major, will return here promptly." The king laughs dryly, thumbing a blueprint before him. "Give our love to the Portinaris."

Claudia's jaw drops. I grab her by the arm and haul her toward the door before she can deliver an undoubtedly witty but entirely unhelpful response.

We have our answers and our orders. We're dismissed.

1287

HEAT STRUCK THEM as soon as they stepped through the portal. The sun burned far ahead within the sphere, not a gem but a mountain of flame. The horses reared and snorted, showing the whites of their eyes, wagons rattling behind them.

"Look away!" Beatrice shouted to the magicians, shielding her face with her hand. "Cast a barrier against the heat and the light!"

They pressed on, Marco at the fore of their party, the roots of his curly hair already dark with sweat. Dante crept close behind him.

They reached the flames far too soon. At once, they were engulfed. "An island!" Beatrice cried, her auburn hair blazing, her skin burning red despite the magicians' charms. Even amid the heat, Dante was frozen to his very core with fear.

The fire was so close. The fire was everywhere. It threatened to burn away every artifice, to illuminate every secret and lie of omission and all his deep-buried cowardice.

The magicians huddled together, hands outstretched, dampness beading on their foreheads. Beatrice's voice grew hoarse as she called out orders to strengthen the barrier against the conflagration, to reinforce the island on which they stood, to summon cold to ward off the blistering heat.

Marco looked alive, vivid in the flames. Dante thought with a sinking feeling that Polo looked like a blessed saint he'd once seen in a fresco—unbowed, unburned even by fire.

He would never have his friend's bravery. Everything within Dante told him to flee once more to Venus, to retreat to its sheltering warmth and gentle song.

He fought to conceal all of this, certain he would fail, when Beatrice turned to him with desperation in her eyes.

"I can't," she breathed. Tears pooled on her lashes and evaporated on the shimmering air.

Dante wrestled with himself. The terror he felt threatened to burn him to ash; but he would not let his beloved see, could not allow the sun to illuminate his myriad insufficiencies.

"You can." He knelt before her, ignoring the fear that pounded in his veins as the flames rose and fell about them. "You have brought us by your will to the very sun, my love, and you can make it safe for us." Dante wiped the sweat pouring down his forehead with the sleeve of his robe, feeling its gold braid scrape his tender, burning skin. "You are a star. You are the door to a hundred worlds, a perpetrator of miracles."

"Do you believe it?" There was desperation in her voice. "Do you, truly?"

Dante took her hands. Hers were stronger than his, more callused. They were hands for tending the sick, for studying, hands for prayer. But they fit well within his.

"You are equal," he whispered, "to all its burning."

Beatrice was a mathematician. But she had traveled with

201

magicians for these many weeks; she had learned from them.

And she had learned from Dante. He had unwittingly shown her a world of feeling, had amplified the spheres' songs for her until every part of her that was not calculation was magic, was melody.

She listened to the sun's music, and let herself feel only Dante's presence beside her.

She could bear them all through the fire, if only he would not let go of her hand.

Beatrice swallowed and closed her eyes.

CLAUDIA

25

"SHE CAN'T DO this," I blurt once we're in the hallway. The scholars who've been waiting to be summoned back gape at my outburst. I don't care.

"Correction." Major's staring at the ceiling, hands clasped around his neck. "She can literally tell us to do whatever she wants."

Rora frowns, pacing. "I don't want to split up."

Amir glances carefully at his parents' advisors filing back into the council room. "Let's get somewhere where we can talk freely," he says, voice low.

"Your house," I retort. "You lead the way." He gestures, and we wind after him through darkened passageways, past darkened windows; most of the palace must be asleep.

I can't imagine resting right now. I can't believe this is happening.

"Here. We can speak privately in my room." Amir opens a door, and I sulk on inside.

Inside his bedroom, I remember what I thought on Mercury, about cities being monuments to their people, and wonder if bedrooms are a personal history of their owners. If this one would tell the story of Amir growing up, if I could cool my frustration enough to read it.

Mounted horizontally on the wall over the fireplace is a series of swords, the one nearest the ceiling hardly longer than a knife. There are other weapons in the room, too—spears propped up in the corner like skis, a curved dagger left out on a side table—plus an intimidating assortment of athletic and all-weather gear. The Portinaris are not outdoors people, unless by *outdoors* you're referring to our annual expedition to Corsica on Nonna's yacht. Of course, if Jack's recent behavior is any gauge, he's probably made his way to the marina in San Vincenzo and sunk it by now.

A bookshelf lines one wall, and I'm studying the titles on the shelf when Amir steps up beside me. He's closer than I expect quicker than I expect, and I try not to show my surprise.

"You're quite a reader," I say. A lot of the titles are on the history of the spheres. Among others—Möngke and Yelü Chucai, Johannes Kepler, Yehuda ben Moshe ha-Kohen—I see her name: Beatrice.

"I haven't read most of them, to my mother's very great disappointment," Amir says. "I'm working my way through them slowly, but I'm not an academic."

It's the reverse of the attitude Jack and I hold toward school. We both take pride in getting good grades, and we have lots of interests.

But we're driven by whim. Amir is driven by duty. By the role that will someday be his and his own insufficiencies, real or imagined.

I think Jack would find Amir kind of boring. Stuffy. A drag. I don't think he'd like him much. But I can't deny that I do.

And now that I've admitted it to myself, we have to split up. Because his parents say so.

"So what are we going to do about this?" I turn back to the others, flopping onto an armchair next to the desk.

"I guess . . . we have to go where they say," Rora says slowly. She glances up at the three of us. "Why didn't you just listen to my song? Couldn't you tell it wasn't Saturnine?"

I don't understand the hurt in her voice. I don't even understand what she's saying.

Major shakes his head. "Rora, you can't hear people's songs. Planets, yes. People—no."

"I can hear yours," she says, looking first to Major, then me. Aggravation burns up my spine as I realize again how little I understand about this place, how little *any* of us knows about what it means for Rora to be an amplifier.

"I'm glad you didn't tell them," I say to her fiercely. "That you're an amplifier. They might not have sent you to Mars if they'd known."

The way I'm feeling about the court right now, I don't care if Rora has the power to fix the spheres. I want her fixed first.

"The king might not have ordered you back to Mercury if you hadn't worked up that story about the Portinaris," Major says to me dully, hands on his knees.

It's not a story, I want to bite out. But of course he'd think that. I'm a Gemini. We're pretenders.

Rora puts a hand on his arm. "I'm sorry you have to stay here."

"What do you mean?" Amir frowns. "Is something wrong?"

"No, nothing." Major flashes a grin that looks like hard work and nods at Rora. "I've just been worried about this one." The reply reminds me of something she said earlier.

Nothing happened, Rora told the queen. *I didn't have anything worth taking.* I'd had to fight to keep my mouth shut then, not trusting myself to speak.

Nothing happened. As though her invisible wounds caused her no pain. As though my best friend's trauma was some minor inconvenience she'd rather not trouble anyone with.

She's hurt me and I'm annoyed at her and still, I want to shake Rora for not seeing that she deserves to be safe, she deserves acknowledgment of her grief, she deserves help processing her suffering.

And Major's brush-off hides the truth, just like Ro's did. I've noticed his discomfort here on Jupiter, but I'd chalked it up to circumstance—our fruitless search for answers about the spheres, Rora's breakdown, the boys being in such trouble. But his hurry to reassure Amir that nothing's wrong tells me something *is*. "I would have considered asking to stay here," I say to him slowly. "But you don't want to."

"Well, you also asked to go to Ulaan Garig with Rora, didn't you? You don't know what these places are like," Major says, his false good humor fraying. "You would've hated it on Mars. The music is regimented and the whole place has a stick up its—"

"Hey," Amir protests.

"And honestly, since Jupiter's going to own me one day very soon, I don't want to spend any more time here now than I'm forced to," Major finishes.

Amir's eyes narrow, confused. "You've never—Major, what are you saying?"

"But it's necessary, isn't it?" I ask. "The exclusion keeps you safe. People have to stay with the songs they belong to, or the things that are happening now would happen all the time."

"That was Beatrice Portinari's reasoning, anyway," Major says grimly. "Speaking of the Portinaris."

I stop dead. Beatrice?

The exclusion was based on *Beatrice's* thinking?

I want to ask for more, but I can't—not if I'm not ready to tell them everything. And I'm not. My heart beats too fast as I try to school my features, hide all my questions.

"Still." Major swallows hard. "*Belong* is a tricky word."

"It is," Amir agrees, and his voice takes on a jagged edge. "Some of us would do anything to belong to the right place."

"Amir, I didn't mean—" Major begins, apologetic.

"You didn't, but everyone else does." Amir's jaw hardens. "We haven't had a monarch born outside Sagittarius in over four hundred years. I only belong to Mars by minor rulership, Major. And really, I belong to Inferno. That councilor, Ingrid—" He breaks off, scrubbing a hand through his hair.

"Is one person!"

"Was saying what half the room was thinking!" Amir gives a harsh laugh. "Do you think those advisors aren't waiting for me to fail? That I don't have cousins ready to step in if enough people decide they don't want a king born under a dark sign?"

Typical Scorpio behavior, Ingrid had muttered during the meeting. The words taste like bile in my memory. And Amir had to just sit there and take it.

He turns to me, like he can't look at Major anymore. "Abu Ma'shar, our founding astrologer, didn't trust Scorpios at all," he says bitterly. "I only happened to my parents because they tried for years to have a child in Sagittarius or even Pisces, who would belong to al-Mushtari. And after losing three babies, they decided they wanted a child, any child, born to any sign."

"And they were lucky to have you," I insist. But the words don't land at all.

Amir turns desolate eyes on his friend. "I'd give anything to have what you have," he says, shaking his head. "To be the king they all want instead of who I am."

"I'd give it to you," Major says, shamefaced. "I'd give it to you in a heartbeat."

"Look," Rora interrupts softly, putting a hand on Major's arm. "It'll be fine. We'll split up. We'll go where we're supposed to go. The Conjunction will pass and it'll be . . . fine."

I frown. "You really accept that explanation?"

"Again, it's not really so much an explanation as orders from our sovereign," Amir says flatly.

"Well, forgive me if I prefer understanding to blind obedience." The words burst out of me. I drag myself out of the chair and begin pacing.

"What do you *want*, Claudia?" Rora asks, exasperation lengthening her words. "We got what we came here for."

"Did we?" I demand. Frustration almost wrenches me out of my skin. "Because—you say you've been looking for answers, but it seems like what you've really been doing is looking for someone to tell you what to do."

"Excuse me?" Rora's words are breathless.

I can't believe I'm saying all this. But I don't stop. "Yeah. You've *always* put more stock in the word of a perceived authority—your horoscope, some random adult, whatever—than in your own intuition or ability to solve a problem, and it kills me."

What hurts even worse is that she doesn't seem particularly cut up about separating, when for me, it feels like carving open my chest and deciding which lung to leave behind.

"That's not true," Rora bursts out. "Claudia, there's a reason I follow the rules. That I *rely on authority*. You don't understand that not everyone sleeps on a bed of money! Not everyone has endless bailouts waiting and parents with nothing to worry about but you!"

"That's not fair," I rasp.

"And if you want to know the truth, it feels like you just want to fix me because being my friend is exhausting," Rora bites out. "And believe me, I get it. Being *me* is exhausting. I would die not to feel like a grenade. Like I'm not going to explode if you bump me. But lately I feel less like your friend than your project. You push and you push and I—" She breaks off, shoulders heaving. "So *explain*. If not to get what we came for—for answers about the spheres, and how to fix me—then what do you want?"

I blink at her, stunned. I don't know what to say.

Because, to be honest, Ro doesn't usually ask what I want or need. And to be honest—should she? Really?

With Rora eaten alive by anxiety, always counting pennies, never getting what I know she deserves, am I—the girl with everything—allowed to want anything?

Except I do.

For Jack to come home, I want to say.

For you not to be lost in your own mind, in a place where I can't go.

"I want you to not accept every crap thing that happens to you as your just penance," I say, hoping my voice won't break. "I want you to fight for yourself instead of settling for being miserable."

Rora's jaw tightens. "Well, that's what I'm doing. I'm going to go to Mars and fight for myself. I hope the way I'm doing it meets your approval. For now, though, I'm going to the bathroom."

"I'll show you where it is," Major mumbles. He scrambles up, and he and Rora head out the door.

I want to follow her. I want to apologize. I don't.

For the first time, I want more than to cling to my twins like life rafts—to keep faithful watch over Rora and to know that Jack's okay. I want those things, too. I know I hurt her, and I'm sorry.

But I also want answers. Because I don't accept the ones we've been handed.

Maybe Mars and iron will help Rora, but I don't think that the Conjunction will end and everything will just fix itself. I don't accept that answers will come that easily.

And there's something else. Something I left in Dr. Qureshi's office that keeps calling to me and won't leave me alone. Someone I keep learning about, who only makes me want to learn more.

Beatrice, Beatrice, Beatrice.

So I'll do what they say. I'll go to Mercury.

And I won't stop till I find what I'm looking for.

RORA
26

I FOLLOW MAJOR out the door and down the hall, past a music room and a few more closed doors. He clearly couldn't be more relieved to be fleeing the scene of my first ever real fight with Claudia.

Inside the bathroom, I avoid the mirror. I don't want to see my own reflection right now, let alone anything else, be it maps, magic, or Bloody Mary.

Major's leaning against the corridor wall, arms crossed, when I step back out. He never changed clothes; his crumpled shirt is rucked up over his biceps and his blond hair has dried curly from snow and sweat. He looks exhausted, his spine bowed, hips jutting away from the wall.

The sight of him waiting for me, draped against the wallpaper, is enough to do me in.

I swallow hard against the dryness in my mouth and punch him awkwardly in the arm. "Thanks for the escort."

"Sure," he says easily, but his smile is barely a nod to its usual self. "Did I wreck everything back there? I couldn't stop myself."

I lean against the wall beside him. "You didn't wreck anything," I say. "Claudia and I had it out right there beside you two. I think everyone's really tired."

"I just hate this place." He says it like a confession, eyes shut, voice so diminished I barely recognize it.

I don't see a life for myself there, he said yesterday outside Dr. Qureshi's office. And being here, hearing this music, I understand why. "And this is the first time you've admitted that?" I venture.

Major nods heavily. "I never bothered. They can't understand how anyone can not want this." He gestures at our grand surroundings—arched windows, rich woven rug lining the hallway. "That's the liability to al-Mushtari's pride. It's such a strong, noble planet, but the other side of that coin is arrogance. And I hear it, Rora. The music is just—it's just *throwing* itself against me."

It's unfair. It's unfair that Amir wants to belong to Jupiter but Major does instead. Just as it's unfair that I was fated to suffer, with Chiron in my chart dooming me to pain from the moment I was born.

I shut my eyes and listen again. And I don't know Jupiter's song like Major does, but I can hear it. Beneath all the wind and all the gold there is an unfeeling, unmovingness, anathema to the easy fluidity of his own music.

I think of the king and queen and their advisors at the council table, all so very certain they knew what was wrong with the spheres, and my blood goes cold. It makes me crave the warmth rolling off him.

Slowly, I unwind Major's hand from his crossed arms. His breath catches, but he lets me. I cradle his hand in mine, tracing the calluses on his palms, his clean short nails, the small white scar on his index finger.

"Are you telling my fortune?" he asks unsteadily.

"No," I say softly. "Just holding your hand."

Major slips his palm from my grasp, and my heart crashes into my stomach for a moment before he winds his arms around me. Gold hair hangs in his eyes as he searches my face for something I'm afraid he won't find.

"Jupiter is not your song," I say softly. "I hear yours almost all the time now, and it's not this music." Tentative, I brace my hands on his chest, as if I can soak up some of his warmth through my fingertips; Major's heart beats fast and hopeful beneath my palm. "I think Queen Inara was right when she said none of this is simple."

Of their own accord, my hands climb up his shoulders, around his neck. "You're grabby," he laughs softly. But he closes his eyes, skims his hands beneath my jacket, over the soft fabric of my T-shirt.

When he looks at me again, I meet his gaze. I hold it, let it wash me in ocean water, bathe me in summer twilight.

"I don't want to leave you," he says simply. "I know this is what's good for you, but I wish there was another way." Major's body is so close to mine, smelling of salt and earth and sunshine. Just as on Kronos, I feel sheltered standing here beside him.

I don't want to leave you, either, I want to say. I don't want to leave Major, and I don't want to leave Claudia. I'm mad at her right now, for reasons that are her fault and for reasons that aren't, but the idea of being separated hurts down to my very bones.

Back in Amir's room, I told Claudia that I want to be strong. To not feel constantly on the verge of breaking down. But I didn't tell her why.

I don't want to be afraid that I'm nothing more than deadweight in my friends' lives. A burden for them to haul around, a fixer-upper for them to distract themselves with, a charity case they'll eventually come to resent.

Right now, with Saturn still filling up so much of my insides, I am lead.

But I want to be iron.

I want to be strong enough on my own to feel the difference between needing my friends and wanting them. I want them to feel the difference between loving me and being obliged to me.

And that means I have to go.

I run my fingers over the downy hair at the nape of Major's neck, just over his collar, and he presses his forehead to mine.

He is close enough to kiss. He is broad enough and deep enough and warm enough to lose myself in. If only I didn't have so much to lose right now, standing on the brink of the cure I've hoped for.

"Can you . . . text me?" I venture.

"I will, but it won't be the same." Major swallows. "Rora, I know we just met. You owe me nothing. But there's something about you that makes all the good things louder and brighter."

I look away. "I'm just afraid I make all the bad things louder, too."

"No. I can barely hear them when you're around." Major gathers me a little tighter against his chest. One last time, I listen hard, like putting my ear to a conch shell to hear the rush of the ocean; and there it is.

I know I'll carry his music with me when I leave.

1287

FOR THREE DAYS, as long as they remained on the sun, Beatrice alone sustained the barriers that protected them from the light and the heat.

As for the magicians and scholars of their party, even could they have found refuge from the endlessly blazing sky (it was far too warm inside the gers with which they traveled), none could have forced their minds to rest. The magicians spent their hours scribbling notes, the secrets of alchemy suddenly clear as day in their minds.

The others found their thoughts fixed on yet higher things. The air rang with novenas and litanies, mantras and prayers and chants. When not absorbed in meditation or worship, the travelers found themselves in lively, vigorous religious debates of a kind Dante had never seen.

He had known petty bickering and thinly veiled politicking and abuse. But here was only goodwill. It was as though all their best understanding, all their best intentions, were perfectly illuminated there by the sun's ceaseless light.

Beatrice remained a little apart from the others. She named their island Helios.

And on their third day, a visitor arrived.

ULAAN GARIG, MARS

WE LEAVE THE castle behind to find the spheres cloudier than ever, mist rolling over the aether and shrouding the blackness and stars beyond. Remembering the way I broke the aether when we left Saturn and fearing what damage I might do again, I force myself to move carefully.

But it's a struggle. Because I can hear the red planet, calling me on.

Mars's song swells through the sphere, thrumming in its crystal walls. Though it doesn't sound exactly like Ad Astra, I hear the similarity Amir pointed out.

This is drive and persistence, the song of gladiators and boxers and fighter pilots. It's *forward music*. Even with the spheres brittle and uncertain beneath me, I can barely resist its summons.

Perhaps this is Mars's weakness: that its ferocity outweighs its wisdom. I should certainly know better. But my feet start moving faster, hurrying me on, until Amir gently grabs hold of my backpack. "Easy there," he cautions, nodding at the translucence swirling around us. But even eyeing the tenuous sphere, it's hard to feel the fear that's always pervaded my brain and bones, in the thirty-one specific forms I know or otherwise.

I listen for the wrongness that has touched the music elsewhere—for that warning disharmony that threatens danger to come. But if it's there, I can't hear it. I hear nothing but the strong melody that calls me on, orders me to move.

I am going home, I think, hope in my heart, oxygen in my lungs, counting on the iron that will soon be in my blood. *I am going home.*

Amir's coordinates guide us toward a deep valley in the planet's side. It's night on Mars, and the sky is cloudy. We burst through the portal and onto hard, brick-colored pebbles and sand. Torchlight gleams on a metal gate reinforced with bars and bolts.

A knock, and a password, and we're through.

"So," I say, panting from our landing. "This is Mars. Ulaan Garig."

"This is our settlement," Amir says in a low voice. "Earth calls this canyon Kasei Valles."

The gate behind us is fitted into a narrow point of the canyon, but the valley broadens as it stretches toward the horizon. Cliff walls striped with rust and russet flank a rocky landscape dotted with round white tents, scattered with bonfires. In the sky, between the thick clouds, I can just make out two pitted gray moons—one low on the horizon, the other much higher.

Amir hefts his bag from one shoulder to the other. "You and Major were gone for a long time earlier," he says, not looking at me. "Did you get lost?"

"Maybe I just spent a really long time in the bathroom," I mumble.

Amir coughs. "Uh. Did you?"

"No." I pause. "We were talking, okay?"

"At least he's talking to someone," he says under his breath.

"Major never *stops* talking."

"Apparently not about the things that matter." Amir stops short, fixing troubled eyes on something just past me. "He never gave me any idea he hated al-Mushtari. Not a single sign."

I swallow hard, wrapping my arms around myself against the chill. "Have you seen his chart before?"

"Yes. Once at his parents'." Amir hesitates. "We were just wasting time one afternoon, poking around his mother's study. I guess I decided to torture myself for no reason."

Yeah, that checks out, I don't say. "And?"

"It's not dominated by Sagittarius. I remember a lot of planets in Libra and Taurus. Maybe I should have known. But I just—didn't." A muscle feathers in his jaw. "All I remember thinking was how lucky he was."

Libra. Taurus. Both governed by Venus. It's so obvious where Major belongs. And he can't do anything about it, and neither can Amir, and it's hard on them both.

"He's a good friend," I offer quietly. "Maybe he didn't want to hurt you."

"He's my *best* friend," Amir says forcefully, expression significant, and I feel my temper flare.

"Yeah? Well, Claudia is mine," I bite out.

The change in Amir is immediate. His gaze darts away. "And?"

"And"—I prod him in the shoulder, forcing him to look at me—"if you hurt her, I'll kill you. I've got nothing to lose." I fling my arms out, my voice rising. "Literally. Nothing to lose."

"All right, all right," he grinds out, glancing around. "Keep your voice down."

I walk on, smiling back at him sweetly. "Don't give me a reason to yell at you, and I'll be as quiet as you want."

We walk for maybe forty minutes after that, no more than a

couple of miles, passing more campfires and round white tents and a cluster of shiny-coated horses nibbling dry grasses at the canyon's edge. "So who lives here, again?" I ask.

"All of us born under Aries and Scorpio," Amir says. "The adults are deployed the majority of the time, but their permanent residence is still here in Ulaan Garig. They live farther east, toward the center of the canyon." I nod, thinking of the red-uniformed guard who arrived on the scene after the train crash in Hermes, the sentries outside the palace in al-Mushtari.

If he couldn't have been born to Venus, I wish Major had been born to Mars. Then, at least, he might have a chance at being assigned to his home. Of spending his life where he's happy.

"This is the training camp, at the canyon's western edge. All of us, the children and teenagers who belong to Ulaan Garig, come here to train on weekends. But we've been stuck here for a while." We pass another campfire, surrounded with ruddy-glowing faces and laughter. Amir looks carefully away as if he doesn't want to be recognized—or recognized returning, when he shouldn't have left at all.

"Well, not you," I correct him wryly, and he arches an eyebrow in acknowledgment. I change the subject. "And are you guys, like . . . the military?"

Amir shakes his head. "We're more like emergency services. We keep the peace, but primarily we respond to disasters, rescue people in danger from the elements. The spheres can be treacherous."

"Oh, I know. Sinkholes, snowstorms. I'm just waiting for the aliens to arrive." I pause. "Wait, are there aliens?"

Amir huffs a laugh, relaxing a bit, and I do, too. "Not so far as I'm aware."

It should be odd to chat openly with him without Claudia or Major here as a buffer. But there's something about Amir that I understand without it having to be explained.

I guess the scholars back on Jupiter would say it's because we both belong to this place and its music. I can feel it thudding through me, steady as a heartbeat, tireless and driving and indestructible. It tells me it won't let me fall, won't let me fail.

But the song I can hear on Amir, now that I'm listening, doesn't feel like the music around us. It's soberer, quieter, a low, serious bass line.

It doesn't sound like Mars. I wonder if it sounds like Inferno.

I don't mention the mismatch. I would keep silent on this subject if absolutely everything were at stake, because I know what it means to him. To belong, at least, to Mars, if he can't belong to Jupiter.

But I wonder if Amir feels at home here—if the minor rulership Mars has over his being is close enough for comfort. Because I was joking about aliens before, but I've felt like one for the longest time, back on Earth. It's on Mars I finally feel human.

We come around a curve in the valley wall, and I shield my eyes against sudden firelight. I move to skirt around the camp, but Amir stops.

"Remember," he says to me in a quiet voice, "no one knows you're an amplifier but the four of us. We need to keep it that way for now, so nobody changes their mind about you being here."

The four of us. Amir and me. Major and Claudia. As Amir moves toward the fire, I pause, feeling my heart ache at their distance. This secret feels too thin a thread to keep them close so far away.

When my vision adjusts, I see where Amir has gone—to a ring of red rocks, to join a few dozen strangers. A tall boy with chestnut hair stands at once. "Where have you been?" he demands. More voices join his; more people get to their feet.

Amir grimaces. "It's a long story that ends with a verbal thrashing from my mother. Is Commander Bao in camp?" He scans the horizon, looking glum.

A white girl with red hair crosses her arms. "Still out near the eastern edge reinforcing the fraying spots in the barrier. Should be back around dawn. You timed your prison break well."

Amir flops down before the fire, expression going wry. "Except I told on myself and she'll definitely be telling him."

"Did you hear he took fifteens with him?" asks the chestnut-haired boy.

"Fifteens?" Amir frowns. "Why didn't he take adults? Or us?"

"It's lucky for you that he didn't, or your escape plans might have needed adjusting," says a slim, graceful Black girl to my left with a shaved head. "Besides, he said they needed the training. I'm Tishala, by the way," she says to me with a friendly smile. I shake her outstretched hand, and offer my name in return.

Amir addresses himself to the group of thirty or so. "I've forgotten my manners. This is my friend Rora."

The rest of the group welcomes me; a few introduce themselves. Tishala is to my left, and Nikolai, who first greeted us, is to her left. He's white, thickly built, with a strong nose and heavy brow. Pale, redheaded Briony is currently sporting a sunburn and a quick smile. Baatar—barrel-chested, with tawny brown skin and angular dark brown eyes—grins and crosses the circle to clap me on the shoulder so hard my knees buckle. "My squad," Amir says to me.

There's no mistaking the pride in his voice. There's no mistaking how *right* he seems here, though his music is an unusual counterpoint to the melody around us.

I miss Major and Claudia. But I feel it, too. That rightness.

"So, what brings you here, Rora?" Tishala's voice is curious.

Slowly, I sit, unsure how much to explain. "Queen Inara recommended I come here to . . . convalesce. Which reminds me," I mutter, rummaging through my backpack, finally lighting on the pills. Across the circle, Nikolai squints at the bottle, then politely looks away. "It's just iron," I say.

Briony brightens, straightening up a little. "I take iron, too. You've eaten recently, right?"

I stop short, the bottle open in my hand. "No, not since—wait. Really? You do?"

She nods and pushes a lock of red hair out of her eyes. "A lot of us do. Even a minor deficiency can make it hard to feel Mars fully."

My jaw works for a moment. "I assumed I was the only one," I finally say.

"Definitely not," Briony laughs. Riffling through her bag, she passes me a handful of crackers and an apple. "Honestly, I think we could all benefit from the supplement."

She's so casual, talking about it. Relief sweeps over me.

I'm not a freak. Not even a rarity.

While they talk, I eat, then shake a dull red pill from the bottle. Take the canteen Tishala passes me. Pill. Water. Swallow.

I'm going to get better. Step one is giving my body the iron it needs.

We all sit up a bit longer. Amir explains that they sleep outdoors most of the time, so we'll be staying here for the night.

No one talks to me overmuch, or asks me a lot of questions about myself, and I know it'll be a while before I get all their names straight.

But I'm relieved for the first time all day to sit *in* a circle instead of at its center. To just be one of a group, instead of the thing everyone's staring at.

Both moons are high in the sky when everyone settles onto bed-rolls. Amir fetches his own from one of the round white tents nearby, finds an extra for me. Tishala cracks a grin. "Early to bed and early to rise—"

"Means you won't get destroyed when Commander Bao comes back," Baatar finishes. "Training's going to be brutal tomorrow. Always is when he returns from scouting the barrier."

Amir laughs at this. He's completely comfortable here, sprawled on his bedroll a few feet to my right, hands behind his head. He's a far cry from the person he was at court.

I let myself drift away on the squad's jokes and on Mars's song. I try to tell myself that maybe this music remains untouched by whatever has soured the others. That if I'm an amplifier, like Major and Amir say I am, then maybe this place will work doubly well on me.

That maybe, at last, I have found a safe place.

I tell myself I can be fixed, and the Conjunction will end, and the disasters threatening the spheres and home will stop. That if Chiron fated my harm, Mars is fated to help me.

Staring up at the clouds, I roll onto my back, the iron pills rattling in my backpack beneath my head. I try not to think about the war between Mars and Chiron that Queen Inara read in my chart, about Saturn's ash-gray skies and the lead I still feel lingering inside me, about the people I miss.

I've got a broken body to fix, and training to start, and a destiny to work out.

Step one was giving my body the iron it needs. And I'm here, ready to let Mars work on me. Work in my blood, and give me the strength I'm lacking.

Step two is sleep.

HERMES, MERCURY

RORA AND AMIR are gone to Mars. Major and I head out as soon as they've left.

Welcome back! Mercury's song seems to say as we enter its sphere, and I try to rally my spirits. This place belongs to Geminis and Virgos, I remind myself. To witty, bright young things like me.

But its sparkle feels a little faded. Hermes seems different, like a club in the hours near morning, when you don't care about the lights anymore; when the music feels too loud and too buzzy, but somehow all you hear are girls crying in the bathroom and all you feel is ready to go home.

I shuffle after Major onto a train to the Centrum, making flat eye contact with strangers, jostling shoulders here and there. My feet ache despite the low heels on my boots, and I'm too hot in my coat. It's not so different from getting the subway home after a long day in Manhattan or DC, I guess.

It hurts too much to think about all the ways that's not true. About all the people who aren't waiting for me, wherever we're headed.

Neither of my twins is here, Mercury reminds me. And my heart is just as quick to point out that neither is Amir. It's just me and Major, a boy I barely know. His blue eyes are vacant as we cross the platform and exit the station together.

I'm used to Major blurting out the first thing on his mind, constantly bubbling with jokes and ideas, a smile never far from his face. To see him so subdued sets an ache throbbing in an unexpected place in my chest.

I count 134 steps down from the platform to the street, 862 steps over the cobblestones and east of the college courtyard. One clock on the skyline that reads a little after 9:08 p.m. Eight steps up to the door of a turreted and silver-stoned building, and two flights of stairs, and I find myself in their dorm. Major fumbles for a switch and turns on a gas lamp, then has to shut the old wooden door three times before it catches.

Their dormitory has a fireplace and bare wooden floors and a low plaster ceiling striped with dark wood beams. "Toilet is just there, and Amir's room's through there. You can sleep in his," Major says, talking around a mouthful of something retrieved from a dusty-looking cupboard over an old gas hob. Fishing a jar of jam from the icebox, he holds up a half-eaten slice of bread. "Want some?"

"Not hungry." I clear my throat. "Do you have to head back yet?"

Major rolls his eyes. "They're not going to miss me. I'll go back in the morning."

I nod, not arguing. I'm dreading the moment I'm finally left alone in this empty dorm, in this too-quiet city.

"The train was less crowded," I offer, staring at the kettle, trying to decide if I feel like making tea. Assuming they have tea; that cupboard looked full of more cobwebs than food. "Than last time, I mean. I guess it's late."

"No. I imagine they did what they threatened to do and sent everyone back to their corners. Probably only Geminis and Virgos left, and the rest have gone home," Major says dully. He takes another bite of bread, then nods again at the bathroom. "Want to get cleaned up?"

"Yeah." Someone cleaned our clothes on Jupiter, but I never had time to clean *me*. I shrug off my coat and start toward the darkened bathroom door. But I stop when Major speaks.

"You would have hated it there, you know." His voice is lower now. He sounds lost. "I know you wanted to go to Mars, and I'm sorry they said no. But you would've hated it."

I swallow. "Yeah?"

"Yeah."

My head seems to nod itself. He's probably right.

But we both know we would've been happy to trail after our friends. If only because the alternative is exile.

I don't know what else to say, though, so I take his proffered consolation prize and go take a shower. Space apparently has hot running water; I take the win. I try to lose myself in the steam and the soap and ignore the mild layer of grime that says *boy bathroom*. Once I'm clean, I dry off with a towel from a dusty stack on a shelf and pad barefoot to Amir's room, turning on the gaslight, shutting the door quietly behind me.

I've already analyzed Amir's bedroom on Jupiter. I could analyze this one all night if I let myself. I could search for meaning in the way his curtains are drawn, or the state of his desk, or the way he's organized his shoes in front of the closet door.

But I can't do that tonight.

I can't think about Amir. I can't think about Rora.

A quick rummage through his dresser drawers produces a soft oversize shirt. I pull it on, step back into my cleanish underwear, and sit down on the bed.

But I've only been awake for four hours. My body is exhausted, but I'm not sleepy. Mercury still buzzes fluorescent in my brain, the quiet of the dorm too like the quiet of my house after Jack left. My parents busy, and me alone.

I sit at Amir's desk, wondering if he has anything fit to read. I tell myself I'm not searching for titles about Beatrice, so I'm not disappointed when I don't see any. Instead, I light on an English-language copy of *Introduction to Horoscopy*. With the memory of Rora's chart burning in my mind, shimmering red over her arm, answering all the queen's questions, I flip it open and skip several chapters ahead to the instructions for calculating natal charts.

My own chart didn't explain what was going on out in the spheres. But I wonder once again if calculating Jack's chart and comparing it to mine might explain what happened to us.

The clock outside has chimed ten, and eleven, and midnight before I'm finished constructing the most basic version of Jack's star chart. As best I can remember, it looks like my own, the only difference being that my ascendant sign is Virgo and Jack's is Leo, because we were born forty-five minutes apart.

But that only tells me what I already know: that I come across as focused, a purist, and that Jack shows a bold, impulsive face. And even this speaks only to appearances, not realities. Not even feelings kept on the inside. Frustrated, I turn down the light, make my way back to the bed by feel, and pull a pillow over my head.

I try to shut off my senses to Mercury's song; I don't want to hear it anymore. I try to block out the smell of Amir that lingers on his sheets. The knowledge that he is far away, and so is Rora, and so is Jack.

I remind myself that I came here with a plan, consoling myself with memories of learning to research alongside my nonna and with the answers that I might find about the woman we're both descended from if I just look hard enough.

I ignore the voice whispering that answers are cold comfort when all I want is my friends.

1287

THE VISITOR HAD come to issue an invitation.

The man was perhaps in his early twenties, light-brown-skinned and brown-eyed, dressed in loose black trousers, a black tunic embroidered with jet beads, and a black turban. Those who had come from Suvd Uls at once recognized the court on Jupiter as the provenance of his language and clothing.

When he spoke, Beatrice, who had studied some Arabic along with her Greek and Latin, did not look to Marco for translation.

This time, it was she who understood.

"Sabah al-khair," the man greeted them. *Good morning*, it meant, though Beatrice was not at all sure it was morning.

"Sabah al-nur." *A morning of light,* she replied, as was proper, with a wry glance at the endless blaze around them.

The man smiled. "My name is Syed. I have come from the court of my king, two spheres hence, where I serve as minister." Beatrice introduced herself and a few members of their party, and he nodded courteously.

"My king has watched your progress and is most impressed by the strength you have displayed here. He is pleased to issue you all an invitation to al-Mushtari, to consult with us, if you will. If nothing else," he added with another smile, "perhaps you would like to rest somewhere comfortable. You have traveled far."

Beatrice returned his warm expression. At her side, though, Dante felt a frisson of fear at the prospect of being watched.

She thanked him very much for his king's invitation and for his trouble in coming, and Syed did not wait for them to discuss their answer. "Ma'a as-salama," he said, and was gone.

They left Helios later that day, making for the settlement the Khaan's explorers had established in a deep canyon on Mars. The planet they called Ulaan Garig—*red planet*—and so Beatrice and the others began to refer to the camp.

Human travelers and their horses alike seemed to breathe easier in Mars's sphere, relieved at last to be again surrounded by a balance of light and shadow. Relentless illumination was exhilarating, but the thrill had left them raw and weary—Beatrice most of all, as she alone had sustained the charms that had protected them.

But though they slept for the first time in three days on Mars, their rest on the planet did not make them dreamy as Luna or Venus had. Their thoughts were steady, tactical, only slightly defensive or combative.

Among themselves, they debated the invitation issued by the king from al-Mushtari. "I don't like the idea of being watched," Dante said when Beatrice raised the subject, voicing his earlier fear.

"Well, of course he's been watching us," one of the travelers from Suvd Uls said evenly. "He'd be a fool not to."

"And watching us doesn't indicate ill intent. Only caution," Polo added. A few others nodded. They all thought in silence for a moment.

"I should like to learn what they know, especially about what lies beyond," Beatrice finally said. She was thinking, always, of the pale blue planet that lay beyond Saturn. "I do not mistrust Syed or the king he represents, and surely any risk we may face in a strange city is dwarfed by what might await us in the unknown spheres." Murmurs of agreement rose; even Dante could not deny the logic of what she said.

Another member of the party from Suvd Uls spoke. "I do wonder what this king will think of playing host to emissaries of Kublai Khaan. You, from Siena, are a party of scholars; we are essentially a conquering force." He grinned at Beatrice ironically, and she laughed.

They would talk for some time more. But Beatrice already knew what she would do.

She was weary, and craved rest somewhere comfortable. But she craved knowledge of what lay beyond even more.

RORA

29

DAWN IS A cold red haze over Ulaan Garig's brick-colored canyon walls. The air smells like dust and smoke, like a perpetual desert autumn. I wake up slowly, the last but Nikolai to stir. My topknot is drooping out of my hair tie and I've sweated and gotten cold again in my leather jacket.

"Morning, Rora," Briony says with a smile. She's already dressed with her long red hair braided, and the others are packing up. Panicked at the prospect of falling behind, I haul myself out of my sleeping bag, roll it up, and rummage in my backpack for the mini toiletries that make Claudia call me a human minivan.

Thinking of her, I realize at once why the morning feels raw and forlorn, despite Mars's song still thrumming strong and uncorrupted around me.

How many times, I wonder as I tidy up, have I done this in the morning with Claudia beside me in the mirror? How many times in the past two years have I woken up with her drooling on a pillow a foot and a half away, satin eye mask slipping down her face? I couldn't even begin to count. Enough times that even someplace this far away might feel like home if she were here.

In the bleak light of dawn, with the red walls and the barrier the color of a cat's-eye marble far above us, my hope feels more brittle than it did last night before the fire.

"Rora!" Tishala tosses me something. I react just quickly enough to catch what turns out to be a packet of dried fruit and tear into it; my stomach's growling. "That's all we have time for, for now," she explains.

I chomp an apricot. "Why's that?"

I glance up at the crunch of footsteps on the red-pebble ground. A black-haired, light-brown-skinned middle-aged man is approaching, five or six teenagers a bit younger than us trailing after him.

"Because." Amir sighs. "Commander Bao is back."

Amir's squad is thirty or so strong, but not one of them speaks when the commander pauses at the edge of our circle. He's got red marks and soot all over his hands and the grimmest smile I've ever seen.

"Yes, he is. Good to have you back, Amir," Commander Bao says. His eyes are deep-set and dark and I don't see anything promising in them at the moment.

I'm shocked to find my legs doing a thing where they stand up by themselves and my mouth opening on its own. "Can we skip this part?" I blurt out.

Bao's black eyebrows rise so high they nearly hit his hairline. "Excuse me?"

Oh good God. What have I done.

"I said, 'Can we skip this part?'" It sounds so much worse the second time. I stuff my hands in my jacket pockets because they're horrified at what my mouth has started and are totally going to give me away.

"Who are you?" asks a blond boy, one of the teenagers crowded behind the commander.

"He knows who I am," I interject, nodding at Bao. "If you know enough to shred Amir, you already know who I am."

Commander Bao frowns, crossing his muscular arms. "You were considerably more traumatized and less mouthy in Queen Inara's letter."

I shrug. "Sorry, I guess?" I clear my throat. "How did you burn your hands?"

"Repairing deteriorated patches in the barrier around the camp," Bao answers, still looking disgruntled. "The barrier here is formed partly of fire, because the planet beyond is cold. The fire magic tends to be difficult to control, with all the oxygen inside the barrier."

Amir bites his lip, glancing concernedly at the kids behind the commander. He's wondering the same thing I am. And as I'm already being rude to the point of insubordination— "That's work for fifteen-year-olds?" I ask.

Bao ignores this, turning to Amir instead. "Are you ready for an endless stream of questions? Because once she joins your squad, she's your responsibility."

"Yes," Amir says. To his credit, he only hesitates a second.

I stop short, shake myself. "Wait. I'm sorry. Join his squad?"

"Yes. Did you take your iron?"

The commander's voice is brisk, efficient, and my brain is skipping like a scratched CD in the nanny van's old player. "Yeah, but—"

I break off, but Commander Bao doesn't say anything. He puts his head a little to one side, waiting patiently for me to speak.

Except I'm not sure what to say. I joked last night with the others that I was here to *convalesce*, but what did I expect? A yoga retreat? A training montage with my own Jedi master? I twiddle the zipper on my jacket, feeling my cheeks turn red.

"Look, Rora." Commander Bao's voice shifts, firm but not unkind. "We don't do individual work here. It's Amir's squad or another, much younger one. The choice is yours."

Tishala steps up behind me. "Rora's with us. She'll be fine. Right?" she asks, nudging me.

"Yep." My jaw is locked. I bite the words out. "I'll be fine."

"Good," Bao says. "We'll get you iron to wear soon, but for now, just keep taking your pills. The queen asked for updates soon. Report back to me in a few days."

"Yes, sir." Amir nods.

The commander strides away from the campfire without a backward glance.

I'm feeling too raw and embarrassed to make eye contact with the others as we cluster after Amir through the canyon, passing the remains of other campfires and the dozens of massive tents that make up the squad residences—gers, as Nikolai informs me they're called. The others talk a little, stretching and loosening up as we weave through them, the brilliant colors and patterns of the gers' carved doors gleaming in the dawn light. I can't quit tugging at my borrowed uniform.

I want to talk to Amir about what's to come, and about everything else I wondered last night—about how Mars feels to him, whether he senses any of the disharmony we encountered elsewhere in the spheres. But he's leading the group, several bodies ahead of me.

I wonder what's happening out beyond the barrier, out beyond our sight. If the storm has begun to abate on Kronos, if the Conjunction is nearly here, and nearly over; or if things have only gotten worse.

Here and there, other squads of children and teenagers train around us. They run in loops and straight lines, or gallop and jump on horseback; in the distance, one group climbs a section of the canyon wall. Much farther off, another squad seems to be flying enormous kites. Their red wings flutter on the air, bobbing and diving like my nervous stomach.

Amir leads us into one of a row of massive white gers like the squad houses, with fierce animals and weaponry patterned onto the doors. It's hot inside, brightly lit with torches fixed to the tent frame, but the crowd would warm up the space even without them. A cluster of elementary-aged kids are doing push-ups along one wall; a line of teenagers a little younger than me wait to tumble across a mat; and dozens of kids my age practice hand-to-hand combat in pairs as an instructor calls out orders. Though all kinds of bodies fill the room, they're alike in their eagerness as they move, as if they can't bear to be still with Mars's song on the air.

Our group heads to an empty mat, where they scatter and begin stretching. I flop down next to Briony and Tishala and half-heartedly begin loosening up my arms, noticing a rack of spears set into the ger's wooden frame alongside swords, staffs, and knives. Unstrung bows and arrows and throwing stars fill a case in the corner.

"Standing arm bar!" barks the combat instructor on the next mat, a short, full-figured woman with high cheekbones and copper-brown skin and a sling around her left arm. One of each pair of students throws out an arm; every opponent seizes the outflung limb and wrenches it around, tucking it against their chest.

"Down, knee to stomach!" calls the instructor again, and the students who initiated the attack are prone on the floor, their defending opponent's knee buried in their belly. Their instructor paces the mat, dark hair swishing in her long ponytail, uninjured hand repositioning limbs and nodding here and there in approval. "Remember," she calls, "the warrior most in control is the one who never has to swing her fist."

"Commander Atlacoya." Briony casts her an admiring glance. "She broke her arm two weeks ago when her climbing gear gave out. She managed to rappel back down the canyon wall afterward with one hand. I got to watch them set her arm."

I grimace. "Ew."

"First aid training is important," Amir insists, getting up to stretch his hamstrings. "No good rescuing someone if you can't keep them alive until they're back to safety."

The little kids across the room have progressed from push-ups to sit-ups. One boy is fudging his while his instructor's back is turned. "What else do you learn here?"

Amir pauses, switching legs to stretch out the other. "General fitness, combat, weaponry. But primarily search and rescue training. That means climbing, rappelling, spelunking, swimming, horseback riding, firefighting, flying—"

I hold up a hand, startled. "Flying?"

"We'll get to that eventually, I promise." He grins. "Flying, and building temporary magical protection for when people are lost outside the barriers."

Suddenly, I frown at the children across the room. "They aren't too young for all this?" Their coach weaves across the mat, gently smacking the knee of the boy who wasn't doing his sit-ups right.

Tishala shakes her head. She's rolling out her wrists, putting pressure on them this way and that. "They start coming for weekends as soon as they start school on Mercury, but until they're twelve or so, they mostly work on strength, flexibility, teamwork, self-control. How to judge their own limits and capabilities."

"And what about the fifteens earlier, out at the barrier?" I ask suddenly. "Working with fire magic seems really dangerous for . . . I don't know. Not-adults."

Briony and Tishala exchange an uncomfortable glance.

"I don't know," Amir admits. "I would expect Bao to pick students our age, but who can say? Our program can be brutal, but so is life. And lives depend upon our preparedness." A muscle twitches in his jaw, and he turns away to speak to someone else.

There it is again—that weight on Amir's shoulders, a nearly tangible burden. He's tougher on himself than any trainer or program could ever be.

But is he wrong for that? Amir will be king someday. And in the meantime—I think again of the kids who were killed on Mercury. Rescuing people in that kind of danger is what he and the others born to Mars will spend their lives doing.

I wish I could talk to Major about it. About how we could help him. I wish I could talk to Major about anything.

I push into child's pose and close my eyes. I get now why Major said he didn't like it here. Why he didn't think Claudia would, either. But though the chaos of the training room ought to rattle me, it's calming, somehow. Orders issued, teammates calling out to one another, the heat of the torches; it all settles onto me like a weighted blanket.

Baatar slaps the mat and I jerk my head up, blinking. "All right, Amir," he says. "Time for that rematch."

"Rematch?" I ask no one in particular.

"Boxing." Briony pushes herself off the ground, offers me a hand. "Amir destroyed him a few weeks ago and he's still not over it."

"Wait." My nerves kick up as I study them side by side. Baatar's friendly-looking, but his arms are as big as my thighs. "Amir beat—?"

"He didn't *destroy* me," Baatar protests.

"Of course not." Tishala palms her shaved skull, nonchalant. "You just took an impromptu nap on the mat in the middle of training."

I elbow Amir. "You knocked your squadmate out?"

He shucks off his jacket. "It was an accident!"

"Enough talking," Baatar says, rolling his neck. "Amir, let's go."

Amir catches the pair of padded gloves someone tosses him. The rest of us move to the edge of the mat, except for Tishala, who stands between them. "All right, guys, you know the rules. No low blows. Nothing permanent."

The boys pound their gloves together before backing up a few steps. And then they begin to circle.

I'm used to holding back. I'm careful as I push through a crowd not to shoulder-check an unsuspecting stranger, not to tread on any toes. When I nudge one of the Miller kids or swat Claudia's arm, I'm gentle, so aware of the damage thoughtless contact can do.

I think that's why a gasp escapes me when Amir's first punch connects with Baatar's side. Why I *feel* a hit to someone else's body.

It's astonishing to see their blows connect. To watch Baatar not pull his punches as he swings for Amir's ribs, to watch Amir grapple unrestrainedly for Baatar's waist or thigh. There is no shyness about bodies, no fear of hurting one another.

I wonder if this is callowness, or if it's the beauty of being equally matched. Of absolutely trusting the other person in the ring.

"I know," Briony says. She's watching me at my side.

"What?" I ask.

"I'm from a long line of Aries, so I'm used to this. But you never get over your first fight." Her mouth quirks. "There's so much artificiality everywhere in the worlds. But what you do on the mat? What you feel there? It's real. And we're all here for the same reason."

Amir gets Baatar around the waist. I gulp, marveling and horrified at the unwilling embrace of the two fighters. Amir delivers one, two punches to Baatar's ribs before he wrenches away. "And what reason is that?"

"To experience pain."

I blink at her. "Excuse me?"

"Pain," Briony says again, shrugging. She's facing the fighters, but her eyes are unfocused. "To feel pain on the mat, on the climbing wall, in the range and in the ring. To eat in pain and go to bed in pain, and get up in pain and go to work again."

My horror comes out a confused scoff. I shake my head, stepping back a little. "But *why?*" I demand. "Why would you want that?"

"Because it's the only way to get stronger." Briony smiles at me, and it's a real smile, loose but steady, with no trace of cynicism. "To feel pain, to . . . carry him around in your arms and legs and on your back. To make a comfortable friend out of him." She jabs a finger at the air. "*That's* how you become unafraid of suffering. That's how you make yourself brave enough to fight."

I clear my throat, glancing back at Amir and Baatar. Her earnestness makes me a little uncomfortable, and coming from me, that's saying something. "It sounds like masochism," I say. "Or just being jaded."

"It's not, though. We never stop being humans with bodies, so pain never stops hurting." Briony puts a hand on my arm, her eyes intent on mine. "But it stops being a fearful unknown. And the enemy isn't bodily pain. The enemy is dread." Her gaze narrows. "And if I'm any judge, you're here because pain and dread are already both old friends of yours anyway."

Pain and dread. Mars and Chiron. Exactly what Queen Inara found in my chart.

I suck in a sharp breath.

My heart's beating pretty hard for someone standing still.

"The thing about dread," I say slowly, "is that it's born up here." I point to my temple.

"Exactly," Briony says firmly. "So you move the battle. Move it from your mind to your body. Give your thoughts a rest."

I absorb her words. They're everything Queen Inara told me to do.

"I'm afraid I can't," I finally say, my voice brittle. The others jostle around us as Baatar and Amir circle faster. Sweat pools on their foreheads. "I'm not like you guys."

If knowing your body's limits and abilities is essential, like Tishala said, then I'm out of luck. I know nothing. I feel constantly betrayed by this thing that carries my soul around—betrayed by its screwed-up chemistry, by its perpetual urge to run.

My body and I are not friends. I don't trust it, and it serves me as little as it has to.

"You *can*," Briony urges me. "You can do this, because you're here on Mars now. You have your iron. You have his song," Though she's close, she has to raise her voice now over the shouts of the squad. Baatar delivers one, two, three jabs to Amir's jaw and chest. Amir sways and stumbles a little, but rallies enough to send a quick punch beneath Baatar's chin.

And just like that, the match is over.

Baatar collapses—not passed out, just exhausted—and doesn't rise before Tishala pounds her fist on the mat four times. Amir crumples beside Baatar and nudges a cup of water at his squadmate before drinking any himself.

Briony's right. I don't know if I can feel the iron charging through my blood, but I can feel the red planet beneath my feet. I can feel his song drumming against me, muscle and bone.

Mars is offering himself to me. Him or Chiron: the choice is mine.

Briony twitches a braid over her shoulder, eyeing me. "Get comfortable with pain. Because you hurt a little, and then you recover."

"And then?" I ask. Baatar and Amir are still prone on the mat, exhausted.

"And then you do it again," Briony says firmly. "And every time you do, you take a little bit of dread's power away."

CLAUDIA
30

I WAKE UP, and my first thought is that I'm in his room, and he's there. I feel myself smile before I've even opened my eyes.

And then I realize Amir's shirt and his sheets may smell like pine soap, like him, but I'm all alone.

Bleak artificial light creeps through Amir's bedroom window over his dark blue comforter and the beams in the pale plaster ceiling, across the books and papers stacked on his desk and Jack's natal chart, half-crumpled where I abandoned it around midnight.

The dorm is still quiet. I can't remember the last time I woke up to such absolute stillness.

Mornings at my house are excruciatingly loud to non-morning people. My dad's always up early to check on the day already closing in the Asian markets; Jack's usually scrambling to finish his homework, club beats pulsing out of his laptop by 7:00 a.m.; my mom's got her bullet blender roaring as she makes her green juice, her voice rising over the sound as she video-chats with Nonna or her own parents because it's early afternoon in Italy. When Rora stays over, she usually pulls the duvet over her head, and I'm reduced to luring her out with the promise of chocolate chips in her oatmeal or something.

But—no. Even that's not true anymore. It used to be, six weeks ago. Now my parents and I tiptoe around each other, not acknowledging that everything is different. Mom and Dad don't even call Nonna when I'm around, because Jack might pop up.

The silence is lonely. It asks questions I'm afraid to answer.

Amir had me pegged with the star chart he conjured just two days ago in Dr. Qureshi's office. Castor and Pollux floated there in silver light—the twins, the emblem of Gemini. Their whole identity is attachment. Being paired. No one ever refers to them individually.

I don't know who I am on my own, in this silent place. Alone in a boy's bed, with a twin who won't speak to me, with an un-twin who's left me for a totally separate path.

Because a twin without a twin isn't a twin. It's just a star alone in the sky.

In a burst of misery, I push the thoughts away. I climb out of bed, trying not to think about Rora or my brother as I clear a spot on the floor, trying not to thwack my arm on the wardrobe as I reach into a sun salutation.

Yoga, shower, clothes, food: this is my morning routine. The shower water is hot, and the button-up I steal from Amir's dresser fits, somehow. I move efficiently around the apartment, knotting my wet hair into a bun, trying to let Mercury's song energize me.

Queen Inara and Dr. Qureshi wouldn't give me answers, so I'm going to get them myself. And when I have, I'll be able to help the people I love, and bring them back to me.

Before I leave, I knock on Major's door. He groans something indistinct, so I just go inside. His room is cluttered but not dirty—books and clothes are scattered across the dull hardwood floor, but the little row of lemon tree topiaries in the window smells pleasant and clean. Major lies mostly asleep in a yellow-blanketed bed in the center of the room.

"Hey." I bump the foot of the bed with my knee. "Hey. Major."

"Yup."

"I'm going to the library, okay?" I pause. "Be safe going back to court."

His mouth works for an answer, smacking a few times, but all that comes out is ". . . Yup." Then he turns over and goes back to sleep, just like Rora probably would. I wonder if Amir's a morning person like me; I wonder what he's doing.

The thought comes quick as a paper cut. Stings like one, too.

I brush it away, order my mind. I zip up my boots, swipe Amir's academic robe out of his closet, grab my purse and a mostly unbruised apple from the cupboard, and head toward the Astronomy College.

According to the clock tower, it's not even eight in the morning when I reach the courtyard. It's entirely empty, a far cry from the plaza crowded with laughing, talking students we crossed just two days ago.

An unpleasant memory pops into my mind, of the first time I drove to school without Jack after he left. The morning ride had been an eternal war between us, me insisting EDM was too much before sunrise, Jack rolling the windows down because he "couldn't breathe" around the smell of my "weird tea" and Marc Jacobs perfume. I'd begged my mom for my own car so I could get to school on my own, but even she wasn't impractical enough to agree to becoming a four-car family in a city like DC.

That morning—no bickering, no obnoxious music—was all I'd ever wanted. I cried the whole way to school.

The courtyard feels the same now. Mercury's song may be clearer without the interference of other songs, but the school somehow feels less itself.

My heels crack over the cobblestones like breaking chalk, the sound echoing between the ancient buildings, and Amir's robe swishes around me as I slip into the Astronomy College. There's no signage in the silver-stoned building, but I find the library without wandering for too long.

The Astronomy College library covers at least two or three interconnected rooms, centered around a reading room with books shelved all the way up the walls, past platforms reachable only by rickety old ladders. Wooden buttresses brace the star-frescoed ceiling, and old wooden tables and an empty librarian's desk fill the floor. Gaslight flickers softly over the whole scene, empty but for two girls sitting opposite one another at a table in the corner. Even the sound of setting my coat and purse down on a table is loud in the quiet.

Steeling myself, I make for the stacks in one of the adjoining rooms. The librarian's desk is empty and I don't see a card catalog anywhere, but maybe I'll figure out the organizational system of this place if I browse a bit.

"Buenos días." An elderly man in a tweed jacket bustles past with a stack of books, smiling pleasantly. He is mostly bald, with gray hair and a whiskery gray beard, and his skin is olive-toned like my grandpa's.

"Ah, buenos días," I return, a little surprised.

"Can I help you find anything?" he asks, and I grimace. Though I can understand him through the language charm, I can't respond to him in kind.

"I'm sorry," I say, "I don't speak Spanish."

The man laughs, gesturing at a trio of ribbons on my left shoulder. "Apologies. I saw your robe and thought—but perhaps you're just beginning?"

I shake my head, confused. "I'm sorry," I say again, like I'm turning into Rora. "I borrowed this from a friend," I add quickly, pulling the sides of the robe out like a gown.

But even if the robe's borrowed, any student who lived here would know what the ribbons meant, and we both know this. The man studies me for a long moment, then nods at my shoulder.

"The red ribbon is for Castilian Spanish, and the lilac ribbon is for English, which you do appear to speak," he says with a smile. "The yellow ribbon is for Arabic—hal tatakallamina al-arabiyya?"

"I think you know by now that I don't and this is just a cruel game you're playing with me," I say, crossing my arms and biting back a laugh. The man shifts the stack of books from one hip to another, studying me. "Do you want to put those down? They look heavy."

The man rasps a laugh, a smoker's cough at the back of it. "An insult, yet so polite. A fellow Gemini, by all appearances, so by rights you should be here." His brown eyes narrow. "And yet, you don't know the rules, and I've never seen you here before. And you show up just when most of them have cleared out."

"Do you know all the students who come in here?"

"Of course I do," he says simply. "I'm the librarian."

There's no avoiding it. He's too quick. "I'm Claudia Portinari. Queen Inara sent me here." He pauses again, considering me, and I brace for another barrage of questions, but it doesn't come.

"I'm Baldassare," the old man says, dipping his head a little. "How can I help you?"

I hesitate only a moment.

"I want to research the Great Conjunction," I say. "Specifically the events it's foretold."

He squints at me. "What makes you interested in the Conjunction?"

"Because." I hesitate. "I heard the king and queen's scholars discussing it. And I have questions about what it means."

"Very well," Baldassare says after a moment. "Come with me."

To my relief, the library fills a bit more as the morning stretches on, and low conversation and the soft rustle of pages allay the quiet. From behind his desk, Baldassare helps the dozens of students who pile into the reading room and trawl the stacks for material. Hermes may have cleared out, but either classes aren't canceled or, like me, everyone else has their own reasons for being here.

The longer I work, the sharper my mind feels. Mercury's music may not be what it was before, but still it drives me, pulsing through my thoughts as I sit at my table with the short stack of English-language books Baldassare helped me find. Deep in focus, I jump when the chair across from me screeches back over the floor.

"Major?" I demand, my voice just above a whisper. Because he's standing over my table, robe rumpled and hair dark with water. "What are you doing here? You were supposed to go back."

He shrugs stubbornly. "I decided I didn't want to."

"What happened to *orders from our sovereign*?"

"What happened to the girl who didn't care about that kind of thing?"

He's right. I thought it was harsh to drag him back to Jupiter, and I think it makes sense for him to stay. It's comforting to have someone else around who can ignore rules when they hurt instead of help.

Most of all, I don't want to be alone here.

"Whatever." I shrug, giving a short laugh. "But you're going to get caught. That blond head is a beacon."

Major rolls his eyes. "They have more to worry about than me right now." Then he grins, gesturing at his wet hair. "Besides, like this I'm practically incognito."

"Taking a shower before you leave the house does not count as exercising forethought in this situation," I say dryly. "Anyway, if you're staying, come sit down. I'll show you what I've got."

Major plops into the chair opposite mine, gesturing grandly. "Proceed."

I hold up the first book Baldassare brought me. "*The Great Conjunction: Omens and Portents*." The book is so old, the *s*'s in the title look like *f*'s.

Major arches an eyebrow. "Investigating Albrecht's idea?"

I nod. "I power-read this book using my brother's signature method. You read the whole introduction, then the intro and conclusion to every chapter until you find what you're after."

"Your brother is a genius. And?"

I hesitate. "I may've found what we're after."

And? Major gestures, impatient, and I open the volume to the chart I've been puzzling over. He rises and rounds the table to sit beside me. "So this book is really old," I begin. "Like, it was published in 1552 here on Hermes."

"And that matters because . . . ?" Major's forehead wrinkles.

"Well . . ." Again, I pause. "I'll get to that. Here, look at this."

The page is less a chart than a table of dates, nearly fifty of them, spanning from before AD 900 to the time of publication. I've been studying it for over an hour.

16 April 1206. Prophesied the rise of Chinggis Khaan and the Mongol Empire, leading to the arrival of Möngke, Yelü Chucai, and party.

23 July 1265. Portended the birth of Beatrice Portinari (1 February 1266) and Dante Alighieri (21 May 1265).

31 December 1285. Beatrice begins her study in earnest, leading to her arrival.

On and on the dates run, foretelling scholars assembling in Spain under a rabbi named Yehuda ben Moshe; portending the birth of Mexica emperor Ahuizotl in modern-day Mexico City, who would send a party of explorers into the spheres around 1490; predicting Copernicus's theory taking hold on Earth.

Major blinks down at the book, leaning over it until I swat him and scoot him back. "You're gonna drip on the page! There are languages younger than this thing."

"Sorry," he mumbles. "So—it's old. You mentioned that before. Why does that matter?"

"Well, looking at this chart—these aren't all bad." I grimace. "I mean, sure, Genghis Khan burning and pillaging his way across Asia was terrible, but a lot of these entries just seem like big events. Things that weren't always good or bad, just significant." I pause. "Maybe something shifted later? Maybe—in the centuries after the book was published, the Great Conjunction began to predict *only* bad things, never good or neutral ones?"

Major frowns. "But you don't think that."

"No, I don't," I say. "Albrecht said that the Conjunction portended bad things, and that it was only to be expected, because the convergence of two songs was dangerous." I pause, shaking my head at him. "But looking at the events in this book, it seems more like—the king and queen's scholars have this hypothesis, that the convergence of two songs is dangerous, so the Great Conjunction must *necessarily* bring bad things. They organize the facts around their hypothesis, rather than the other way around."

Major pushes back from the table, chewing on his lip. "This is big. This is good, Claudia," he adds, nodding at the book, forehead furrowing in appreciation.

"Thanks," I say, abruptly shy.

All morning, I've felt the buzz of Mercury's music in my brain, firing from synapse to synapse, pushing me to keep reading, to keep questioning. But it's more than the music. It's been a long time since I've let myself chase ideas for myself instead of worries for others.

I don't hate the way it feels.

1287

IN THE END, most of the travelers from Suvd Uls remained in Ulaan Garig. Some fifteen, though, chose to leave the Khaan's service and travel on with the party from Siena.

Not, of course, that the Khaan would be informed of such. But the distinction would be important to maintain for the sake of the king who awaited them at al-Mushtari.

They spent a week on Mars to satisfy Marco's curiosity, climbing through the russet canyon, admiring the cat's-eye sky, riding through the dust that sometimes swirled up to obscure it. As always, Beatrice thought Polo throve on the exploration, on the pressure and physicality of searching out unreachable places and remarkable sights. It pleased her to see his appetite sated, even a little.

Seven days after their arrival, a considerably smaller party bade farewell to those who would stay in Ulaan Garig. Some kissed goodbye, some shook hands, some merely nodded warmly.

Beatrice was sad to leave them behind. But she was even more eager to press on.

On Jupiter, they landed in the midst of a shallow sea, water slapping the hems of their robes and their horses' fetlocks as they sloshed toward the walls of the towering city before them. Beatrice explained the nature of their visit to the guards at the gates, and no sooner had she mentioned Syed's name than they straightened and welcomed the travelers inside.

Up, up, they climbed, wagons rattling behind them. They passed great buildings of sandstone, and arched doors carved with scripted letters, and minarets and domes of violet and crimson and gilt enamel. And all the while, a strong wind blew, lifting the hair off Beatrice's neck and cooling her skin.

The citadel dwarfed both Siena and Florence. And the palace defied her every expectation.

Again, at the mention of Syed's name, they were welcomed inside at once, guided past salons and staterooms and observatories into a library. Beatrice felt her heart race at the sight of hundreds—perhaps thousands—of books, more than she had seen in all her life.

Before she could translate the first of the titles she bent to study, the door to the library opened, and the king was announced. King al-Radi, they called him: al-Radi, *the Content*. A party of five black-clad men accompanied him, including Syed, who welcomed them warmly.

Beatrice strode to the head of their company, feeling her mouth go dry. She was uncertain how to greet a king properly in Arabic; the ancient texts she had studied had not advised her in this. Then again, she would scarcely have known what to do confronted with the podestà of Siena.

So she inclined her head and shoulders, hoping it would compensate for any slight when she spoke. "As-salamu alaikum." *Peace be with you.*

"Wa alaikum as-salaam," al-Radi responded as she straightened. *And upon you, peace.* The king was not much older than her own father, with dark hair and brown skin, dressed in loose white trousers and a tunic of deep purple embroidered with agates. On his head he wore a turban the color of the sky outside. "Whence have you come?"

"The university in Siena," Beatrice said. Then, remembering her world was small and his much larger: "North of Rome. Some of our fellows have come from Suvd Uls," she added, gesturing behind her.

"They allow women at your university? How marvelous!" The king glanced at Syed before turning back to her, eyes lit with interest.

Beatrice shook her head. "They . . . do not." Feeling herself go red, she did not explain.

"Ah. I see," the king said kindly, and Beatrice suspected he did. He gestured to the couches behind them. "Please, be comfortable. You are all very welcome."

At this, Beatrice breathed a sigh of relief. She had been unsure how he would receive the members of their party who had formerly served the Khaan, but al-Radi seemed entirely unthreatened.

As attendants brought in tea and sherbet and almond-studded cookies fragrant with spice, their company settled onto couches. Heart racing, Beatrice reached for Dante's hand behind one of her skirts where no one would see. His palm was as damp as her own.

"We were told—" Beatrice began haltingly; she had read in this tongue, but rarely spoken it, and never in such glittering company. "Syed told us you had foreseen our coming."

"We did," King al-Radi agreed. "The Great Conjunction of Jupiter and Saturn a year and a half ago promised great changes—the arrival of a bright new star. And here you are."

Beatrice felt two things at once: the sensation of her mouth growing dry again, and that of Dante staring at her, unconcerned with anyone else who might be watching.

She had witnessed this very conjunction from her window in Florence some eighteen months before. She had waited and prayed for a clear evening, and watched the skies in wonder when night fell.

It had been that event that had firmed her resolve. She had gone to her parents the next day and begged for a twelvemonth in Siena before she married Simone dei Bardi.

"And whence came you, Your Majesty?" she could only ask. It was an impertinent question; she hoped the king would not take offense.

But al-Radi only smiled, shifting comfortably on his couch. "We came from the city of Baghdad," he said, "and we were the first."

The party of explorers had crossed into the heavens over four hundred years earlier, led by Abu Yusuf Ya'qub ibn Ishaq al-Kindi. He had been a philosopher; he had become their king, taking the regnal name al-Hadi, *the Guider*. And like the city of Baghdad, in whose House of Wisdom he had served, al-Kindi had founded their city under the auspices of heaven.

"On the instruction of his friend, the astrologer Abu Ma'shar, the first stone was laid when Jupiter was in the ascendant and the sun was in the ninth house," al-Radi finished. "And I am his six-times grandson."

"How fascinating," Beatrice said, glancing around at her party. "I have calculated our natal charts, but the horoscope of a city—!"

"It is with such great things that we primarily concern ourselves," Syed answered, speaking for the first time. "The rise and fall of houses, of lands. The coming of famines and droughts and wars."

He glanced out the screened window, where the tide was now rising, and smiled slightly. "Sea changes, if you will."

"My son is correct," King al-Radi agreed.

Ah, Beatrice thought. Though Syed had been respectfully quiet during the king's story, standing unmoving at his back with the other ministers, she had not failed to notice their resemblance.

"There is much you know that I do not," she said, doing her best to wrap her eagerness in courtly courtesy. "There is much I should like to learn."

RORA
31

WHEN THE BOYS are done, the real work of the day begins.

The squad starts drills as soon as Baatar and Amir have peeled themselves off the mat. I imitate them as they shift from one exercise to another, warming up properly for the day. Again and again, I hear Briony's words in my head.

Get comfortable with pain.

And I really do try.

When they do conditioning exercises, I try until I'm red in the face, until sweat runs down my forehead and into my eyes. The rest of them aren't even winded, but my chest shudders with my breathing, my arms and stomach and thighs shaking under my own weight. When they head to the lake for swim practice, I follow them and try not to flinch when it's my turn to fling myself in.

I'm the slowest of all of them by full laps, entire minutes. The horses drinking at the water's edge lift their heads to watch me straggle behind the rest of the squad. While the others practice rescuing dummies, I manage not to drown. That's all that can be said in my favor.

The work feels endless. But after we haul ourselves out of the water, it's barely noon.

I'm drained. I want to cry, sleep, collapse on my sofa and bury myself in cookies and TV. I can hardly talk to Amir's squadmates during lunch for the shame that heats my face.

Maybe I was wrong. Maybe this place isn't going to heal me at all.

And at the back of it all, as much as I try to live in my body and not in my mind, fear is always waiting. Fear that if I'm not getting better, maybe nothing else out in the spheres is, either.

We head back to the training gers after lunch, and Commander Atlacoya barks at us to pick up staffs for sparring. But Amir stops me as I reach for one. "Wait. You look like you're going to pass out."

"I'm fine," I lie.

Tishala shakes her head, a slim hand on my arm. "You need to slow down."

I stare at them, feeling the hope leak out of me.

Amir's squadmates and the rest of the Aries and Scorpios are of all shapes and sizes. But there's something about all of them, in their bearing—their posture is trained, their muscles powerful. There's a friendship with their own bodies, a connection with this planet, an eagerness to move and test themselves.

I'm neither thin nor fat—just soft. And my body is not my friend. And neither, it seems, is Mars.

The planet's song pounds on the air, relentless, urging me on. But it all feels like it lives somewhere outside me. I feel no different, feel no sign of the strength it's supposed to build in my body.

It aches, this fear that we've gotten it wrong again. But I can't quit or slow down. I have to push Chiron away.

"I can't be fixed if I stop." I look away, feeling myself flush with embarrassment. "I thought Mars was supposed to change me."

"Patience," Tishala says, completely unruffled. "He will work, and more quickly than you think. But you've been here less than twenty-four hours. You have to allow the song to build in your blood."

"The song *and* the iron." Amir knocks my shoulder companionably.

"You said to get comfortable with pain," I say to Briony. "I'm trying to push myself. To bring the battle to my body, out of my mind."

I haven't felt anxious all day, I suddenly realize. Embarrassed, exhausted—but not the lightning bolt of anxiety through my heart. Not the depression heavy as lead that tells me nothing matters, so I might as well let myself crumble to dust.

I'm afraid to stop pushing. I'm afraid that if I do, those things will seep back in.

"And you are." Tishala is confused. "Rora, you've fought hard today."

"And it's keeping my head clear," I say to her, desperate. I face Amir, knowing he'll understand. "I'm not ready to be turned inside out again. I have to keep moving."

But Briony doesn't let him speak. "I also said you have to let yourself recover," she insists. "You threw yourself in with us. But now you have to give your body a break."

"Briony's right," Amir agrees. "Chiron's influence is not going to set in again the moment you allow yourself to breathe. It's all right," he says, and the words aren't an empty consolation. They're full, solid enough to lean on.

They're exactly what I would say to him if he were staring down his fears, instead of me staring down mine.

My throat feels thick. I look away. "I hate not being able to keep up with you guys," I grumble, but I've nearly conceded.

"Progress looks different for everyone," Briony insists. Then she pauses. "Hey, Baatar," she calls over her shoulder. "When's the last time you fell short in training?"

"You mean, since Amir trounced me this morning?" Baatar asks, sounding unconcerned. "My lap time was long today. I felt off." He stretches one broad arm across his chest and shrugs.

"Nikolai?" Briony asks. She's still watching me.

"I'm failing at this maneuver, right now." Nikolai fumbles with his combat staff, but his frown looks mostly like concentration. Commander Atlacoya adjusts his grip and he repeats the move, dropping the staff once more. But he just picks it up and tries again.

"Do any of them look embarrassed to you?" Tishala asks quietly.

I shake my head slowly, surprised to see that they don't.

"That's because we protect our squad." Her dark eyes fix on mine. "We fight for each other so hard that no one's embarrassed to fail, or even to progress slowly. That's what it is to be one of us." Tishala smiles, almost smug. "And you're one of us now."

One of us.

I swallow hard. "Tell me what to do."

"You leave the shame where it belongs, for a start—behind you." Briony paces, watching me with almost ferocious kindness. "I don't know if that's Kronos or Earth or somewhere else, but it weighs you down. It's anathema to our song."

At this, I can't help but smile back at her. "Anything else?" I venture.

Amir gives me the ghost of a grin. "Stretch," he orders me. "Drink some water. Sit for a while and meditate on the song."

So I do. While they train with staffs, I loosen up my worn-out muscles, the stiff rounds of my shoulders and the taut expanse of my back. I drink water. I find the facilities and pee. Then I stretch a little more gently, basking in Mars's music.

Because I've done all I can today. But I'll be back tomorrow.

The next morning, I wake stiff and cold to a dawn that comes a bit too early. My muscles ache, but campfire and movement warm them as I eat quickly and change into gear.

Briony and Tishala were right. I feel better today.

Just like yesterday, I follow the squad to the training ger, and just like yesterday, I do all the squad's drills; but when Atlacoya comes to our mat for sparring practice, I know it's time to step back.

I try not to let desperation rise up to claim me. I try to remember what Briony and Tishala said, about healing and patience with Mars's song.

"Tell me what to do," I ask Briony. I hope the words don't sound like pleading.

She looks me up and down, chewing her lip. "What hurts least?"

My thighs and stomach feel weak from the morning's drills, and I have a scrape on my leg from climbing out of the lake yesterday. "My arms."

So Briony shows me the punch Amir dealt Baatar to end their match yesterday, a shot to the chin called an uppercut. "You have to drop your shoulder and let your heel come up as you punch to really give it heft," she explains. Then Tishala comes over, and she teaches me how to jab and hook, putting all my weight behind my punches.

Briony tapes up my knuckles and steers me to a sandbag hanging near the edge of the mat, and the two of them leave me there. And as they pick up their staffs and join the rest of the squad, I train right alongside them.

The bag hardly moves as I throw myself at it—*hook uppercut hook uppercut, right left right left right.* I don't think of missing Claudia, or of Major and the song it's hard to imagine now that he's gone away. I don't think of Chiron or the Conjunction that threatens us. I punch until my shoulders and sides are weary, until the knuckle over my right forefinger splits and bleeds through its wrapping and stains the bag. And then Briony teaches me how to kick.

I tape up the tops and arches of my feet and practice roundhouses and back kicks until Commander Atlacoya dismisses us. And all the while, I stare at the bloodstain I left.

The sandbag may have broken my skin. But I left my mark on it, too.

On and on we train. I do what I can, wherever we are, for two more days of iron pills and ever-easing pain.

If the squad swims in the lake, I paddle determinedly beside them, trying not to mind how much slower I am. I clamber up cliff sides, twisting like a fish on a hook in my climbing gear, refusing to look at anyone else's progress, focused only on the top.

On the top. On the goal. On the song all around us, driving me on, compressing and expanding my heart and lungs on my behalf.

Mars's song no longer feels like it lives outside me. I can feel it migrating inside my very being.

But even if I'm no longer comparing myself to the squad, I can't help but notice a subtle change in them since I arrived. Maybe they don't sense it—increased speed as they swim and run, heightened focus as they fight and climb—but they grow sharper and stronger before my eyes. It's as though Mars is singing more clearly to them than ever, calling harder to their blood and muscles, drawing them closer together and building them up stronger. I even catch Commander Atlacoya and Commander Bao muttering something about it to one another, but they stop talking as soon as they notice me eavesdropping.

I say nothing. Amir and I agreed to keep the secret of what I am. But it builds up something bright and fierce inside me to watch Mars's song amplified in my squad, and to know that I've helped them.

I'm on the sidelines, but I'm still one of them. And this piece of the fight is mine.

I don't stop.

When they spar, Briony and Tishala teach me a simple kata to do on my own. I go through the movements of the choreographed fighting routine again and again, my punches and kicks growing weak as I wear out.

I don't stop.

Briony and Tishala and Amir call out encouragement when they see me falter, just like they do to one another.

You can do this, they say to me, to each other.

You should rest, they say sometimes instead.

I confront the pain. I make a friend out of him. Then I stop, and greet him again when I've recovered.

For once, my body and I are on the same side. And Mars is fighting alongside us.

The planet coaxes strength into me, healing me impossibly quickly, leveraging the iron in my blood and transmuting my bones from lead into a fiercer metal.

Forward, Rora.

Ad astra per aspera, Rora.

Because Mars's song isn't just the music of gladiators and boxers. It's the music of tired girls who push on. Of anxious boys who don't give up when everything whispering in their ears tells them they'll never be enough.

As I bed down at night beneath Mars's black sky and red rocks, I think of Queen Inara and Dr. Qureshi and the other scholars. Of the conjunction of Saturn and Jupiter, and whether it really is the cause of the disruption in the spheres, and when it will end. Of how Mars is fighting Chiron for rulership over me.

It's only as I shut my eyes and drift off that I let myself think of all the other songs that have darted through my brain or wrapped me in their arms over the last four days. I reach for quicksilver in my thoughts, wondering if Claudia's come to terms with all that's happening outside our control; and my heart and my blood and my soft parts dream of sunlight, of summer and salt, of being wrapped up close to someone. I let myself think that, grateful as I am for the strength of Mars's music, there is still something missing here.

Something—someone—to be missed.

CLAUDIA
32

I SPEND A quiet day in the library with Major, then follow him home to make sure he actually goes back to the dorm and doesn't get caught. After a quick trip to a shop for some groceries—their pantry is exactly as empty as I suspected—we eat an easy dinner in his and Amir's kitchen, smack-talking Jupiter's scholars over mozzarella and tomatoes on focaccia, mixed greens that Major barely touches, and raspberries with mascarpone.

"So you're going to check Dr. Qureshi's office next," Major asks, reaching across their rickety wooden table for my unfinished dessert.

"Yeah." I prop one hip against the counter as the copper kettle hums and shivers on the hob. "I don't think the Conjunction hypothesis holds water, but I don't have any other ideas. Albrecht and the others were just all so . . . sure of themselves."

He snorts. "Rora said she thought they were all pretending to be more confident than they actually were."

I straighten. "What? What do you mean?"

"Al-Mushtari is strong. Proud. And the downside of that is arrogance." He arches his eyebrows. "You know. Like a council chamber full of adults insisting that they know what's wrong, and we couldn't possibly help."

Rora never told me she wasn't totally convinced by everything they said. I can't decide if I'm hurt that she confided in Major and not me, or if it serves me right for pushing so hard when she was probably already overwhelmed. Then I pause. "Wait, *when* did she tell you this?"

Major rubs at the back of his head, looking uncomfortable. "Uh, when she went to the bathroom. We just talked for a minute."

"Uh-huh." I narrow my eyes. "Listen, I've been meaning to ask you about that—"

"Oh boy," he mutters.

I jut a finger at him. "Don't you *oh boy* me. You'd better not just be messing around with Rora. She doesn't flirt. She doesn't even *speak* flirt. One of Jack's friends tried to hit on her one time and it didn't even register." Major dips his head, grinning, but I just snap my fingers at him. "No. No smiling. I need you to acknowledge that I will *bury* you if you break her heart."

But that smile doesn't fade; Major laughs, incredulous. "I'm not going to hurt her, Claudia. I mean, I might, somewhere down the line by accident. But I really, honestly, very much like Rora." He pauses, cocking his head in a way that makes me uncomfortable. "You have a hard time trusting anyone else with the people you love."

"Yeah. Well. I'm not going to apologize for that." I lift my chin, challenging him.

Major just shakes his head. "You shouldn't," he says frankly. "You're a good person. It's a good quality."

"Oh."

The kettle begins to whistle. I blow dust out of two teacups before pouring scalding water over sachets of dried verbena. Quiet presses against the plaster walls, against the low-beamed ceiling.

"Just remember to live in your own life. It can be easy to try to forget your own problems and live someone else's," Major says to my back. He pauses. "But it all comes to the surface eventually."

"I know." I sit, and we drink our tea quietly.

I still can't help recalculating Jack's chart before I fall asleep.

I set out even earlier the next morning, armed with a new language charm from Major. I don't head for the library. But I run into Baldassare anyway.

"Buenos días," he greets me with a teasing grin, clad once more in tweed, sipping from a cup of what looks like hot chocolate. "Are you coming to open the library with me, Portinari girl?"

"No, I'm researching elsewhere today," I hedge, not certain if a college employee would take issue with my rummaging through a professor's office.

Baldassare adjusts the leather messenger bag over his shoulder. "I saw you yesterday with Major Vieira," he says, studying my face. His gaze is quicksilver-clear. "It looks as though he and Amir made it to Earth after all."

I stiffen. "How did you—?"

"People with questions always seem to find their way to me," Baldassare says, waving a hand. "I'm more curious about what the royal family thinks of another Portinari girl befriending their son, given what happened last time."

"What happened last time?" I ask.

"Never mind that." Baldassare shakes his head, smiling slightly, casting his eyes in the direction I was headed. "Only take care you turn down the lights when you leave Nadeema's office." And then he turns toward the library, and I'm alone.

Everything in Dr. Qureshi's office is just as we left it when the text from the guards appeared and we had to run: chair tucked in, maps and models of the spheres in their places, leather-bound books stacked on her desk. For a moment, loneliness is a tight band around my heart.

But I push those feelings to one side. I've made actual progress, and I've got more ground to cover. I can't cover it if I'm eaten up with missing them.

Rora. Jack.

Amir.

I sit down at Dr. Qureshi's desk, shift her stack of books in front of me, and start to read. It must be hours later when Major appears in the doorway. "Hey," I greet him. "How'd it go?"

"Mostly like we expected." He puts something wrapped in a napkin in front of me. "Leftovers of the focaccia. Ah, so I found some more books on the Conjunction in Castilian and Arabic."

"Language charm?" My brows arch. "Or do you speak—?"

I'd only been able to scour Dr. Qureshi's library books, most of which weren't in English, via the language charm Major put on my eyes last night. It was strange to read the text in its own language while magically understanding all its intent—the straightforward writing as well as idioms and expressions.

Major nods at the ribbons on his shoulder, identical to Amir's. "Yeah, my family speaks Castilian, so I help Amir with it. He helps me with the Arabic. Anyway," he continues, "I was mainly looking at projections for ten or fifteen instances of the Great Conjunction in the seventeen hundreds."

"And?"

"There are both good and bad predictions," he says, shrugging off his bag. "A mix. Auspicious for some things, inauspicious for others, like we thought yesterday. But no one talks specifically about songs encountering other songs." He flops into the chair in front of Dr. Qureshi's desk and I follow his gaze to the ceiling, its deep blue gilded with the constellations Gemini and Virgo, the zodiac signs Mercury rules.

"Maybe the Conjunction brought you," Major finally says. "It brought on so many arrivals. Al-Kindi, Yehuda ben Moshe. Itzcoatl and Kepler and Möngke and Yelü Chucai. And . . ."

"And Beatrice," I finish.

It feels foolish even to imagine such a thing—that Rora and me sneaking onto this grand stage could have been foretold. That it could matter enough to be portended by the movements of the heavens.

But is it any less foolish than accepting that Beatrice is my ancestor? That she left something behind for me to finish?

I wonder what Beatrice's sign was. Where would she have thought she belonged, as she discovered planets that weren't even known on Earth at the time?

My stomach growls again, interrupting my thoughts, and I take another bite of the focaccia folded around tomatoes and cheese. "Thank you for this," I say to Major. "You ate, right?"

He nods. "Back at the dorms." Then he scans the titles in front of me, frowning. "I thought you read all these before."

"Yeah?" I raise my eyebrows, swallow another bite of sandwich. "You thought I read six books in thirty minutes while you flirted with Ro in the hall?"

"No," Major says patiently. "I thought you read three books in thirty minutes while I flirted with Ro in the hall. Obviously, Amir read the other three."

I choke on a laugh and, thankfully, not the last of my food. "Okay. So the truth is, I barely had time to touch any of this stuff before. Half of it wasn't in English. Amir helped, but I was upset." I hesitate. "Rora and I don't usually argue. I was just poking through Dr. Qureshi's material, hoping a single decent idea would occur to me."

"Fair," Major concedes. He glances down at the books again. "So. Did you find anything?"

"I think so." I hold up *Celestial Conjunctions: The Pace of Planets.* "Yesterday while I was in the library, I remembered Dr. Qureshi had requested a book about conjunctions, so I thought I ought to take a look."

The corner of Major's mouth lifts. "More power-reading today?"

"No, I read this one pretty closely. But an hour in, I noticed that the most interesting part is right on the cover." I point to the author's name, giving Major a significant look.

"*Albrecht Schreiber,*" he reads aloud, then straightens. "Albrecht, the scholar from court?"

"I think so. The book's in German; his English had a German accent." I shrug, hesitating. "Anyway, the book was illuminating. Apparently, there are all kinds of conjunctions all the time—between different planets, at varying distances." Major nods; this isn't new information to him. "But what struck me most was Albrecht's method. It's terrible, Major."

He plants his elbows on his knees, blond brows contracting. "What do you mean?"

"I mean this book is really light on data and really heavy on opinion and framing," I say. "He's cherry-picking information, whether he means to or not. Albrecht writes about a conjunction between Mars and Jupiter that supposedly brought about a lot of political unrest on Earth a few years ago, but a really important UN convention was signed around then, too, protecting the rights of an ethnic minority that had been under attack for years. The conjunction wasn't all bad news, but he doesn't report anything good."

"Do you think he's misleading people on purpose?" Major asks.

I grimace. "I don't know. You don't have to be a bad person to be misinformed. But you run into problems when you can't hear any evidence contrary to what you think you know. When you're not teachable anymore." I hesitate, tracing the book. "I think some of the advisors have bought really hard into this worldview, and they can't see the facts from any other perspective. That maybe they're not even seeing all the facts anymore."

"So we still don't know what's causing this." Major swallows, leaning back in his chair. "Didn't you say things only took a turn for the worse on Earth six weeks ago?"

"Yeah." I frown. "I'm not sure why there's such a difference in the timelines."

"Did any of the other books help?" he asks.

I hold up *Many Moons: The Great Planets and Their Satellites*. "Well, this was the next one in the stack."

"That looks . . ." Major pauses. "*Exceptionally* dull."

I jab a finger at him. "You, sir, are correct! But I was reminded that all the gas giants have lots of moons. And that where Jupiter pulls detritus into its orbit fairly often—because like its namesake, it is extremely promiscuous—Saturn rarely does so. I didn't read much more than that. Very niche content. Not sure what Dr. Qureshi was looking for here."

"Okay. What else?"

"Well, then I started reading about Beatrice." I swallow hard. "You know. The books were here. Felt worth looking into." Major gives me an odd look, and I know I'm protesting too much. I hold up *The Settling of the Spheres, Volume III: Beatrice and Her Companions.* "But I didn't get much farther than the introduction of this one, either." I push the book across the desk and watch him read the passage I've nearly memorized.

> Deep in the caverns of the Moon, Beatrice and her companions rested in Suvd Uls, the camp of the explorers from the court of the Khaan, a waypoint for travelers weary from voyaging.
>
> On Mercury they founded the underground city of Hermes. As the spheres filled, its inhabitants would educate their young in this fleet-as-thought city.
>
> On gentle Venus, they planted an ocean. Mexica explorers, led by the astronomer Itzcoatl, would later establish the city of Quetzal-coatl on its shoreline and settle it with shapers of beauty and lovers of land, to create and to grow and to dwell in peace.
>
> On the bright surface of the Sun, Beatrice and her cadre made their first contact with the court of King al-Radi. Before departing, they named their island Helios, where later would settle alchemists and theologians who neither slept nor slumbered but worshiped eternally with open eyes in the land where there is no night.
>
> On red Mars, they rested in a deep scar along the planet's side, in the settlement called Ulaan Garig. The fiercest would make their home in this canyon one day, to study peace and safety.

From valiant Jupiter reigned King al-Radi with his noble astrologers. They welcomed Beatrice and her company warmly to al-Mushtari, and there the party remained for many weeks.

On sober Saturn, Johannes Kepler founded Kronos, where philosophers and astrologers would devote themselves to quiet contemplation in its monastery.

On brilliant Uranus, in Acuto, the best and strangest students would commit themselves to discovery and the endless pursuit of magic and science.

On quiet Neptune, storytellers dwelled in the village of Tarshish founded by rabbi and astronomer Yehuda ben Moshe. There they kept the tales of the past ever in their souls and spun the stories hidden in their hearts.

The party from Siena only briefly visited dark, distant Inferno's belt. Itzcoatl's party built a small settlement around a monument on Pluto, calling it Teopanzolco; but few would reside there, though many would visit to clear their minds with the songs of Stellare and the Primum Movens beyond.

I don't know what I was looking for. Maybe for an explanation of Beatrice's legacy, of where the exclusion of the spheres came from.

Or maybe I'm just looking for her. For Beatrice herself.

I stare at the ceiling, trying to make sense of it all. Trying to understand why I feel so connected to an ancestor who lived so far in the past—what she can possibly have to do with me, today. "Amir's ancestors were already well established by the time Beatrice and Dante arrived. So how did she convince them to begin the exclusion?" I ask the gilt constellations overhead. "I just don't understand."

"I don't know," Major admits, pushing the book back in my direction. "I always got the sense that she was just . . . influential."

"I know the rule—the exclusion—makes you unhappy," I venture. "But do you think she could have been right? That it's for everyone's good?"

I think of Rora, my best friend and my polar opposite. Of Jack, the twin I can't understand.

We're not alike. And they've both hurt me. But do we belong apart? And what does it mean that Jack and I are so different, but share a sign?

"Beatrice may not have had bad intentions," Major finally answers. "But I think the exclusion makes choices for people that they should make themselves."

I bite my lip. This is an impossible conversation to have with Major. He's too close to it.

He acted so strangely yesterday in Queen Inara and King Sameer's castle, shuffling around, barely raising his voice. He stares into a corner now, and the shadows there seem somehow to settle below his eyes. "I look at my future, and all I see is myself waiting in al-Mushtari for Amir. For decades, possibly, until he moves to court to take his parents' place. But shouldn't there be a path for *me* when I look ahead?" he asks, sounding troubled. "A future where I might be happy, instead of just music that wrecks me and one friend with his own life to live?"

I think of what I asked Rora yesterday. *Are a series of choices where you* never *get the help you need really the right thing?* I demanded. I feel like asking the same question now.

Can it be for the best for Major to be headed somewhere that makes him so miserable? And how many more people out here are like him, stuck on paths they have no way of escaping?

Belong *is a tricky word.*

Frustrated, I slump in Dr. Qureshi's chair. I've learned so much today, but I still don't have any answers. And even if I read this stack of books cover to cover, could I really know who Beatrice was and what she was thinking?

Across from me, Major's tangled blond head is bowed, his hands flipping through another book, over pages he doesn't read.

Watching him, I decide right then what I have to do.

"I really am related to her." My voice is hoarse. "To Beatrice. I wasn't making it up on Jupiter. My nonna told me we were when I was little. It took me all this time to believe her."

Major doesn't look up. But his fingers still.

"I want to figure out what's wrong out in the spheres. But I want to find out who she was, too," I say. There's a piece of me that needs to understand Beatrice as badly as it needs Jack to come home to me, as badly as it needs Rora to be okay.

"I need to know for me," I say. "And I need to know for everyone else."

When Major raises his head at last, I almost can't handle the hope in his eyes.

"I need to know," I finally say, "if there's any hope of changing what she's done."

1287

IN A MATTER of days, Beatrice was the darling of King al-Radi's court.

She spent her hours in the libraries, or in the observatories, or in the salons of the court scholars. The king was much occupied with the work of governing his city, but Syed seemed pleased to keep her company. Beatrice learned that he was King al-Radi's second son (after his older brother Salim), that he was engaged to be married to a young woman who was the daughter of one of his father's advisors, that at twenty he was one year younger than Beatrice herself. She also learned that he was familiar with many of the astrological techniques she wished to study.

"And so a solar return—this can predict the sort of year a person will have?" Beatrice asked, studying notes she'd already taken.

"Season by season, month by month," Syed agreed.

Sitting back, Beatrice counted on her fingers. "You have taught me Masha'allah ibn Athari's means of divining the answer to a question *and* Abu Ma'shar's lots and solar returns, all of which speak of the future of persons. I thought you were only interested in *sea changes*."

"Perhaps I spoke too generally," Syed said easily. He seemed to do many things easily: to speak, to smile, to please everyone at once. "Of course we each concern ourselves with choosing the most auspicious paths. Enterprising men and women want to undertake business endeavors at the wisest time; farmers want to plant when the stars dictate the best return. But you seem much more concerned with what the stars say of a person's essential nature."

"That's precisely it," Beatrice said, straightening.

Syed thought, tapping his long fingers on the desk. He seemed to wish to give an answer that would satisfy her. "We do calculate natal charts for newborns, of course. I was born when the sun was in Libra and the ascendant was in Pisces."

"Dante's is Pisces, as well. But I do not know my own ascendant. No one marks the birth of a daughter so precisely," Beatrice said, only a touch of bitterness in her smile. "I assume your birth was observed with much fanfare."

He inclined his head, grinning ruefully. "It was. Though recall, Beatrice, that I am myself only a second son. Most families in the city have an astrologer present for the births of children, as we set great store by the ascendant sign." Remembering how ill-suited to his nature Dante's sun and moon seemed, in devious, slippery Gemini, Beatrice privately thought this wise.

Syed's smile grew sunnier. "Perhaps natal charts could be your particular study," he offered. "One could spend many years on the astrology of personality and disposition."

One could spend many years.

It was an appealing picture of what the future might be. Here, at work, with Dante at her side.

Something warm and solid swelled up inside Beatrice.

"Your Highness," an attendant interrupted. "The scholars you requested have assembled."

Syed turned to Beatrice, eyes alight. "I hope you don't mind," he began eagerly. "I thought to summon a group of our astrologers so that you might calculate the horoscope of Florence. Or perhaps its solar return, if you do not know the hour of its founding!"

Beatrice beamed. "Florence's birth was not marked quite so well as yours, or your city's," she said. "But we shall see."

As Beatrice watched the stars and read her books, Dante watched his friends, keeping an eye to how they fared as King al-Radi's honored guests.

Beatrice was radiantly happy ensconced among al-Radi's libraries and scholars; moreover, the court adored her. Marco, on the other hand, seemed stymied. There was no landscape to explore, nothing to be tamed, merely a citadel set above a sea where the tinder of his endless energy could not catch and burn.

For his part, Dante found the city alluring, inviting. Its towering sandstone buildings and fountains and gardens stirred in him a craving he had forgotten.

He had thought that, with Beatrice at his side, he could lack for nothing. But al-Mushtari's grandeur and Jupiter's music reminded him of the person he had been before he left Florence. Of things he had once desired.

It reminded him of ambition.

As Beatrice studied and Marco struggled, Dante honed his wordcraft. Sometimes, he recited poetry in the palace salons—his odes to the heavenly spheres they had passed, to the stars that made bright cathedrals above, to Florence behind them, to the holy vision that Beatrice made as she worked.

Al-Radi's courtiers received his efforts politely. But Beatrice took in every word Dante spoke. In their time alone, as Beatrice showed him the path forward she had planned, he shared more of his writing with her; and more and more, in those quiet hours, Dante talked of Florence.

It seemed impossible to Beatrice that Dante could think of any other place. But Dante cast his mind back more and more, speaking with a strange new longing of the city he had been so eager to leave behind.

"Will you ever come home?" he asked suddenly one day. Many of their hosts were at afternoon prayer; the two of them sat alone on a hill outside the palace, watching the waves crash against the city wall.

Beatrice was reclined in his arms; but at this, she drew away. "Home?" she asked. "To be wife to a man I hardly know and run his household? No."

Beatrice had thought little of Siena since entering the spheres, and less still of Florence. And as al-Mushtari sang to her, as she learned from Syed and the other scholars, she had imagined only her future there with Dante, among the stars.

"But you wouldn't have to," Dante insisted. His eyes were bright. "Things could be different. When we tell them what we've seen, things *will* be different. We could—"

Beatrice sat up, speaking slowly. "Dante, I don't want to go back. I could never lead there the life I lead here." She shook her head. "It's impossible."

Dante laughed, and the sound seemed to ring off every stone in the city. "Impossible? For you?" He brushed a hand over the hair that hung around her face. "What could be impossible for the girl who breached the spheres of heaven? For you, who have so enchanted an entire court?"

Something in his voice unsettled Beatrice. Unease curled in her stomach.

"My Dante," she said to him, "might we talk of other things?"

"Of course," Dante said easily. He waved a hand, indulgent. "Perhaps we shall stay."

At this, her smile returned. "We have, after all, more stars and spheres to search." She lifted her eyes—not to the heavens, but to the palace behind them, where her work and new friends awaited. "We have more worlds yet to seek together."

RORA
33

THEY WAKE ME up in the middle of the night. Before I'm even properly conscious, I'm scrabbling backward, my hands slipping on my bedroll, fearful of the shadows moving around the campfire.

No matter where I go, it seems I'm still afraid of the dark.

"It's just us," Amir says quietly. "It's fine."

My heart beats jaggedly, nothing like the planet's steady rhythm. I force my breathing to slow, reminding myself that I'm one of them. That I'm at home here, and that I am more than thirty-one fears, and that if there is any safe place, this is it.

"What's happening?" I ask when I've steadied myself. "What's wrong?"

But Briony grins. Her braids swing as she crouches beside me. "Nothing's wrong. It's time for you to get your iron."

I glance around the circle, and with my eyes finally clear I see what I didn't before. Excitement.

Tishala squats beside me, holding out a wristband. I hold it up to the firelight.

"It says *hic manebimus optime*," Amir says from across the campfire. The squad faces him, and he begins to pace, hands on his hips.

"Hundreds of years ago, when the Gauls attacked Rome, many

members of the Senate wanted to evacuate somewhere safer. But one centurion refused. 'Hic manebimus optime,' Marcus Furius Camillus said. 'Here we will remain, most excellently.' That's our squad's motto. And that's our question for you, Rora." The firelight washes over Amir, casting everything into shadow behind him. "Will you stay?"

"I—" I stare around, startled. I never thought of *staying* in the spheres. I suddenly realize that I have a matter of days before my nannying excuse runs out and I'm supposed to be back in DC.

When I finally manage to speak, my throat sounds like it's full of gravel. "I don't know if I can. My family—they don't live here. I can't leave them."

"You can be *with us*, even if you're not here," Tishala says. "Our squad may be split up when we're done training. Most of us won't live here in Ulaan Garig; we don't have any choice about that. For some of us, our postings will be uncomfortable—in a place where the song pushes against who we are. But we won't run from that, either."

"What's important is that you plant your feet." Briony shifts at my side, settling in the dust. "That even if your heart falters, you subject it to your will."

"We don't run from danger," Amir says. His voice is low, but I don't miss a word. "We don't give in to fear. We persist. We remain."

I swallow hard. When I reach for the armband, Tishala passes it to me.

The iron is cold beneath my fingertips, power drawn to its circle. As it slides around my wrist, I feel Mars's song bind itself to me, muscle and bone.

I want to not feel like a grenade. I want to be resilient. I want to be indestructible.

All those wishes burst out of me a few days ago, fighting with Claudia. But they don't feel like wishes anymore.

They feel like my fate, cast in iron. As if, with this song ringing through my body and pounding in my heart, I'm destined to become everything I always wanted to be, and nothing that Chiron threatened in my chart can touch that.

It's a powerful feeling. It's almost enough to make me believe I could never need anything else.

We celebrate for hours—longer and later than we should. A few people dance; some of the squad send a flask around, though I pass. It must be after midnight when the laughter and the black night make me bold enough to approach Amir and pose the question I've been wanting to ask him for days. "If I wanted to text the others, could you help me do that?"

Amir glances up from where he sits on a rock, reading. "You want to text Claudia?"

I stop short. "To—Claudia. Yeah. Yes, of course I meant Claudia. There's no one—who else?" The words trip out of my mouth like clowns piling out of a clown car. "But, like, if I wanted to text Major, how would I . . . ?"

Amir and I stare at each other for a long moment. He presses his lips together really hard, like he's doing his best not to laugh.

Thinking about Claudia, I wish I felt like laughing. I've been trying these past four days not to remember how we left things back on Jupiter. We haven't gone this long without talking in two years.

But whatever needs to pass between us, I'm not sure I can put it in writing. I'm not even sure I'll be able to say it when I see her again. Words have always been her forte.

Which makes what I'm about to do incredibly intimidating.

"Do you have a pen and paper?" Amir finally asks. Teeth gritted so I don't say anything *else* to embarrass myself, I hand him both, and he scribbles down two sets of coordinates.

Amir passes me the folded sheet, mouth quirked. "One is for our dormitory. The other is for my room at court. Major's probably staying there, making a mess of all my things."

My face is tomato-red. "Got it." I nod and start away, but Amir speaks once more.

"Hey, Rora?"

I turn. "Yeah?"

"I'm glad it's worked for you. Being on Ulaan Garig." He swallows, fingers riffling the pages of the book. "I was wrong before when we were talking to my mother. You belong here."

I nod. For once, I don't have to hope he's right; I know. The evidence that Mars rules me is in every split in my knuckles, each of my aching limbs. "Thanks," I say, because I can't give voice to everything else I want to say to him. To everything I want *for* him.

I wish he believed he belonged anywhere, instead of feeling like a fraud. I wish he could see that his song, so disciplined and serious, is a gift to everyone around him. That it makes him a good squad leader, and that it will make him a good king someday.

I don't know if Amir reads any of this on my face. He grins faintly and extends his fist, and I knock my knuckles against his and return to my sleeping bag.

But when I try to write, I can only stare at the page.

If we were texting—*actually* texting, with phones—I could be cowardly. *Hey* would be enough to test the waters. But I've only seen this done once; I don't know exactly how it'll work, or how quickly

Major will find it. He might not even notice a one-word message.

The blank page stares back at me; my pen shakes a little in my fingers. Trying not to think too hard, I jot down a few words.

> *I got my wristband tonight. Only been four days here on Mars, but it feels much longer.*
> *All good here. Hope you're okay. Miss you.*

In the end, I chicken out and add *both* to the end of my last sentence. I scribble the coordinates of Amir's room on al-Mushtari and sing a quiet, gold-soaked note toward my writing. Nothing happens.

I drum my fingers on the packed dirt, waiting, waiting.

A few minutes pass. I wonder if I should ask Amir if I've done something wrong, then decide I'd rather chew my own arm off. I don't even know what time it is in al-Mushtari; Major could be busy or asleep. But I feel flat with disappointment after so much buildup.

And then another thought occurs to me.

Would Major really have gone back? As miserable as he was on Jupiter, as lonely as Claudia would be without us?

I scratch out the first set of coordinates and scribble in the ones for the dormitory, and hum the note Major played for us so many nights ago in the 9:30 Club bathroom.

Almost immediately, words appear beneath my own.

> *Nicely done, soldier.*
> *Also, I guess if you're sending this here, you guessed I stayed. You had me pegged from the beginning, pretty girl.*
> *It feels like more than four days. Claudia and I spend all our time in the library. We're making progress.*

You're probably running around from dawn to dusk. You're
probably so busy you don't even have time to miss me.
I think I need a little more convincing.

I can hear Major's voice as I read the words, imagine the grin on
his face. I bite my lip, feeling myself flush.

His mention of Claudia stings, and I try not to miss her down
to my very bones. But it's not hard to focus instead on that last line,
the one that makes me fizz like a soda can. On the challenge in his
words. *I think I need a little more convincing.*

Cheeks heating, I prop myself on my elbows, glancing around
our campsite. Half the squad has gone to sleep; the other half are
laughing and whispering and, I suspect, still drinking.

But I don't want Dutch courage. Mars's song and the cover of
night make me bold enough. Before I can lose my nerve, I scribble a
reply and send it off.

Of course I have you figured out. A thought's out of your mouth
before it's fully registered in your brain.
Is it proof enough that I keep kicking myself for not making more
of the five minutes we had alone at the palace?

Those few minutes with Major feel like they were ages ago. But
I can still remember the sound of him. The in-out of breath in his
lungs, the warmth of the melody that clung to him.

I bury my face in my pillow, my heart thumping against the hard
ground. I wish I had three little dots to tell me he was typing, that
my note hasn't disappeared into the aether. When words appear on
my paper, I pop up so quickly I whack my elbow on a rock.

Should have kissed you then. Next time I see you, I think I will.
What do you think of that?

I roll onto my side, not fighting my smile, curling up to shield the words from everyone around me. Because they're from him, just for me.

I read them over and over. I can't stop imagining Major's tanned hands on my waist, his mouth searching mine out. Blond hair falling around his forehead, his eyes soft as dusk.

All that warmth. All that summer. His breath mingling with mine.

The imagining works on my mind like a drug; it's a long moment before I can even try to respond. And when I do, though Mars's song still thrums all around me, I don't reach for it.

Another song comes to me as I think what to write—one that enveloped me days ago. It settles into my heart like sugar in a teacup. It tells me what I already know I want to say.

I wish you would. Just the thought of you feels like unwinding.
Tell Claudia I miss her.

There's almost no room left at the bottom of the page. I pause, then write one last line.

Give me three good things, before I call it a night?

I bite my lip, send it off, and wait. And wait.
And wait.
I flip my page over. But nothing has appeared on the back.

Dread is rising in me like a cold tide when Amir comes to stand over my sleeping bag. He clears his throat, once again fighting a grin. "I think this was intended for you. Major's handwriting. Showed up on a blank page between my chapters."

Blushing furiously, I snatch it out of his hands. "Thank you. Go away."

Two short lines wait for me on the torn scrap of paper. My heart beats faster as I read them again and again.

I tried to think of three, but I can only really think of one.
All of them are you.

CLAUDIA
34

I SPEND THE next day reading the books on Beatrice. I don't power-read; I soak up every word, reveling in her dreams of miracles and her chosen mantra—*as above, so below*. I don't find anything in *The Settling of the Spheres* to tell me how she developed the idea of the exclusion, but I don't let myself be discouraged. I just pick up *Beatrice and Dante: Notes and Letters* and keep reading, the language charm slowly recalling to me the Italian I spoke better as a child.

Beatrice's and Dante's names have been familiar all my life, but I hadn't thought of them much since until a couple of years ago, when my world lit class read Dante's *Commedia*. One morning when Mom was video-chatting with Nonna, I mentioned it while I hurried around the kitchen, toast in one hand, paperback in the other.

"How is school, Ombra?" Nonna shouted over the whir of the espresso maker. "What are you learning?" She already had a tan by late April; there was sweat in her short gray waves like she'd been out walking or gardening.

Mom passed me the phone, and I propped it up on the counter. "Fine," I said, chomping my toast, holding up the book. "Look. Your favorite."

Inferno and *Purgatorio*, Dante's tales of hell and purgatory, were a little dark for my taste. But my interest had flared when we reached the *Paradiso*, where Dante met Beatrice, who would be his guide into the heavens.

Nonna squinted through her wire-framed glasses at the cover, an enamel painting of Dante and Beatrice. With their hands almost touching, Beatrice gestured at the sun and the stars above them, the sky at their backs an impossibly deep blue.

Then she smiled enigmatically. "Your great-great-grandmother."

I nearly choked on my food. "Nonna. Come on. Not this again."

"Portinari, Portinari. I've been telling you this for years." She shrugged, gesturing between herself and the illustration. "Why do you think all our women keep their name?" She had, when she'd married Grandpa. She'd even given it to Dad.

I shrugged. "Feminism?"

"I was too busy raising three children and getting my doctorates to be a feminist," Nonna muttered.

"If you were—then—okay," I broke off, scrunching my eyes shut. "Besides, great-great-grandmother? That's four generations."

"You were always a very literal child." Nonna's grin creased her whole face, affection in every line. Then she winked. (For her part, she had always been remarkably whimsical for a physicist.)

"What are time and space to a Portinari?" she asked me, smiling mysteriously. "We are the keepers of doors. Of *worlds*."

I hadn't been quite sure what to say to this. So I laughed, and told her I loved her, and hurried to school.

Shared surname notwithstanding, I hadn't really believed Beatrice was my ancestor. I hadn't even been entirely convinced she was a real person, despite the records Nonna swore she'd seen, despite my dad's family still living in Tuscany.

More to the point, I hadn't cared. Family history so deep in the past meant nothing for my present life. It had nothing to say about my abilities, my choices.

Because I've never believed in destiny. Even religious faith can be a stretch for me.

But before, I didn't know this place existed. I didn't know that Beatrice was a real person, a scholar—anything more than the embodiment of a man's desires in a work of fiction.

I know now, though, why King Sameer assumed I was joking when I told him my name was Portinari.

It was because Beatrice Portinari was a real person. Not a symbol, not a metaphor, not a mirror where a poet could admire himself. She was an Aquarius with a mind like a steel trap, a strange and remarkable woman for her time.

She guided Dante and Polo to the stars. She grasped the heavens, stood on the face of the sun, left her mark on this place, for better or worse.

Beatrice Portinari is my forebear, a real woman who made real discoveries, and I know with certainty that her life means something about mine.

More than anything, I want to tell someone about it all. I share some of it with Major, and even consider confiding further in Baldassare. He's Gemini to the core, sharp and silver-tongued as Jack and I could ever hope to be, and he clearly knows more than he's letting on. The library feels less lonely with him around.

But he's not Rora, who barely feels like a second person when we're together. He's not Amir, who quiets my mind and helps me think. They're the ones I really want to talk to.

I miss them. I miss Mercury the way it felt the first time we came, before it turned too high, too fast, too sharp. My thoughts tremble and buzz as I read, like I've had half a dozen shots of espresso and half as many hours of sleep. And as I cross back and forth from the school to the shops to Major and Amir's apartment, my boots clacking too loudly on cobblestones in the too-quiet city, I can't help but wonder if the city's very emptiness could be why it feels this way.

On our fifth morning in Hermes, Major slides into the seat across from me, pushing an apple and a folded piece of paper in my direction with a look that means absolutely nothing good. "Morning."

"Good morning. What's this?" I reach for both items.

"An apple." I roll my eyes at him and he laughs. "The text came last night. You were gone before I could give it to you this morning."

"Thanks," I say distractedly, unfolding the paper and peeking inside.

"You forget to eat when you work." Major grins crookedly. "Also, uh, I quit reading that once I realized it wasn't for me."

I don't ask who the text is from. I can guess who sent it from the cautious, even writing. Heart floating toward my throat, I stick it in my robe pocket until I find a private moment.

"Speaking of which, how goes the reading this morning?" he asks, nodding at my notes.

I can hear him trying to keep the hope out of his voice. He wants to understand Beatrice's reasoning as much as I do.

"It's going." I drag a hand through my hair. Major arches his eyebrows, and at his prompting, I admit the truth. "I miss them today. I just keep thinking about my fight with Rora."

Major shakes his head. "One fight isn't going to put a dent in years of friendship."

But *was* it just one? Or was it months of argument, built up and released into one moment? In my thoughts, I see Rora—the frustration and hurt on her face at my too-brutal honesty, refusing to back down again while I pushed and pushed. She must have felt so relieved at just the possibility of getting better, and my response was to demand more from her.

I can still see the windburn on her skin, after the frost had disappeared.

My heart gives a little lurch. "Do you remember," I begin slowly. "Do you remember the red mark on Rora's cheek after we'd been on Jupiter? After the frost from Saturn was gone?"

Major nods. "Of course."

Of course he remembers. If I haven't forgotten, neither has he.

"Why do you think it did that?" I ask quietly. "Why would Jupiter heal her, if she doesn't *belong* to Jupiter?"

He shrugs. "It can't have."

"But it did," I insist, keeping my voice low. "Jupiter helped her when she was hurting from Saturn. Your song did the same thing," I add, realizing the truth as I say it. "I told you to sing something else on Saturn. And you picked her up and you sang Venus to her and it kept her from falling apart, even though it wasn't *her music*. It was like the songs corrected one another, or balanced one another out."

Sing something else! I remember shouting at the Abbot, at the boys. I sensed the truth even before I understood it.

"Whether it did or it didn't, it's—Claudia, you can't say stuff like that," Major says, glancing around anxiously.

I wave a dismissive hand. "We're spitballing."

"I don't know what that means. But you have to remember how they talked at the court," he insists. "They were unsettled by the mismatch in Rora's sun sign and her natal chart. People belong to one sign and one song, and as far as they're concerned, any other music is irrelevant."

"I know, I know," I concede. Major picks up a book at random, looking troubled.

I try to turn my attention back to my notes, where I've been tracking Beatrice's references—Aristotle, who proposed the spheres were made of *aether*; Pythagoras, who defined the movement of the planets within them; and Kepler, who revolutionized the subject later. "Uh, I have to go find something," I say, holding up my notes.

Major still looks concerned. "Want me to do anything?" he asks.

I push volume three of *The Settling of the Spheres* his way. "Read this, if you want," I say. "Keep an eye out for anything interesting."

My mind races as I hurry toward the stacks. Could the spheres be able to correct one another, balance one another out? Could their music together protect one another from extremes?

Could the presence of so many songs—of all of the signs and all their melodies—be why Earth has only been suffering for six weeks, when the rest of the spheres have been seeing the effects of disharmony for nearly six months?

I stride through the shelves, mind racing, reaching for my apple once I'm out of view. Baldassare may be cool, but no librarian would condone eating in the stacks. But when I put my hand in my pocket, I find Amir's note.

I can hardly focus for thinking about this new idea. But then I open it and begin to read.

I finished another one of my mother's books tonight. I don't read as quickly as you, but I'm trying. I should've read so many more of them by now.

This is what I usually think about when I lie down at night: my shortcomings. Or the things my mother will ask me later about the books I have and haven't read.

But tonight, I can hardly remember what I read. Because I can't stop thinking about you, and the night I got to run my hands through your hair.

I've never met a more loyal friend. I've never met a more brilliant, beautiful girl. And you have no idea, because you're not even watching yourself. You didn't look at a reflective surface once in twenty-four hours, but I watched you check to be sure Rora was okay a hundred times.

Your wit, your mind—Mercury suits you. And I'm here on Mars, with my squad, where I belong. And it defies everything I've ever been taught to wish things were different. Everything that's protected us these hundreds of years.

But I couldn't help thinking that tonight would have been better if you were here. And I didn't want to go to sleep without telling you.

I hope I see you soon.

Amir

Making no sound, I slide down the wall between the shelves and read the letter again and again. *I didn't want to go to sleep without telling you.*

My gaze slides away as I imagine Amir last night. Sitting beside a fire, book in hand.

Until I'd sat beside him and he'd set the book down. Because he would have.

No one has ever made it so difficult for me to deflect attention. No one has ever made me feel so specifically noticed. The thought of his eyes on me sends a shiver over my skin.

I imagine him next to me, so close to my side that I can feel his shoulder rise and fall with his breath. So close that if he touched my hand, no one would see.

I imagine being the thing that finally breaks his calm.

Then I remember again what Baldassare said the other day. *I'm more curious about what the royal family thinks of another Portinari girl befriending their son, given what happened last time.*

Does he mean Beatrice's edict, or something else?

I come back to myself and fold the note back up. Then unfold it, reread it, fold it again. I drum my fingers on the ground, restless.

A week ago, a note like this would have been my starting pistol— my cue to run away. I might have denied ever getting it.

It's so full of feeling. It's so deeply sincere. But strangely, I don't feel like bolting.

Stranger still, it's as if even spheres apart, Amir and I are in the same place. As if, in the perfect quiet of his mind, he is asking the same questions I am.

My hands are trembling when I push myself up and get back to work.

A few minutes' search finds an annotated copy of the Kepler book where it should be. I flip it open, and when I come to a chart on the musical ranges of each planet, alongside their sizes and angular velocities, I jot it all down on the back of Amir's note. But suddenly, the pen stops in my hand.

I'm almost finished copying the chart. But my mind is blank.

I can't read the table in the book or on my own paper. I can't wrap my thoughts around what I was just about to write.

It defies any attempt to describe it in words. Because that is what it is: an utter failure of words. Babel.

I clamber to my feet, clutching the bookcase, panic swelling inside me. Two boys and a girl across the aisle gape, their mouths working but making no sound.

Like startled prey, I sprint away from them, tearing around corners, knocking volumes off the shelves. A tall girl slams into me and she doesn't apologize, doesn't say she's sorry, because she can't. She gives an animal howl and pushes past me.

I look down again at the paper clutched in my hand. Amir's note is on one side, the table on the other.

I can see it. But I can't read it.

The letters remain in their right places but I can't make any sense of them and it is the single most frightening thing that's ever happened to me. I feel like I'm having a stroke, but I know that's not what's going on.

What's going on right now is what's been happening over and over across the spheres. This is the evidence of the error in their music. The product of their creaking disrepair. Only this time, something is about to break.

Screams rise as I race into the reading room where quiet hovered not five minutes before. The shrieks aren't words; they're feral, formless, void of meaning. I dash between tables, catching my hips and thighs on corners and chairbacks, colliding with other students in robes, until finally I find Major.

I grab at him and he seizes my hand, both of us horrified, both trying to speak to one another. But the sounds are babble. Major talks at me, and I respond, and we're yelling over one another, twin fountains of senseless sound.

My skull throbs. I summon words—*you, me, sit, floor*—but they don't come, and I'm so scared. I slide down a panel between shelves and Major crumples beside me on the carpet, and neither of us tries to speak again until it passes.

And after fifteen or so minutes, it does pass. The chaos fades like a migraine, leaving me drained in its wake, tears streaming out of my eyes. Major crawls toward me and wraps me in a hug, limbs shaking as Mercury's song buzzes around us, searing and aching and too loud in my brain.

"We have to get out of here. Somewhere we can think clearly," I say, when I dare to speak again. "This is it, Major—we may not have much longer. Whatever's wrong out in the spheres, we have to figure it out now, before things get worse."

"They already have," he gasps, blue eyes tight with fear. "Two minutes after you walked away, emergency texts appeared. Quetzalcoatl and Helios just—their islands just dropped where they hung in the sky. I've been trying to text my mother but I haven't gotten anything back."

My whole body is shaking. "I'm so sorry."

If Major were Amir or Rora, he would collect himself. He would tell me now is not the time to take risks, that we should sit tight and wait for orders.

But he's Major, and he's like me. Nothing matters more than his people. His family.

"Where can we go?" I ask him.

He presses his palms into his eyes, looking as wrung out as I feel.

Then he drops his hands. "The introduction."

"What?" My voice comes out in a rasp.

"Just—here." Weak and hollow as fever patients, we hoist one another up and stagger back to the table where Major left the book he was reading. *The Settling of the Spheres, Volume III.*

He flips through the pages, broad hands trembling so hard I'm afraid he might rip them. "There!" he gasps, slamming the book open. He points to the passage I showed him just a couple of days ago, the one I've nearly memorized.

> *The party from Siena only briefly visited dark, distant Inferno's belt. Itzcoatl's party built a small settlement around a monument on Pluto, calling it Teopanzolco; but few would reside there, though many would visit to clear their minds with the songs of Stellare and the Primum Movens beyond.*

"*To clear their minds,*" Major says. "That's it. That's where we've got to go."

"The edge of the spheres?" I whisper. "Are you sure?"

Inferno. The sphere farthest from the sun, farthest from the center. The sphere that truly governs Scorpio—that would rule Amir, were Mars not the more acceptable place to belong.

Rora told us on Jupiter that she heard songs emanating from each of us. Somehow, I know that Amir's song is what clears my thoughts when we're together.

If I can't be with him right now, I can at least have his music.

I nod to Major.

"Inferno," I agree. "Let's go."

1287

JUPITER MADE SCHOLARS and celebrants of them all. But after six weeks in the court of al-Radi, Marco could remain no longer.

"We must press on," he told Beatrice and Dante one night when they were alone. He paced like a caged animal in their sumptuous quarters, staring out the screened window at the tossing night sea, as if to fling himself on its waves might provide some relief.

Beatrice had befriended and learned much from King al-Radi and Prince Syed and their court's scholars; she did not yet wish to leave. But Polo was her friend, too, and she could not win her happiness at the expense of his misery.

"A few more days, to make our goodbyes," Beatrice finally said, looking first at Marco and then at Dante. Dante nodded, just once, expression encouraging. She took her leave then, contemplating preparations for their departure and resolving not to burden Polo with her own sadness.

"Will she be all right, you think?" Marco asked, after the door had shut behind her.

"The bean counters and fortune-tellers will miss her," Dante said, a hard edge to his tone. Marco arched his eyebrows, and Dante waved a hand, schooling his expression; he had no wish to tell his friend that three of the king's astronomers had left in the middle of his poetry recitation that afternoon—to meet Beatrice, as he had later learned. "She will be fine," he said more evenly. "She wants to see what lies beyond as much as any of us."

Marco nodded. "You know her best," he finally said. "I am sure you are right."

Five days later, King al-Radi, Syed, and a dozen of his other ministers escorted them and their horses and wagons beyond the city gates. All twenty-seven scholars from Siena and Suvd Uls would depart, none remaining.

Beatrice was the last to step with them onto the sand.

"Thank you for your hospitality, Your Majesty," she said, taking one last glance at the citadel at his back. "I could never have imagined such a place existed, and I am the happier and wiser for knowing."

"Any of you are always welcome," said King al-Radi, ever gracious.

Prince Syed bowed slightly to Beatrice. "Ma'a as-salama, ya sadiqati." *Go in peace, oh my friend.*

But she shook her head, smiling. "No, no. Arrivederci." *Until we meet again.*

Deeper they roved within the known heavens. Dante felt himself as relieved as Polo, but he was not sorry they did not stay long in Saturn's sphere. The gray planet they found calm, sober, and utterly empty, and no sooner had they conjured an island upon which to stand than a mountain rose above it and snow began to fall.

Dante wondered if the snow might be the incarnation of Beatrice's loneliness at departing the court. But he told himself it could not be so. All the same, four days later, they moved on, seeking more comfortable climes.

But past Saturn they came to parts unknown.

Al-Radi's astronomers had confirmed to Beatrice that a pale, strange blue planet lay just beyond Saturn, the most distant planet known to Earth. They did not expect, though, to meet a foreign body in its sphere.

Beatrice recognized it at once. Knew it by the name she had given it in a moment alone in Hermes.

Chiron.

It appeared with no warning, shrieking high over their heads, careering back and forth against the aether, which transformed from incorporeal substance to brittle crystal in an instant. The horses bucked and screamed. The mere sight of it left Dante sick with terror, and its sight was not the worst of it.

Chiron's song was agony. It spoke of shame, of pain, of humiliation.

Marco stood frozen as it ripped overhead, for once unable to move. Bice crossed herself. Dante shut his eyes and gathered Beatrice to his chest, pretending he did so for her safety, pretending he was not clutching her like a talisman of light against the dark. And though the sphere healed quickly enough from Chiron's rampage, the cracks sealing in the briefly crystallized aether before it grew immaterial once more, the comet left a burned, frosted path behind.

Dante saw each of the others shiver as they crossed its trail. But he could not know as their robes or shoes or fingertips brushed the damaged aether that they each pushed down a rising private shame, a whispering secret fear, just as he did.

RORA
35

WHEN COMMANDER BAO makes his rounds the next morning, I'm the only one who wakes. I squint against the rising sun, blinding against the white felt sides of the gers.

But I realize at once what woke me, and it isn't the commander's footfalls. I feel it. A change in the music.

Something's wrong.

Mars is hammering harder and faster than ever and its major chords have slid into harsh minors. The same eerie rhythm pounds in my heart and for one blinding second, I am terrified that I have done this. That somehow, my coming—my secret, my ability as an amplifier—has done this.

"Where are the sixteens?" the commander barks. I meet his eyes, shaking my head. I have no idea where they are. Silence is his only other answer.

"Amir!" Commander Bao calls sharply. A few feet to my right, Amir jerks awake.

"Sir. Yes. What is it, sir?" He stumbles over his words, wiping his eyes.

"Where are the sixteens camped?"

"Um. About half a mile east. Along the south canyon wall. I think." Amir blinks hard, scrubbing his hands over his cheeks. "No, I'm sorry, that's not right. Did you want squad one, two, or three?"

Bao's voice is crisp. "Whichever is closest."

"Across the way, then," Amir says, pointing at another camp of sleepers fifty yards off.

Commander Bao strides toward them, not hesitating. "Squad sixteen-two! Everyone up."

It doesn't take any more than that. They're awake instantly, all thirty or so trainees shucking off sleeping bags and staggering to their feet. "Where are we going, sir?" asks a petite Black girl. Her eyes are barely open, but she's looping her braids out of her face and packing up her gear.

"The western barrier."

"The barrier?" I turn to Amir, frowning. Dread is a slow, warning drip inside me as the music around us pounds feverishly on. "Does it normally have to be patched twice a week?"

"No." Amir's staring at Bao, expression unreadable. He pushes up off his knees and strides toward the camp of sixteens.

Mars's song still beats roughly on the air. Instinct tells me to stay back—no, to hide. Because whatever's coming, it's not good. But I follow Amir.

"Commander Bao, wasn't the barrier just seen to?" he asks. "Did the fifteens—was there some sort of mistake?"

Another camp is rousing nearby. At Amir's question, one of them lifts his chin and crosses his arms—a blond white boy, one who'd gone to help the commander that first day. "Why would you think we made a mistake?"

Amir frowns, scratching his cheek. "I don't. I mean, I wouldn't. It's just we don't usually have to—"

"But of course, you do." The boy stalks toward Amir, gold hair gleaming, teeth flashing like a warning. "Of course, we couldn't do anything right. We're just fifteens. And none of us are the son of Queen Inara, heir to the throne and the spheres. Why could *any* of us be counted on?"

"I didn't say that." Amir stretches his hands out, cautious. He glances back to me—not to one of his squadmates, but to me—and the warning klaxon blares again through my thoughts.

The music on the air is angry. Defensive. Aggressive. This is larger than me, than whatever strength I have as an amplifier.

Something is *wrong*. The kind of wrong we've seen raise blinding snowstorms, open cracks in the ground, carve irreparable holes in the aether.

I've let my own comfort with Mars's music lull me into forgetfulness about the danger out in the spheres, the conjunction that looms between Jupiter and Saturn. But no more.

The pretty Black girl from the squad of sixteens speaks up again, hoisting her pack. "Well, you didn't have to say it. Your criticism was implied. Next you're going to say my squad can't be trusted with the job. And we can. We're just as responsible as you are. You're only a year ahead of us."

The blond boy from the fifteens surges to the center of the canyon. "Are you saying you can do what we can't?" he demands. "Commander Atlacoya told our squad just the other day she hasn't seen motivation like ours in a group of fifteens for *years*." He glances back at his squadmates and they nod in agreement. They're standing close together, sidling up behind their spokesman, all wearing the same expression—offended, angry, combative. And then everyone's shouting at once.

"So you fifteens can do what—"

"You're reading things into—"

"I'm not reading into anything, you just don't have the training—"

I need a moment of sanity. A second of eye contact with Briony or Tishala or someone who can hear what's happening. Glancing back to our camp, I find both girls and the rest of our squad are already crossing the canyon floor to stand behind us, pressing us toward the fray.

Nobody's avoiding my gaze intentionally, but no one meets it. It's as though I'm the only one who can hear the change in the music, who can feel Mars's iron rhythm hammering rigid, brutal, too harsh, too fierce. *Wrong wrong wrong wrong.*

My heart is beating too fast, like a bomb ticking down.

I'm not sure who throws the first punch.

But the next blows follow so close on its heels, it's clear everyone was ready to start something. Blood and dust fly and an elbow hits my cheekbone and I'm reaching for Tishala and—

"STOP!" Commander Bao's voice cuts through the furor, sharp and clean. Everyone freezes in place, shoulders heaving, palms pressed to cuts and bruises.

"Back up, all of you," he bellows. "Fifteens, you did not make a mistake. Go get ready for training. Sixteen-two, you're with me. Seventeen-one and seventeen-three, afternoon activities are canceled. Report to Command after lunch."

The squads stare around at one another, still panting, eyeing each other in confusion. "Go!" the commander barks, and we all limp back to our individual camps. Everyone but me.

307

I back toward my squad, but I can't look away from Bao's face. Because I see anger in his eyes, but I see something else there, too. That moment of sanity I was looking for.

It scares me more than I expect it to.

The commander meets my gaze, and there is fear on his face. Because he heard the music go wrong. He heard what I heard, too.

CLAUDIA
36

TEOPANZOLCO, INFERNO

WE BREAK AWAY from Mercury for Inferno, the sphere scattered with Pluto and other dwarf planets. Its song is an immediate release.

Inferno's song isn't like any I've heard on our travels so far—a slow, gravelly bass, with something cold and clear shimmering above it. Though Pluto's surface is a sunless, frozen mud flat that's maybe the ugliest place I've ever seen, I want to starfish on the ground and drink the music in.

Some of the glitter had rubbed off Mercury's song on our second visit to Hermes, but I'd never hated its music the way I did in the few moments after the words came back. For fifteen minutes, the planet's bright, buzzing music was grating, formless, uncontrolled; and even when the order and the sense returned, the noise was unbearable. It made me want to be anywhere else, somewhere completely outside myself.

It made me wish for Amir. And this place—this place that truly governs his sign, Scorpio—feels like him.

I search the muddy plain. A single pyramid of gray-brown stone rises in the distance. "This way," I say to Major. I don't stop when we reach its base, though I can't see the top and its steps are narrow and slick.

"What are you going to do when you get up there?" Major pants as we climb, expression grim. I know he's thinking of his parents and his sisters on Venus. They haven't texted him back since he got word that Quetzalcoatl fell.

I swallow. "Not sure."

With Major so worried, I can't bring myself to tell him that something about the sky here calls to me. That I want to stand as near it as I can, want to strain my ears to catch the high, silvery top note that seems to soar over the sphere's calming, low bass.

But when we reach the top, we find we're not alone.

Dr. Qureshi has beaten us here.

She wanders around the seamlessly fitted stones of the pyramid's top, a song hovering soft on her breath. Its notes are varied, ranging from low to high, and she repeats it as she circles.

Major and I watch as something awakens slowly before us, like city lights at the end of the day. Like neon signs buzzing to life, like apartment lights flipping on as people arrive home or lampposts at dusk.

A model of the spheres materializes, hovering translucent at shoulder height. When Dr. Qureshi spots us through the shimmering field, she lifts a hand, looking resigned.

"You're supposed to be on Mercury," Dr. Qureshi says, watching the planets drift through the air as I come to stand beside her. But there's no judgment in her tone. "And *he* was supposed to return to court. You're lucky Baldassare texted me, or I'd have been worried."

I reach into my bag for one of the two books I took from her desk and hold up *Beatrice and Her Companions*. "Mercury was hit again. I asked Major to take me somewhere I could think."

"Then you came to the right place." I follow her stare to the dark sky around us, to the endless expanse of icy mud. "When Itzcoatl led the Mexica astronomers to the spheres, they felt a kinship between this place and their god of night, Tezcatlipoca." She pauses. "But above the music of this sphere, they could hear the music of another. That's why they built Teopanzolco."

Major comes to our side. "What's why they built this?"

Dr. Qureshi's gaze darts skyward. "You can hear them from here," she says simply. "The outermost spheres—the Stellare and Primum Movens. The stars, and the Prime Mover. So they built the pyramid to be nearer to the sky. Just like on Earth, humans can't help reaching upward when they catch glimpses of what lies beyond."

Thinking back to Beatrice's notes, I recall that Ptolemy identified the spheres that lay beyond Inferno, though no one—not Beatrice, nor anyone before or after—could suggest how to cross them. Stellare was populated with untouchable stars, and the Prime Mover was whatever lay beyond it all. Some called it *the Unmoved Mover*. Dante called it *the Love that moves the sun and the other stars.*

This is a listening kind of place. But is it because Inferno's song quiets the mind, or because that other music somehow feels like the only thing worth listening to?

I shake myself. Whichever it is, I have to do what I came to do.

"Major, can I borrow your pitch pipe?" He nods and pauses scribbling another text to his mother to pass it to me.

I'm grateful he's here. It feels like good luck to have a friend here in the dark.

Because it should really be Rora attempting this. Rora, who feels the music in a way I can't even understand.

But Rora's not here. I have to believe I can do this on my own.

I force myself to breathe as I cross into Dr. Qureshi's model, slipping Amir's text out of my pocket, turning it over to the chart that I copied. It's almost complete, lacking just the last details on Inferno's music.

I begin at the center.

Earth lies at the heart of things, its song round and harmonic, as known to me as the sounds of my own house. I've never listened out for it before, but I can hear it now.

Behind my shut eyes I see the rest of the songs like plotted equations, unique in their rise and fall: the warped, wavering notes of the moon; Mercury a sharp, twinned rise and fall like an absolute value equation; Venus, a gently rising curve, exponential in its abundance. All of them are midtones between the chasm-deep song of Inferno and the high, lucid notes of the Unmoved Mover and the stars beyond.

I spiral through the model, arms outstretched, trailing my hands through the air. And as I pass through each sphere, I play the note for every planet on Major's pitch pipe and compare it to the music around me.

Without Rora's ability to intuit the rightness or wrongness of the music, I feel blind—but I have to trust myself. My process.

Music is an aesthetic expression, but it's also just math. Math is how Beatrice crafted her path to the spheres. It's how my nonna studies the universe. It's how I reason and make decisions.

This can work my way, too.

None of the songs emanating from the planets in the model are quite in tune with the calibrating notes from the pitch pipe, and it occurs to me that the model must represent the spheres and their music as they truly, presently are. But none of them are quite wrong enough to give me real pause. None of them are wrong enough to seem like causes—just effects.

And then, suddenly, I hear a false note in the symphony.

I glance up sharply at Major. He's been checking for texts from his parents every few seconds, but he watches me now, alert. "What is it?"

I listen for a bar or two, then play the note again.

There. It's wrong. The sound is so corrupted I can't believe I didn't hear it before.

"Yes," Dr. Qureshi says to me when she sees where I stand. "There."

I cast about and find her seated on the stones, her eyes despairing. She looks a bit like my mother did the night she and Dad told Jack he had to go. She looks the way I feel.

"You see," Dr. Qureshi says. "You see my problem."

I've told myself not to cling too tightly to any one hypothesis. Now I have to remind myself not to dismiss a result simply because I don't like it.

I've located the break in the harmony. And it upends everything.

But I push my feelings aside. I have to work out my proof, the equation that will confirm what my ears already know.

I take out Amir's note again, brace it against the hard backing of *Beatrice and Her Companions*, find a clear spot to write.

Pythagoras and Kepler agreed that the music made by the planets was the product of their sizes, their speeds, and their distances from one another, as well as their spiritual and astrological traits. It's strange, archaic math I'm playing with, here at the edge of the worlds, and I have little to go on to assess how far the corruption of the song has progressed besides skimmed theories, hasty estimates, and my own imperfect human hearing.

It's all looser than I'd like. It all demands I trust myself more than feels wise.

But Beatrice made her way here after barely a year of study. She forged her own keys to escape a world that didn't believe in her right to open doors at all.

When I'm done, my calculations crowd around my hand-drawn chart, and I have my proof.

The sphere out of tune belongs to Saturn.

"It can't be." Frustration draws out my words as I rise and cross the model. "It can't be Saturn and Jupiter in conjunction. All the data defies it. And wouldn't Jupiter be out of tune as well?"

"I know," she says dully. "I knew the Conjunction wasn't the problem before I ever left for al-Mushtari. I don't understand it, either."

I blink at her. "You knew?" I demand. "So why didn't you say something?"

"Of course I did." Dr. Qureshi's tone sharpens. "Claudia, the spheres operated harmoniously for four hundred years before Beatrice arrived and determined that the signs and the songs needed to be excluded from one another. Inara and I have been studying the earliest principles of the al-Kindi court for almost two years now, and we were going to speak up when we were fully prepared, and not before—you saw how that council behaved," she adds in an ominous voice. "But the need for exclusion? We haven't found any thinking to that effect before the Italians arrived."

"I know," I say softly.

Now it's her turn to be surprised. Dr. Qureshi stops short, confronting me with her clear, dark gaze. "You do?"

"Yes." I flush, choosing my words carefully. "Earth has seen falling sea levels and shrinking mountain peaks just like the spheres, but it only began six weeks ago there. I wondered why, when the spheres have been suffering for six *months*. Then it occurred to me that people of every sign live on Earth. All the songs are present there." I swallow hard. "I thought, too, about how Venus and Jupiter cured Rora of Saturn, even though she doesn't belong to either planet."

Across the model, Major's eyes widen. He shakes his head at me, and I remember him warning me on Mercury not to give voice to thoughts like this.

But Dr. Qureshi started it. And besides—this is for him, too.

"Thinking about all that, I wondered if the spheres had the power to balance or correct one another. If multiple songs and signs in one place could be protective, not dangerous." I hesitate. "And no matter where I looked, I couldn't find any analysis—any real mathematical explanation—from Beatrice that contradicted that."

Major crosses the model, his chest rising and falling heavily. "What are you saying?"

"I looked," I say simply. "And I think Beatrice was wrong."

I'd planned to tell him my suspicions after I'd finished checking a few references today. But I never got the chance.

Major studies me, a dozen emotions flickering across his face— hope, doubt, desperation, resignation, and hope again, tender as a seedling. Out beyond the model, I can feel Dr. Qureshi watching me in disbelief.

"Regardless," she finally says. "Regardless of what may or may not have protected Earth or exacerbated the issue in the spheres, we haven't identified what's happened to Saturn. What, if not the Conjunction, would have changed its music."

"I know," I say again, turning away from Major, frustration sinking in once more.

You came here to think, I tell myself. *So think.*

I shut my eyes to both of them. I still all the thoughts buzzing

Gemini-fleet through my mind.

For long moments, I don't think; I listen.

Saturn's shape and size and melancholy nature say its music should be deep, low, slow, philosophical. But the model tells another story.

Notes that should be parabolic swoops balanced by gentle rises are catastrophic dives; those that should be steady run jagged, chaotic as the storm in Kronos, as the babel in Hermes. I heard that same chaos in Jack's voice, loud and wild as he fought with my parents over being sent away. I heard it in Rora's voice the night she was attacked.

I think suddenly of the council room on Jupiter only a few days ago. Meeting Dr. Qureshi and Queen Inara. Their conjuring Rora's star chart, all of it so entirely unexpected and opaque to me. The conjunction of Mars and Saturn, the quincunx between Mars and—

Chiron is a harbinger of pain.

I stop short.

Chiron, manifest in Rora's chart. Chiron, and their shock at its presence.

I still my thoughts, work back to the beginning. Think of Rora as my microcosm.

"Chiron," I whisper. "Could Chiron have something to do with all this?"

Even in the dark, I see Dr. Qureshi pale.

She strides into the model, toward an asteroid belt between Saturn and Uranus. Her eyes are closed and she is listening. But I've already moved on.

While the professor is distracted, I play a sharp, high note on the pitch pipe, focusing my intentions on my skull, my brain, the very synapses firing inside it. Dr. Qureshi doesn't look up as my own star chart appears over my head.

"What are you doing?" Major whispers, looking from the blank page in his hand to the silver rings that graze my hair. But I've found what I was afraid of.

I've found the key to a door I don't want to open.

I dispel the chart before Dr. Qureshi can see it and return my focus to her, watching her face for the shift that will tell me she hears something wrong. But it never comes. Instead, I see a different change in her features.

Her search hasn't turned up a problem of presence, but of absence.

"He is not where he should be," she says slowly. "Chiron dwells between Saturn and Uranus, and he is missing from his place."

I wish I were surprised. But I'm not. Because when I searched my chart just now, I found exactly what I was afraid I would.

Major's rushing through the model, asking rapid-fire questions of Dr. Qureshi. I'm still, but my mind is racing.

If Chiron is at fault for the havoc that has settled over the spheres, and Chiron appears in Rora's star chart—I don't even have to think about what to do next.

"I have to get to her," I say. "I have to get to Mars."

Dr. Qureshi dismisses the model and texts the king and queen, and Major and I hurry down the pyramid after her. "When Helios and Quetzalcoatl sank, their advisors feared al-Mushtari might be next, so they sent Their Majesties to Ulaan Garig for safety. We will meet them there."

Major grimaces, and as we scramble down the steps, he checks the sheet of paper in his pocket yet again. "My parents!" he gasps, stopping short.

"His family lives in Quetzalcoatl," I explain to Dr. Qureshi. "Major, are they all right?" He nods, still scribbling.

We give him a few minutes to write back and forth to his mother, to confirm that all of them are safe. While we wait, I try to focus on what's to come. But again and again, I find my attention straying toward the sky and the music that hangs there.

The high, pure tones of the Stellare and the Unmoved Mover are a thousand shimmering points on a scatterplot, piano-bright and harp-clear, both melody and percussion. An overwhelming presence, and not one simple to grasp. But what sends a shock through my brain as I listen is this: unlike every other song—every other piece of the harmony of the spheres—their music seems undamaged.

I don't know what's protecting their melody from the ruin Chiron has exacted everywhere else. But when I try to hear it the way Rora would—when I lift my face to the glittering sky and try to listen with more than just my ears—I *feel* something.

The song is almost impossible to describe, except to say that it feels a bit like mornings at my house used to feel, and it brings to mind words I once heard from a priest.

It feels like being seen and known. Like viewing my own life from a great height, and yet not disappearing or being lost.

Most of all, I know that having heard this music once, I'll never forget it. That I'll be just a little different from now on, because wherever I go, I'll be listening to hear it again.

It gives me hope.

I try to carry it with me as we leave Inferno.

1287

WHEN CHIRON HAD fled, their company staggered on to the cold, strange planet the color of an aquamarine. Beatrice and her magicians tugged their robes tighter around themselves and conjured an island upon which to stand, as they had before. Then they conjured another, and another, until they had a constellation of firm spaces in the clouds.

They arrived shaking in fear, but the fear soon left them.

The planet made geniuses of them.

They did not talk endlessly and spiritedly, as they had on the sun, or sink into sober philosophizing, as they had on Saturn. Instead they drifted absently, thinking and breathing in the misty air. But though their mouths stilled, their hands and their minds worked furiously.

The sun rose, and the sun set. The horses never quite seemed to settle. But beneath a sky the blue-green of the Mediterranean, though paler and colder than that sea had ever been, the humans worked.

Absorbed by the planet's weird music, Beatrice spent hours conducting experiments. Fixed on no one subject, her work wandered between meteorology and mathematics and physics, inspired by the whim of the moment and wild bursts of curiosity.

She had seen as in a mirror, darkly, on Earth; now she saw clearly. She saw all.

Classical astrologers had placed her sign of Aquarius under the reign of Saturn. But Beatrice had known since she had seen this strange planet from Hermes—had known beyond doubt—that she and the rest of her sign belonged here.

While Beatrice experimented, Marco directed the magicians as they built their newest city. Sweat misted on his brow as he raced back and forth between islands, calling out orders to the enchanters and seeming to grasp ideas as if they were falling bolts of lightning. The city rose toward the aquamarine sky, growing taller and more towering than any they had built, gleaming like so many razor-edged knives.

Beatrice called the city Acuto—sharp, keen, acute.

And Dante—while the others chased genius like a comet in the heavens, Dante disregarded them, bearing down with unshakable focus. He began to sculpt into his own image the universe he'd witnessed.

Dante began to write.

ULAAN GARIG, MARS

WE SET OUT through the spheres again, and I can't help the startled glance I shoot at Major at their sound, at their groaning and
creaking like ice threatening to crack on a lake. But I only clutch my
coat tighter around me, hurrying after him and Dr. Qureshi. *Doesn't
matter, doesn't matter, doesn't matter.*

Rora needs me. And the rest of the spheres need what we know.

Mars's music confronts us as we enter its sphere, landing on its
surface outside a massive iron gate. Dr. Qureshi offers a password
and accepts a letter from the sentry, and we're inside.

"Their Majesties are at Command," she says, scanning the note.
"We'll head directly there."

I barely hear the professor. I'm distracted by the new, thudding
pressure of this song, by the high red canyon walls all around, like in
the deserts out West; except this sky is a mottled topaz where ours
is an infinite blue.

We cross the canyon packed with kids and teenagers and meet
the king and queen outside a tent the size of a single-family home.
Midmorning light glows off its white felt exterior, its red carved
door; I catch glimpses of green-and-gold brocade on its walls inside.

Dr. Qureshi kisses the queen's cheeks, and Queen Inara presses a hand to the professor's shoulder. "You said you had news. Did you solve it, Nadeema?"

"*Claudia* solved it," Dr. Qureshi says adamantly. She hesitates, glancing down at me. "Inara, she'd come to the same conclusion we had. The exclusion is only exacerbating the damage to the spheres."

"And the source of the problem?" Queen Inara presses.

"Chiron." The word bursts out of me like poison expressed from a wound. "Chiron, in Saturn's sphere."

The queen presses a hand to her chest, looking faint, then steadies herself. "It makes sense," she finally says, exchanging a glance with King Sameer. "Given what it's all come to."

I want to ask what she means. But before I can, Queen Inara turns on me, spearing me with her gaze. "Whatever else you've learned, you have to keep it to yourself," she says in a low voice. "Exclusion has been law in the spheres for centuries."

I stiffen. "But don't people need to—?"

"In my time," the queen says evenly. "When *I* am ready."

For a long moment, I stand very still. I don't fidget as I consider.

I think of Beatrice, of her influence on this very queen's ancestors. Of how assured Beatrice must have been, and how much harm she may have inflicted in her certainty.

I've walked a little way down the path Beatrice trod before me. But I don't want to go everywhere she did. I don't want to be a guest shaking the foundation of someone else's home.

I don't want to make decisions that are not mine to make.

I nod. "When you think the time is right, Your Majesty. I should warn you, though," I can't help adding. "I think Amir may already have ideas. Ideas that didn't come from me."

"That doesn't surprise me." Queen Inara's voice is soft. "Watching Amir suffer is what made me question the exclusion in the first place."

My jaw drops open. I want to ask her a dozen more questions, but King Sameer cuts in. "After the competition," he insists.

Dr. Qureshi frowns. "Competition?"

"The storm on Kronos has progressed," Queen Inara answers, and I remember what she said only a moment ago. That Chiron being responsible made sense, *given what it's all come to.*

"And Commander Bao and Commander Atlacoya couldn't choose who to send." King Sameer hesitates. "They're all so young. I still worry this is a mistake." He shakes his head and his eyes drift closed, and all I see is Amir in three decades, wearing the weight of worries and a kingdom. Then he straightens. "We should go. They'll have started by now."

Dr. Qureshi glances around the camp. "One of the training centers?"

"No," says King Sameer. "Farther."

It must be the song on the air, the music that urges me to jump first and think later. Because when the queen conjures a portal, I follow her through it without question.

RORA
38

COMMANDER BAO WON'T let me compete, and I'm not surprised. But I still feel a pang as squad seventeen-three gets ready around me.

We met at Command after lunch, per his orders. No one knew why we were there. But he and Commander Atlacoya were waiting.

I hadn't understood what was happening as the commanders traced coordinates in the dirt, conjured a portal. Surely we weren't leaving. Surely it wasn't safe yet to travel. But this portal hadn't led us out into the spheres.

"Competitions are normal," Briony reassures me as I stare up at the mountain. "We do this kind of thing all the time."

We're near the center of the canyon, standing before a mountain so high that the caves and switchback paths and twisting cedar trees at its top seem to brush the shimmering cat's-eye barrier above. One side is a sheer cliff.

Commander Bao didn't explain why we were here. Instead, he gave us three rules: that squad seventeen-one and seventeen-three would compete against one another. That whichever squad met three challenges and rescued his iron wristband from the summit would win. And that no magic was to be used until the third challenge.

Around me, both squads prepare. The air is electric, humming with the same aggressive energy that surged through Mars's music this morning. It snaps and pops, anticipatory and confrontational as they smear themselves with paint, tape up their hands and feet, check their climbing gear.

I don't know how I know. But there's nothing normal about this day.

My heart won't sit still. I pace as the paint dries on my arms. Seventeen-one, our opponents, have daubed themselves with indigo to distinguish themselves; we, seventeen-three, wear green.

Green for permanence and planted feet, Amir said; *hic manebimus optime*. Baatar wears it on his palms. Tishala's smeared it in long, graceful-looking lines down her biceps. Briony's covered in splashes of the color; some has migrated into her long red braids. She was the one who insisted I put on paint, too, even though I'm not competing.

They're all buzzing. Eager to begin.

I want us to win. But somehow, I'm afraid of what will happen if we do. And too soon, the squads are forming two lines, one hundred yards of desert away from the foot of the mountain.

I stand alone, heart thumping in my chest.

"Seventeen-one," Commander Atlacoya calls. "State your aim."

The leader of the opposing squad shouts something about persisting and not quitting; through the language charm, I recognize the words as Mongolian—Baatar's native language. The squad echoes him in chorus, their voices rumbling like rocks in a landslide.

Bao nods and turns to Amir. "Seventeen-three, state your aim."

"*Hic manebimus optime*," Amir shouts.

"*Hic manebimus optime*," our squad calls back.

Commander Atlacoya's hand in the air becomes a fist. I watch her, holding my breath.

Atlacoya brings her arm down. The two squads of seventeens take off across the canyon floor, dust flying beneath their feet as they converge on the mountain.

At the base of the cliff, Amir reaches for something small and white pinned to the stone. He rips it away, unfolds it, reads it aloud.

Is it a riddle? Is it instructions? I can't hear. I don't know. But in seconds, both squads are pouring up the cliffside.

They are quicker than seems possible, picks and clips and taped hands and feet finding their way into crevices and crannies. Where I twisted at the end of my rope in training, their bodies are strong and certain.

I wonder for a moment if it hurts to dig their feet and fingers into the rocks, but I push the thought away. Pain is an old friend to everyone here.

Still, my palms sweat just watching them climb.

I trust their skill and their training. But there is so much air and so little else between their bodies and the hard canyon floor.

I wish I could be up there with them instead of safe on the ground. Mars's song is hammering at me and the green paint is drying taut on my skin and I am completely useless here on the sidelines.

Back and forth, I pace. My squad is a third of the way up the cliff. Tishala and Amir are doing all right, but I gasp as Briony misses a handhold.

I've left the commanders behind and made my way to the base of the cliffs before I realize I've moved at all.

"Come on," I hiss to myself, frustrated.

Isolation threatens to settle cold and gray in my stomach. I can't go to them. I can't protect them. I can't fight for them. I'm trapped here, at the edge of the competition.

And then I remember what I've been doing on the sidelines all along.

A week ago, I would've felt too shy to do anything but stand and watch for fear someone could end up watching *me*. Even now, I don't know what moves me to practice the kata Briony and Tishala taught me. I only know, somehow, that I need to be part of their efforts.

A kata is a drill, a choreographed form of punches and blocks and kicks students learn for practice. The girls taught me an easy one, one they learned when they were young. It moves in a circle, a symbol of the spheres, a symbol of their power.

If the squad's going to work, then I have to work, too.

Restless, I begin.

A little capoeira to distract your opponent, Tishala said as she taught me the opening steps to the kata just a few days ago. Red sand and pebbles scuff my soles as I shuffle right and left, lunging and dodging, loosening my joints.

Neither Commander Bao nor Commander Atlacoya pays me any attention. Their eyes are fixed on the mountain, on the squads climbing its sheer face. They are two-thirds of the way up its side.

The kata shifts, drops. *You have to be quick*, I hear Briony say as I crouch low to the ground, shooting forward, reaching behind my invisible opponent's knees like a desert mirage.

But I am the only person at the base of this mountain. I'm competing against myself, competing alongside my squad.

The kata picks up speed. I punch and block and kick, my heart throbbing—but not a knife in my chest.

I'm nearly stopped short by the realization, and by the one that follows on its heels: my body isn't a traitor to me anymore. My body is my weapon.

Most shocking, most subversive—my body is my friend.

Go, go, GO. Don't stop. My squad has nearly reached the clifftop and I can't see Tishala but I can hear her urging me on back in the training room. *Focus. You can do it, Rora.*

The form turns into a series of kicks and turns, *back, front, side, back, front, side.* Dust rises in the air, iron red like the iron in my blood. I catch glimpses as I rotate—my squadmates hauling themselves over the edge at the cliff's top, their bodies heaving with exhaustion, unhooking themselves from their gear.

My body wants to sag with relief. I don't stop.

I realize, suddenly, that I'm singing.

Beneath the thump of climbing gear discarded and the shouts of my squad and the stamp of horses at the clifftop, my singing is barely audible. But I hear Mars on my voice, Mars in its rise and fall and range and force. Hoofbeats ring through the canyon as the two squads gallop up a treacherous, winding hill.

I am halfway around the mountain when the dust storm begins.

Red clouds billow on the air, choking me, blinding me. My heart plummets.

My squad is up there riding blind and I can't do a thing about it.

I can't do a thing—except this. I shut my eyes. I don't stop.

Strength in your legs and in your gut, Mars exhorts me. I can't see, but I can tighten my abdomen. Lengthen my legs through the kicks as I turn. Drive my heel out with all the force I can gather up.

And don't forget to gather your voice, Amir had said. *Use it to focus your strength.*

If I can fight hard enough here on the ground, it will keep my squad safe. If I can defeat the invisible enemies who never cease to stalk me, somehow, I can protect my friends.

Mars wraps his melody around me like tower walls. I gather my voice.

"HA!" With every kick, a cry breaks from my chest, the sound of all my strength. Mars is guitar, it's synth, it's bass, it's drums hammering hard as my pulse.

Then the song changes, and the dust storm ceases as abruptly as it began. I open my eyes, scrub my palms over my cheeks. My squad has summited—or I think they have. But then it seems they've found a higher point to ascend.

They disappear. Not around a corner, or into a cave, but into thin air.

My body continues mechanically as my eyes strain after them, unwilling to accept what I've seen.

But I know what's happened. They've passed outside the barrier.

This is the third stage of the competition. And it's taken them outside every semblance of safety.

I want to go to them. I don't know any magic that will protect them from what lies outside. But every muscle in my body strains toward the mountaintop.

Focus, the music reproaches me just as Briony did.

So I do. This is all I can do. I remain within my sphere of control. I pour all my will, all my music, all my desire for their safety into my fight.

I push forward. The drum pounds on, Mars's relentless rhythm, and so do my fists. With every kick and block and punch I gather a cry from the very pit of my stomach and send it onto the air.

BOOM, the drums order. *Forearm block*, my body answers.

BOOM. *Roundhouse kick.*

BOOM. *Side kick.*

My friends are still nowhere to be seen.

I'm frantic with energy, with all my fear for my squadmates. Pebbles scrape my bare feet and my bun has slid down to my neck and Mars still swells in my blood, his music fierce and bombastic and swaggering. I throw my arms forward, throw my body forward with a running kick. Forward, forward, again and again.

I've nearly rounded the mountain.

Gray, treacherous fear tells me *nowhere is safe*, but I refuse to believe it.

This is my planet. These are my friends. I will make space for us, will *make* them safe. *Hic manebimus optime.* I am alive and Mars is singing, singing, singing in my blood.

"HA!" I finish the kata with a block and a cry I feel in my teeth and fingernails. Dust swirls around me. I'm covered in it.

"What are you doing?" A hand seizes my shoulder. I'm facing Commander Bao.

Cheers and shrieks ring out from the mountaintop. Squad seventeen-three pours back through the barrier. Amir brandishes something that flashes silver in the sun.

"YES!" I jerk away from the commander, race a few steps toward the foot of the mountain, throw my fist in the air.

They've done it. They're safe.

"Rora!" But it's not the commander calling.

I turn and Queen Inara is striding toward me, King Sameer and Dr. Qureshi close behind, Commander Atlacoya racing after. What are they all doing here?

"Explain yourself, Rora," the queen demands. Silver beads on her white dress glitter in the strong midday light.

"Explain what?" I'm panting. There's dust in my hair, all over my arms and legs. "I didn't think I'd distract anyone. I just couldn't keep still—"

"Distract?" demands King Sameer. "Couldn't you hear your song? Rora, didn't you see what you were doing?"

"A kata for children?" I ask, helpless.

"This isn't right," Commander Atlacoya snaps. "The rule was no magic until the third stage. We'll need to start again."

Commander Bao throws up his hands. "Atlacoya, they're spent. It wouldn't be the same."

"Tomorrow, then," she presses.

"Tomorrow we leave. It's done." King Sameer pauses. "You wanted the competition to choose its instrument, and it has. Squad seventeen-three has taken the victory."

There is a finality in Amir's father's voice that does nothing to disguise the fear in his eyes.

"Because she turned the tide with her song," Atlacoya says, gesticulating at me, frustration in every line of her face. "Nobody told me she was an amplifier."

"A *what?*" Queen Inara gasps. I scramble for a response.

It never occurred to me my practice on the sidelines would affect the competition's outcome. I had no idea I could amplify the music for my friends through my own intention.

"I wondered how long you'd be able to keep the secret," says another voice from behind the adults. "Honestly, I'm impressed, Ro."

It's that voice that freezes me where I stand. A voice I'd recognize anywhere, on any world.

She's here.

I push past the king and queen and the professor and the commanders and she's here; her coat is muddy and her hair is completely flat but *she's here*. Before Claudia can speak again, my arms are around her.

I remember everything I said to her before we split up. Every unfair judgment, every true thing that could've been said more kindly. Every question that could've come from a place of more trust.

I want to apologize. But first the words won't come, and then they come out in a rush. "You're here," I choke out. Tears hang in my throat. "I'm so glad to see you."

"I'm glad to see you, too." Claudia's voice is muffled as she crushes me in a hug. "I'm . . ."

She breaks off. Neither of us knows what to say.

Not everything is right between us, and some of that's my fault, and I'm going to fix it. But for now, we just hang on to each other. Because this hug is the axis of my entire universe.

Nothing on this planet has called to her. Nothing about this place beckons her.

She's just here. For me.

"Amplifier?" asks Dr. Qureshi. Claudia releases me and begins rapidly to explain, not justifying, not asking forgiveness for the secret we kept. As she speaks, Major steps up beside us.

I want to blush at the memory of my own boldness writing to him last night. But I'm so glad to see him, I can't look away. His blue eyes are lit up like summer bonfires.

"Their having an amplifier changes things," Commander Atlacoya insists again.

But Commander Bao shakes his head. He raises his voice, loud enough to be heard by all the seventeens who stand at the top of the cliff, preparing to rappel down. "We have our victors. We have a squad to send into the fray."

The sounds of celebration peter out. No one moves. No one realized, before, that winning meant anything.

No one but me.

King Sameer's throat bobs, his eyes fixed on his son, standing motionless at the clifftop.

My mouth is suddenly as dry as the dust beneath my feet. "Do you know what's going on?" I ask Claudia. "I know you do. You always do." I count on that. On Claudia being one step ahead of me.

But she shakes her head. Her face is bloodless.

"Squad seventeen-three," says Commander Bao. "You will travel to Kronos, in Saturn's sphere."

"And is she prepared to go with them?" Atlacoya demands, nodding at me. "Their victory is down to her."

Kronos.

Because of me.

I don't understand what's happening, but whatever it is, the knowledge that *this is my fault* sits heavy on my shoulders, sharp in my bones. I reach for Major and Claudia before I realize my hands are moving.

"We'll brief you all shortly," says Queen Inara. "But . . ." She looks to me, questions in her eyes. And I know what I have to do.

I straighten, fix my eyes on the adults looking down at me. "I have thrown myself against the spheres, and I was not the one who broke. I've come to Ulaan Garig to heal, and I've done so." I pause, fight to keep the shaking out of my voice. "I will go with my squad to Kronos."

1287

DANTE WORKED FURIOUSLY, feverishly, obsessively. He had seen the great celestial spheres and he imagined Heaven and Hell and Purgatory after the same fashion, imagined himself led by the great Virgil through winding rings populated with his friends and enemies and acquaintances and heroes.

He had traveled to the spheres for Beatrice. But this work was for him alone.

It would be the making of him.

Pen in hand, Beatrice looked up at Dante from where she'd been scratching out calculations. Her fingers shook with fatigue; she'd been working for hours.

"My head's so clear," she said, voice hoarse. "I haven't rested but I can still think. This place is amazing."

Beatrice paused. When she reached for his hand, Dante let her take it.

Some mixture of pride and trepidation had stopped her on Jupiter. But here, in Acuto, she could be direct. Her thoughts were clear, and so were her words to Dante.

"I want to stay in the heavens forever," Beatrice said to him. "I want us to join King al-Radi's court. We can work with his scholars from here or in al-Mushtari. The others can stay if they wish. We can have everything we've dreamed of."

Dante did not reply. His eyes were dark and full.

Beatrice thought she could read his heart in them.

RORA
39

WE PASS BACK through the portal and make our way to Command.

Mars's song and my own guilt still hammer in my ears. I cling to Claudia, drag at her song, bright and loose and nimble. "Please," I whisper to her, and I have to clear my throat. "Please let's never go four days without talking ever again."

"Never again," she mumbles, and squeezes me tighter as we cross through the ger's red door, only releasing me when Dr. Qureshi summons her. The professor and the queen stand at the head of a yellow-painted table as we file inside, and the king, the commanders, and my squadmates and I sit. Major pulls out the seat beside mine, and when his knee bumps my thigh, my stomach gives an unexpected dip.

Everything around us is wrong. Mars's music, my dread of what I've brought on my squad.

But Major is so close right now, it's impossible not to feel a little less leaden. I memorize the earnest expression on his face as a charm against what's to come.

Because just like Claudia, he's not here because anything on this red-dust planet calls to him. He belongs to the beach, to eternal summer, to his mother's art and his family's orchards.

Here, in this desert, he's my very own sea breeze. He looks like a hundred good things.

Queen Inara and Dr. Qureshi conjure a glowing gray planet I recognize all too well over the center of the table. As it rises, ringed and vast and trailing moons in its wake, I take comfort in Major's closeness, and try not to shrink away from the choices I've made.

"You all know," Queen Inara begins, "that travel has been curtailed for some months, due to the increased fragility of the spheres." She waves a hand and a white spot swirls to life on Saturn's surface. The storm.

"Approximately every twenty-eight and a half years, the Great White Spot rises. But though this storm's recurrence is predictable, the circumstances surrounding it are not." Queen Inara plants her hands on the edge of the table, chewing her lip, the expression just slightly less controlled than seems right on her face. "We came today to choose a squad to enter it, because the Abbot inside the monastery has ceased responding to our attempts at contact."

I remember the storm. Its ferocity, its leaden weight. I can't imagine it worse.

Briony's face is pale beneath her freckles. "Why us, Your Majesty?"

"Because you are the only ones left." Commander Bao passes a hand over his forehead. "We have met disaster after disaster across the spheres. Our forces are stretched too thin."

Commander Atlacoya clears her throat, looking subdued, and abruptly I ache for an abrasive reply from her. But none comes. "What few fully trained squads we still had here traveled to Quetzalcoatl and Helios this morning, when falling pressure caused their islands to drop."

Quetzalcoatl—on Venus. Major's home. My heart stops.

"They're safe," he whispers. But I can't bear the grim set of his mouth.

"That's why you've been using fifteens and sixteens to repair the barrier." My voice is hoarse. Commander Bao grimaces. His nod is so slight I almost miss it.

"There's more," Dr. Qureshi says, stepping forward. "We previously attributed the disharmony of the spheres and its effects to the Great Conjunction, due to occur tomorrow." She takes a long breath. "But we were wrong."

My nerves jolt. What else can there be?

I seek Claudia out at the far end of the table. She looks strangely right beside Dr. Qureshi, shed of her muddy coat, swathed in a black academic robe. But why is she there, I suddenly wonder, standing beside the professor?

Dr. Qureshi clears her throat. "This morning, Claudia discovered the source of the disharmony." The room falls completely silent as Saturn's moons whirl to life around it, their glow catching the gold brocade on the ger walls.

For the first time, Claudia speaks. "Jupiter commonly attracts passing meteorites and debris and brings them into its orbit. Saturn, however, rarely does so." She fixes her eyes on the ash-colored planet hovering over our heads. "Which is why Saturn's drawing Chiron into its orbit is such a cataclysmic event."

"Chiron?" The word is out before I realize I've spoken. The blood drains from my face.

And suddenly I'm not thinking of disharmony at large but the specificity of my own fear one cold night in late October. Of the individual kind of silence that follows the unlocking of the safety on a gun.

Chiron is a harbinger of pain.

I've known all along he and Mars were fighting to rule me.

I just didn't expect to have to face him again so soon.

Claudia and I watch one another, and it's like there's no one else in the room.

"We do not know why Chiron has left its path to cling to Saturn. Perhaps it is their likeness, as they are both melancholy bodies." Dr. Qureshi pauses. "But Chiron is a bearer of anguish, and he cannot be allowed to persist in Saturn's wake. That cannot be his place."

Into the long silence that follows, Queen Inara speaks again. "Our plan is, thus, twofold," she says. "Dr. Qureshi, Claudia, and I will return to al-Mushtari. From there, we and our scholars will attempt to free Chiron from Saturn's orbit by magic. In the meantime, our concern is the monastery, the village, and those who live there.

"Your squad has today met a series of extraordinary challenges— you have scaled a cliff, passed through a dust storm, and crossed outside of Ulaan Garig's barrier while maintaining protective charms of your own." Queen Inara swallows hard. She's been watching Amir, but now she forces her gaze away. "You must demonstrate these skills again tomorrow by traveling to Kronos and passing through the storm and up the mountain, where you will rescue the sunken monastery's inhabitants. You will return with them to the village and reconjure the barrier for their protection. Rora will travel with you to amplify Mars's song against Chiron's and Saturn's music."

"But the village was so strange and quiet before. What if things aren't any better there than at the monastery?" My voice breaks as I speak. "And the Abbot and everyone else—what if we can't get them out?" *And what if I cave to Saturn's song again? What if I'm as powerless against him as before?*

King Sameer presses his lips together, seeming to steel himself.

"If your squad cannot recover those inside, they may be lost to Saturn's altered song forever."

Nowhere is safe, comes a threat from the darkest place in my brain. This is my nightmare. This is the fear that follows me wherever I go.

Give me your wallet. Now. The man had taken me by surprise.

A cry had built too low in my gut to climb to my throat, my throat too constricted to set it free. My neck had wrenched back and forth, eyes searching the quiet Georgetown street. There had to be someone—

But there was no one. It was only nine at night but there was no one to watch over me but perfect brick homes and perfect little gardens.

Hey. Look at me. He'd snarled the words, lifted the gun to my eyeline and unlocked it.

But I couldn't. I couldn't look at him. The black barrel was too close for me to focus on anything past it.

The eight dollars, the Metro card, the photobooth pictures of me and Claudia and Jack in my wallet—they'd just made him angry. He'd thrown it all on the ground and spat at me before telling me to go, and I'd scraped my knuckles clutching it all up off the bricks. I'd finally begun to cry as I limped away, the sound harsh and animal in my mouth.

Even now, a million miles away, tears prick my eyes as I remember the feeling. The small, cold certainty that I was going to die.

It has been difficult, in the aftermath, to leave that certainty behind. To believe anywhere might be safe for me.

Some of that suffering was earthly—all too mundane. The natural product of trauma and my innate bent toward anxiety.

But now I know it was magic, too. It was larger than me, at its root.

And its root is Chiron.

Chiron in my chart, Chiron out of place in the universe. Chiron, harbinger of pain, attached to the heaviest planet, making misery of Saturn's natural melancholy.

"Rora." Amir's voice bleeds into my hearing. I think he's said my name a few times.

"Yeah?" I come back to them all, my hands shaking. Major's eyes are blazing with concern beside me.

"You don't have to go," Amir says. His jaw is tight. "You don't have to do this."

He might understand better than any of them. Amir, the mourning prince. Amir, minorly ruled by Mars, the ashamed son of Scorpio, the boy with the low, grave song.

The thing is, though, I do have to go.

It was smart to run, that night. It was survival. Just like it was smart to move the battle these past few days from my mind to my body, to give my thoughts a rest and confront pain with muscle and blood instead.

But if I never turn and look back at what happened—if I never face up to the dread that is a permanent shroud over my thoughts— then nowhere *will* ever be safe for me. I'll be running forever, forever trapped in the dark of that night.

I will never be the friend I need to be. I will never become the person I want to become. And the spheres and those trapped on Kronos will pay the price for it.

Chiron wounded me. Now it's time to lift the bandage and clean out the wound.

I shake my head, meeting Claudia's eyes. *"Hic manebimus optime."*

She doesn't belong to Mars. But I know she understands what I'm saying.

I'm done running.

CLAUDIA

40

MAJOR AND I camp out with the squad that night. The sky is incredibly clear; Phobos and Deimos, the planet's moons, whose names mean *fear* and *panic*, rise unobscured by clouds. And though Mars's song is strangely heavy and regimented—too strong to suit me, too much itself without the music of the other signs to balance it—it's a relief after Mercury's scattered melody. It's good, too, to see a sky after so many days underground. And it's even better to be with Rora.

As we settle down for the night, I want to tell her I'm sorry. That I wasn't being fair, back on Jupiter and even before; that I should've let her handle things in her own time. I just don't know how to tell her *why* I've clung so tight. Pushed so hard.

Because to explain would be to expose the gaping hole in my side. To peel off all my armor and show her I'm only half a person, alone. And I can't bear to do it yet.

For now, it's enough to be together again.

Rora lays out bedrolls for the four of us while her squad makes dinner, all speaking the language I thought sounded like Welsh back on Mercury, but which turns out to be Mongolian. She squares up to me as soon as we've served ourselves.

"Okay," she begins, bowl balanced on her knee. "I want to know everything you've learned. How did you figure it out? That it was—Chiron." She falters over the word for a moment, then steels herself. "Tell us everything."

In her borrowed red uniform, with her bangs pinned back and color in her face, Ro looks so different. Mars, the planet where she belongs, has so obviously been good for her, I feel a moment of doubt in my idea about the exclusion.

I feel a moment of doubt about *her*.

Will this new, stronger Rora be even more distant from me?

Her voice, only slightly too bright, tells me she's remembering our argument, too. But her eyes say *I missed you*.

So I swallow my worry and explain how Major and I studied the Conjunction and the moons and Beatrice's notes, how we traveled to Inferno to analyze the music. I show them all the calculations I worked and only realize belatedly that I've spread the paper with Amir's text out before them.

My work is all on the reverse of the sheet, not the side with his letter. But I see from Amir's suppressed smile that he recognizes it immediately. Cheeks burning, I stuff the paper back in my pocket.

Rora doesn't notice anything. "That's amazing," she says. "Claudia, your brain is . . ." She shakes her head, eyes lit up with admiration.

There is no doubt in her voice. Rora has nothing but faith in me.

I'm suddenly too shy to look directly at the boys. But I can sense Rora's enthusiasm building in them, too.

Rora, a bottomless well of trust and confidence. Rora, our amplifier. This is what she does.

"Do you know how much I love you?" I ask her impulsively. And though I try to keep my voice light, it breaks a little over that word. *Love*.

I'm terrified that any minute now Rora is going to pull away, to retreat inside herself to tend to all her fears or to new hopes I know nothing about. But she just scoots forward over her sleeping bag and throws her arms around my neck. "I missed you, twin."

I still at the word. She's never called me that before.

It braces something inside me. Stitches up a wound that's been gaping, too long, in my side.

It's enough to quiet the whisper in my thoughts that I could still lose her. For now.

Rora pushes her sleeping bag close to mine when we crash that night; we are back to back as the fire sinks to embers. The sky is pitch black and the night is freezing, desert-cold around us, despite the magic woven into the barrier overhead.

I try to close my eyes, to force myself to sleep. But when I give up and open them, Amir's eyes are on me, only a foot or so away.

He doesn't speak. But the silence between us feels like words; it's full, heavy with intent. I'm afraid to interrupt.

I pretend not to stare after him as he stands, puts another log on the fire, and crawls back beneath his covers. The flames gleam against his dark hair, make beguiling labyrinths of shadow on his skin. I strain to catch any sound from his direction.

The whisper of his bedroll against the pebbles of the canyon floor. A breath in, as if he's about to speak.

Across the campfire, a tall, slim girl with a shaved head laughs at a redhead with French braids, and I startle. Rora shifts at my back. Amir's still quiet beside me.

I can't bear any more silence, but I don't know what to say. So I choose the topic I can never banish from my mind.

"She's getting better," I venture quietly. "I can't believe how quickly she's changed."

I can't bring myself to be brave. To ask him about the text he sent me.

I can't stop thinking about you, and the night I got to run my hands through your hair.

"She's been taking her iron," Amir says simply, as though there's been no agony of waiting between us, as if I'm continuing a conversation, not beginning one. "When people finally find where they belong, things fall into place. She belongs here." He studies my face. "But I think maybe you belong with her, too. So does Major."

I blink. "You do?"

He nods steadily. "The two of you together, and the two of them . . ." Amir pauses. "He's always watching her, and she doesn't even know it." Flickering light burnishes his mouth and nose and cheekbones, leaving his eyes in shadow. I catch at my breath.

He's talking about Major and Rora. But his gaze is fixed on me.

"I think . . ." I hesitate, beginning to tremble. "I think, maybe, she knows it."

The dark is soft, soft between us.

"And as much as he's always been afraid of having no control over where he belongs," he says slowly, eyes troubled in the firelight, "he's even more afraid now of a different prospect. Of living in a world without her."

I couldn't help thinking that tonight would have been better if you were here.

I remember the minutes after I read his text. The mindlessness and chaos in the library. The animal fear I felt, how absolutely repulsive Mercury's song sounded when it was over.

A place filled with people like me, a place shaped to fit every contour of my personality—and still, I felt trapped. Until I found my way to Inferno, to the low, slow bass song that finally gave me space to breathe.

"I think he makes her happy. I think—I think everything about her is clearer and better when they're together." Again I hesitate, tracing idle patterns into the red dust canyon floor. "I don't think she wants to be without him, either."

Amir puts out a hand, stilling my fingers. "Is that what you really think?"

"You'd have to ask her." I try to smile, but I'm trembling. Amir rolls onto his side, his hand still wrapped around mine, his eyes watchful. Like the coward I am, I look away.

"I am," he says quietly.

My heart races as his fingers slide between mine.

I think again of his text. Of the questions we'd both found ourselves asking, spheres apart. *It defies everything I've ever been taught to wish things were different. Everything that's protected us these hundreds of years.* And again, I want to tell him everything. To tell him I know, somehow, that Beatrice was wrong.

Then I remember my promise to his mother and Dr. Qureshi, to let them reveal the truth in their own time. "You're going to be king someday," I hedge. "That's where you belong." It's the only true thing I can say. I'm too afraid to say anything else, too afraid I might give away what I feel or what I know.

"I am." He swallows, lets his gaze drift toward the stars. "And that knowledge has been on my shoulders my entire life. I am made entirely of that responsibility. I can't change my future, and I wouldn't want to." He pauses, and looks back to me. "But I've begun to wonder if maybe— if other things can change. Not my place, but who's there beside me."

I can't stop thinking about you, I can't stop thinking about you, I can't stop thinking about you

I am terrified at how easily he sees me. And yet, with his eyes on me, cutting through my every defense, all I want to do is show him everything.

I remember how I imagined us after I read his text. So close, only shadow between us.

And I didn't want to go to sleep without telling you.

"I'm a city already built. An omen already cast," he says quietly. "Someday I'll live behind those walls, in that palace, whether I belong there or not. But if I could choose who was with me, I would choose you. The most loyal friend. The most beautiful girl. The most brilliant mind."

He was so cool, days ago, when he conjured my chart on Mercury. I was so frustrated that he shook me up and I did nothing to him.

There is no trace of that *nothing* in his eyes now. No sign of all that cool.

He's as unsettled as I am.

What are time and space to a Portinari? Nonna asked me once. *We are the keepers of doors. Of* worlds.

He makes me feel equal to her words. To every door I've been afraid to open and pass through alone.

"It's okay," I say, the words as much breath as sound. They stir the dust between us. "It's okay, if you're set in stone. If you're a city, if your walls are built."

I squeeze our laced fingers and bring them to my lips.

"Because as long as you want me there," I say softly, "I'll always find a way inside."

I don't know if I deserve his confidence. But hope strikes like a match behind his eyes. Our hands are still linked together between our sleeping bags when I finally drift off.

And when I sleep, I dream of doors, every one of them open to me.

1287

THREE WEEKS LATER, when the explorers had utterly exhausted themselves, they left Acuto and traveled to the next sphere, to a dark blue planet that sang to them quietly of beautiful things. There, their feverish brilliance simmered into music as slow and dreamlike as breath.

Where in Acuto they had conjured a constellation of islands, here they conjured just one, casting a barrier over themselves like a blanket and crowding all their number into what gers they had brought. It was only when they woke some hours later, with snow falling softly outside the tents, that Beatrice remembered it was Christmas Day.

They lacked the strength to build another towering city, but they assembled a few more temporary shelters, creating a globe of quiet amid the snowbanks and outcroppings of ice that covered their small island. Beyond the barrier, diamonds fell like rain in a sky the color of sapphires; and within it, the company wrote stories and composed melodies and created art, small wonders blooming from the frost.

Beatrice watched Dante flourishing there, amid the endless cerulean and the snow. And just as she had known that the pale blue planet was the true ruler of her own sign, Aquarius, she knew that the deep blue planet must govern Pisces, Dante's ascendant sign. She still disbelieved what his sun and moon sign suggested, possessed as they were by duplicitous Gemini; but Pisces seemed to thrive here, where Dante told Beatrice his tales in the night, and her lips spoke to his, after her own fashion.

When Beatrice kissed him, she spoke silently of remaining there among the stars. She thought Dante heard her. But Dante was lost in a dream.

He wrote. On and on, he wrote.

RORA

41

I WAKE UP in the night. Not for any magical, interesting reason; I just have to pee.

For as long as I can, I lie still. The fire burns low and the stars are brilliant, clear, cold overhead.

Will they guide me tomorrow? Or is the path I'm fated to walk already bound into me, muscle and bone, into whatever makes me able to amplify a song?

I wonder what was powerful enough to pull Chiron from his course. If, whatever it is, it might do the same to me, and bind Chiron and me up together for good.

Too soon, I can't hold it anymore. Shivering and grumbling, I drag myself out of bed and make for the toilets, hurrying back as soon as I'm done.

The canyon smells like woodsmoke and sweat and dust and the cold burns the inside of my nose. I freeze when I'm about halfway back, startled by a firelit silhouette.

"Rora?" Major's voice is quiet.

My whole body relaxes immediately. "Oh," I breathe. "It's you."

"Just me." He's smiling, but his eyes are a little tired, a little forlorn. "I woke up and you weren't there."

Hands tucked in his pockets, he stops right in front of me, but I don't. I walk directly into him, curling up against his torso until he wraps his arms around me.

"You're like a cat," he grumbles good-naturedly, squeezing my ribs. "I've never met anyone else who just *demanded* to be held."

"Hmm. Well." I press my face into his chest. "I guess you don't have to."

He's quiet for a beat, his music filling the silence between us.

"Are you all right, Ro?" He speaks the words into my hair. "How do you feel?"

His arms are solid around me. He feels like a safe place to come apart.

"Good, here on Mars. Guilty, because we're going to Saturn because of me." I pause. "But I've been so clearly not okay for so long, even the mixed feelings are a relief." I tilt my head back to look at him. "Are *you* all right?"

Major shrugs, his muscles shifting beneath mine. Furrows sketch themselves between his brows. "I'm worried," he admits. "I'm worried about you and Amir. I'm still worried about my family in Quetzalcoatl."

I frown. "But you said they were okay." I pressed him for details as soon as we left the meeting; their home had sustained some damage, but none of them had been hurt.

I can't imagine how scared they must have been. How he must have panicked, waiting to hear from them.

"They're all right today, but a lot of people weren't. And what happens next?" He shakes his head, staring into the black. "If the

351

queen and Dr. Qureshi and Claudia can't dispatch Chiron, no one will be safe. Not my family, or the city I love. Or anyone's family, or anyone's city."

"They will," I whisper. The words feel like too little.

"I love them so much, Rora. I miss my home." Then his expression tightens, belying the shrug he gives, the flippancy of his next words. "Though it was never meant to be mine, anyway. And if I'm never going home anyway, maybe it should be all the same to me."

His tone is hopeless, his expression shuttered. His nonchalance rings so false it hurts. From nowhere, a fire springs up inside me.

"Hey," I say sharply. "Nothing is going to keep you from going home. Nothing is going to happen to your family, or to anyone else. There are going to be no more disasters, because we're going to solve this tomorrow."

Major, cut off from the song he belongs to—I banish the idea. It's unthinkable.

He will always have orchards and artwork and ocean breezes. I don't care how far or fast I have to ride to his rescue.

But disquiet still lingers in the lines of his mouth. "Hey. Look at me," I insist. "Don't think about that stuff." I borrow all of Mars's iron, go on tiptoe to force his eyes to mine. "Three good things, Major."

"Yeah?" He bites his lip, waiting.

It's only when he doesn't speak again that I realize he needs me to conjure them.

I hold up one finger, thinking as quickly as I can.

"Sometimes, in the summer, when I don't have to nanny, Claudia and I spend the whole day by her pool," I begin, not sure where I'm going. "We have chips and sodas and music and magazines. She

352

hassles me nonstop about SPF. The best part of the day is sunset, but the whole thing is just . . . perfect." I clear my throat. "Good thing. Think about that."

Major's gaze had fallen. He lifts his eyes to mine again now. I put up a second finger.

"Two, back to the present. I've been training. Claudia has studied. We have a plan now," I say, trying to sound more confident than I am.

"And three?" he asks quietly, when I don't say anything for a moment.

Trembling a little, I let the dark make me bold like I did the night before. "Three," I say slowly, "when all this is over, you're going to take me to Venus and show me your mother's artwork. Because it's all going to be there, just like you left it. Safe and sound. Safer than it was before."

The corner of Major's mouth turns up, just a little. "Yeah?"

"Yeah," I say, more breath than word. "I want to know what a monthlong sunset feels like."

Major takes my hands and holds them to his chest. He looks like he wants to tell me something, but he doesn't speak for a long time.

"Do you know," he finally asks, "why I liked you right away?"

My heart begins to race. My fingers are shaking in his. "I assumed it was my stunning charm," I deadpan. Major barks a laugh. "Honestly, I thought you were teasing me. Being nice to the bitter girl because it was funny."

"No. It's because there are no half-truths with you." A smile spreads over his face, slow and inexorable as the wash of the ocean. "You feel what you feel. You refuse to be dishonest or apologize for it."

"Some people would call that selfish," I mumble. "Or attention-seeking."

"I call it relentless. You're a comet. Totally unstoppable." Major's smile is a firefly caught in a jar, a secret told between camp bunks, a leap off a dock into a lake.

"You don't think maybe destructive comets are a bad analogy right now?" I ask weakly.

Neither of us can stifle a laugh at that. We're helpless, our arms winding back around one another.

His heart beats beneath my ear. It's a little faster than usual, just like mine.

"You know—" I begin again impulsively, my heart pounding even harder. "You know that promise you made me in your letter?"

Major puts his head to one side, frowning. "Promise?"

My mouth goes dry. Can he have forgotten?

I've memorized his texts. The paper is already worn, red dust ground into the creases where I've folded and unfolded it.

Should have kissed you then.

Next time I see you, I think I will.

Major's face splits into a grin. "Your face," he whispers, leaning close, shaking with laughter. I shove his shoulder, my cheeks flaming, but he catches my hand again.

"I haven't forgotten." His throat bobs. "I couldn't."

"Why do you love embarrassing me?" I groan, hiding my face in his chest.

"You don't have to be embarrassed, Ro." Major brushes my hair behind my ears, biting his lip. "It's just me. Just us." His voice is tentative, uncertain. An offering.

My lungs swell almost painfully as I meet his eyes.

It seems silly to think there could be a *just us* in such a short time. But my brain makes that argument alone.

My muscles, my blood, my soft flesh, my bones—they know that it's true. Because Major is warmth in the cold, an ocean in the desert.

They know that he has seen me spiteful, ashamed, broken, afraid, and he hasn't run away. That he is safe to trust. That together, we are just ourselves.

They are what draw his chest to mine, what draw him down so I can press my lips to his.

Major doesn't stumble as he walks me back toward the canyon wall, braces me against it. One warm, tanned hand cups my face, smoothing my hair back to kiss my temple and my cheekbone and the corner of my mouth; the other arm wraps around my hips, scooping me up as easy and confident as if he's done it a hundred times.

The red stone is cold, but I don't feel it at all as I memorize the contours of his chest and shoulders with hungry hands. When my chilly fingers find his back beneath his shirt, he hisses a little at the contact.

His answering laugh to mine is low, throaty; it rolls against me like a buoy bobbing on the water, like something solid enough to hold me up if I cling to it.

Major towers over me, sheltering me from everything else in the world, kissing my palm, the inside of my wrist, never looking away. "Rora," he whispers against my neck as I fist my hands in his shirt and pull him in again, and I remember again why I wait all day for sunset.

Because by the time it arrives, my skin is warm to the touch, maybe a little burned. I'm sleepy and loose-limbed and prone to unprompted laughter. Completely unselfconscious.

This is how it feels to kiss Major. Like seeing the sun behind my eyelids, like a warmth so complete it seems winter could never touch me, like falling asleep to a song I've memorized without meaning to. Like a never-ending sunset.

Though the canyon smells of smoke and dust, he still smells like summer, like the ocean. Though Mars's drums never falter, the music that never leaves him is perfect comfort, the warmest welcome.

I am drunk on the taste of him.

It's why I don't push him away when I know I should.

I know I should focus on the work ahead of me tomorrow, on Kronos, on what's to come. I know I shouldn't let myself want more than one thing—dwell on more than one song—at once.

If I fill my ears with salt breezes and sunset, Mars's music might slip away from me. But I can't resist the call to rest, just for a little while, before I get up to fight again.

Here in his arms, I can believe that even if there is no safe place in the universe, there are safe people.

The boy holding me is all surprises, all comfort, nothing like me, entirely perfect. I feel his every heartbeat, feel the laugh he gives when I have to pull away for a second to breathe because it's been too long. When we finally break apart and walk back to the campfire, I bask in him like sunlight, in his talk of the terrace his mother will retile at home in twenty shades of blue, in the steady rise and fall of his chest as he falls asleep first.

When he's drifted off, I stare up at the sky again. At Phobos and Deimos, the moons anchoring either end of the sky. They remind me of the fear and panic that wait for me on Saturn, that remain close at hand as I sleep.

But I don't dread the omens hovering overhead. They're there, I know. With all of us here around the fire and Major so close I can hear him breathe, it's just too warm to worry much.

CLAUDIA

42

THE MOONS ARE still in the sky when I wake; sunrise hasn't even begun to brighten the horizon.

The Great Conjunction is tonight.

I'm not sure precisely how many hours are left until Jupiter and Saturn—Fortuna Major and Infortuna Major—are at their closest, or whether I'll be watching it from Jupiter or somewhere else. Whether I'll watch it with my friends or alone.

Earth, Mercury, Saturn, Jupiter, Mercury again, Inferno, Mars. I've seen nights and days and sunrises and sunsets on five planets over the past five days. I ought to be exhausted, but all this running, all this searching, has only made me hungrier for the truth.

It feels like the only thing that might fill up a little of the emptiness that lingers inside me.

Rora has repaired herself. But I still feel just a little bit hollow. Just a little bit afraid that if a hurting Rora doesn't need me, a healed one will be gone before I know it.

So while the squad sleeps, I tug *Beatrice and Dante: Notes and Letters* from my handbag and crawl toward the banked fire, stoking it so I can see to read. I pore over the final chapters as the sky turns from black to gray and the sleepers around me begin to stir.

I don't believe I'm going to find what I've spent the past few days looking for—some clear mathematical reasoning from Beatrice to justify the exclusion. But still, I search her notes and letters for a way to make sense of it, grasping for a reason why even after I've turned the last page.

Before the others wake, I finish the book and put it away, trying not to be discouraged by the end the explorers from Siena met. By Beatrice, and her final diary entry, and the sadness that still throbs in every word she wrote.

They had their grand adventure, and then they went home.

I know what Amir and I said last night. But in the end—won't Rora and I do the same thing? Go home, and put all the magic behind us?

I tell myself things will be different for us. *We* are different.

We have to be.

1287

EVERY HOUR WITHIN their little globe rendered the company from Siena and the Uls dreamier, quieter. Only Beatrice grew more unsettled as time passed. Dante could not see why.

In truth, he gave it little thought. His work consumed him.

Marco kept busy. He worked at carving out sturdier shelters for the Sienese travelers, exploring the world within the barriers they had cast, investigating the icebergs that dotted their island and the rain of diamonds that fell outside it. But after five days and nights, Dante and Beatrice came to sup in his cottage, and he proposed they move on. "I can find no other way to be useful," he said frustratedly. "And I have covered every inch of the confines of our village."

Reluctantly, Beatrice confessed the truth.

"You know that the next sphere is the last we can travel before we reach the Stellare." She hesitated. "But there isn't a planet in the next sphere."

Marco frowned. He scrubbed at the shorn curls he had asked Beatrice to cut back on Acuto, when they had begun to get in his way. "I don't understand."

Beatrice watched Dante, waiting for him to react. But he only made a few more notes to his manuscript, not glancing up at either of his friends.

"There isn't one planet in the next sphere, but a thousand-thousand," she finally admitted. "In order to explore it with any pretense at thoroughness, we'd have to scatter. And I don't think we should," she added hastily.

At last, Dante spoke, frowning. "But what will people say if we come back with an incomplete tale?"

Beatrice blinked. "I didn't think—"

But she was so stung, she could not finish her thought. Dante watched her for a moment, then turned back to his work.

She had not thought of what other people would say. She had not thought of returning at all.

She had thought Dante had agreed.

Beatrice did not know what stories he had been telling himself in the dark after she fell asleep at night.

Marco grimaced, shaking his head at the softly falling snow outside his little cottage. "I am bound to explore the heavens," he said firmly. "If we must divide to conquer, then divide we must."

Beatrice looked again to Dante. But he did not speak. He was not listening at all.

"Very well," she conceded. But her throat was so tight she could hardly speak the words.

RORA

43

MAJOR'S GONE THE next morning when I wake. I scan the canyon for him as I pack and get ready, but he's nowhere to be found, even when we line up outside the gates in threes, waiting for Queen Inara to conjure the portal. Amir's mother insists three is the largest number of people who can safely travel the spheres at once.

Fear circles my heart in its familiar grip at her words—familiar, and yet a little strange. Anything could have happened to the four of us before. But fear has seemed to lose a little of its hold over the past few days of befriending pain. Of iron pills, and iron music.

I've tried to focus on Mars's song this morning. But others keep slipping in when I'm not paying attention. Claudia's soft Mercurial scatter, Major's song like sunset.

It's been so good to hear these songs, to have my friends here. But though I've missed their music, I push it away now. I can't let it distract me as I set out.

Mars's song must drive me forward. I have to be entirely iron to bear Saturn's leaden weight. If I don't, nowhere will be safe. Not for any of us.

Queen Inara traces our coordinates in the dust and Claudia holds my hand as I wait at the back of our ranks with Amir and Briony. A drum hangs around my neck from a leather strap; the queen thought it would help.

I try not to search the canyon for Major. I try to focus on the task ahead of me.

Three by three, we pass through the portal. Tishala, Commander Bao, and Baatar go first.

Every few rows, my squadmates have to smash a new entrance into the aether.

"Don't let Kronos sing to you," Queen Inara says, drawing near us. "Sing Ulaan Garig right back to him. Remain strong. We in al-Mushtari will be working to dispel Chiron. Text us when you've secured the monastery's inhabitants."

Before Dr. Qureshi and King Sameer returned to Jupiter last night, the professor advised that I be last in line to minimize my time on Saturn. The less time I spend there before we retrieve the Abbot and the others and reconjure the barrier, the better. I can only nod and do my best not to think about Queen Inara and Claudia traveling back to Jupiter after we've gone.

I don't know what Major's decided to do. I wish I could've spoken to him this morning.

I can't stop hoping he'll be here before I leave.

Only three rows left to pass through. We're wearing thick gloves to protect against the brittle aether as we break through, and heavy coats and boots to protect us from the blizzard waiting on Saturn.

I won't be returning there unprepared, with nothing but a beat-up black jacket and warm thoughts from a boy who didn't come to say goodbye.

Two rows left.

One.

Claudia hugs me tightly. "Be safe," she says. "Please, please, please be safe, twin."

"I believe in you, Claudia." I squeeze her tightly in return. "I'll see you soon."

Amir punches through the portal. When he, Briony, and I step into the spheres, they rattle beneath us like old windows in a storm.

Forward, I tell myself. Softly, haltingly, I begin to sing Mars's song to the aether. But I can already hear Saturn—and Chiron—in the distance. The fear I've tried so hard to push away rises like a flood in my belly.

I am afraid this will be the last trip I make through the aether. That I'll end up trapped on Kronos, away from Claudia and Major and my family. Trapped, with no view but the awful gray of Saturn's storm and the darker snarl of my own heart, its thirty-one fears left to grow and spread like mold.

The hole I left in the sphere four days ago is still visible, just barely patched over from Amir's repairs. The damage I did—it hasn't healed.

I walk faster, racing against my anxiety. "Rora," Amir cautions. But I rush on.

That's when it happens.

The edge of the hole cracks. And slowly, with a horrible creaking sound, it spreads.

The three of us stop dead. A vein pulses at Amir's temple. Briony's face is bloodless.

"*Go*," Amir whispers.

We shouldn't run. We all know we shouldn't run. But we tear forward, arms swinging, breathing hard. The sphere's music is layered with the ragged sound of our panting, with the rustle of our heavy coats and boots. When I finally dare a backward glance, the aether is spiderwebbed like a broken old mirror.

Horror keeps me running. It's the *snap* that stops me cold. I whirl around.

Briony's foot plunges through the sphere with a sound like breaking bone. One foot, and then the other.

Her cries echo off the brittle aether. She's supported only by her elbows, waist-deep in the night beyond, feet kicking ineffectually at the dark.

Just like yesterday, my every instinct tells me to run. But I crouch and slowly crawl to her on my elbows, trying to distribute my weight.

My heart feels like a shotgun, pumping relentlessly, preparing for the end.

I'm going to suffocate, I'm going to die, nowhere is safe, nowhere is—

I wait for the aether to shatter like diamonds beneath me, for blackness to rush in, for the breath to be sucked from my chest. But I don't stop until I'm at her side, reaching for her.

Briony wrenches away from me, trying to haul herself up, red braids swinging around her face. "No. No, you can't stop. Amir, Rora, you have to go!" Though her expression is fixed, absolutely rigid, her damp palms squeak across the aether.

Something ferocious sparks in me. "Would you leave one of us?" I demand.

Hic manebimus optime. Not a chance in hell.

I seize Briony beneath her arms and lift, but I can hardly budge her. The drum clatters around my neck so I wrench it off and shove it away. And then Amir is beside me, grasping at Briony's rib cage, muscles straining beneath his coat. Jagged shards of the aether hook into her uniform, slicing at her torso, but together we finally free her, and Briony clambers back inside the sphere.

Falteringly, I sing Mars again to the shattered aether smeared with Briony's blood. Some of the rough edges smooth out; part of the hole patches over. But it's far from repaired.

I retrieve my drum. Amir, Briony, and I turn our eyes toward the ash-colored giant looming in the distance.

Hearts beating hard against the aether, we crawl toward the battle we know waits for us.

AL-MUSHTARI, JUPITER

I HURRY AFTER Queen Inara. We land on our feet in the shallow sea.

Al-Mushtari looks just as we left it—the crimson-and-gold clouds sweeping across the darkening sky, the domed citadel rising high over the tossing sea. Trepidation fills me as I follow the queen through the tide, wind tugging at my hair and water soaking the hem of my coat, and try to gauge the music around me.

The exclusion pushes songs to their extremes. At its best, Jupiter's pride manifests in nobility and strength; at worst, in stubbornness, in arrogance. Which waits for us inside the castle?

Thinking of how Jupiter's song affected me at the council table just a few days ago, I wonder how it's worked on Queen Inara over the years. I wonder how it's felt to watch her scholars and courtiers sneer at her son for not belonging to this place by sign, by birth.

It would have driven me to ask questions, too. To look for better answers than the ones offered to me.

The guards jump to attention when Queen Inara and I reach the citadel walls, swinging open the gates for us. Through the sandstone city and the halls of the palace proper, it's the same. *Salute, salute, salute.*

She walks with purpose a little ahead of me. I match her step for step in the slippers the attendants traded for my shoes, trying to hold my chin as high as she does, trying to keep my shoulders as straight.

Some women diminish others to make themselves look taller, smarter, more beautiful. But there's something about Queen Inara that makes everyone around her more confident. Broader and stronger and more queenly. It feels like a queenly quality itself.

Bypassing the council chamber, we head up an elaborately carved staircase, climbing one, two, three flights before emerging onto a lamplit marble rooftop. The palace's topmost dome of gold and crimson rises over us to one side, and the city spreads out toward the seawall on the other, a balustrade and four watchtowers marking the rooftop's edge. Dr. Qureshi starts up from the table at its center, rushing to the queen and kissing her cheeks. "You're— oh, God be praised. You made it."

I watch the pair of them for a long moment, the beautiful two-headed monster they make, and pity any who dare to rise against them.

I pity myself, missing my twin and my not-twin and the boy who sees me entirely too well.

But I shake the thoughts away, order my mind. Jack is beyond my reach for now, and I can only do one thing for Rora and Amir and their squad as they evacuate the monastery: locate Chiron in Saturn's orbit, and cut him loose.

This is what I've prepared for. This is what I have to focus on.

As in the council chamber a few days before, the queen's scholars surround the table, a model of the spheres at its center. But tonight, others have joined them.

A young Black woman with dark curls sits with her knees drawn up to her chest, a glass of tea untouched before her.

A blond boy and a Black girl in Mars's red gear stare at their taped hands in their laps.

An elderly white woman with tired eyes. A younger white woman with a hand pressed to her pregnant belly. A thin, brown-skinned man eating from a plate of food, seeming not to taste anything he puts to his lips. And still others.

As the queen takes her seat beside Dr. Qureshi, Albrecht appears at her back. "Are we ready to begin, then?" he asks.

"Yes." Queen Inara nods at me, her expression unreadable. "Claudia is the last of them."

1288

ON NEW YEAR'S Day, Beatrice distributed coordinates to each of the twenty-seven members of their party, assembled on a snowbank beneath the cerulean sky. Her auburn hair was bound up in its net of pearls; her face was set like stone.

She had chosen twenty-seven of the most sizable objects in the sphere for their company to explore. All was ready. "I will travel to the largest planet," she said. "Travel by the figures and the tone I've indicated. Follow them to the minutest detail. If you are off by even a hair, you will be lost. Return within three days."

She passed instructions to Marco and then to Dante last; both men nearly had to tear the paper from her fingers.

One by one, the scholars and magicians traced their destinations on the great gleaming chunks of ice that surrounded them and disappeared.

Beatrice pressed one hand to Marco's shoulder. "Be safe," she said to him.

Finally free to roam, he only grinned his devil's grin. "Of course," he said, and was gone.

Then she turned to Dante, and kissed him. "If your charm begins to fail, come home quickly." Her eyes were anguished. "Just come home."

Beatrice had to force him to meet her gaze; though he had torn himself away from his writing, he was still lost in thought. "Of course," Dante echoed Polo.

But she feared, in her heart, that Dante had already gone and come back—had gone farther than his appointed destination, had overshot the point of return.

She feared he was already far away, in a place that called to him alone. A place where she could never belong.

KRONOS, SATURN

MY NOSE BEGINS to run as soon as we hit the surface. With the blizzard screaming across the air and turning the world to white, it feels strange to notice this; I only do because the snot dripping onto my upper lip freezes immediately.

I turn, surveying the landscape. The mountain path is more or less visible for a dozen feet or so, but it's impossible to see the village. And the song around us has only decayed, slunk further toward ruin. Phrases that should run smooth turn jagged and snarling; an unrosined bow drags itself across strings gone out of tune. The music is all minor chords, all misery.

As I listen more carefully, though, I seem to hear not one melody line, but two. Layered through Saturn's sober melancholy is Chiron's decay, wave upon wave of grief.

Amir and Briony break into a run toward Commander Bao and our waiting squad, jolting me back to Queen Inara's orders.

Don't let Kronos sing to you. Sing Ulaan Garig right back to him.

I rack my memory, scraping the walls of my brain for echoes of Mars's song, sing under my breath as I chase after my friends.

"Do we have to make the same climb we made before?" I ask

Amir, already breathing hard. "All the way up the mountain?"

I'm terrified at the prospect of fighting off Chiron's and Saturn's melodies until we've summited. I try not to think of that climb.

Major isn't here to comfort me now.

"Not this time." Amir nods at Tishala, who holds out what looks like an enormous kite. Its sturdy canvas is rust-red as Mars; it bucks against the wind.

"Stretch out your arms," she says, teeth chattering.

Commander Bao calls from the front of our ranks. "All accounted for?" Amir gives the order, and our squadmates begin to count off through their rows.

Before I know what's happening, Tishala has lashed my body to half of the kite, rope winding around my torso and between its ribs. She ties Amir to the other half. All around me, the rest of squad seventeen-three are pairing up and doing the same.

"Thirty," Briony counts at my side.

There's a beat of silence, and Briony arches her brows. "Oh." I shake my head. "Uh, thirty-one."

"Thirty-two," Amir says, absently finishing the count. Then his chin jerks up. "Wait. Thirty-two?"

"What?" I ask. "What's wrong?" He frowns, scanning our ranks, and I suddenly realize what he's wondering: How can there be thirty-two of us when there are only thirty-one members of squad seventeen-three?

"Amir?" Commander Bao shouts.

Uncertainty flashes across Amir's face, then exasperation. He presses his lips together for a long moment. "Thirty-one. All accounted for!" he hollers.

I blink at him. "But—"

Amir just shakes his head.

I want to argue, to ask him what's going on. But ahead of us, pairs of my squadmates are breaking into sprints and taking off in flight. There is only time to breathe a short string of curses Jack taught me before Amir tells me to *run*.

Mars's iron rhythm pounds my feet into the ground as we dash forward and lift into the sky, red canvas catching the wind, the gray planet falling away from our feet.

The wind claws at my face as we soar toward the summit; it rips tears from my eyes that freeze in my lashes and flash in my vision. My nose is streaming, and the storm bats the drum against my stomach.

When the skin of my right cheekbone grows suddenly taut and numb, I reach up and find a familiar rime of frost beneath my fingertips.

The frost reminds me what I'm here to do: to fight Saturn's music. But when I reach for Mars's song, other melodies come to the front of my mind instead.

Mercury's light, witty staccato. Venus, and a song like falling asleep in the sun.

No. I push their music away. Mars and Chiron are the only songs that matter right now: the one I have to clench in my fists, and the other I have to push away with all my might.

I grab at Mars's rust-red song, at relentless strength. They are all that will help me now.

I pour Mars's music into the snow as it buffets our squad, my friends dipping and soaring on the air like a flock of canyon-colored birds. Grit flies into my eyes and wind slams into my body, demanding every ounce of control I've practiced. I tense my muscles, angle my limbs as Amir instructs me, as his magic carries us along on the current.

And as this planet's bottomless melancholy settles like lead into my bones, I hammer Mars's song into the mountain.

Forward. Ad astra per aspera. Hic manebimus optime.

Just ahead, Briony is still bleeding. With every dip on the wind, with every controlled rise, red blood drips onto the dirty snow far beneath her, like a sacrificial offering of iron and strength to this crumbling-ash world.

Catching Amir's eye, I nod at her wound. He grimaces, but jerks his head at the summit above. I know what he means without saying a word.

We can't stop. Not for a while yet.

We are making for the monastery as quickly as we can, before time runs out for those inside.

CLAUDIA

46

"THE LAST OF *whom?*" I cram my perfect grammar out of my orthodontically perfect teeth because correctness is all I have at the moment. Queen Inara pulls out a chair beside the Black girl with the curly hair who's still staring down at her tea. I tuck my hair tightly behind my ears. "What exactly am I doing here, Your Majesty?" Albrecht arches his eyebrows, judgment in every line of his face; Dr. Qureshi looks concerned.

The queen reaches for my hands with the air of a priest hearing confession. "You're here to help us dispel Chiron, as you said you wished to," she says calmly. "You're here to speak for Mercury, the final sphere we lacked."

"How?" I stare pointedly at the table, empty of the tools of inquiry.

"In order to dispel Chiron, we must first locate him within Chiron's sphere," Queen Inara says. She lowers her voice. "You suggested that Earth was slower to suffer because it was protected by a multiplicity of songs. It led me to believe that Chiron might be simpler to track and defend against if we employed something of the same strategy."

I clear my throat. "So?"

"So," she says, "everyone here has been affected by Chiron's presence."

I stiffen. "I wasn't—"

But at Queen Inara's look, the words die on my lips.

"Neither was I, exactly," says the Black girl to her neglected glass, the only one close enough to hear us. "But my brother's not here to tell his own story."

A low wave of panic laps at my nerves. I'm overcome, suddenly, by the wish to back toward the door. "I can't tell Rora's story."

The queen's eyes narrow. "You know you aren't here to."

I say nothing. I can't speak.

Queen Inara stares just above my head, her brown eyes so like Amir's that my breath hitches in my throat. "I may not have conjured your chart," she says, so quietly only I can hear. "But you have. And you have seen him there."

I don't bother protesting. I know what she means.

She means the key I found. The one I hoped to leave hanging on its hook forever.

The one that, if I use it, will unlock my memory, will unlock my tongue. Will expose wounds I hoped, somehow, to keep secret.

1288

MARCO POLO STOOD in Inferno's sphere and looked out onto the Stellare beyond, and knew that he could go no farther. He'd been compelled to travel to the edge of all things, to scour this final planet, to be certain they would meet no other explorers in the spheres. And now it was done.

The field of heaven stretched before him, and a strange, hollow feeling yawned inside.

Polo turned his face toward the sapphire planet and his heart toward Earth.

He had seen what he'd come to see, done what he'd come to do. When he returned to Earth, he was determined to see and do so much more.

He was determined to keep moving.

Dante Alighieri stood on the ice-brown planet, tugging at his coat, wishing he had a new one. He thought longingly of the cloth and fur coats fashioned so beautifully in Florence.

He was uncomfortable. And though he'd fretted over returning home with an incomplete story, he barely noticed the world above his head or beneath his feet.

Dante had once thought the spheres resembled a cathedral wrought of night and stars. But what good, he thought, was a cathedral without crowds? What good was worship with no witness to one's piety?

What was a story with no one to hear it?

It was inferno. The dark, the emptiness, the absence of listeners and admirers: that was hell.

He hurried over the rocky planet, jotting perfunctory notes, determined to see what there was to see and be done with it. If there was music, he did not hear it. He heard nothing but his own thoughts.

Stories and plans slid through his mind as his feet slid over the icy rock, and he fell, mud staining his coat. Dante groaned, then shook off his discontent.

He would be rich enough to buy a new coat for every day of the year when he made it home to sell his tale.

In two days, Beatrice had scouted the planet she had chosen in its entirety—its mud flats, its ice fields. Now she had nothing left to do, and anxiety gnawed at her. It took all her will not to turn her back on its eternally dark sky and return to wait for Dante. But she could not leave the sphere prematurely.

She feared—she sensed, somehow—that she had little time left in the heavens.

So she gazed into the Stellare beyond, piecing together bright new constellations, humbled by the stars' beauty and their fire.

Beatrice knew what part Dante had played in her mathematics and in her magic, how he had amplified the music in her mind. Apart from her love for him, it was why she had dreaded their parting to explore this sphere: she had questioned what, if anything, she would be able to hear without Dante at her side.

But to her surprise, as she watched the distant stars, Beatrice found she could hear their music—or, perhaps, that of what lay past it: the sphere of the Unmoved Mover. So named by Aristotle and the ancients, the Unmoved Mover was mysterious, unseen; but it kept the spheres in motion, surrounding and sustaining them all.

All Bice knew was the startling joy of the songs beyond. All she knew, as she sat for a full day, was the love she felt despite this small planet's emptiness. She caught it in strains and snatches, a love persistent, all-surpassing; a love that bound together things determined to fall apart.

The very sound of it made her ache.

When Beatrice turned to face the blue planet once more, she was determined to fight for the friends she so loved.

RIDING THE SCREAMING wind, we summit the mountain in far less time than Major, Amir, Claudia, and I did on foot. But it takes us twice as long to find the monastery, looping back and forth on the air above the path.

When we finally touch down on the mountainside, I tear off my kite, break rank, and sprint up the path until I stand at the lip of a pit.

The last time we were on Kronos, not even a week ago, the building's bottom floors were buried in a slick of frozen mud and rock. But now it's sunk entirely.

This chasm is all that's left of the monastery. I can't even see the bottom.

Briony races up beside me, and my questions die at the helplessness in her face. Ash-gray snow settles on her shoulders as she squats, panting, staring into the dark.

Saturn's song is so much worse. Contemplation, sobriety—the traits this planet possesses at its best—are buried beneath frozen ground and Chiron's influence. And the Abbot and the monks are buried, too.

We have no way of knowing if they're safe. I know without asking that we have no way of getting them out.

Mourning music sinks deep into my bones as I stand, unable to move, at the edge of the abyss. I'm not sure when I quit singing Mars's song against it.

At a shout, I jerk around. Commander Bao is yelling and waving his arms. I glance at Briony. "What's—?" But her guilty expression stops me. And then my stomach plunges.

Commander Bao is yelling at Major. Baatar is crouched in the snow beside them, pain contorting his features.

I'm moving before I can tell my legs to go. "Major!" I exclaim. "Major, what are you doing here?"

My voice is ragged. I can feel the horror on my face as I take in the scene—Nikolai untangling himself and Major and Baatar from an overloaded kite. Tishala bent over Baatar's ankle, grimacing at its already swollen state.

"He wanted to look after you," Briony pleads. I ignore her, slog through the snow, push past the commander to Major.

He's hopeful, expectant, ready to defend himself. But it all falls away when he sees my expression. "Rora," he falters.

The anger in Commander Bao's face only just hides his rising worry as he barks an order to Baatar and stalks off. Amir remains at Major's side, loyalty and frustration at war in his eyes.

"Thirty-two," I accuse Amir. He presses his lips together.

He knew. He knew immediately that Major was here.

Panic rising, I turn away, testing my grasp on Mars's song, singing experimentally below my breath. I can't think about the commander, Amir, Major, any of them. Only Mars can own my thoughts right now.

The music is there, if I stretch hard after it. But Mars's song is a distant thing.

I whirl on Major. "How could you?" I demand. "How could you do this?"

"I'm sorry." He shakes his head, shamefaced, determined. "I just . . . I had to be sure you were all right."

He is all concern for me. And I am all desperation.

The golden melody rolling off him is the only thing I can hear. It thaws my bones. Angry as I am, I want to lean my head against his chest. I want to sun myself in his music that speaks of morning glories unfurling at dawn, of jasmine sighing onto the air at night.

And it terrifies me.

Because Venus offers comfort I cannot accept right now. She will drown me, will dilute the song that I need.

With Major here, I am deeply afraid that I will fail to do what I came here to do.

I bite down on my anger and my dread. "I can't," I say.

I leave Major standing on his own and return to the edge of the pit.

It's dark below, where the monastery has buried itself. The wind howls against the frozen walls of the abyss. It's a hollow, hungry, aching noise; it sounds like I feel.

Everything within me is reaching for the boy I've pushed away.

"It's too deep to rappel." Commander Bao's mouth is a tight, anguished line. "It's too deep to get any of them out."

No one says anything. No one knows what to say.

We're a few mere mortals pitted against cosmic rage and pain. Thirty-one teenage soldiers, their commander, and their friend.

Amir catches Major by the arm, draws him in with the squad. It's too cold to stand apart from the group.

Even huddled together, my friends' faces are pale, their lips purple from cold, their complexions of every shade all leaden in the wolf-gray snow slashing at our bodies. They look so different from when they crowded around our campfire to give me my armband, their faces all bronzed by the light of the flames, or from when they competed yesterday, smeared with green paint and Mars's iron-red dust. I think of the circle of our campfire, of circling the mountain.

"I have an idea," I suddenly shout. The squad turns to me.

"If we can't go down to the monastery," I say slowly, "we'll have to raise it."

CLAUDIA

48

QUEEN INARA HASN'T seen my chart. I know she hasn't.

But I have.

And I saw Chiron's key-shaped icon there, lurking in Gemini. The key to a door I have no wish to open. The symbol of my hurt where I'm joined to the people I love.

My whole being recoils from the table, from the heavy sincerity between these strangers, already threatening to smother me. Nothing in me is willing to stay here. Jack would have bolted already.

"Claudia Portinari, are you a brave girl?" Queen Inara asks abruptly.

I've been called so many things. Clever. Witty. Sophisticated.

Brave's not one of them.

I wasn't brave enough to talk to Amir about anything that really mattered until I had Rora at my back last night. Without her beside me, it took me days to tell Major the truth about my research—that I was trying to understand the exclusion and bring it to an end, because his and Amir's pain hurt me.

I've never had the guts to swim in emotional waters without her. It's not what I do.

But Rora's far away right now, facing her own darkness. She's

384

being brave. I'm thinking of her when I answer, "I can be."

"Good." The queen nods again at the chair she's drawn out. The only other sound is the tide against the city walls. "Now, sit. Everyone's been waiting for us."

I take the seat.

Queen Inara begins to pace around the table, and the crystal model of the spheres slowly wakes. When she stops just behind my neighbor—the Black girl with the curly hair—the queen puts her hands on the back of her chair. "Now, Nour, if you would be so kind as to begin."

1288

BEATRICE MADE HER case. All twenty-seven of their party gathered together in her cottage on the sapphire planet to listen as the snow fell gently outside.

"We should remain here in the heavens, all together," she said. Her eyes were bright, her cheeks flushed with cold and the memory of the music of the Stellare and the Unmoved Mover. "We can take residence in King al-Radi's court, or in the Uls. Explore the planets further, and their moons. We can encamp in the next sphere—"

"Inferno," Dante interjected under his breath.

"Inferno," Beatrice repeated, faltering a little before she collected herself again. "We can return there and listen to the music from beyond. Perhaps one day we might discover how to travel the field of stars and reach the Unmoved Mover itself!"

Some of the party felt her excitement catching; even Marco seemed to consider what she said. But Dante avoided Beatrice's eyes and said nothing more.

He had heard nothing of the song she had described.

As the others began to talk excitedly of remaining, of where they might live, the spark left Beatrice's eyes. "You want to go back," she finally said to Dante. Because he would not say it himself.

"Beatrice . . ." He glanced about, embarrassed for the others to listen. The rest of the party began to gather themselves and trickle out into the night, back to their cottages or gers.

Marco seemed to think of following the others as they beat their retreat. But he only settled more firmly into his chair.

"I made a promise," Dante said, gaze flickering about once more. He swallowed. "I made promises to Gemma and the Donatis. And so did you, to your own betrothed."

Dante spoke low and discreetly; but Beatrice hardly noticed the emptying cottage. "I did not. To *be* promised is not *to promise.*" Her voice was fierce, but it trembled. "And if you made a promise, surely you rendered it void long ago by your leaving."

"I think . . ." Dante trailed off, shaking his head. "The planets do not draw me as they draw you. I do not think my journey ends here. I think I am meant to return to my home, to Gemma." He dropped his eyes. "As you are meant to be someone else's wife."

In truth, he had thought little of Gemma. But he had thought much of Florence, and what he might achieve within its walls with the Donatis at his back and his story to sell.

"I am meant to be where my heart belongs," Beatrice said. She pushed back the tangles of her auburn hair and reached for Dante's hand, for Marco's. "You are my friends, and this—our work, we are perpetrating miracles!"

Et quod est superius, est sicut quod est inferius, ad perpetranda miracula rei unius. She had said the words to him in Siena and many times since. It was her favorite phrase, the song of her heart.

Marco smiled wanly. Beatrice seized upon it, attacking with renewed vigor. "You're explorers!" she said. "There are worlds upon worlds left to seek out!"

Dante tugged his hand away. Not sharply, but away all the same. "Bice—"

"Dante, you're—" she began.

"I'm not an explorer!" Dante burst out. "I'm—I'm not an explorer," he said again. His voice was a whisper. "I fled a skirmish at Arezzo, where I had gone with the Donatis. I could not return alone to Florence. I did not know what else to do."

He could hardly look at her. At Marco.

When he met their eyes, he saw nothing of what he had expected. There was only surprise in Polo's gaze, and confusion. And in Bice's, there was none of the judgment or disappointment he had expected.

"And now?" she asked.

There was no judgment, no disappointment in Beatrice's eyes. There was only sadness.

Because he loved her, but not enough.

Dante tugged from his pocket the copy of Virgil's *Aeneid* he always carried and flipped blindly through its pages, choosing a line at random.

"What are you doing?" Beatrice asked, blinking fiercely.

Dante read the line to himself and scoffed. "Do you see?" he asked, pointing at the page.

"Sister, the Fates have vanquish'd: let us go
The way which Heav'n and my hard fortune show.
The fight is fix'd."

"Fixed," Beatrice repeated. "I do not believe our fates are fixed. Only your will."

Dante's voice grew quiet. "I must put away childish things," he said. "I must become a man."

"Joy," Beatrice said hoarsely, "is not childish. Nor am I, for wishing to be loved. To pursue a life that I love." She turned away. "And if you think so, perhaps we are less alike than I believed."

Bice left her cottage, and left the two men alone. Marco studied Dante as if he'd never seen him before. Dante looked back at him but did not speak.

For once, he didn't have anything to say.

"THE PIT. WE have to march around—no." I hesitate, watching my squad. "The kata. We have to circle the pit doing the kata I did during the competition. I'll sing Mars."

She turned the tide, Commander Atlacoya said just after my squad had won.

I don't know if I can replicate what I did yesterday. It's a testament to their trust in me that they do as I ask. Their trust, or maybe just our lack of options.

We form ranks. I stand at the back, Major and Amir and Tishala ahead of me.

And as our company begins to circle the pit, I begin to truly sing.

My voice is not beautiful. My wordless notes are fragile, threatening to snap off and break like icicles in Saturn's air.

As one, my squad moves in front of me, dropping into a squat, their shoulders and arms swaying left and right, bobbing and weaving in unison. Their red uniforms shift like sand dunes in the snow.

This is one of the elevens' katas, Briony told me. Six years ago, this squad learned it together, practiced it together, corrected one another as they trained. All their strength is bound up, together, in this form.

My hands are grim purple with cold as I mark time on the drum.

Major walks beside me, heedless of the rhythm I set forth.

I tear my eyes away from him, tug my gloves off with my teeth; I can't feel the drum with my fingertips muffled. I focus on Mars, bear his rhythm to Saturn, offer the gray planet all his strength.

The kata changes. As one, my squadmates drop toward the ground, shooting forward, arms reaching out to catch the knee of an opponent. Wind pounds our ranks, but their bodies are close together, darting forward again and again.

I sing alone into the blizzard air. The cold is so dry my knuckles have split, and tiny rivulets of blood freeze across the backs of my hands. Frost tightens the right side of my face, scaly and cold from temple to jawline.

Ahead of me, my squad is an interlocking clockwork machine of spinning bodies, of kicking legs. Snow flies up from the ground to join what's already gusting through the air.

Gather your voice, Amir told me during training. I clung to those words during the competition yesterday.

So I marshal my voice, scrape it together with bare, bleeding hands, push it into Saturn's air. I push away every other melody until my throat is hoarse and my hands throb.

I reject Saturn's song, all around us. I reject Venus's song on Major at my side, and the deep, grave music that emanates from Amir a few rows away, and the half-dozen other melodies that cling to my squadmates, that I can hear even now.

The winds of the blizzard slow a little beneath our progress, and a few icicles fall from the scrubby trees on the mountainside—but only a little, and only a few. The snow at our feet melts into icy sludge and seeps through the seams in my boots, freezing again as my lone voice begins to falter.

And always, always the pit beside us. Dark, despairing, unchanging in its depth.

Saturn resists, but I push on. We have to close the circle. Surely, things will look better when we've made it around the pit.

My squadmates press forward, forcing their legs through the snow as it piles around their feet. Tears freeze to my cheeks as my voice grows shrill and feeble. Major walks a few feet away, his blue eyes worried. Warm music hovers around him, still offering itself to me.

I force it out of my thoughts. I focus on Ulaan Garig, on the strength that built me up, and pour it into Saturn's ashes. Brute force, blind forward motion: they are all that will carry me now. All I have is the fight in my muscles, the iron in my veins, the tape around my wrists, and a squad around me who are just like me.

We finish the circle.

But the monastery is still nowhere to be seen.

For a moment I try not to stop, to keep singing, keep playing. But the drum's vellum head has grown brittle with the cold. A button on my coat punctures the instrument's taut surface, and it tears beneath my palms.

My squad has confronted the cold and the misery of this place. We fought so hard even to get here. And it's made no difference at all.

With a scream of pain and frustration that I feel in my nails and teeth, I rip the drum from my neck and fling it into the pit.

MY WHOLE BODY strains away from the table. We're outdoors, with Jupiter's sky darkening overhead, but the air is still much too close. And then Nour begins to talk about the morning she woke up to find that her brother, a researcher in Acuto, had taken his own life.

I forget the urge to run as she speaks. Her story makes me forget myself entirely.

"He kept sending me these messages, and they worried me," she whispers toward her lap. The distant sound of waves nearly drowns out her words. "He was in the lab day and night. His advisor told him to take a break, but he didn't think he was making progress quickly enough.

"He pushed himself too hard. He was a genius, and he worked himself to the bone, and it—" Nour's voice breaks. "It looks like he finished his experiment. He was researching ways to increase the life span of octopi in Quetzalcoatl's ocean," she says to me. Perhaps she's already shared this detail with the others. I nod, wanting her to see that I'm listening.

Nour's jaw tenses. "His research was inconclusive. He'd been working on it for two years. It must have broken his heart."

Genius is the defining trait of those who live on Uranus, I

remember reading. Maybe pressure and hyperfocus are the draw-backs to that sort of brilliance.

But she's telling us more than that. Nour's story is more than Chiron's effect on a given sphere. She is offering up her particular suffering, and her brother's.

The model whirls on at the center of the table. No one else speaks. Queen Inara paces around the table, watching the miniature spheres, watching us.

Nour crumbles.

"I wish I could have told him it was all right," she sobs. "I wish I'd told him to come home for dinner, that I would make whatever he wanted, that there'd be another experiment, that he was only twenty-six. That he had his whole life. This shouldn't have been the end."

I try to clear my throat, but the sound is wet. My eyes are damp.

Before I can second-guess myself, I squeeze Nour's forearm, just once.

Missing Jack is like missing half my brain, but he's just somewhere else, not gone forever. Nour's pain is an unfathomable well. But I can fathom it a bit now, because she has drawn from its depths and poured her grief out for us.

I see the shape of her pain, and I see her, and I am so sorry.

I say so. Nour nods without speaking, and I drag my chair a little closer to hers, its legs scraping the marble floor.

"Look," the older woman across the table whispers.

At the center of the table, where Saturn hovers ash-gray and forbidding within the crystalline model, one of its ghostly moons begins to glow.

Queen Inara is still pacing. "One story," she says, "and then another."

1288

BEATRICE COMPLETED HER calculations in silence the next morning, feeling none of the dreaminess that had settled over her when she first lay beneath the sapphire sky.

All of their party—those from Siena and those from the Uls— had elected to remain in the heavens. Some had chosen to return to Luna's sphere; some would repair to Ulaan Garig, the settlement they had vacated on Mars. Others would migrate to Hermes or to al-Radi's court. Only she, Marco, and Dante would return to Earth.

So eager was Dante to be off as Beatrice finished her work that he did not hear Marco approach.

"Why did you lie?" Marco asked quietly. "About traveling."

Dante had avoided him all the night before—Marco, his friend, the companion who had been almost a brother. There was no avoiding him now.

"Because your tales were exciting, and you made people listen. Because I had no stories of my own to tell," Dante finally said, unable to look his friend in the face. Then he straightened and spoke firmly. "But now I do."

Marco nodded, expression unreadable. "Indeed," he said. "Now you have your story."

Beatrice summoned the others. She traced the coordinates for five paths in the ice, produced her little panpipe once more from her pocket, and bade their company a subdued farewell.

She had brought them thus far, but would go with them no farther.

They left the deep blue planet unnamed—both the planet itself, and the little ring of stone cottages they abandoned to the quiet and the snow.

One by one, the four parties left them.

Marco, Dante, and Beatrice were the last remaining on the snowbank. The three of them looked at one another for a long moment.

When Beatrice put the pipe to her lips for the fifth and final time, the note she played to return them to Earth was a siren song to Dante. For once, its appeal had nothing to do with the woman who played it.

When the portal opened to them, Beatrice nodded to Marco Polo. "Lead the way."

As she stepped into the aether after him, Beatrice hung her head. She did not look at Dante.

She could not bring herself to look upon the marvels of the spheres as they traveled back the way they'd come.

RORA
51

THE DRUM SAILS into the pit, and I sink to my knees.

I am freezing over. I am failing Kronos and Ulaan Garig, failing Major and Claudia and my squadmates and everyone in the monastery I cannot save.

Even as I clutch Mars's music in my fists, I wonder if somehow I've made matters worse by coming here. If, by suggesting the kata—or by my very presence—I've only amplified Saturn's painful song.

At Commander Bao's voice, I turn. "Maybe—" He eyes the chasm behind us, clears his throat. "Maybe it's best we return to Ulaan Garig."

It's not an order. I'm as terrified as I've ever been when I realize he's making a suggestion, because it means he doesn't know what to do any more than the rest of us.

Squad seventeen-three stands behind me, lips purple, faces gray. Briony wraps her arms around herself. Nikolai's hair is full of snow. They look fearful and cold and too young.

Because even while I sing to Saturn, Saturn sings to them. They are looking into the pit, and the pit is looking back.

But leaving would be abandoning the monastery and everyone inside it.

Amir crouches at my side. "They can't keep this up much longer," he says below the screaming wind. "Rora, we have to finish this or go back."

"We can't leave the monastery." Tears fill my eyes, and I dash them away before they can freeze again. "Amir, I know what it's like in there. We—we have to think of something else."

"What?" Amir runs a gloved hand through his hair, looking utterly helpless. "We can't retrieve them. And Mars's song—" He breaks off, eyes hollow with misery. "Rora, I'm afraid it's not enough to heal Saturn. We aren't—*I'm* not strong enough."

Somewhere low in my stomach, I know he's right.

I'm afraid for my friends. I wish I could spare them this.

I suddenly wish I had come here alone.

I'm so hollow inside that when Major sits beside me, I don't pull away.

Amir glances between us, then rises, retrieving a pitch pipe from his pocket. "I'm going to assess the music," he announces to the squad. "Let's see if we've managed to shift it at all." Over Major's shoulder, I watch him walk away, play a note, listen; the squad confer among themselves.

Major and I are alone at the edge of the abyss.

"Are you all right?" he asks, just as he did last night. His expression asks nothing of me, offers me himself. For the life of me, I can't imagine why.

"Why did you come?" I can't stop myself from asking.

"I wanted—" He hesitates, hands twisting in his lap. "I wanted there to be someone here who cared more about you than about your plans."

The words are achingly gentle. They would thaw me if I would let them.

"I'm sorry I ran away from you earlier. I know you were trying to help me." I swallow. "I'm just trying to do the right thing."

I bite my lip, thinking of why I was so eager to go to Mars in the first place. I wanted to be strong enough not to drag my friends down, full enough not to drain them.

It never occurred to me that I might be pushing them away with my own two hands.

"We're very different people," I say, eyes on the pit. "I might hurt you."

"We are different," Major admits. "We belong to different places. I don't have half of your power."

I bark a bitter laugh, feeling the pit taunt me with my helplessness. All my strength, come to nothing. "I don't feel powerful."

"Every song is so much stronger around you. So much more itself." Major's gaze lifts to mine, blue and warm like the night just after sunset. "Being with you, it's like I can see the world the way it wants to be seen. Like *I* can be seen that way."

My heart is raw from cold and my own failure. But he is so, so warm.

He feels safe enough to trust with my fragile parts when all my strength is gone.

I don't want to push him away for some greater good, to pretend his music is anything but safety to me, that I'm not happier when he's near. That I don't care for this golden boy who followed me into the dark.

I don't wait for him to move. I put my arms around him, press my forehead to his shoulder.

Summer is coming.

I'm tired of trying to keep myself warm.

CLAUDIA

52

NOUR HAS TOLD her story, and it is the hardest. One after another, the others tell theirs.

The man who left his family on Inferno, because he was furious all the time and didn't trust himself.

The elderly woman from Tarshish, on Neptune, who felt so lost inside her own mind she couldn't get out of bed for weeks.

The girl whose sister drowned swimming in the ocean when Quetzalcoatl plummeted in the sky.

Inferno's severity turned to rage; Neptune's thoughtfulness turned to depression; Venus's richness in collapse. The queen has assembled one of us for every sphere, for every song, for every incarnation of Chiron's ill effects. And as the others speak, I begin to understand.

We are here to establish the mass of our pain, to outline its exact dimensions in every song. To delineate from each planet the specific angles of our wounds.

We are here to take Chiron's measure.

While Rora rescues those in danger on Saturn, we will excise this bullet. We will eliminate the source of the ill in the spheres while she and her squad mitigate its worst effect.

So we give shape to our pain before a listening room. We admit our sins and our sufferings and hope our chosen confessors will absolve us, or grant us miracles.

And as we speak, Chiron's outline within the model grows clearer.

I dread the sight of him. But I know instinctively his brightness does not mean Chiron himself is growing stronger.

It means he is growing more known to us.

When the woman from Suvd Uls finishes, we've circled the table. Someone belonging to each sphere has spoken. Except, I realize, for Mercury.

Everyone turns to look at me.

"I don't know what you want me to say." I give a nervous laugh. "It's Rora's story. She was assaulted and—"

"Rora is confronting her pain on Saturn," Dr. Qureshi says. "Do you mean to say you have none of your own?"

She doesn't have to say anything else. I know my protesting is cowardly. A slippery Gemini's last-ditch effort to avoid uncomfortable honesty.

Rora is meeting her pain face-to-face. And I've been avoiding my own by being consumed with hers.

But I've seen Chiron in my chart. I know what he means.

I have no distractions here, and no sarcastic comment will deflect the people waiting for me to speak.

"I just—" I pause. My breath is halfway to a sob; it rattles on its way out. "I feel so selfish even explaining this now. Nour, you lost your brother."

Nour frowns, turning sober dark eyes on me. "Claudia, pain isn't a competition."

"How?" I gasp, laughing uncomfortably. "How can you say that?"

"Because it's true," Dr. Qureshi says evenly. "Pain is specific."

I already know that. It doesn't make this any easier.

I stare at my hands. I don't have a phone or a pencil or anything I could pretend to be busy with. Nour pushes her tea toward me, and I take a drink to steady myself.

Everyone else at this table has laid themselves bare for the sake of identifying the bomb in our collective wreckage. On the horizon, a gray moon has begun to rise. And within the model, Chiron waits, bright but not quite substantial.

If he is to be found and dispelled, then it's left to me to tell the truth.

I have to be brave. I have to do what all the rest of them have done.

"My twin brother, Giacomo, and I were born forty-five minutes apart," I say, "and that was the last time I ever gave him so much space." I have to begin here, I think.

"My nonna calls him by his name—Giacomo, never Jack like the rest of us—but she calls me Ombra. *Shadow.* Because I used to follow him around so much when we were little. I never knew what I wanted to watch on TV, or what I wanted to play. I just did whatever Jack did, because I wanted to be near him. He was mostly okay with that."

Tears press at my eyes. This sucks. But I don't stop.

"I know how Jack is feeling by the outfits he chooses in the morning or the music he picks on the way to school. It's seemed for years like we were growing into different people, but about seven weeks ago, something just changed, and my parents sent him to live with my nonna. And I miss him, and I am so mad at him, because it is *his fault.*" I feel sick to my stomach, all the anger I've repressed curdling in my belly. My words grow thick and damp. "And I *need him.* Not in Siena. With me. I am so, so lonely with him gone."

402

I finally dare to raise my eyes to the table. I'm terrified.

My hurt is so small, compared to theirs.

But there is no irritation or discomfort, no judgment. I find only compassion in the eyes of those listening.

Deep breath. I'm halfway there.

"As soon as we moved to Washington, I made friends with Rora. There's no one like her anywhere. She's sharp and interesting and sweet and even though she doesn't need anyone, she wanted to be friends with me, too. And I *needed* her after Jack left, but suddenly—" I take a shuddering breath. My head hurts from trying not to cry. "Suddenly, I felt like I couldn't find her anymore."

Chiron is throbbing at the center of the table, ember-bright, like a bullet hole.

"Rora was mugged the same night my parents decided to send my brother away, when Chiron broke everything. She was completely shut down for weeks before she traveled to Mars, and I couldn't do anything about it." I blink hard, dragging the backs of my hands across my eyes. "And I could feel I was losing her when she was sad, but now that she's better, I'm afraid she's not going to come back. And when she doesn't," I ask, my voice hoarse, "who will I be?

"I don't know who I am without the people I love. I don't know how to be a twin without a twin." Tears leak down my cheeks. "What's a shadow without the thing that cast it in the first place?"

I think of Rora showing up at that party, her face slimy with tears, locking herself into the bathroom to hyperventilate while I stood outside the door. I think of Jack, who should have been there, the shouting as he fought with my parents, the echoing silence of his room after he left.

Merciless emptiness presses down on me.

"This is a problem. This is a problem for me." My nose is running, but I'm still not quite crying. "My total inability to exist as a person by myself. The whole reason I agreed to travel to the spheres was not to protect them, but to help *Rora*. Because I wanted to fix her, so I could keep her, because I'm too cowardly to be alone."

Nour presses a hand to my shoulder. "You are *not* a coward."

"Oh yeah?" The words come out sarcastic. Even now, I'm too afraid to be anything else.

"Yes," says Queen Inara fiercely, her eyes boring into mine. "You are Claudia Portinari. You are the descendant of Beatrice Portinari. You are a brilliant mind, the daughter of a great family, and—I imagine—of a few people in particular who are very proud." She sweeps her hand around the table, at the representatives of each planet who have helped us find Chiron, and her eyes go wide. "Just look what you've already done. What you helped us learn."

I lift damp eyes and lashes to the queen. "But Beatrice—"

"Was an intelligent woman, whatever else she may have been," Queen Inara finishes. Then her voice grows soft. "And you may belong to Mercury, but you are not a shadow. Not only a twin, or half a pair. You are a whole person, Claudia. Perhaps not self-sufficient, though who of us is?" She gives a small laugh. "But a whole self."

Her words are so honest. So kind. They sound like the truth.

My chest squeezes, and the emptiness feels a little—a little—bit smaller.

And when Nour puts an arm around my shoulder, I feel her take a little of my pain away, as I took a little of hers.

1288

DANTE HAD FELT overwhelmed when he'd fled Arezzo and come to Siena not six months before. The new city had felt so brave and adventuresome and different from Florence, though it looked much the same. But as they passed into Earth's sphere and inside the Studium Senese once more, it all felt diminished.

His world was larger now. Dante was prepared to conquer it all.

In the days that followed, he, Beatrice, and Marco made a complete report to the university masters, who swore to keep secret all they were told—about the settlements the party had seen and established, about the king and the explorers who already dwelled in the heavens, about their own scholars who had chosen to remain.

Beatrice did not acknowledge the masters' worthless compliments as they completed their testimony, or remark on the fact that they were largely aimed at Dante and at Marco. She would receive no position for her discoveries; she would never be credited for her work. Worse, her family was humiliated, furious at the sisters of Santa Petronilla for not keeping better watch over her, furious at Beatrice herself for risking her betrothal to Simone dei Bardi. They had concealed her disappearance only by convincing Simone that Beatrice had pleaded to remain in Siena through Michaelmas (and then through Christmas, and then through Epiphany) and by threatening the sisters of the convent, who spread the rumor that Beatrice was cloistered in prayer before her wedding.

Beatrice had not defended herself to her father's and mother's rebukes. She did not interrupt the masters as they talked around her now, planning future meetings and further voyages into the stars.

With Dante, her amplifier, so close at hand, she could still hear the music from beyond, and it broke her heart.

The masters would send explorers of their own who would hear the music she so loved. They would see the great planets, wander the spheres; no door would be closed to them.

And she would go home.

When all was finished, the matron who had been sent to chaperone Beatrice at the meeting beckoned. Beatrice followed her out, passing Marco and Dante silently on her way.

She followed her chaperone to her parents' waiting carriage, and climbed inside. Instinctively, almost idly, she reached for the spheres' music, to which she had become so accustomed.

But the only sound was her parents' continued reproofs.

The heavens, at last, were silent.

RORA

53

I'VE BEEN SUCH a fool.

"What is it?" Major asks as I stare at him. At my answer.

I stagger to my feet, and when I slip a little in the snow, he reaches to steady me. I glance down at my feet. My heart stops.

All around us, where Major and I have been sitting, the snow has melted.

Summer is coming.

"It isn't just Mars," I say to him, shaking my head. Amir and a few of our squadmates edge back toward us. "It isn't just Mars!" I say again, my voice rising, almost frantic with realization.

Major puts a hand on my shoulder. "Rora. Slow down. What do you mean?"

"Mars's song won't be enough to fix this alone," I say, my voice cracking, hope rising like the sun in my chest. "We need to sing the others. *All* of them."

"What makes you think that?" Amir asks. "The exclusion . . . It forbids it. We've never done things that way." But there's no wariness in his eyes, no dismay at an idea that borders on heresy. Only wistfulness, and a guarded kind of hope.

I think of the first time I came to this planet. Of the gray that dumped me in a grave and tried to bury me alive.

Hours later, Queen Inara told me where I really belonged. But it wasn't Mars that hauled me out of that spiral, that held me in its arms and bore me away so I could breathe.

It was Mercury's song on Claudia beside me. It was Jupiter, where Amir took us, that melted the frost from my skin.

And it was Venus. Venus, rolling off Major, golden enough to break through the dark that smothered me, warm enough to keep me from freezing. When he wrapped his arms around me that night, he was such a threat to Kronos's ruined music that the Abbot refused to let him sing it.

All along I wanted to be strong enough not to need my friends, not to drain them. But I think of the monks I pitied, alone on their beds, all with the same weaknesses, with no one to carry them to safety, and I am grateful I was not alone here that night. That I was with people so truly, miraculously different from me.

"The planets have nothing but their own songs to heal themselves," I say. There is frozen snot above my lip and frozen blood on the backs of my knuckles and my throat is raw, but hope rings in my voice. "What if only ever hearing one song—spinning toward an extreme, ever since Beatrice laid down her rule—is what's brought us to this point? What if it was Saturn's grief, Saturn as its worst self, that *attracted* Chiron in the first place?"

When my chart showed me that I had to choose between Chiron and Mars, I thought it was simple. That one would drive out the other.

Mars was enough yesterday—enough to turn the tide in a competition, to sway something so small. But it will not be enough to raise this pit, to light up the dark. Not on its own.

My own heart would have told me that, if I'd been listening.

I watch Amir take this in, watch his unquiet thoughts. Watch him weigh what he's been told forever against the evidence before him.

"I know it's hard," I say. "The first time we came here, we tried to heal me with Saturn. But that only made me worse. It took Venus and Jupiter and Mercury and Mars all together to fix the damage. And then I came back, and tried to confront Saturn with Mars, to push all this strength at it, like we could *force* the planet to pick itself back up. But it's not enough," I say helplessly. "I know that bringing all the songs together goes against all your rules. But *none* of the songs would be enough on their own. And—"

"And I had begun to doubt those principles anyway," Amir suddenly interrupts. His eyes are fixed on Major.

Major falters. "You had?"

"Why?" I ask him. But Amir doesn't look away from his friend.

"Claudia—" Major begins. He clears his throat. "Claudia had doubts, too."

I startle at her name and seize Major's arm. "What?" Quickly, he explains how Claudia began to doubt Beatrice's theory of the exclusion—and how Queen Inara asked Claudia to let her be the one to tell the truth.

"My *mother* believes this, too?" Amir asks quietly. His eyes are still full of light, of desperate hope.

This means everything for Major; for him, the exclusion has only ever meant being cut off from the place he loves. But it means everything for Amir, too.

Amir, the someday-king on Jupiter, born to Inferno. The mourning prince bound to rule the proudest planet.

If it's true that all the songs need one another, then Amir, the Scorpio prince, has never been any less than he ought to be. He has only a new kind of strength to offer his people.

As Amir struggles to clear his throat, Major steps closer to my side. I wrap an arm around his waist, borrow his warmth, revel in the glow of Fortuna Minor that never seems to leave him. Venus's beautiful, confident, affectionate son, who is everything I am not, who is exactly what I need.

How could I have ever thought his music would make me less powerful, less true, less myself?

"So," Amir finally asks. "What do we do now?"

QUEEN INARA GLANCES again to the model at the center of the table. And there is Chiron: its outline sharp, its place clear amid Saturn's moons.

I'm just thinking of the outer spheres—the Stellare and the Prime Mover—and wondering if there will be anyone to speak for those songs; and then I realize why there won't be. Because they were untouched, incorruptible, undamaged by chaos.

When I shut my eyes, I don't have to reach far for the songs I heard coming from beyond Inferno. I remember the clear, piercing music that made me think of how mornings at my house felt before, of words I heard once from a priest; and as I listen to my memory, I recognize what I heard.

Those high, glassine notes had sounded like light. Perpetual light. *Lux perpetua*, the priest had said in his prayer, head bowed. And standing there in Teopanzolco, high on the top of that pyramid, I'd had the sense of being more than just half of something strained and needy; I'd felt like part of a great whole, surrounded by a family larger and fuller than two twins alone.

I think of how tightly I have squeezed Rora to protect her, how

I've tried to shield Jack from his choices. I did it because I was afraid, because I felt like half a person, a mere shadow.

But beneath that perpetual light, I didn't disappear. My sadness required no justification, invited no comparison.

I felt surrounded. Safe. Known, and not forgotten.

And all at once, I understand.

Clinging to the people I love will not make them stay. Controlling them will not keep them safe. And if, God forbid, they drift away from me someday, I will still be me.

I have to remember that I am not a shadow. I have to remember everything I've seen these past days—everything I've reminded myself I can do, and all the wonder I've felt.

I have to trust that the ones that I love, love me, too. I have to trust the Love that moves the sun and other stars to hold them securely, as it holds and moves everything in all the worlds.

I get up and pour Nour a fresh glass of tea. This time, she drinks.

1288

DANTE SAW BEATRICE just once more, two weeks after their return. He was in fine form that day, one of Folco Portinari's many honored guests at Beatrice's crowded wedding feast.

"So," Beatrice said listlessly as the dancing began and Dante took a seat beside her. She toyed with the gold brocade of her gown. "You've returned to Florence."

"Yes," said Dante. "For good, I believe." Many wonderful things were happening: his tale was already garnering great interest; even the Donatis were looking more kindly upon him.

Beatrice was beautiful in her wedding gown, her skin as lustrous as the pearls in her auburn hair. The dress itself was crimson—the color she had worn the day he had met her, he thought with some small regret.

He had forgotten how lovely she was. In fact, Dante had almost forgotten Beatrice entirely in the days before he received the wedding invitation from her father, as if Beatrice herself did not exist outside his thoughts or his company.

Dante faced her now, his voice growing indulgent. "Why so sad, Bice? You've had your adventure—are you not ready to grow up, and be a wife? To have your own children and husband, to run your own home as you see fit? Simone dei Bardi and his people will make you comfortable, at least."

He felt a moment of guilt for changing his mind out in the spheres. He hoped she was not hurt. But he could not help what was fated and what was not.

He had misunderstood, all those months ago. Destiny had not led him to Beatrice; it had led him to the tale. She was merely a character in it, just as he was.

But Beatrice would be fine, Dante reassured himself. She had what every woman wished for. And if all Beatrice had wanted was a comfortable life, it would have been enough.

But it was not, and they both knew it.

"Polo lied, too, you know," Beatrice said, catching Dante off guard. She nodded slowly, taking in the surprise on his face. "The tales he always told belonged to his father and uncle. He had learned Mongolian from them as well. One of the party from the Uls told me before we departed Mars that pieces of Marco's story—details about their timing—did not ring true. He spoke to others who'd arrived on Luna more recently and said that they had heard of Niccolò and Maffeo Polo, but that no one knew of a Marco. It was why he constantly pushed us onward, why he avoided their camp so diligently."

Dante gaped at her for a long moment. "Why did you not say anything?" he finally demanded.

Marco had left Siena not long after they had given their report. Dante had hardly been able to look his friend in the face as he embraced him and they parted ways.

Dante had thought Polo headed east, pushed on by his endless need to explore, but now he could not be sure.

"Because I did not care," Beatrice said simply. "His stories were borrowed. But Marco was always the person he professed himself to be." Dante's face flushed, from anger or embarrassment or both.

Before he could reply, a woman drew near, touching Dante none too lightly upon the arm. She was dark-eyed and dark-haired, in an umber gown Beatrice thought did little to flatter her thin figure; but she found the woman had rather a pleasing expression, frank and efficient and unfussy. "My dear Dante," she said in a clear voice, loudly enough to be heard over the musicians and the laughter of the guests. "We must not occupy too much of the bride's time on her wedding day!"

Dante's face turned redder still. "Indeed," he said, but did not move.

"You are Gemma Donati," Beatrice said, smiling politely at the woman. "I hope you are enjoying yourself?"

Beatrice hardly heard Gemma's reply in the affirmative, but not from any feelings of rancor. She had no quarrel with this woman. Gemma had not taken anything from Beatrice.

Say what he might, Dante had not returned for Gemma, or for anyone but himself.

Gemma finished her courtesies and turned away, gesturing for Dante to follow. But Beatrice leaned nearer him and spoke low before he could follow his betrothed. "I have married Simone. You will do as you wish. But do not pretend you have acted in my best interests, or out of any great wisdom or maturity," Beatrice said to him.

Dante swallowed hard, and said nothing.

"My adventures are only just beginning," Beatrice said to Dante,

415

and she said it like an oath, like an ended prayer, like a shut door.

She had been his friend, and she had loved him. Her words now stung. But Dante consoled himself as he walked away. All the world lay before him.

Dante did not know what he left behind as he rose to mingle through the wedding feast, to greet his many admirers.

RORA
55

I CAME TO this planet with just Mars's music—just my own kind of strength. But we will need so many other kinds to lift this darkness and raise the pit.

Amir beckons the squad closer. "We need the other songs," I say to him quietly, scanning their faces. Tishala. Briony. Baatar. Nikolai. So many more I barely know. "We need Jupiter, we need Mercury, we need Neptune. Each of the spheres has its own gifts. We need them all." Amir nods.

"Seventeen-three," he calls. The squad snaps to attention at once.

Amir is every inch our leader. Every inch a someday-king.

"Carry on with Mars's music, if it's all you know. All you love," Amir bellows above the wind. "But we can love many songs. We can belong to many different places."

He looks at Major, his expression full of meaning. "And if the place you were born still calls to you, or your heart belongs somewhere outside your sign—then follow it. Because we will require every sphere's song to save those trapped in the monastery."

The squad eyes us nervously. They're freezing and exhausted, and no one in Amir's position has proposed this in hundreds of years.

"But I only know Ulaan Garig," Briony says, faltering. "I grew up there. I belong there."

"That's all right," Amir reassures her. Considering, he turns to Baatar. "But weren't you born in al-Mushtari? The girl you're seeing—doesn't she belong there?"

"We ended things." Baatar looks away. "There was no future in it."

"Do you miss it?" Amir asks. *Do you miss her?* he doesn't add.

Baatar doesn't hesitate. "Every day."

"My mother still lives in Suvd Uls," Tishala offers quietly. "I worry about her. I miss it there, too."

"Then you know what to do," Amir says to them both.

One by one, we account for all the spheres. I'm surprised by how many of the others admit to missing other places, other music. By how many have been nursing unspoken hurts caused by the exclusion.

Major and Amir are far from the only ones who have suffered quietly under this rule.

"What will you sing, Rora?" Major asks as we reassemble ourselves, Amir moving to the head of our numbers. The shins of my pants are drenched, but with the summer and salt water and green life rolling off him, the aching cold has receded a little from my bones.

"I don't know," I say honestly.

Whatever we do, our path forward will not be dictated. Not by the stars, not by the hour of our birth.

We will choose our path. And I will choose who to walk beside.

I take Major's hand, and we begin again.

We straggle around the pit, not quite in ranks, just keeping together. The snow is up to our knees, but everyone seems a little less daunted than before.

Songs rise in fits and starts. There's no order to our progress. But no one is ashamed to falter in front of anyone else on this squad, and soon, we find our voice. We sing the songs of our stars and our hearts, the songs that are our birthrights and our own choices.

A few rows ahead of me, Briony—born to a long line of Aries— sings Mars, iron-strong as ever, still pouring strength into the gray planet beneath our feet. But I feel the other songs at work at once.

The moon is calm to Chiron's wild grief on Tishala's voice; Baatar's Jupiter is bracing, like a strong sea breeze. Nikolai offers the gray planet a light-drenched song that can only belong to the sun.

Mercury speeds and enlivens Saturn's slow anguish. Neptune soothes it. Uranus reminds the planet of its own curiosity.

Major pours out Venus beside me, warm as ever.

And Amir—Amir sings Inferno.

Pieces of him belong to various spheres. To Mars, the home of the squad he loves. To Jupiter, where his future as king has shaped him, weighed him down, built him up. Their influence is there in his music—iron-strong, proud and peerless.

But the song on his voice is grave, low and slow; it is solid, unshakable ground for a sinking city. And finally, finally, he can sing it without shame.

Suddenly—I don't know when it starts—I'm not walking anymore.

I'm not a good dancer. But my feet begin to take their orders from the music rising around us. And soon, everyone else is doing the same.

Our squad encircles the frozen pit, a multitude of rhythms and volumes, ten different songs and more because they're all distinctive on our voices. We stomp and clap, singing until we can't breathe, twining arms, spinning past one another.

We sing differently; we move differently; it ought to be cacophony. But together we are harmony. We are a symphony. We are wild, joyful, disorderly, and free.

The ground softens beneath my feet. Hope rises like a comet in my chest. And whatever it is within me that loves each of these songs, that makes them broader and louder and more themselves, amplifies them all until we are the only storm on Saturn.

And then I realize my own song has shifted.

I try to remember where I've heard what I'm singing—a song with words, a song I know. I almost laugh when I realize it's an Ad Astra song. "An Early Cold," my favorite.

Amir said Ad Astra sounded a little like Ulaan Garig. But as I shut my eyes and summon the memory of the concert, that night that feels like forever ago, I hear something different.

Mars's music is fierce, regimented. And Ad Astra's music is those things. But it's scrappier than Mars. More earnest. I've called their stuff my marching orders for forever.

But Earth's great power—our true magic, our cardinal virtue—isn't strength. It's hope.

Hope brought me to the 9:30 Club in the first place. It made me believe that even if there was no place safe in the universe, there were songs where I could feel entirely at home.

It makes me believe, now, that Earth has its own kind of magic to offer this place.

Ad Astra rises on my voice, headstrong and happy, as true and mine as if I'd written the words myself.

> Winter comes, it will not fail
> But do you fear the early cold?

Run, run, make your blood flow
Build your bones up sevenfold

Major spins me around, laughing breathlessly. Snow cascades off a tree branch nearby. Frost melts down my cheeks.

I jump and throw my fists at the sky, defying omens and storms and signs and portents. Let them make their threats; I have Claudia, I have Major, I have Amir, I have every good thing.

The sludge in the pit begins to dry and, spiraling, to ascend.

Kronos's monastery rises whole from the abyss, turrets and towers and slate gables, guardian chimeras and crows of stone. Its rock walls are weather-stained but solid, its windows unshattered.

And as we slow, panting and clinging to one another, we watch the mountainside become as whole as if the great abyss were never there.

1288

FLORENCE AND THE Donati clan welcomed Dante with open arms. In short order, he married Gemma and began climbing the city's social ladder, becoming known for his poetry.

But no matter how Dante rose, the center of things always seemed just beyond his reach.

He pressed on. He became an important man, moving in Florence's inner circle, in a sphere of politicians and rulers. Eventually, he became prior of the city. But those who dwell on high often fall the farthest.

Dante was lucky for years and years. But one day, he misstepped.

He put his foot on a brittle place and broke through the sphere of the favored into the night beyond. No longer basking in the sun of good fortune, he found himself lost, adrift, alone.

Dante was exiled from Florence, from the place that had made him famous, whose admiration he had chosen above the only person besides himself who he'd ever loved.

He fell off the edge of the world.

CLAUDIA

56

PAIN IS A social animal, a hardy disease. Pain is a comet, a bullet, a bomb.

It wrenches itself from one body into another, adaptable and contagious, wreaking havoc as it travels faster than light or sound.

So how do we unburden ourselves of pain without unleashing it on others? How do we dislodge a destructive body without destroying others in the process?

The answer is by caring, and with care. By keeping our hearts open to the incorruptible music, to the Love that moves and sustains all things.

Our experiment began with mourning. With trust. In sharing our stories and our suffering, I watched leaden mass converted to energy, the weight of grief turned into compassion for others. Somehow, as we sat here, we each felt kind words alleviate our pain just a little—without passing it on to anyone else.

It's the purest alchemy in the universe. It shines like perpetual light.

We see Chiron now. Our words have drawn him out, enabled us to measure him, time him, track his path. Now we can compel him to leave orbit at precisely the right moment and speed, so that he does not damage Saturn or anyone else.

He is our pain, and together we understand him, and together, with care, we will dispel him.

Someone pulls the lamps closer to the table so we can see better to work in the dark pavilion. I accept a task from a scholar at the far end of the table and set to work, my fingers racing to keep up with my brain. Some of the other scholars calculate his path alongside me; the rest take our math as quickly as we can produce it and turn it into magic. They circle the table, hands outstretched as directed by Queen Inara, glancing again and again at the gray moon coming over the horizon.

At last, I hand over my results. "Chiron's moving roughly thirty percent faster than Saturn's nearest other satellite," I say. "But he shouldn't catch up to it for another six hours."

The scholar scans my work, then nods, seeming satisfied. "Thank you."

And then my job is done, and I don't know what to do. I take another sip of Nour's tea and glance over at her.

I haven't seen Jack in seven weeks, and I've hardly spoken to him in that time, but I've missed him every hour. Nour will not see her brother again in this life.

Sadness for her is a weight in my stomach. I'm suddenly, deeply aware of all the chances I still have.

"I'm sorry." I push a plate of cookies closer to her; they smell like cardamom and almond. "You should eat."

Nour picks one up. I'm relieved when she bites into it. "It still doesn't feel real," she says in a low voice. "That he's gone."

"I can imagine." I pause, then correct myself. "No. No, I can't."

Nour shakes her head. "I'm glad you can't. I don't want you to."

I drink some more tea. Dr. Qureshi and the queen sing and sing. Their pace rises, mirroring Chiron's progress.

"Forgive your brother," Nour says quietly. "Talk to him. Whatever it takes, fix it. Chiron does not need to have the final word in your story."

She's right. Chiron may have hurt us—may have strained and twisted my relationship with both my twin and my un-twin in one fell night. But we still have the chance to fix things between us. To rise above what the stars predict.

"I promise." I nod at her. "And I—if you ever need to talk, I know you don't know me, but I hope I'll be back."

Nour doesn't smile, but the twist of her mouth is grateful. She eats another cookie and I give her a little space, fishing both textbooks about Beatrice out of my bag. With all our talk about grief, sitting around this table, the passage I read this morning in *Beatrice and Dante: Notes and Letters* has been nagging at me.

And suddenly, I understand.

It's that final passage—not Beatrice's analyses, but her aching last diary entry—that explains the exclusion.

I'm furiously making notes on the book's last pages when the scholars suddenly stop talking. I set the volume down as we all stand, glancing first down at the table like angels watching from heaven, then looking to the sky like the mortals we are.

The gray body we saw on the horizon is not a moon at all; it has rings and moons of its own. The Great Conjunction has brought Saturn almost close enough to touch. Its cool, sober light wavers over al-Mushtari's endlessly shifting tides.

In the model and in the heavens, Chiron is a small gray orb, soaring out of Saturn's proximity. From where we stand, it seems to narrowly avoid another moon before sailing toward its old place in orbit.

I can see from the path it cuts that it won't cause any more harm as it makes its way home.

1290

ON A FINE summer day in 1290, Beatrice Portinari died in child-birth.

Or rather, that was what her family told the world.

This second pregnancy had been difficult. Only by the grace of God and the skill of the midwives had she been safely delivered of the babe.

A hollow had persisted in her chest since she had left the heavens behind. Beatrice could not have imagined that it could be any deeper, or why it should be. Her baby boy had been born squalling merrily, and she had wept with gratitude at his cries.

And yet, inexorably, the hollow grew.

Enough, Beatrice had told herself, chest heaving on her bed as maids bustled about her, carrying her boy away to Simone to be cel-ebrated among his friends, to be named for a litany of saints and deceased family members.

Enough.

She spent two days gathering her strength and her recollections. Then, after the household had gone to sleep—the servants to their quarters, Simone to his own bed—Beatrice kissed her tiny daughter, Francesca, and her newborn son, and conjured herself away.

The sun was rising over al-Mushtari when she returned, the shallow sea swirling around her feet and legs in welcome. The gates were opened at once by citadel guards who recognized her.

Beatrice climbed through the carved sandstone city with wet feet and wet lashes. And she found still more tears when she reached the palace and pled an audience with the king.

She was waiting in the library where King al-Radi had first met their expedition when he entered alone. Beatrice rose, frowning. "Syed?"

"Bice!" Al-Radi's second son greeted her, swiping at his eyes, leaning heavily against the arched doorway with his other hand. "I'm so glad you've come. How did you know?"

The sunrise through the screened window showed Syed's eyes were red and ringed with shadows, his lashes damp as hers were. He looked thin, as though his appetite had fled.

Beatrice shook her head slowly, misgiving growing within her. "Know what, my friend?"

A fever had taken the city, and King al-Radi had died. Syed's own beloved wife, his oldest brother, and many of their people had gone with him.

Sitting on the hillside where Beatrice had once sat with Dante, watching the waves crash against the city wall, the two of them shared the grief they had felt—Beatrice after returning to Earth, Syed after losing his loved ones and ascending a throne he had never wanted.

"I feel like a fool," he said to her. "Al-Qadir, *the powerful*. That is the regnal name my advisors chose, and I feel like a fool wearing it. I was never even supposed to be king."

Beatrice shook her head, watching the crimson-and-gold horizon. "You are not a fool," she said softly. "But I will stay and help advise you, if you wish me to." She paused. "I believe I can help protect others from the harm I have suffered. And I believe you could use a friend."

She was grateful, in a way, that they were alike in their pain. Returning to a jovial al-Mushtari—even a city overjoyed to see her—she would have found insupportable.

"I could," Syed answered readily. Then he cocked his head. "What sort of changes?"

She laced her fingers together, organizing her thoughts. "Do you remember the day we discussed natal charts, and you told me what great store you all set by the ascendant sign?"

He frowned dimly. "I believe so."

Beatrice shook her head. "I believe I was misled by that ascendant sign. That it is only a face we choose to wear, and that we ought to attend more closely to the truths revealed in the sun sign."

She saw clearly now what she had not seen when she first reached Jupiter. That she had been deceived by Dante's ethereal Pisces ascendant, not perceiving that he truly did belong to Gemini. That he was slippery, a tale teller, duplicitous to his core.

"Perhaps if I had been more honest with myself about Dante's essential nature, I would not have been hurt. He might not have had the chance to cause such harm, confined to Venus, surrounded by others like him." Beatrice paused. "Perhaps those of varying sun signs ought to confine themselves to those planets where they belong."

Syed looked at her, alarmed. "Beatrice, I do not—"

"I only wish to spare others pain," she insisted. Beatrice paused, considering her friend, and said what she knew would convince him.

"I do not wish others to be wounded as I have been. To suffer as we have."

Syed did not understand yet. This was no surprise; she had been like him, once. Lying with Dante beneath Venus's eternal sunrise, she could never have known the pain he would cause her. That the differences in their essential natures meant it could not be otherwise.

"We have both suffered much," Syed finally agreed, softening. "And I should be grateful if you would stay."

He could not comprehend at present. But he was good, and tender-hearted. He would see that this was the best way to protect his people. She would help him to see.

"I will stay," she said to him.

Beatrice thought, once more, of Earth. Of the husband and children she had left.

Then, in her heart, she locked the door behind her.

RORA

57

THE ABBOT'S WALKING stick clanks against the stone stairs, frost melting off his clothes and beard. At the bottom of the monastery steps, he pauses, seeming to shake the cold out of his bones. Then he bows to Amir.

"Highness," he says simply, "I cry your mercy."

Amir shakes his head. "There's nothing to forgive, Abbot."

But the monk grimaces. "I am old enough to know better. I ought to have recognized the signs sooner." He looks back at the other monks emerging on unsteady feet, shielding their eyes against the light. "I ought to have taken better care of them."

"You are the wisest of us," Amir insists, his tone of respect never growing reproachful. "If even you can find yourself lost in shadow—I will not be the one to blame you."

I don't expect the Abbot to recognize me, but his cataracted eyes narrow on my face. "I am sorry for the despair with which I burdened you." He leans on his cane, draping his long gray beard over his shoulder. "Clear of mind, I would never have sung to you. I would have sent you on to Ulaan Garig, where it appears you found your way, regardless."

"I did." My tone's a little absent; I'm more interested in the change in him, his new bearing. I cock my head. "You're different."

"Of course I am," the Abbot says kindly. "I was sick. I've gotten better. As, it seems, have you." He pauses, gesturing around us. "How did you do it?"

"We surrounded the depression with all the songs," Major says. "We tried Ulaan Garig alone at first, but when that didn't work, Rora figured it out."

Because of you, I don't say. But the Abbot remembers Major, too.

"Son of Venus," he says, smiling slowly. "You rescued her when I put her in danger, though I chastised you. My apologies, dear boy, and well done. Fortuna Minor has you well in hand." Major bites his lip, and the Abbot looks again to the monastery, musing aloud. "Yes, I'll have much to discuss with Their Majesties when they arrive."

"Are they coming?" Amir blurts, eyes wide.

The Abbot's brow wrinkles. "Well, aren't they?"

Before any of us can answer, a gentle snow begins to fall.

Soft sounds of panic come from my squad, but the Abbot raises a hand. "Don't be afraid." His voice is stronger now than it was even a moment ago.

And as little snowflakes land on my cheeks and nose, I find I'm not. This isn't the blizzard of despair we came to calm.

This is soft, sober, peaceful. This is Saturn as it should be.

The contingent from Jupiter arrives soon after, and the king and queen and their scholars immediately move into private talks with the Abbot, Commander Bao, Amir, and—to my surprise—Claudia. I spot her at once, and I want to ask her what's happened, but I content myself with seeing that she's all right. While more industrious members of squad seventeen-three run around setting up pavilions and building fires, I wait for her, my eyelids drooping.

"Take a nap," Major urges me.

"Can't," I say thickly, blinking hard. "Claudia might—"

"I'll wake you up when she's out," he promises me. "Rest."

"I'm never going to be able to fall asleep," I grumble.

But of course, I'm out in minutes. And when he wakes me sometime later, there she is.

Sleep makes me clumsy, but I'm up like a shot, wrapping Claudia in a hug that's certainly too tight to be comfortable. "You did it," I gasp out. "You absolute genius. You did it."

"Rora, *you* did it." Claudia stares around, taking in the calm skies and the healed castle, her expression turning so earnest I almost don't recognize her. "This place was a graveyard. You brought it back from the dead."

"I didn't do it alone." I glance over to where Queen Inara and King Sameer stand with Amir and Major, Amir's parents wearing expressions of love, exhaustion, and pride.

Claudia gasps. "Major was here?"

"He snuck in with us." I clear my throat. "We couldn't have fixed this without him. I fought his music for so long, even though it made me feel happy and safe. Because I thought needing him—letting myself lean on him—would make me less myself." I pause. "But the thing I realized today is that the truest, strongest version of me still needs the people I care for."

Claudia stills. "Yeah?"

"I haven't been a very good friend lately." My voice is very small; Claudia doesn't love this sort of thing. But to my surprise, she doesn't brush off my seriousness, or try to make a joke. "I'm so sorry. I've been absorbed by my own stuff and forgot you very much had your own stuff going on. More than anything, I was afraid if I let you see how bad things really were, you'd cut me loose." I hesitate, daring to meet her eyes. "I need to learn how to fight for myself, like you said. To find healthy coping mechanisms. And maybe, like, a doctor. But it was a mistake to lock you out for fear you'd just leave on your own anyway."

And it doesn't have to be this way anymore, I vow to myself. *It can be so much better.*

"I'm not going anywhere," Claudia says softly. "And I forgive you. While you were raising the pit, I dealt with . . . some things on Jupiter, too. That's how we released Chiron."

I blink at her. I've never known Claudia to admit needing to *deal* with anything. "What kind of things?"

"Jack things. Neediness things. Self-worth things." She swallows. "Half of the process was weird magic. An exercise in vulnerability." Claudia's visibly nervous at all this intimacy; I'm still waiting for her to bolt. But she doesn't. She's right here.

I think of the first time I saw Amir box—with Baatar, that first day on Mars. I was amazed at how clean and unrestrained the fight was. And it was that way because they were well matched. Because they trusted one another.

I'm lucky to have someone I trust here in the ring with me.

"What was the other half of it?" I ask, squeezing Claudia's shoulder.

"The most exciting research experience of my life." Claudia offers this statement with zero irony, a breathless grin spreading across her face, and if she were anyone but herself, I'd lose it. "We had to calculate Chiron's size, speed, path. It was like working in a NASA lab, except, you know. With archaic science and magic. I can't believe I got to help."

"I can," I say, maybe a little too aggressively. "You're brilliant, Claudia. You're so smart and so strong."

Claudia's been down since Jack's left. I wonder if maybe she also forgot how much she had to offer on her own.

I'm a day late and a dollar short with this realization, but I'm determined not to let her forget anymore.

I hug her again, breathing in the smell of cashmere and the last hints of Marc Jacobs. "Thank you," she mumbles. And I thank all the spheres and all the stars that we've found our way back to each other.

When Claudia pulls back, her eyes are gleaming. "There's one other thing," she says. "Amir told me how you recovered the monastery. With all the songs."

"I think the exclusion is the problem. I think it exaggerated Saturn's song so horribly that it pulled Chiron into its sphere." I pause, grinning a little. "Major said you were on the trail before I ever got there, though."

"And other people were there well before I was," Claudia says, darting a glance to the queen and Dr. Qureshi.

I shake my head. "How did you even figure it out?"

Claudia hesitates. "Beatrice Portinari," she says, lowering her eyes. "I wasn't making it up before, Rora. I really am related to her."

She doesn't say it like it's a point of pride. It's a small, difficult truth on her voice, something precious and sharp she puts in my hands, asking me to be careful.

"At first, I just wanted to know who she was, and what that meant about me. Then I found out what she'd done." She pauses again. "In the end, I just wanted to understand why, so I could undo it. So people like Amir and Major wouldn't have to suffer anymore."

"And you did this in a matter of days," I say, awe filling my voice. "Claudia, I am—so proud of you." I shake my head, trying to clear it. "Tell me more. I need to know everything."

"Okay." She glances back to Major and Amir again. "I should show you guys what I found."

1288

Excerpt from Beatrice and Dante: Notes and Letters

I wed Simone this morning. Dante attended the wedding feast this afternoon with his own betrothed.

I ought not to write which excited me more, even here where only I will read it. I ought to be meditating on how to run my household, on the children Simone and I will have.

But I find I can only dwell on the past.

On another world, I might have been glad to run his home, have his children. There, with him, it might not have been to the exclusion of everything else I care about.

For now, I can think only of how happy I believed we were, and how mistaken I was. But no matter how many times I turn over the events of our journey, I cannot see if our problems began in Acuto, where he began to write—to dream dreams without me—or if they began sooner.

I suspect that some of us are planets, moving predictably and safely. And some of us are comets, destined to break whatever we touch.

I believed Dante and I were the same. But we are not.

Perhaps I only ever hoped we desired the same things. Only ever wished that we were alike enough in mind and soul not to harm one another so grievously. My thoughts were too fixed on the avenues between heaven and earth, on the infinite miracles we might perpetrate.

Perhaps I ought to have dwelled more on the proper place for things and not dismissed what the stars told me, for the safety of my own heart.

CLAUDIA
58

"THIS IS SO sad," Rora says, sliding *Beatrice and Dante* away from her.

I nod. "Dante picked the stained-glass version of Beatrice over the woman herself. He traded a person for a symbol, because of ambition. And it hurt her." I gesture at the diary entry, the image of Beatrice's cramped, scrabbly handwriting.

Major shakes his head, flexing his fingers on his knees. "I still don't understand what it means, though."

"Well, what's *missing* is as important as what's there," I begin, glancing between them. "I'd been wondering how Beatrice found her way to the rule of exclusion. Where was all the analysis that led to it?" Amir nods, sitting forward.

"I'd already been thinking about the spheres' need for balance after what happened on Mercury," I say. "After we banished Chiron—which we were only able to do by bringing all the songs together—I was thinking how hard it is not to let pain become a cycle. And then I reread this." I point to the page.

"This is Beatrice's last diary entry on Earth. And this insistence on *the proper place for things* at the end, on putting things where they belong—that never comes up in her early research; she was always so focused on *as above, so below,* on the harmony of the music and how everything holds together." I pause. "But she stresses it here, and Dr. Qureshi told me she absolutely hammered it when she returned to al-Mushtari. And then the exclusion of the spheres became law less than a decade after her arrival. But reading this diary entry—it tells me she was just hurt, and she didn't want anyone else to feel the way she did."

Major pushes hair out of his eyes. "And no one ever thought of this?" he finally asks.

"She was wounded and embarrassed," I say. "No one was supposed to think of it. So it's been that way ever since."

Things are going to change, though. After talking to Amir, the king and queen have already put an end to the travel ban.

I'm glad his parents and advisors are finally listening to him. I'm glad to have helped put an end to some of the harm the Portinari line has caused.

Mostly, I'm grateful Amir doesn't hold my heritage against me.

I'd been afraid to tell him the truth about being Beatrice's descendant because of all the suffering she'd caused. Because of the choices she made and the insufficiency Amir had felt his whole life as a result. But when I confessed just before our meeting earlier, he'd refused to blame me.

You aren't her, Claudia. You're choosing to be different, and better. To undo what she did.

The truth is, *he's* better. He's too good to punish me for someone else's mistakes.

Everything—every*one*—is getting a fresh start.

And I'll be here to see it happen. Dr. Qureshi has already asked me to come back and study with her. Across our little circle, Amir's smile is steady, coal-bright, warming the pit of my stomach.

He's already asked to see me again.

"LOOK!" Rora bursts out.

I jump at her shriek, so close to my ear. "What?" I demand, on edge for her out of habit. "What is it?"

"Sorry." She blushes, pointing at the sky. "But—look."

I have already watched Saturn rise in Jupiter's sky. But it's an entirely different thing now to watch Fortuna Major rise above Infortuna Major's horizon. To know now that neither means the other any harm.

As the sky fills with Jupiter's golden light, the camp around us fills with delegations from other planets. Queen Inara told us they'll stay until Saturn's music feels completely balanced.

Maybe they'll stay after that. Maybe they'll go. It'll be their choice.

"What's at the edge?" Rora asks after a while. "Past all the planets?"

"The Stellare." Amir smiles again, so contained you'd miss it if you didn't know exactly where to look. "A boundless sea of stars."

"And after that, what the ancients called the Unmoved Mover. *The Love that moves the sun and other stars*, as Dante puts it." I pause. "I could hear it from Inferno, when Major and I went there. Both of their songs."

"What did they sound like?" Rora's voice is wistful, like she wishes she could have heard it. I hope someday she will.

"It felt like seeing all the way to the end," I finally say. "And knowing everything will be all right."

And it will. I squeeze Rora to my side, and I know—it will.

RORA

59

WE CAMP OUTSIDE that final night. Claudia sleeps with her back to mine. My best friend, with the sharp tongue and the brilliant brain.

I've missed her so much. I'm glad we're both back where we belong.

Major lies awake on my other side. It feels like he and I are the last ones awake in the world, beneath Jupiter like a gold coin in the sky. My heart swells every time I see him remember that it's there, and then remember it doesn't own him anymore.

"I can't believe I can go home," Major says for what must be the twelfth time. "I can go home. I can do what I want with my life."

"What will you do?" I ask softly. "Run the orchards? Learn art from your mom? Sail all day?"

"Any of it. All of it. Whatever I want," he says, as if he can hardly dare to believe the words. I watch his lips move as he speaks, watch his sun-bleached blue eyes.

When he smiles, it calls to me, and I answer.

It feels natural as can be when Major reaches out a broad golden hand, traces the shell of my ear, strokes my face with his thumb as he cups my cheek.

He's luminous in the dark, the endless summer I've been waiting for.

"You know," I say quietly, "when I first met you, I went with you guys on the hope that the things that made me sad were . . . extraordinary. That my pain wasn't this mundane thing. Except—it was, and it wasn't." I glance at Major. He's still, his only movement the rise and fall of his chest. "The thing that happened to me happens to people every day. But so do things like this." Gold hair tangles at his temple, hangs in his eyes. I push it away.

"That can't be true." Major scoots nearer to lean over me, brushing my bangs aside with gentle fingers. "There's never been anyone like you and me, Rora."

"There has been," I insist, smiling. I tug at his hand, press a kiss to his palm. "People fall for each other every day, Major. People suffer every day. But just because something is ordinary doesn't mean it's not also catastrophic, or magical."

I smooth the lines in his brow, trace a finger over his lips. But he shakes his head. "You can't tell me we didn't discover this," he says softly. "It feels brand-new." One corner of his mouth lifts before he bends to kiss me.

As his mouth moves over mine, my hands find the nape of his neck, his shoulders, his chest; the heartbeat beneath is my metronome. I plan to set my clock by that rhythm.

These past few weeks, I've been spiky, defensive. I've felt unbearable to be around.

And yet when Major pulls back, shaggy blond hair falling around his face, he looks like he sees someone who's easy to care for. The same way I've seen him all along.

We kiss until we're sleepy, until we're just lying face-to-face, watching each other out of half-shut eyes. I hold one of his hands in mine, counting his fingers, back and forth, his steady-thrumming pulse lulling me toward dreams.

"What will we call you now, if you won't live on Jupiter?" My voice is drowsy. "Minor? Like Fortuna Minor, for Venus, instead of Fortuna Major?"

"Mpphh. Minor is a terrible nickname."

"Oh yeah, so much worse than Major." I think of our first conversation—*Major what?*—and laugh.

"Major's fine, I guess." His eyes are closed. Blond lashes splay across his cheeks. "Been called that for years. Too much work to change it now."

"What's your real name?" I wonder aloud. But his breathing has steadied; he doesn't respond. I prod him in the cheek, on the nose. "Hey. Major. Hey. What's your real name?"

He cracks open one eye, catching my rogue fingers in one hand, and smiles at me sleepily. "Felix," he says, the word clumsy and sweet on his voice. "It means *happy.*"

I wake in the middle of the night. Claudia's back is still pressed to mine, shifting evenly with her breath, but Major's not beside me anymore.

Frowning, I look to the sky—and there he is, standing over me. Behind him and Amir, the moons cast the monastery in soft, endless light. "Wake up," Major whispers.

My heart plummets, out of habit. "What?" I demand, still half asleep. "What is it, what's wrong?" But when I see he's smiling, all the starlight and all the moonlight caught in his eyes, something in me steadies.

"Don't be scared." Amir crouches beside Claudia, reaches for her hand. "We have a surprise. My father had an idea for a last hurrah before you go home."

When I reemerge from the monastery, changed out of my borrowed uniform and dressed in my leather jacket again, they're waiting for us. Amir's parents. My commander and the professor. Even the Abbot. We pass thanks and farewells back and forth, but there are too many things I'm not sure how to say.

Thank you for listening to me when I was hurt. Thank you for teaching me to fight for myself. Thank you for helping me find my place, and my people.

I smile instead. Shake the iron pill bottle at Queen Inara and promise I'll keep taking them. Pass Commander Bao my uniform. "It will be waiting for you," he says.

Mostly, I'm grateful the long goodbyes don't feel necessary.

I'll be back soon. Though Earth's music beckons me, I won't be able to keep away from Mars—or from Major—for long. Not now that I know where I belong.

Amir traces figures in the snow, and I sing a note that I know will lead us home.

The spheres are transparent when we enter the portal, their aether made truly aethereal. We don't need to smash our way in; they don't creak or rattle as we walk.

I've sung a note to take us to Earth, but we find ourselves in Inferno's sphere, looking out on the Stellare.

I turn to Major, confused. "Where—?" But he smiles.

"We're taking the long way." He stands behind me and nods beyond the aether, arms wrapped around my middle. Nebulae and black holes blossom like flowers in a field, every color and no color amid a thousand points of brilliance. And I can hear the song Claudia tried to describe.

The music is bright and clear, like pianos and harp strings, like light made sound. Light so absolute and inexorable, it's impossible to fear the dark—not the familiar dark inside me, not the unknown dark beyond.

I suck in a sharp breath and hold it, holding on to the feeling of it all: the stars a city of light before us, Claudia and Amir safe beside me, Major holding on to me and not letting go.

When the ache has passed and my heart is full, I take Major's hand and break into a run.

"Wait. Where are you going?" Claudia shrieks, sprinting after me. "Don't make me run, I have boots on!" I laugh in answer.

We are swifter than a solar wind; we are comets in the night. We are safe now.

We sprint beneath the field of planets that make up Inferno, their music like Amir's song, a low, grave bassline beneath the glittering high notes of the Stellare and Unmoved Mover.

We race through the sphere, complete it, and move on to the next.

Neptune. Her music's slow violin slide hits my ears as soon as we pass into her kingdom; it speaks of a hundred hearts with stories, a hundred ears to listen. She glows sapphire-colored in the distance, and my breath frosts as we race by.

The music turns unpredictable, wandering, curious, woodwind-clear as we run past Uranus—the genius thunderstorm, the sphere in endless pursuit of progress and science and magic. As we pass the shivering aqua pearl of a planet, Claudia crosses herself, like a prayer, like a promise.

On, on, on we run.

And there is Saturn again in the distance. Infortuna Major is a cello to Neptune's violin, perfectly tuned, measured in his melancholy.

The first time I saw him, my heart quailed in my chest. The second time, it pounded like a drum, steady as Mars. Now my soul warms as I look on Saturn's soft gray sobriety, as I think on the mountain of Kronos where I know a gentle snow is still falling.

I squeeze Major's hand as Jupiter appears in the distance, brilliant purple and red and gold as the trumpet fanfare that rings out around it. *This planet doesn't own you*, I say silently, and I think he hears me.

Jupiter isn't Major's home. But I eye it gratefully as we pass, knowing it *is* home to so many, and that the music of the spheres depends upon its song just like every other.

I hope that a strong wind still blows over al-Mushtari's walls and its water, and that all is well there.

The asteroid belt is a few brief bars of percussion before Mars's drums hit our ears.

I run toward the red planet, the home that makes my heart strong and speaks to me in iron tones. Amir and I race each other, glad to see again the red flag that tells us all is well, the red light that tells us to go.

We press fists to our chests, not stopping. *"Hic manebimus optime!"* I shout, even as we run forward, toward the sun shining in the distance, toward harp music and burning fire.

The sun. How many days has it been since I've seen its light in a blue sky? We shield our eyes until we've passed it, unable to comprehend its brightness but knowing that somewhere on its blazing surface is a city, home to brilliant alchemists and fearless worshippers.

We complete the sphere, racing the sunlight stretching out before us.

And then we see *her* in the distance. Fortuna Minor, Venus herself.

I've never seen her before—her rose-gold sand, her oceans, her endless sunsets. But I've heard her music, rushing on the tide of Major's heartbeat.

His eyes are lit up as we sail past his home. I can't wait to meet her someday.

And then Claudia darts forward, feet fleeter even than her thoughts, racing toward Mercury. I chase her just to see her face brighten at its high chimes, its quicksilver brightness.

The moon's sphere is last, its wise, gentle light and its panpipe song that draws the ocean almost as familiar as home. We slow as we approach, panting, calmed by her gentle face.

We complete the sphere.

Slowly, slowly, our steps begin to flag. And then we reach it. Earth's song is a choir, a happy crowd, as wonderful and familiar as concerts and Metro announcements and phone calls from friends.

We stumble out of the portal and into the 9:30 Club's bathroom stall doors, reeling and laughing. We're home.

1321

MARCO POLO WAS an old man when Dante saw him for the last time. Marco had aged, his tanned skin grown leathery, grown wise with his travels.

Dante was an old man himself.

He had orbited one great house after another, exiled, isolated from his wife and children. He had become a well-known artistic hanger-on, and an even better-known poet.

His work was famous—the tale of a man who traveled through hell and purgatory with Virgil of the *Aeneid*, who circled the heavens with a beautiful woman named Beatrice, a holy vision in a brilliant red dress.

And when Dante Alighieri arrived with a party from Ravenna for diplomatic negotiations in Venice and found himself opposite Marco Polo, he knew he looked as though he'd been to heaven and hell and back.

Dante had been forbidden to speak during the meeting at all—in his old age, as when young, he could argue any point, justify anything, and the Doge of Venice dreaded debating him.

It didn't matter. The sight of his old friend Marco stunned him into silence.

Dante knew he was paler and more angular than in years past, his eyes more calculating than they had been when he was young. When they'd been friends. When he was happy.

If only he'd known it.

When the deal was done, Dante and Marco and the other men rose. Amid the momentary shuffle of chairs and papers, Marco extended a rough hand to Dante, expression carefully neutral. "I have read your poetry, Signore Alighieri."

Dante smiled. "My politics created quite a stir in Florence. Hence, my exile."

"I don't care about your politics," Marco said quietly. "But your Beatrice..." He trailed off. "I don't hear the music anymore. I haven't since a few years after we returned, though I've searched for it everywhere."

To this, Dante said nothing. He had never been able to hear the spheres' music from Earth. He had scarcely listened to it as they had traveled the heavens. Even to describe the song of the Unmoved Mover—*the Love that moves the sun and the other stars*—he had had to speak in Beatrice's words.

"Perhaps others will find the way again." Marco wet his lips. "Perhaps others will remain where we could not."

Dante nodded vaguely. "I have heard rumors."

All attempts by Siena's university masters had failed to breach the spheres, but there were whispers that others had succeeded—most lately the rabbi Yehuda ben Moshe and his companions from Toledo. They had been assembled to translate tables on the movements of the heavens and had briefly, mysteriously disappeared. A few of their number had returned bearing whispers of a snowy village on a sapphire-blue planet that they had named Tarshish.

More would follow them, word of whom would never reach Dante's ears: the Mexica astronomers of the New World drawn to the stars as they counted days into the future; the scholars of the Holy Roman Empire who would one day follow a man named Kepler into the heavens.

"I tried to go back, just once," Marco said suddenly. "But I couldn't remember the figures. I couldn't remember the songs."

Dante had as well, and had failed. But he would not admit as much. This time, Marco would be the one to confess weakness, and not he.

Beatrice Portinari, the door between worlds. Dante had left her, and she had shut him out.

It was his own fault.

Dante swallowed, nodding. "To lose it—to lose her—was quite a loss, indeed."

They both knew, though, that she had not been lost. That Dante's Beatrice had gone where her heart drew her. And that Dante himself had chosen the glitter of fool's gold over the brilliance of stars when he had them in his very hand.

"Yes." Marco nodded. That was all he said.

Signore Polo took his leave. Signore Alighieri departed in the other direction.

Dante was surprised, after so many years, to feel his heart ache. But it did, as he remembered how he and his friends had found the bright center of all things in the midst of the three of them.

CLAUDIA

60

THE CENTER

AS THE PORTAL spits us out and we tumble against the bathroom counters, relief hits me so hard I could almost kneel and kiss the ground. We're home.

But then I see Rora laughing at Major, her backpack hanging off one shoulder, and Amir watching me as though I've done something incredible, and I know some part of me had already found its home, even worlds and light-years away.

I slip my phone out of my bag, power it on, and pull the three of them close. Just as the bathroom door swings open.

A man in a 9:30 Club T-shirt crosses his arms. "Hey!"

"Mirror selfie!" I shout, and Major and Rora grin at our reflections as I snap the photo. When I shove them toward the exit, I expect Ro to look upset, but Major's the one looking apologetic.

"Sorry, sir," Rora says in a stage whisper, wincing theatrically as she seizes Major by the hand. "He was just soooo cute, I couldn't—"

"*Don't* finish that story," says the club employee, shaking his head. "Out."

"Useless kids," another black-clad staffer chuckles.

"At your service." Rora gives a little salute.

As we trip over each other out the door, I look at the picture on my phone. Major and Rora are laughing. Amir's just looking at me.

We're talking over each other, snorting with laughter as we tumble down the hallway and past the empty bar and merch tables and through the front doors of the venue. Eyes on the night outside, I prod Rora down the front steps—right into Jude London.

"Whoa there!" he laughs.

Rora's face goes white. "Oh, wow."

I frown. "But—how—?"

"The Solstice Show," Rora says, heaving a sigh of relief. "We made it."

We've traveled through the stars and back and still caught Ad Astra's second stop through town. Only ten days have passed.

"Yeah, you made it." Jude London blinks at us, pushing shaggy hair out of his eyes, and I know he's wondering if we were taking more than selfies in the bathroom. I laugh.

Rora rummages in her bag. "Will you sign my—" But her hands only find a copy of a magazine with their band's photo on the cover. She passes it to him, wincing, and Jude raises his eyebrows. "I know," she exclaims. "The review was crap. Ad Astra has meant everything to me these last few months."

Jude thumbs through the magazine. "Well, everyone's entitled to their opinion," he says, shrugging easily. He looks younger up close. When he comes to the article where Rora's scrawled *JEEEEEERK* across the name of the writer, he barks a laugh and nudges the guitarist. They fumble for a Sharpie, and his bandmate draws devil horns on the photo of the writer and scribbles a little note to Ro.

"I know," Rora finally says. "Music is so—"

"Individual," Jude finishes.

"Exactly!" says Rora. "Not everyone is at home in the same song."

He grins. "That's a nice way of putting it."

Rora's beaming as she seizes Major by the hand, introducing him and Amir to Jude and the others. I reach for my cell again, snapping photos of Rora's flushed cheeks and bright eyes, the friendly band members and the club's front steps.

About twelve texts pop up from my parents when I pull my phone off airplane mode. They're pissed, but less than I expected. Huh.

I fire off a quick reply, telling them I'm sorry for taking off and that I'm back from Shenandoah with Rora and the Millers a few days early. *Bad reception out there! Home soon!* Then I drag all the photos into another text.

DC misses you, I type.

Ro and I do, too. Especially me. Then I send it to Jack. Somehow, my battery's holding out at 12 percent.

A response appears immediately. *Don't cause too much trouble.*

I almost drop my phone. Fingers shaking, I try to tap out a reply, but another text comes through too quickly, then another.

I told Mom and Dad I was sorry.

They said I could come home for Christmas.

Christmas. I can't stop the smile that breaks over my face.

It's only four days away. I can't wait to show Rora.

She's saying bye to the band, thanking them for making music, joking that she'll frame the horrible article. The guys laugh and I snap a photo of them hugging her. It's a great shot.

Rora turns to leave, then pauses. "Hey!" They stop and turn toward her again, grins still clinging to their faces. "Look up this Latin phrase." She scribbles something down on a page from the magazine and shoves it into Jude's hand before hurrying back to Major and Amir and me.

"What—" Jude begins. *"Hic manebimus optime?"*

"You're going to love it!" Rora hollers back. She ducks beneath Major's arm, too shy to watch Jude London stare at the words a moment longer, then carefully fold the paper and put it in his pocket.

"That doesn't count as giving away official magical space secrets, right?" Rora asks Amir, leaning around Major.

Amir shrugs, deadpan. "Why start following the rules now?" Then he groans, rolling his eyes at Major. "It's finally happened. You've corrupted me."

Rora ignores this, eyeing me significantly. "14th Street? Ted's Bulletin? Pop-Tarts?"

"I've got a little time." I turn a curious glance on Amir. He nods, eyes alight with the same questions, hair tousled and perfect, hands stuck in his pockets.

"Plenty of time," he agrees. His voice is as warm as his eyes.

I put an arm around Amir, and Rora skips ahead with Major. She's chanting *Pop-Tarts, Pop-Tarts* and people are staring but Major joins right in with her. Amir turns his face into my neck as he laughs. Another text buzzes in my coat pocket, and I know it's Jack.

The streets ahead are crowded with people and voices, neon-bright.

It's good to be back. To come home to the center of my universe.

The concert's over, and my ears are ringing. It's eleven o'clock, and the night is endless.

We round the corner, and the lights go on forever.

AUTHOR'S NOTE

This story takes liberties with history—great ones, like fabricating a friendship between Dante Alighieri, Beatrice Portinari, and Marco Polo, and small ones, like building a bell tower in Florence that doesn't appear to have existed until the mid-1300s.

For what I've related faithfully, I'm indebted to A. N. Wilson's *Dante in Love*, C. S. Lewis's *The Discarded Image*, Michael Ward's *Planet Narnia*, and Ali A. Olomi's podcasts on Islamicate astrology, as well as various other books on modern astrology. I'm also grateful to several wonderful authenticity readers. Any inaccuracies or shortcomings are entirely mine.

The translation of Dante's *Paradiso* referenced is Longfellow's; the translation of Virgil's *Aeneid* is Dryden's.

Finally, this book makes heavy reference to my own experiences with anxiety, depression, and other mental-health issues—your mileage may vary. But therapy and medication have helped me mightily. Whatever your experience, please believe that you deserve help if you are struggling, that you are wanted and needed and valuable, and that I am rooting for you. Hard.

If you need someone to talk to, the following resources may help:

Crisis Text Line: Visit www.crisistextline.org, text "HOME" to 741741 (US/Canada), or 50808 (Ireland), or text "SHOUT" to 85258 (UK)

List of International Suicide Hotlines: Visit www.suicide.org/international-suicide-hotlines.html

National Suicide Prevention Lifeline: Visit www.suicidepreventionlifeline.org or call 1-800-273-TALK (8255)

National Alliance on Mental Illness Helpline: 1-800-950-NAMI (6264)

ACKNOWLEDGMENTS

I owe a debt of gratitude to so many for this project. Here are a few in particular.

Stephanie Stein: I was nervous sharing this bit of my heart with anyone. Thank you for understanding what I meant to say from the very beginning and helping me say it.

Elana Roth Parker: so much of this story needed translation. Thank you, thank you for believing in it and helping me tell it. You are the best teammate I could ask for.

My wonderful team at HarperCollins, including Louisa Currigan, Sophie Schmidt, Jon Howard, Vanessa Nuttry, Corina Lupp, Michael D'Angelo, and Lauren Levite: thank you for every painstaking read of the manuscript, for all the clever descriptive copy written, for your beautiful design work, for every social media post. Thank you for making my story a *book*.

Corina Nika: the cover is stunning. Thank you for lending me a bit of your magic.

Naseem Jamnia, Tselmegtsetseg Tsetsendelger, and Dr. Anne F. Broadbridge: Thank you for correcting my Arabic, my Mongolian, and my faulty renderings of the world outside my experience. I am indebted to you all for making me aware of my blind spots and for helping me adjust this story accordingly!

My One More Page family—Eileen McGervey, Lelia Nebeker, Rebecca Speas, Rosie Dauval, Amanda Quain, Lauren Wengrovitz, Eileen O'Connor, Neil O'Connor, Kelly Dwyer, Trish Brown, Amber Taylor, Sally McConnell, and Jeremiah Ogle: from falling-down Post-its to the Wall of Thirst and Quotes, I have to believe our little corner of Booklandia is the best of all. Thank you for making it special.

The 9:30 Club, U Street Music Hall, the Black Cat, Rock & Roll Hotel, the Fillmore Silver Spring: thanks for the memories and all the magic still to come.

To the musicians who made it all easier, especially Tom DeLonge and Angels and Airwaves: thank you for the songs. I wore them like armor when times were hardest, and they live in my pocket and in my heart to this day. Your art made all the difference.

Patricia Riley, Shannon Price, Grace Li, and Jessica James: you each read early drafts of this project and provided invaluable feedback and encouragement. Thank you from the bottom of my heart for your kindness as I kept working.

Sara Faring and Katie Blair: thank you for the infinity-long phone calls and texts about life, work, and more. I am so grateful for you and love you both dearly.

The Pod—Steph "Stephinephrine" Messa, Laura Weymouth, Jen Fulmer, Joanna Meyer, and Hannah Whitten: the Pod, the Pod, the Pod forever. Your words, whining, and ride-or-die love make my day every day.

C.S. Lewis: you were long passed before I was ever born. But I am always reaching for that lamppost moment. Thank you for your beautiful work and for baptizing my imagination.

My family, close and extended: so much of this book is about a world that feels uncertain. You have never felt that way. Thank you for always being a safe place.

Wade: I am not the person I was when I began this book, thank the Lord. Thank you for being my rock through those difficult years. I would not be where I am without you. I love you.

Caroline: you were not even dreamed of when I first imagined this story, but I carried you through ten demanding months of writing it. So in a way, it belongs to you, too.

It will be years before you're of an age to read this book, but I hope there are parts of it that never entirely make sense to you. I hope that darkness never comes for you. But if it does, know this: I will help you fight a thousand kinds of darkness if you ever lose the light. I love you already and always.

To my Heavenly Father: You are before all things, and in You all things hold together. Thank you for the music and the words, and for holding me securely.